THE GIRL IN WHITE GLOVES

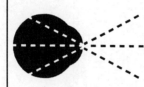

This Large Print Book carries the
Seal of Approval of N.A.V.H.

THE GIRL IN WHITE GLOVES

A NOVEL OF GRACE KELLY

KERRI MAHER

THORNDIKE PRESS
A part of Gale, a Cengage Company

Copyright © 2020 by Kerri Maher.
Thorndike Press, a part of Gale, a Cengage Company.

Thorndike Press® Large Print Basic.
The text of this Large Print edition is unabridged.
Other aspects of the book may vary from the original edition.
Set in 16 pt. Plantin.

LIBRARY OF CONGRESS CIP DATA ON FILE.
CATALOGUING IN PUBLICATION FOR THIS BOOK
IS AVAILABLE FROM THE LIBRARY OF CONGRESS

ISBN-13: 978-1-4328-7623-4 (hardcover alk. paper)

Published in 2020 by arrangement with Berkley, an imprint of Penguin Publishing Group, a division of Penguin Random House, LLC

Printed in Mexico
Print Number: 01   Print Year: 2020

This one's for you, Dad —
for always believing.

Fairy tales tell imaginary stories. Me, I'm a living person. I exist. If the story of my life as a real woman were to be told one day, people would at last discover the real being that I am.

— GRACE DE MONACO

If Gracie can marry a Prince, every American girl can. . . . I am sure we will truthfully say some day — "and they were married and lived happily ever after."

— MARGARET MAJER KELLY

PROLOGUE

March 1955

"Remind me again why we're here?" Peggy asked Grace, shielding her pale eyes with her hand flat like a table over her sunglasses. Though it was only spring, the sun in Jamaica was already intense, more like the iris-searing heat that beat down on the Hollywood hills in July.

"Sister, darling, we're in paradise. It seems pointless to ask *why*. Just *enjoy*," Grace laughed, and picked up the creamy white telephone to call for a pitcher of pineapple juice. She'd been about to ask for daiquiris made with the local rum, but then remembered that Peggy had been talking lately about wanting to dry out a bit, and Grace herself had to keep in mind the arrival of Howell Conant and his cameras later in the day, and of the Oscars later in the month. It was impossible she'd actually win, of course, not when it was so clear to everyone that

Judy Garland would take home the coveted statue for *A Star Is Born*.

But the nomination was quite a compliment, and one that Dore Schary, head of MGM, couldn't ignore for long — even if *The Country Girl* hadn't come out of his studio or fulfilled part of her precious contract with him. If he wanted her in his stable, Schary would have to make a few sacrifices. Even he had to see she'd lose all her star power if he kept putting her in rubbish like *Green Fire* just because it was an MGM film. By the same token, if Oleg Cassini wanted to be with her, wanted to spend his life with her as he claimed, he'd have to curb that intolerable jealous streak of his. She'd worked far too hard to take any of that lying down. This was her life, and her career. She needed to make Schary and Oleg see she was to be taken seriously. After seven years of standing before the camera's eye, she knew a thing or two about its power, and Howell Conant was the perfect instrument with which to wield it.

Peggy padded into their cabana, leaving Grace alone on the stone patio that opened onto the expansive white beach — sand for miles that curved around the gently lapping blue water in an embrace. She could feel the grit of the sand beneath her bare feet, and she wiggled her unvarnished toes. Hands on her hips, she squinted out into the white noonday light and inhaled deeply, feeling her shoulders rise effortlessly as her lungs filled with hot, salty air. This was what freedom felt like.

A memory of walking the Ocean City boardwalk floated to her mind — the sand between her toes, the rush of the Atlantic on the beach, seagulls squawking overhead. She'd felt free there, too, in that narrow New Jersey town where her family had spent every summer of her life. As long as she was outside, supposedly exerting herself on bicycles or in the surf, not inside the cool stucco walls of their Spanish-style house staging one of her plays with dolls or reading a novel, her parents left her alone. Unattended, she spent long hours playing mermaids and pirates with other like-minded children, and as she got older, she learned to stuff a book under the towel in her bag, then pedal far enough down Bay Avenue that her siblings wouldn't spy on her so she could read in peace under an umbrella.

This beach holiday, though, was entirely her own. No one to fool, and no one to please but herself. She had every intention of enjoying it with her older sister, who

11

could use a break. Clapping her hands and shouting, "Peggy! Let's have a swim in that divine water!" Grace headed into the cabana.

It was a marvelous week. The waves were warm, the local people friendlier than anyone she'd met in Los Angeles or New York in an absolute age, and everywhere she looked there were sprays of tropical flowers in all shades of orange, red, and pink. Heaping piles of fruit abounded. At every market, she ate a mango or an orange on a stick, each peeled and cut to perfection.

Even Peggy, who'd been increasingly depressed back at home, was having a ball. Grace was happy to see that her sister didn't even bother ordering a beer or a glass of rum at their favorite restaurant, the one that served the astonishing jerk chicken dish they couldn't get enough of. It was something of a dive, little more than a dirt floor with plastic tables and chairs under banana leaves woven into a tight fabric, but Howell convinced them to try it. "A journalist friend of mine said it's the best on the island," he'd promised. Grace was rather proud of herself for giving it a go the first time, and wrote a letter to Hitch the following morning laughing about how her prim character from *Rear Window,* Lisa Fremont, could certainly tend to globe-trotting photographer Jeff Jefferies as he took pictures around the world if Grace and Margaret Kelly of Philadelphia could eat spicy chicken with their fingers in Jamaica.

Howell captured it all — swimming, lazing, eating, laughing, the water a constant rippling backdrop. "The real Grace Kelly," he kept saying, shaking his head in appreciative disbelief. "At home in her own skin. No one's ever seen a star this genuine before, this honest." She couldn't wait to see the shots when he developed them.

Close to the end of the week, she was sitting with Howell and Peggy on the patio at sunset, having just enjoyed a meal of perfectly grilled hamburgers, which were still her favorite, no matter how delicious any other dish might be.

"I want to thank you," said Howell, raising his cup of rum to her glass of water. "I thought it was something of a risk, having me do this shoot with you on vacation. Never been done before. But when people see these shots, I have a feeling it'll be the start of a trend."

"I thought I'd kill two birds with one stone," Grace said. She felt full and content, languid in the damp night air that made her hair stick to the back of her neck.

"What two birds are those?" Peggy asked, seeming to suddenly remember the question she'd asked at the start of the week, then promptly forgotten in the lull of island life. *Remind me again why we're here?*

"Well, relaxing and getting away from the Hollywood scene," Grace replied, "and also giving Howell here the cover for *Collier's* he's been asking for. I just didn't know when else I'd fit it in, and look how well it's turned out having you here with us. We'd never have eaten that chicken without you —"

"Or found that amazing beach on the other side of the island," Peggy agreed.

"And if we teach Schary a thing or two in the process, all the better," said Howell, with a knowingly raised eyebrow.

"Now, Howell, you think me so Machiavellian?" Grace asked, innocently tilting her head as she'd done so successfully before so many cameras. *Ingénue.* How she detested that word, which had come to be synonymous with her name. But at least she'd learned how to use that girl's manner to her advantage.

Howell laughed and knocked back the rest of his rum. "Oh, Grace, woe betide the man you marry. He won't stand a chance."

"Don't you worry about her husband,

14

Howell," said Peggy sleepily. "The Kelly women have always been pliable where the men are concerned. Daddy made sure of that." Grace winced inside. Jack Kelly was the last man she wanted to be reminded of at that moment. *He* wouldn't be impressed by this photo shoot; he wasn't impressed by anything.

She didn't sleep well that night, and when Howell photographed her swimming the next day, she felt off, her arms and legs gelatinous. So much of the strength she'd been feeling throughout the week seemed to have drained out of her.

As she lifted her head out of the water, Howell knelt in the waves and tilted his whole body left, his face hidden behind his thirty-five-millimeter. He said, "You look gorgeous, Grace. And you're smarter and more talented than anyone gives you credit for. Think of the look on Schary's face when he sees you win that Oscar." And just for the smallest of moments, the time it took for his camera to open and close its aperture, she curled her lip in the faintest of smiles and believed the impossible was hers.

CHAPTER 1

1969

Forty. She'd never felt tempted to run and hide on a birthday until this one. It was still months away, and Rainier and the children and the staff of the palace wanted to know how Her Serene Highness would like to celebrate.

"I wouldn't," she told Rainier in the chauffeured black Mercedes on the way to another official dinner. Small enclosed spaces, shuttling between events — these seemed to be the only circumstances under which they saw each other these days.

"Come now, Grace, that's not like you," said Rainier, putting his hand on hers. She withdrew it and set it on her lap, which was cocooned in peach silk shantung. The dress would be featured in all the columns the next morning — columns that would focus on the fine stitching and embroidery of her ensemble and say little or nothing about the books she'd read to sick children at the hospital that morning, or the many hours she was spending on the upcoming Red Cross Gala, practicing the art of tedious diplomacy to ensure no donor's toes were stepped on, and everyone important was appropriately flattered.

"Forgive me, Rainier," Grace said, employing her most dulcet tones. "I'm just . . . not myself, I suppose." Vagueness was her best strategy with her husband. He wasn't interested in depth of feeling or her thoughts. For so long, this had eaten at her, this sense that he misunderstood her and wasn't even interested in understanding her. Recently, though, she'd come to realize how much easier his limitations made her life in Monaco. If he didn't ask, she didn't have to explain herself; that way, she could preserve her strength for the times when they did disagree.

"Could you try to be back to yourself by November the twelfth?" he asked. "Because our subjects would very much like to pay tribute to their Princess on her special day. I fear they won't understand if there is no celebration." His tone was patient enough, but she knew it would not be in another week if she didn't relent. For now he knitted together his dark brows and pursed his

18

full lips in a pouty smile meant to suggest that of course he knew why she was feeling impatient with having to share a private moment with a principality, but they both knew what was best, what must be done.

Still, Grace felt the irony of her own birthday so strongly: if Rainier made too big a fuss, she would be perceived as self-aggrandizing and even less recognized for her hard work in the principality. A veritable Marie Antoinette with an Hermès bag and diamond tiara. But if she were to do nothing for her birthday, and simply go out for burgers with her family dressed in her favorite jeans and sweater, which her old friend and favorite costume stylist, Edith Head, referred to as dumpy Debbies, she wouldn't be doing credit to her chic principality — the subjects of which *expected* her to look like a fashion plate at all times.

She found it amazing and depressing that after thirteen years of marriage and sovereignty she was still dealing with this catch-22. Just last week, she had gone to the hospital, which she'd renovated and modernized with the same care and attention most women applied to the building of their own homes, transforming Monaco's medical establishment from ill equipped to enviably advanced. Knowing she'd be photographed as she visited patients on the cancer ward, she had dressed in a tidy summer skirt suit, along with her chambray Keds — her "ugly" sneakers as twelve-year-old but still fashion-conscious Caroline insisted on calling them. She asked the photographers not to capture her feet, explaining that she'd worn the sneakers instead of heels so that she could visit as many patients as possible without landing herself in the orthopedic ward!

She'd thought the joke would lighten the mood, but she noticed several attending nurses frowning, and one shaking her head so that Grace could see her disapproval. That nurse had been very old, the lines from many summers spent on the beach carving deep grooves into her tanned face. Grace stifled a sigh at this common and often conflicted reaction to her presence — reverence for her motherhood but judgment of her educational choices; gratitude for her charity but resentment of her wardrobe; and most of all, pleasure in her beauty but animosity that it hailed from a country across the ocean, a nation they resented as imperial and in cahoots with France, which sought to keep Monaco under its thumb.

The mixed reactions these days were, she supposed, better than the outright hostility that Rainier had sensed early in their marriage, and used as a reason to ban all her movies in the principality. But Grace despaired that the Monégasques would ever truly embrace her as one of them, no matter what she did as their Princess; they had proved much tougher to impress than the moviegoers she'd longed to captivate as an actress.

But then one of the youngest nurses, who spoke French with a strong accent, chuckled and pointed to her own large white shoes, saying, "You're not alone, Serene Highness."

Grace replied with as warm a smile as she could conjure, and said, "Thank you for understanding." Perhaps this younger generation would be the one to make her feel at home.

"Do what you think is best, Rainier," said Grace with a light sigh, knowing it was pointless to delay her acquiescence. Something else she'd learned: give in when she could, and as soon as possible. Doing so made everything move more smoothly, made for fewer uncomfortable discussions. "I'm sure that between them, Marta and Meredith," she said, referring to both their secretaries, "will throw a lovely party."

"Is there anything special you'd like?" he

asked, approval making his voice warm and suggestive. She recoiled inside — it was a good thing he'd be too exhausted for anything more than sleep after this dinner.

"Peace on earth? Goodwill toward men?" she quipped, dodging the amorousness as skillfully as she had with Hitch and everyone else all those years ago. Little had she known then what good training for wifeliness her years in Hollywood would be. At the time, she'd feared the opposite.

Rainier smirked, his slim mustache curling up on the right. "I was thinking of something everyone can share. A small public garden for your beloved flowers? Or maybe a statue along the promenade?"

"Please, Rainier, nothing for me, or of me," she said, making her voice both alarmed and embarrassed, hoping this conversation would not spiral out of control. "If you must, donate something in my name. A garden might be nice. Or a new wing of the library, a series of plays at the theater that might be free and open to all . . ."

"So that you can star in them?" he asked jokingly, but the familiar derisiveness was unmistakable.

She laughed, keeping it amused and fizzy. "I should think not! Who wants to see an old broad like me on the stage?"

Though the wisecrack she'd made at her own expense gave her a momentary flutter of regret, it calmed quickly when she saw that she had succeeded and the conversation was over. Rainier nodded, then turned to look out the window of the car into the neon-lit night. How she hated those lights — every one of them a blight on the dramatic coastal beauty of her adopted homeland. Thank goodness Rainier had finally seen sense and slowed the building of more such abominations.

"Don't forget your glasses," he said when the car stopped at its destination. The swell of people and cameras readied themselves outside their car. She frequently forgot she was even wearing her glasses, as the pleasure of actually being able to see more than five feet in front of her seemed perfectly natural when she had them on. But Rainier never forgot that she should take them off in public.

"Thank you, darling" came her automatic reply, as she plucked the tortoiseshell spectacles off her face and set them in the discreet leather box between them. Immediately the world went fuzzy, and when the door was opened for her, she was glad for the usual explosion of flashbulbs so that she had an excuse to squint as she smiled and waited for Rainier's arm to lead her into the night.

Few things were as soothing to her as the sight of her tidy desk. With the stationery, pens, ink, tissues, clips, and all the other instruments of correspondence neatly stored in small containers within its drawers, the top surface was simply a glossy, inviting expanse of varnished wood. She breathed a sigh of relief at its simplicity.

As she had no engagements that day, she could sit in her upholstered chair in the luxurious comfort of her softest jeans, bare feet, and cotton cable-knit sweater. She took out a stack of paper and her favorite fountain pen, given to her by her uncle George when she left Henry Avenue for the American Academy of Dramatic Arts in 1947. Like all well-made things, it still worked as well as the day it was given to her twenty-two years ago. "I want you to write and tell me all your adventures," Uncle George had said. "Even the naughty ones," he'd added in a low, conspiratorial voice to the dagger-eyed annoyance of her mother. Grace had giggled girlishly at his mischievous remark, hardly able to fathom what sort of naughtiness he might be talking about.

Imagine. Now she was worried about Caroline getting into the same kind of trouble. And unlike her own mother, who really had little foundation for worry in Grace's case, Grace had every reason in the world to be concerned about bright, willful Caroline. She didn't even want to consider what Caroline might be like at seventeen, the age Grace had been when she left home. And the world had changed so much, too — forget the relatively innocent naughtiness of her own youth! Grace shuddered to think what debauchery lay in wait for her oldest child, with the vulture paparazzi always ready to capture it on film.

Though Grace had many other more pressing matters to attend to, she decided to take a few minutes to write a quick note to Uncle George in California, narrating the latest anecdotes about the children and asking how he had celebrated his own fortieth birthday. He'd always been an inspiration to her — perhaps he could give her a few ideas for her unwanted fête.

Hours passed in contented, productive silence, and when she started to feel hungry, she wandered into the kitchen she'd insisted on having in their wing of the palace, a kitchen where no servant was allowed unless explicitly invited. She made herself a peanut butter and jam sandwich that she ate standing up, leaning cross-legged against the counter and looking out the large window at the sparkling sapphire blue of the Mediterranean that met the paler blue of the sky at the horizon. At the peripheries of both sides of her vision were the craggy slopes of their piece of the Côte d'Azur, gradual green climbs up and up, with red tile roofs and ancient stonework nestled among the flora. The water was dotted by white yachts of varying sizes, though from her height and distance they all looked roughly the same, except for Aristotle Onassis's behemoth, the *Christina O.* At this time of day, the sunshine was bright white and glinted off the water like thousands of tiny, glimmering gems.

Washing her sweet, sticky lunch down with a glass of cold milk, Grace experienced one of those precious and rare moments of feeling that life was, well, fine. In the last seven years, since she'd said her official goodbye to acting in that wrenching time when she'd had to turn down Hitch's offer to do *Marnie* in 1962, she'd built just this life for herself: a daily schedule of correspondence and meetings in the mornings, mostly about the children and her charity work — the hospital, the Red Cross, AMADE, and her flour-

26

ishing foundation for the arts. She found patronizing dancers and artisans to be satisfying work, even if it did not touch that same part of her soul that acting had. She didn't admit that last part to many people. To anyone? No, she wouldn't dare. The last thing she'd want anyone to think was that she was ungrateful.

And in the afternoons, she tried to be as available to her children as possible. In a few hours, she and four-year-old Stéphie would attend their weekly music class with some other Monégasque mothers and children, after which they would drift to a playground, and then home for dinner with Caroline. Grace enjoyed their simple little dinners together. Noodles and carrots, fish sticks and French fries, tickling and laughing — she liked to indulge in all manner of casual American impropriety when she was with the girls. Pity Caroline was almost too old to enjoy these sorts of silly moments, but Grace planned to cling to them as long as possible.

She pushed the thought of Albie, in school and its related sports teams for all the daylight hours, out of her mind, as it was too painful to think about. He came home late, utterly exhausted, only to kiss his mother on the cheek and collapse into bed.

How much her son would enjoy dinner with his mother and sisters — after all, he was only a boy, just eleven years old! How much she wished he were there.

Would she also see Rainier in the evening? It was hard to say, and she tried not to dwell on the question and its inevitable and disappointing answer too long.

Just as she returned to her desk, her private line rang.

"Hello?" she said, her heart speeding up as it always did in that fragment of a second between her greeting and that of the person on the other end of the line. Who could it be? What escape might the call provide?

"Gracie? It's Prudy. How are you?" Her friend's voice was buoyant, effusive in its long American vowels. She seemed pleased to have reached Grace on the first ring. They had been talking on the phone for nearly twenty years, since the end of their Barbizon days when they'd lived down the hall from each other, and Grace was so grateful for this piece of plastic that allowed them to stay in touch across continents and oceans.

Grace blew out a gust of air and slouched back in her chair. She, too, was glad to be speaking to an old friend. A small but wonderful escape. "I'm all right, Prudy.

Can't complain, except about turning forty in a few months. Rainier's after me for a gift and a party."

"You know you sound like a princess, right?" Prudy teased.

"Oh, I know, and the worst kind, too. Still. This business of getting older is nothing to sneeze at. What did you do for your fortieth?"

"I took myself to a movie and ate a tub of popcorn in the dark, then went home and drank a bottle of very good red wine."

"You mean Arthur didn't do anything for you?"

"I told him not to. Careful what you ask for. If I were you, I'd ask for a trip to India. You used to love to travel to exotic places. Or Egypt. See one of the Seven Wonders."

The trumpeting whine of an elephant and the windy flap of its ears flashed to Grace's mind. She'd gone all the way to Africa just to make a movie with Clark Gable and celebrated her twenty-third birthday in the French Congo. "You know, you're right," said Grace, feeling something inside her loosen at the suggestion that she could be that girl once again.

Then it tightened as hard as a rock. Rainier preferred not to travel much farther than the States, and she suspected that going to India by herself would raise far too many eyebrows. But, "I'll think about it," she told Prudy, and wondered if her old friend knew she was lying.

They talked more about what each of them had been up to — Grace was very interested to hear about Prudy's foray into flower arranging. She was even to have the honor of arranging a large vase of winter branches and berries to be prominently displayed in town hall during the holidays. Grace had always loved flowers, and was learning more about them by working closely with the head gardener to rehabilitate the plantings around the palace.

"And it's just terrible about Josephine, isn't it?" Prudy eventually said.

For a moment, Grace was confused. "Josephine?"

"Baker. Remember meeting her at the Copa years ago?"

"How could I forget? She was treated abhorrently." Grace felt the grip of injustice in her chest just as she had then, when one of the world's greatest singers was barred entrance to the snobby club because of the color of her skin. "What's happened to her recently?"

"I read in the paper that she's been evicted from her home in France. Some château or other."

"What?" Grace exclaimed indignantly, her hand tightening around the receiver of the phone.

"She and all her children," Prudy affirmed.

Grace opened the lower desk drawer, where she kept her enormous, frayed-fabric address book, which was stuffed to bursting with envelopes and business cards. She was sure she had Josephine's number in here somewhere. She licked her finger and thumb and began paging through.

"Gracie? You still there?" came Prudy's voice in her ear.

"Yes, yes, I'm here," she said distractedly. "I'm trying to find Josephine's number. I have an old one under Baker, and I'm sure that's not it, but . . ." *Aha!* "Yes! I found her last Christmas card." And it had what looked like her most recent phone number. Hopefully the phone hadn't been disconnected.

She could hear Prudy laughing on the other end of the line. "That's the Gracie I know and love," she said, "not the one who feels bested by a birthday. Go get her, tiger."

It took a few days of phone calls to real estate people who spoke such regional French she could barely parse a word, to the gendarmes in the Dordogne, where Josephine's château was located, and to former neighbors both sympathetic and utterly prejudiced who referred to her as *le négro.* Grace was infuriated with them, and with herself for allowing Josephine to become a Christmas-card friend. Knowing exactly why she'd let it happen made it more unforgivable, and made her more determined to find and help her old friend. Fearless and iconoclastic, with a decadeslong list of stage and musical credits, and France's highest honor for service during the Second World War, to say nothing of the broken hearts she'd left in her wake, Josephine Baker had long reminded Grace too much of what she was not. She also knew Rainier was skeptical of Josephine, not so much for her risqué performances as for her large family of adopted children from places as far away as Japan and Colombia.

This had been a mistake, and one that needed to be remedied, Grace realized with a galvanizing determination she felt in her gut and her limbs.

When at last she got Josephine on the phone, Grace found herself blathering and hoping for forgiveness, almost like she was in a confession box, "Oh, Josephine, I'm so sorry I've been out of touch. As soon as I heard what happened to you and your children, I started trying to reach you. How can I help?"

"Grace! What a surprise! Don't feel bad! Goodness, don't you have a country to run?" She laughed, in that smooth, musical voice of hers that remained unaffected and American despite all the years of living abroad. "Tell me all about you and those gorgeous children of yours."

Grace raced through her usual highlights — Albie's intensifying interest in track and field, Caroline's budding interest in politics, and little Stéphie's free-spiritedness — then said, "And I want to know more about your own children, so we should look at our calendars and schedule a time to meet. But first, I want to find out where you are living and if you need . . . anything." It was such a sticky thing. She didn't want to presume too much, nor to embarrass this *legend,* her friend. But she couldn't stand by while the same legend might become homeless, either.

"You've always been very kind, Grace."

"I wish I'd been more than kind. I wish I'd been a better friend," said Grace.

"Hush, you," said Josephine. "Now, then. I can't possibly ask you to put up my entire brood, even if you do live in a palace."

"What if I could find you another place?

Someplace big enough, and close by, and . . ."

"Affordable."

"We'll sort that part out later. I'd like to help you in any way I can." Grace paused, her heart beating loud in her ears and chest. "If you'll accept it," she added. "I'd understand if you couldn't, or didn't want to."

For a few beats, there was silence on the other end of the line, and Grace gripped the receiver, waiting for a reply.

When it came, Josephine's voice was quieter, wetter, rockier. "I can't think of it as charity, Grace. I'll need to pay you back."

"You can pay me back by singing again," Grace replied, feeling that the full truth — *It's me that needs to make some repairs, Josephine* — would only create more discomfort between them. "Have you been singing?"

"Well . . . I've been meaning to get back to it."

"That's wonderful to hear," said Grace, her body filling with a humming kind of gratitude.

Once she'd gathered enough information, she prepared to approach Rainier. She made a point of serving him a favorite dinner after the children were in bed, and over the roasted chicken, he commented, "You seem happier this week. Have you given any more thought to your birthday?"

Carefully, she smudged a shine of tarragon sauce from her lower lip, then set the pressed white napkin back in her lap. She had purposely not changed out of the bouclé suit she'd worn to the Red Cross earlier in the day, to remind her husband of the good she did every day in Monaco, in his name. "I hope I seem happier when I'm working for others." She smiled, then took a deep breath.

"You remember Josephine Baker?" she asked.

"Of course," he said. "I have always enjoyed her songs, and she was very important in the war. You two used to be friends, did you not?" He smiled at her, and in his smile, she glimpsed what was best in him — the charity in his heart, his desire to be part of positive changes in Monaco, the father who wanted all that was best for his children.

"Yes, we were, and I feel bad that I let the friendship slip until recently," said Grace. He seemed to be in an open mood. Now was as good a time as any to make her request. "I discovered the other day that she needs some help. You see, it seems she and her children have lost their home in the Dordogne."

Rainier frowned. "Her *Rainbow Tribe?*"

"You don't have to say it like that." *Here it comes. Stay calm.*

"She has twelve children of different nationalities. She had to sell tickets to her château and show off her tribe like zoo animals just to make ends meet."

"She hardly treats her children like animals, Rainier. And anyway, how can you say that as if your own zoo animals aren't the most important things in the world to you?" *Careful, Grace,* she warned herself. *He knows you don't love the palace zoo as he does, and you don't want to put him on the defensive.* "Anyway," she went on, shaking her head and pushing out all thoughts of zoos, "Josephine wanted to make a point, a profound point if you ask me, that people of any color and background can live together happily. And she sold tickets to see the *gardens.*"

"You can believe that if you like, darling, but it will be a belief, not a truth."

Oh, he can be so arrogant and patronizing! She told herself not to lose her temper. "You're always saying," she went on carefully, "that you want all the people of Monaco to live peacefully and prosperously,

36

not just those who make a great deal of money. It's a mission I share."

"And you want to help Josephine Baker." His face was so hard to read. It was a mix of disdain for Josephine's maternal choices, but also pause and consideration of Grace's points.

"Yes," she said, at last playing her trump card. "It would be the most wonderful birthday present you could give me. A home for my friend near Monaco, ensuring that a French *and* American national treasure is preserved."

She'd hit the right note — she could see it in the way he sat back in his chair, his right index finger pressing on his lips, his gaze fuzzy as he thought.

"I've looked into some properties," she ventured. He liked it when she did her homework. She told him about the lovely villa in Roquebrun, just up the hill from the Larvotto. Then she breathed slowly and silently, waiting.

"All right," he finally agreed, "if it will make you happy. But we must also come up with a more public gift, something I can give you before our subjects."

Grace leapt up from her seat and went around the table to kiss Rainier on the cheek, then kneel beside his chair with her hand on his. She felt truly happy, her chest full of fizzy bubbles rising like those in a champagne flute.

"You can give me anything you like."

He smiled and ran a finger down her jaw. For the first time in a long time, it sent a shiver of something approaching desire down her spine. She kissed him on the lips, and tightened her fingers around his palm. "Thank you," she whispered.

He turned in his seat, then slid off of it so that he, too, was kneeling, and they were facing each other. He put his arms around her and pressed his body against hers as they kissed. Grace closed her eyes and reached deep into her memories to find a moment, a sensation akin to this one, and when she found it, she kissed Rainier harder and let him pull her to the floor.

CHAPTER 2

1949

Her voice was not doing what she wanted it to do. Damn it. She still sounded so *nasal.* Grace flicked her electric kettle on again, and spooned salt into the blue-and-white porcelain teapot she'd purchased in Chinatown her first week in New York. It hardly went with the cups she'd brought from her mother's original china set, a fine porcelain with pink and gold flowers vining the delicate pieces, but both had served her well since she'd moved into this shoebox on Sixty-Third Street. Even though her modeling money could afford her a whole new tea set from Tiffany's, these mismatched pieces worked just fine and seemed like the perfect combination of her Henry Avenue life and her more adventurous city life.

When the water came to a boil, she poured it into the pot and stirred with a chopstick she'd purchased from the same emporium in Chinatown, the farthest south she'd ventured on the island of Manhattan. The place was over a fishmonger's shop and smelled terribly of seaweed and cod, but it was well-known as the best place to go for the sorts of inexpensive housewares a girl needed to outfit her room in the Barbizon. "No sense in picking out a pattern before we meet the right man," Prudy had said judiciously to Grace and a few other girls over breakfast last fall.

She poured herself a cup full of hot salty water, took some into her mouth, then tipped her head back and pooled the liquid in her throat, gargled, then spit it into the awaiting soup bowl. She repeated this two more times, then tried again, starting with an old favorite, Cordelia from *King Lear,* to put the English accent into her ear and throat: "Unhappy that I am, I cannot heave / My heart into my mouth. I love your Majesty / According to my bond; no more nor less. / Good my lord, You have begot me, bred me, lov'd me; I / Return those duties back as are right fit, / Obey you, love you, and most honour you."

Then she switched to *The Torch-Bearers* by Uncle George, trying to bring just a touch of those broad vowels and clipped final syllables to the American character

Florence McCrickett. As always, she tried to speak from her abdomen, from far below any pipe the salt water had cleansed; the wash was just to allow as much of her voice as possible through. The main thing was to "stop speaking out of your sinuses," as Don had put it. He'd offered her a pack of cigarettes to help bring her tones down, but she'd flatly refused. Her voice she could train, but her white teeth and mercifully clear complexion weren't to be toyed with. She'd seen far too many beautiful young woman made positively yellow with those sticks — why, if she had a penny for every stunning bride she'd seen in a photograph who was unrecognizable as a friend's mother twenty years later, she wouldn't have to model to pay her rent.

She'd been making progress without the smoke. The vibration of her voice in her chest and ears was an octave lower than it had been a year ago, surely. And today, something in her accent and intonation suddenly sounded new, something maybe a little like Katharine Hepburn, but *not* Katharine Hepburn. Something that sounded like Grace Kelly, but better. Better, older, sexier, more worldly, more poised, more sophisticated. *More.*

She'd better stop there. Mustn't jinx

herself. And she really had to wash and set her hair before her date with Don. If only she had a mane like Hepburn's, instead of this stringy mop. Well, thank heaven for curlers. She'd take her help where she could find it.

When she stepped out of the shower and into the steamy salmon-pink-tiled bathroom, Grace was delighted to see Prudy and Carolyn leaning over the white sinks adjusting their makeup. Towel clad, Grace approached them. "Well, hello, ladies," she said, draping one damp arm around Carolyn, which her friend shook off with good-natured irritation.

"Hey, watch the cashmere, Kelly," she said of the soft baby blue sweater that hugged her curves in just the way that got her so many modeling jobs in town. It was a marvelous contrast to her dark hair.

"It *is* a lovely shade. New?" Grace asked.

"Nice, isn't it? Gift from Bloomingdale's after the shoot today," said Carolyn, turning around to face Grace and lean against the sink. "And I deserved the bonus. It was grueling, what with Mr. Shoemaker's hand on my bum between every take."

Grace shook her head and rolled her eyes. "Oh, Randy, Randy, Randy," she tutted, "when will you ever learn?"

Prudy giggled. "Is his name actually Randy?"

"Yes," Grace laughed. "Never was a man more appropriately named."

"Little does hopeless old Randy know that some of his regular girls have taken up running for exercise," said Carolyn.

"You might be able to outrun one, but won't you just run into another?" asked Prudy.

"I'd love to run into someone good. Captain Joseph A. Truss from the Copacabana last weekend, remember him? He said he runs in Central Park every day. Mmmmm," said Carolyn, sounding like she had just taken a bite of her favorite chocolate.

"Maybe I should join you," mused Grace, pulling the towel off her head and running a comb through her hair.

"Always room for one more," said Carolyn.

"But you're practically engaged to Don," Prudy pointed out. Her friend was sometimes a little too practical for her own good — always home by curfew, never late for one of the secretarial jobs that supplemented her acting. Grace appreciated and even shared many of Prudy's pragmatic habits, but occasionally she could do with-

43

out the moralizing.

"But I'm *not* engaged yet, am I?" Grace said, more to rib Prudy than anything else.

Her friend shook her head and said, "I should start calling you Sphinxy."

"Why would she want to marry Don?" Carolyn demanded. "Grace could have anyone. Every time we go out, no fewer than three different men, all much more successful and better dressed than Mr. Richardson, will send Grace drinks."

"Drinks aren't love," said Grace, opening her bag of curlers, selecting one of the small ones, rolling a section of hair around it, then securing it with a bobby pin.

"Exactly," said Prudy. "Why trade love for fun at the Copacabana?"

"Because it's *fun,*" said Carolyn. "And who said Grace is actually in love with Don? I don't think you are, Gracie. I think you're just enamored of the idea that one of your first acting teachers liked you enough to want to take you out."

"Nothing wrong with flattery," Grace defended herself, rolling another section of hair around a curler.

"Do you love him or not?" Carolyn asked, as if something in her own life were at stake.

"Maaaadly," Grace drawled, then giggled.

"You're impossible," said Prudy, and

Carolyn agreed.

Grace smiled at her friends, then realized she'd forgotten to use her new voice with them. All this time, she could have been practicing! She mustn't be so careless in the future.

The truth was, she did love Don. She wasn't sure if it was his dark good looks, or his relative age — he was eleven years older, after all — or the way he carried his long, slim body like a loosely draped scarf, but Don Richardson had captivated her from the moment his gaze fell on her in his scene-study class at the Academy. He'd waited patiently till she completed his class before suggesting they go to Katz's downtown to "discuss her upcoming classes," but she'd known the whole semester that he wanted her. And that she wanted him.

It had been thrilling to sit across from this man with a tangle of black curls falling into his large black eyes who knew so much about theater and New York, like the deli where they ate hot, mustardy sandwiches with ribbons of a pungent and delicious meat between slices of dark bread. Well, what was a girl to do? Of course she'd kissed him. Feeling heat and possibility buzz between them, eighteen-year-old Grace had

45

known real desire for the first time in her life.

When Don had finally laid her in his bed one dark, snowy March afternoon, she'd never been more grateful to that sweet, nervous boy in Ocean City the previous summer for doing her the great service of dispensing with her virginity, though of course she hadn't felt so callous about her virginity *then,* and it had broken her heart to realize when he went away to Yale that they really weren't right for each other. How could she possibly marry someone so interested in stocks and bonds who hadn't even enjoyed the one and only Broadway show he'd ever seen? She'd gone to confession as soon as she realized this, and admitted the sin of lust to the priest on the other side of the iron grate, though of course she hadn't been so foolish as to admit she'd acted on that lust. She had her mother, Margaret Majer Kelly, to thank for that pragmatism; though she'd converted to Catholicism to marry John B. Kelly, her mother had been raised Lutheran as the daughter of German immigrants. She'd actually told Grace the night before she first received the sacrament of penance, "You don't have to tell the priest everything. Some things are best left between you and God."

46

Though she'd never admit it to any of her Catholic friends, Grace was far less interested in how her adolescent lust affected her relationship with God than the fact that it had made her forget the solemn promise she'd made to herself throughout her childhood that she would make a name for Grace Kelly onstage, like Uncle George. Though she had another uncle who was a vaudeville actor, Grace had never been drawn to him as she'd been to refined, learned George. Her father's older brother was the one person in her whole family who'd used his creative talents, instead of his hands, to succeed in life. He'd won a Pulitzer for writing *The Torch-Bearers*! Even her Olympian rower father had to admit that was pretty impressive.

So no — however lusty they were, she felt no regrets about her feelings for Don because they were extensions of her love for theater. Still, she wasn't in a rush to marry him. A part of her was curious — yes, just a bit — about what it might be like to go out with men as well-heeled as those who sent her drinks the nights she went out with girlfriends.

But all that felt too complicated, and too private, to explain to even Carolyn and Prudy. So she changed the subject: "Enough about me, girls. What are you two up to this evening?"

"Darling," she greeted Don in the foyer of the Barbizon, where small potted palm trees lent an exotic charm to the otherwise heavy, oaken space, the only area in the entire twenty-three-story building where men were allowed. Her black patent pumps clicked on the spick-and-span floor, and the light petticoats beneath her chiffon skirt tickled her shins. Her smooth box calf handbag dangled from the crook of her arm as she put one gloved hand on his elbow and placed a gentle red-lipped kiss on his cheek.

"You'll need your hankie for that, I'm afraid," she said, nodding and raising her eyebrow toward the lipstick on his cheek. The makeup experts at the magazine shoots all told her she'd have to powder her lips to high heaven to avoid leaving such marks, and she simply wasn't willing to spend that much time fussing over her face. Besides, Don was well trained in carrying the monogrammed handkerchief she'd given him for just this purpose.

As he rubbed away the stain, he said, "You sound different."

"Do I?" she said coyly. So, she'd been right about what she heard earlier. The

48

thought made her a little giddy.

"It's good," he said, with that intense look he sometimes got. *I swear,* Grace thought to herself, as a hot rush of longing coursed through her.

Don smiled, returned her kiss on the cheek, then cautioned, "But you'll need to modulate it. Right now it's a bit much. Too Laurence Olivier."

"Killjoy," she said, smiling right back at him, though she felt her heart drop like a stone into her stomach. While their attraction was close to perfect, their statures were not. She needed to land her first big part: *that* would show him they were no longer teacher and student, no matter what it said in the faculty handbook of the American Academy of Dramatic Arts.

They met two couples, theater friends of Don's who were all between gigs and working other jobs, substitute teaching and tending bar, at a checkered-tablecloth place in the West Fifties where they made their way through several bottles of Chianti and enormous platters of chicken parmigiana and garlic bread served family style. Grace enjoyed getting good and tipsy though she eschewed the second helpings she knew would have helped her head the next morning, hoping that a few glasses of water might instead do the trick.

Afterward, they found their way to Bird-land. It was jumping, but luckily Don knew the man at the ropes, and he let their little group in. "You might have to stand awhile," the tall Irishman in the double-breasted suit told them. Inside, the small nightclub was so smoky, Grace could hardly see the man playing the trumpet on the stage at the front, though the melancholy whine of his instrument pierced the air and landed in her ear like honey.

She'd been reading about this new club for weeks, and this was her first time. The music did not disappoint even though Char-lie Parker, for whom the club was named, was not playing that night. Rumor had it he appeared irregularly because of his heroin addiction.

Between sets, a table for two freed up, and the six of them cobbled together enough chairs to sit around it and order a bottle of whiskey. Grace allowed herself a small glass of the amber liquid; she didn't much like it without ice and soda anyway, so it wasn't a hardship not to indulge. Leaning back on Don's arm, which rested on the slim wood of her chair, she closed her eyes and let the music permeate. The tune was sultry and slow, the piano and trumpet, saxophone and drums coming together in rhythms and harmonies she'd never heard before, and yet heard all the time, all over New York — in clubs from the Village to Harlem, on record players in tiny apartments and penthouses, on street corners where players left out their hats, hoping for change.

Fordie, her family's chauffeur and the only person at home other than Uncle George who was unfailingly kind to her, had taught Grace to always throw as much change as she could spare in these musicians' caps. One day when she was around ten, he'd picked her up from the Philadelphia Museum of Art, and from the driver's seat, he'd handed Grace two crisp dollars out the window. "Throw these in the case," he'd instructed her, pointing at the bass player on the wide stone steps who was plucking the strings of his instrument and making a kind of sad but buoyant music. She'd dropped the bills into the open case, and watched as the green-and-white papers fluttered down and joined the shiny nickels and pennies on the scarlet velvet below. Fordie had been the musician's best patron that day. Men like her father, in their fine coats and felt hats, who could have afforded to drop much more into the open case, passed the musician by without even a glance.

Back in the car, Fordie explained in his velvety tenor voice, "Never know where a man like that's been, Gracie. Might be from New Orleans, or Chicago, come all the way here to make his way. Or maybe he lives on these very streets, and he's saving, saving, saving to get up to Harlem. Your uncle George had support on his way to the stage. It's up to us to support strangers like that player."

Oh, how she missed Fordie.

When she opened her eyes, she saw a commotion on the other side of the club. Someone famous had arrived, and people were getting up to offer the couple a seat. Grace didn't recognize the platinum blond woman, but the wiry young man looked familiar. She couldn't quite place him, so she said into Don's ear, "Who's that?"

"Jack Kennedy," said Don, "and one of his showgirls, presumably. He likes the blondes."

Ah. One of the Massachusetts Kennedys her father was always going on about. "And how would you know he likes blondes?" Grace asked.

"Everyone in the theater knows Jack," said Don. "Or knows of him. Just like everyone the generation before me knew his old man, Joe. He's in Congress now, but from what I understand, he's being groomed for much more."

Grace's father had always admired Joe Kennedy and his ambitious family. "Shows what an Irishman can do when he decides to crush the WASPs under his heel," he'd said on more than one occasion, like when her older brother, Kell, won the Diamond Challenge Sculls at Henley in England, the prestigious solo rowing race his father had been denied entry in 1920 because he was Irish and Catholic. Jack Kennedy was just the sort of man her father would love if she brought him home. How would she ever introduce Daddy to Don?

It might have been easy to put off her friends on the subject of their relationship, but it was harder to put off Don himself, especially after nearly a year together. His divorce would be final soon, and he'd referred obliquely to another marriage once or twice: "I doubt your parents would accept a Jewish husband for their daughter. Or would they? The Irish have been almost as discriminated against as we have, in America at least. Should provide some common ground." And in bed once while the long fingers of each of their hands danced suggestively with one another: "Oh, Grace, there might be nothing for it but to marry you." In both cases, though she'd felt a wild flutter of excitement at his words, she'd thought it wise to keep her mouth shut.

If there was one thing she'd learned growing up striking and blond in East Falls, Pennsylvania, it was that silence was currency. It wasn't enough for a girl to be pretty. If she wanted male attention — and not just any male attention, not the kind that could be gotten at any ice-cream counter, but *real* attention, the kind it behooved her to command — it paid to stay quiet. Grace wasn't sure why it bothered men so much when women were honest. She only knew that it did, and she'd gotten very good at knowing when to open her mouth to get a laugh or when to play her cards close to her chest. It didn't matter if the man was loud and brash himself, like her father, or more artistic and introspective, like Don. Silence worked on them all.

She spent the rest of the evening listening to the jazz quartet and watching the room watch Jack Kennedy. It was amusing, really. So many people wondering what he had and they didn't. Except Grace didn't wonder that. She wondered if her own talent was a match for the trumpet player's on the stage, and if it was, where would it lead her?

As the audience clapped at the end of his

solo, Grace's mind went — as it did so often when she was at any kind of performance — to her own well-worn daydream of standing on a stage and taking a bow as clapping and whistling filled the air. The stage in her imagination was bigger than the one in her high school, where she and her older sister, Peggy, had played so many roles. But now Peggy, her father's precious Ba, was married with a child, and the stage belonged to Grace; it was a Broadway stage, the grandest of them all. She could feel the way the hard black floor vibrated beneath her feet as she stood there, beaming with gratitude at the rumble of applause. Everyone she loved would be there, proud of her, her mother and father in the front row. She would be so happy, knowing that her hard work had finally paid off. Cradling an elegant bouquet of roses in her arms as she curtsied one more time, she felt in her soul the proof that she'd done well at last.

CHAPTER 3

She told herself not to be disappointed that her parents couldn't make it up for every performance she gave in her second year at the Academy — there were so many, large and small, meant to show off the talents of the graduating students. In some ways, they were in-house "debutante" affairs, with agents, directors, alums, and well-known actors invited so that they could vet the new crop of talent coming out of the Academy. These shows were how actors like Gregory Peck had gotten noticed, and Grace had high hopes for herself.

She wished her mother and father could see her lead as Tracy Lord in *The Philadelphia Story,* but since her mother had an event at the club she'd been planning for months, she knew that meant neither of them would be coming. But this performance was not all about applause and congratulations from her parents. She loved acting, the work and craft of it, how it enabled her to leave her own self behind in the dressing room and emerge as someone else entirely: a pampered Main Liner; a shrill hausfrau; even Caliban, the sea monster from *The Tempest*. Anything was possible in a theater. She could be anyone. And the performance was where it all came together, with no stops and starts and new directions to distract her from the serious business of being someone else.

Little had she known as she whiled away the hours of her asthmatic childhood, soothing her embarrassment that she couldn't compete with athletic, golden Peggy and Kell by role-playing with her dolls — then later, staging mini productions anytime her uncle George visited and she knew she'd have an attentive audience — that she'd been teaching herself how to act and direct. She was never happier than when she was immersed in those make-believe worlds. Then she discovered she could do it professionally! Well, she simply couldn't imagine doing anything else.

"It's a hard life," her uncle George had warned her one day when she was in high school. "Lots of rejection. Long, grueling hours of rehearsal with actors that are better than you and directors who never think you're good enough. If you think you might want to do anything else with your life, you should do that instead."

"I just love the theater, Uncle George," she replied, her voice catching with emotion. "There's nothing else I've ever loved so much." In all her twenty years, it was still true. Even the modeling she did to pay her rent at the Barbizon and fund her life in New York couldn't compare. Sure, modeling was fun and relatively easy, and she was compensated well for it in both cash and compliments. But it was just a way to make ends meet so that she wouldn't have to depend on her parents. It wasn't *art*.

There was only one other dream that had ever tugged at her heart: the one of her in a beautiful sundress, standing beside a tall and handsome husband and cradling a swaddled baby in her arms. But she'd never been able to picture this dream as clearly as the one of herself onstage. She'd always assumed this was because she didn't know who the man was; in her mind's eye, he had dark hair and eyes, but his features were blurry. Lately, she'd tried putting Don into this picture of domestic bliss, and the image made her feel nervy, both excited and worried at the same time. She wasn't sure if this was because he was the man for her, or because he wasn't. So she put all her attention on her work to avoid thinking more about it. Fortunately, there was no shortage of acting to execute lately.

It was a freezing March morning, and Grace was bundled into two wool sweaters, lined gloves, and her heaviest coat, plus a scarf and a hat as she rushed between the subway and Carnegie Hall, her daily destination for a year and a half, as that was where the Academy held classes. She felt lucky to be there, brimming with both anticipation and accomplishment every time she pulled open the heavy door beneath the central of five arches forming the entrance of the gracious building, which had some of the finest brickwork Grace had ever seen.

Her play would be in the Lyceum, which seated more than five hundred, upon the largest stage on which she'd ever performed. At least Uncle George would be there. It meant so much to her that he believed in her — and she really did have him to thank for getting her into the Academy, as he'd pulled a few strings after she'd missed the application deadline. She'd been positive she'd be going to Bennington for their excellent theatrical studies program, but then heartbreakingly didn't get in because of her grades in math, of all subjects! "I can only get you the audition," Uncle George said of the Academy. "The rest is up to you." He'd sent a dozen long-stemmed roses the day her acceptance letter arrived in the mail. She couldn't help but stick out her tongue and make a face out her bedroom window in the direction of Bennington. *I'll show you,* she'd thought.

Landing the main role in *The Philadelphia Story* was a further step in the right direction. Grace enjoyed the irony that she was an Irish Catholic from East Falls whose father had made his considerable fortune in construction, a girl who'd never be accepted by the Lord family no matter how many gold medals her father or brother won. And she was aware of an additional, very private irony in her playing this role that Katharine Hepburn had made famous: the father, Seth Lord, was extremely hard on his daughter. Oh, his reasons for lecturing Tracy were different from those of Grace's father, but nevertheless, Grace felt a strong connection to this character, in the way she wanted so much to impress her beloved dad. So unusually, instead of escaping herself when she played the character, Grace gave Tracy a little bit of her own heart. Just enough to make Tracy real, never enough to betray Grace's own dearest wishes. It had been a tightrope to walk as she rehearsed her lines and reacted to her fellow players as authentically as possible, but she was pleased with the result.

That afternoon at the Lyceum, in the dressing room she shared with the other girls who were in the play with her — Janet, who was only a year older than her but who'd donned enough makeup to play Grace's mother, and Bridget, who'd be playing the no-nonsense photographer Elizabeth Imbrie — Grace began to feel nervous and even relieved that her parents were not there in case she fell apart onstage. It would be okay if Uncle George saw; he'd understand. And if she did bungle it, she could stick out the remainder of her time at the Academy, then go home and marry a nice Catholic boy with dark eyes and a bright future. No one who patronized the arts on the wide, grand boulevard of Philadelphia's Benjamin Franklin Parkway would be the wiser.

Get ahold of yourself, Grace. This is what you've trained for your whole life. You're ready.

Closing her eyes, she breathed slowly, focusing on the air moving in and out of her nose and lungs, a centering technique the movement teacher had taught in her first year. *Iiiiiinnnnnn, ooooooooooouuuuut.*

liiiiiiiinnnnnnnn, ooooooooouuuuut.

Then suddenly, it was time. She took off her glasses and allowed her eyes to adjust to seeing only six or seven feet ahead. It was just enough to do what she needed to do; anytime a character was out of her sight, she used her finely attuned ears to make up for what her eyes lacked.

Walking onto the stage, Grace felt the heat of the lights above. Thus warmed, the audience a distant, fuzzy sea, and the set of the Lord mansion her only reality, she felt — amazingly, as she always did in this fraction of a second just after a play began — ready. Between the first scene of her throwing out her first husband, and the last of her happy remarriage to the same man after two other suitors vied comically for her affections, Grace lost herself entirely. She wasn't aware of speaking memorized words, but rather of moving and conversing with the other actors. This was what she lived for. These sustained moments of disappearing into someone else, even when the someone else had so much in common with her.

The applause was a surprise. It broke the spell. Now she wished she could see the audience better, but all she could make out were smears of flesh tones and navies and grays. Very quickly, though, there was a wave

62

— a rise upward for a standing ovation. Grace's heart burst and her whole body thrummed as the adulation embraced her. She barely felt the vibration beneath her feet — instead it was more like she had lifted off, like she could fly.

In the greenroom afterward, someone popped a champagne cork to appreciative gasps and claps, and Uncle George gave her a tight hug. "I couldn't be prouder," he said; then holding her at arm's length, he smiled at her admiringly, the dimple in his cheek carved deep.

William Weagley, Uncle George's handsome, dapper . . . Grace was never sure what to call him. Her family always referred to him as his valet or "his man," and George never corrected them. "How's your man, William?" her father would ask, if he happened to remember his brother had "a man" at all. When William did turn up at a family event, he was introduced as her uncle's "friend," but Grace knew that even this term of vague endearment was woefully inadequate. William didn't visit when George came to Philadelphia, but George often included him on family outings that happened on his turf in New York, and he'd never been anything other than kind to Grace. She embraced him now and said,

"Thank you for coming, William."

"You were really terrific, Grace," he said warmly. "Funny and heartbreaking at the same time. Congratulations."

"I know how much theater you see, so that's high praise," Grace said, bowing her head in acknowledgment. William had an encyclopedic knowledge of literature, including every published script from Ben Jonson to Tennessee Williams. Poetry was his favorite, though, and he'd lately been raving about James Baldwin and Robert Lowell. He and her uncle saw every single play in New York, on Broadway and off.

Uncle George and William invited her out for a congratulatory dinner. "And of course, bring Don," added George with a wink.

Grace beamed and accepted the invitation. How much easier certain things were here, with her chosen people, than they had ever been at home. Another reason to love the theater.

Before she went to her dressing room, she drifted over to a group of classmates who were clutching their cups of champagne and laughing.

"Well done, Grace," one of the girls, Julie Pullman, welcomed her. "Great performance."

The rest of the group cheered their agreement, toasting her enthusiastically with their cups, all except a girl named Faye from the first year, who raised her glass reluctantly and offered no huzzah, and even curled her lip in protest. A few weeks before, Grace had overheard Faye referring to Grace as "the cover girl," with pure derisive hatred in her tone. Grace knew some others at the Academy were jealous of her success outside the walls of Carnegie Hall, the clothing and dinners and clubs her face and paychecks enabled her to enjoy. She put it down to sour grapes. Her whole life people had made snotty remarks about her looks, and she'd had to learn to ignore them.

What got to her was when people really believed she coasted by on her appearance, because nothing could have been further from the truth. She worked every hour of the day, either to make money or improve her acting. Even her relationship with Don, their nights on the town that so often revolved around theater, kept her on her toes, always studying her craft — far from seducing a teacher to get what she wanted, as she was sure some of the girls twittered behind her back, being with Don was a constant challenge. She always, *always* felt she had to impress him. She certainly hoped that performances like the one she'd given that night proved she wasn't just a cover girl. *Be real,* she wanted to say. *The Academy's full of gorgeous people, all working hard to become better actors.*

Still, no matter what she said to herself, Faye's snarl wounded Grace. The whole evening, full as it was with toasts and excited plans at dinner, then passion in Don's arms later, her classmate's words sliced her happiness like a knife, reminding her of what a long way she still had to go to prove that she was more than what she appeared to be.

"You're being paranoid, Don," said Grace as she straightened the blue tie she'd given him for this outing with her parents at the club. She put her hands on his chest and leaned up on the balls of her feet to kiss him chastely on the cheek. The door to the guest room was closed, but it was best not to risk a flare of desire. They'd already come too close to making noise the previous evening when she snuck down to his room to cuddle at midnight. Damn the creaky floorboards.

"I'm not paranoid," said Don moodily, running a bony index finger between his neck and collar. He hated wearing ties. "Your father's barely said ten words to me since I got here. And all he can do is talk about your brother's next race."

"Well, it *is* Henley, Don. And it'll be Kell's *second* if he wins again. It's quite a feat, you know."

"I don't care about rowing, Grace. I care about you. And all Kell can do is ride you for your voice, which you've put so much time into correcting. I'd like to hear him take the bricklayer out of *his* tone."

Let that one slide, Grace, she told herself, though she felt a defensive indignation heat up her chest. Patting Don on the lapels, she shrugged and said, "It's just how they are, Don. Neither of us is going to change them."

"Good thing you left, then," he muttered.

The dining room of the club was flooded with brunch-time light, and a pianist tinkled a Rodgers and Hammerstein medley on the Steinway at the other end of the large room. Their party — Don and Grace; her parents; Peggy and her husband, George Davis; plus Kell and Lizanne — was seated at a round table by the windows so they could look out on the flowering cherry and apple trees outside, which were just reaching their springtime peak. Peggy and George were deep into their second Bloody Marys while her parents were nursing their first. Lizanne was still too young to drink, and handsome, strong-jawed Kell was on a Spartan diet while he trained. Don was waiting for a refill on his mimosa, and Grace was working on her coffee and fresh-squeezed orange juice. She had a feeling she'd need her wits about her, but the awkward silence at the table had her regretting her choice of beverages. Maybe Don wasn't paranoid after all.

"Lizzy," Grace ventured to her younger sister, thinking that high school subjects were likely to be the safest, "how are you liking Mrs. Conyer's history class this year? She used to dress up like pilgrims and presidents when she taught certain lessons. Does she still?"

"Sounds like she has a flair for the theatrical," interjected Don, trying to find a way into the conversation.

Lizanne swallowed a mouthful of eggs Benedict and said, "She's all right. Still dresses up and all. But I like Miss Waverly's math class best."

"What sort of math are you doing this year? Is it geometry?" Grace asked, unnerved by the uninterested clinks of silver against china made by the rest of her family.

Lizanne washed her eggs down with a gulp of milk, then said, "Yeah. Geometry."

Silence again.

"I can't get over how much you girls all look alike," Don said, making eye contact with Peggy and Lizanne, both of whom had the same blond hair, fine noses, and peachy complexions as Grace. In their features and coloring, the three of them were obviously sisters, and obviously their mother's daughters; though Margaret Majer Kelly's hair had darkened over the years, it still had a golden hue that lightened close to blond by every summer's end. Kell had inherited their father's straight nose, wide pearly smile, and darker hair — though not nearly as dark as Don's, Grace could see as they all sat around the table together.

"Too bad that's where the similarities end," her father said, not looking up from his plate, where he was nearly finished with his sausages and eggs.

Grace saw Don's body jerk forward, saw him open his mouth to reply, but she lightly put her hand on his under the table and said brightly, "Yes, I never could handle a tennis racket like Peggy or a lacrosse stick like Lizanne." Don shot her a disapproving look. She'd deal with that later.

"You were a good swimmer," Peggy said jovially. "No one could hold their breath longer than Gracie."

"Thanks, Peggy," said Grace, grateful for her sister's defense, even if it did include a long-standing family barb about her lungs being stronger than her arms. *With a lot of practice,* Grace reminded herself. *No one ever gives me credit for all the hours I put in training my lungs to hold air so long without coughing.*

"Daddy," Peggy said in the playfully reprimanding tone she alone on earth was ever allowed to take with him, "don't forget that Grace's own high school yearbook predicted she'd be a star." Turning to Don, Peggy added, "Don't mind our father, Don. He's never appreciated what it takes to be an actor or actress."

Grace gushed her first real smile of the day at her sister, who had headlined the playbills at several Stevens High School productions.

"I'm sure Grace has told you all about Jack's brother, George," Grace's mother said with a benign smile on her thin lips.

Don nodded appreciatively. "In fact, we met just the other week. Swell guy. You'd never know he won a Pulitzer. So many people in the business get a big head, but George was as humble as can be."

Grace's ears burned hot with embarrassment. She should've warned Don not to mention their rendezvous with Uncle George!

"So" — her dad looked sternly at Grace — "you introduce Don to your uncle before your father? I see how it is."

Don looked at Grace with defeated, apologetic eyes. Peggy's husband, who'd learned long ago to stay quiet at Kelly family events, drained the end of his Bloody Mary and lifted two fingers to signal the waiter for a third.

"Daddy, no," Grace laughed. "Of course not. It's just that Uncle George managed to get us all tickets to *Annie Get Your Gun*," she lied. It had actually been *Streetcar Named Desire,* but she didn't think her father would approve of that one.

Jack Kelly didn't reply. Yes, the silent treatment had always been his favorite punishment.

"So, Don, what do you do to stay fit for the stage?" Kell entered the fray.

"I like to run," said Don. "I find it clears my head."

"I only run to train," said Kell. "Never understood running for the sake of it. By the end of a few miles, I think I might die of boredom."

That's because you have no imagination to entertain you, Kell. "Goodness," Grace joked, "maybe we'd be better off talking politics." But only Peggy and George laughed. Don didn't say anything for the rest of the meal, as John and Kell complained about the "damn Jews and pansies who spread communist filth in the papers," which caused Grace to blanch with embarrassment and be unable to meet Don's eye.

Later, alone on a walk through the winding streets of her neighborhood and up the gentle slope from Henry Avenue, Don seethed with fists deep in his pockets and shoulders up to his ears. "Forget their houseguest. Do they realize they're talking about their own flesh and blood when they say those things?"

"I don't think they understand much at all about Uncle George," lamented Grace, who was still so mortified by her father's comments, she hardly knew what to say except, "I'm very sorry I opened the door to that wretched talk, Don."

"Stop apologizing for everything, Grace," he said, echoing one of the lessons she'd absorbed first year at the Academy: *Never apologize for a performance, before or after you've given it. Never prejudice your audience.* Don went on. "It's not your fault your family's a bunch of small-minded" — he searched for the right, perhaps most polite, word and settled on — *"Irishmen."*

Grace nodded. "It's true," she said tensely, feeling the fist on her heart that clenched whenever he disapproved of her lately. "But I hope they don't affect how you feel about *me.*"

Don stopped walking and pulled Grace close by her hand. Surrounded by the brick-and-stone facades of the houses in her neighborhood, so many of which had been built by her own family, Grace felt shy about showing too much affection for Don. Luckily, he knew enough not to kiss her on the street. "If anything," said Don, "they make me admire you more."

How she wished they were on a bustling New York City street! She'd have kissed him properly, then. As the fist around her heart eased, she contented herself with linking her pinkie finger with his. He leaned over and gave her a quick kiss on the cheek.

When they returned to the house, Fordie greeted them at the side gate. His kind face was downturned. "Grace, can I borrow your friend here for a few minutes? I have something to show him, and I think your mother wants to speak to you alone."

Fear exploded in her throat. Something had happened. Fordie was trying to distract Don, but she couldn't be fooled.

"Of course," she said, releasing Don's hand, and telling him, "I'll see you in a few minutes."

In the front room, her father was pacing — no, stalking was more like it — and her mother jumped up from the chintz couch and ran at Grace, waving a piece of paper in her hand. *"Divorced,* Grace? No, not even divorced yet! *Still married!"*

Grace went numb. She plucked the paper from her mother's hands and saw that it was indeed from the courts in New York. "Where did you get this?" Grace asked, her voice as thin and trembly as it had been before the Academy.

"Never you mind where I got it," her mother said, her voice low and grave. "Did you know?"

No acting class could have trained Grace well enough to lie in that moment. Not to her mother and father. "Yes," she admitted. "But, Mother, they've been separated for years. The divorce is just a formality."

"Maybe to the courts, but not to God," Margaret spat. Grace had never seen her mother this angry. Nor her father, who'd stopped pacing to glare at her from a few feet away. "And I can't even mention what else that . . . *adulterer* had in his bag," her mother finished.

Grace felt tears flood her eyes. *Oh, good Lord, she found the French letters, too — and I told him it was pointless to bring them. I wasn't going to sleep with him under my parents' roof!* Pressing her lips together, she tried to keep from crying outright.

"You will not be going back to New York," her mother said, enunciating each word deliberately.

That was too much. "But, Mother, the Academy! I'm about to graduate!" she cried. "And my jobs! I have a whole line of modeling shoots coming up!"

"Peggy will accompany you to New York the few days you have left to complete your remaining rehearsals and performances, but all your nights will be spent here. If your father had his way, you wouldn't ever return to that den of corruption. As for the modeling, you'll have to cancel."

"That little fantasy world you've been living in your whole life is too much," her father added, finally piping up. "Dolls and plays," he growled, shaking his head. "We indulged you too long. Get your head out of the clouds, Grace. It's one thing to aspire to the stage, and another to bring the stage home. It ain't the real world, little girl. If you want to pursue this thing, you'll have to prove to us you still have a good head on

75

your shoulders and your feet are firmly planted on the ground."

Grace couldn't hold it in any longer. As the dam on her sobbing broke, she covered her face and ran to her room, where she lay on her bed and cried so hard, she nearly made herself sick. The house was silent for hours except for the sound of Don — and someone else; she hoped Fordie and not Kell — coming up the stairs, making some hurried, shuffling noises in the guest room. Blood and tears throbbing painfully inside her skull, Grace got up from bed and cracked open her door as quietly as possible so that she could peer down the hall toward the guest room. It was her brother standing on the threshold, arms folded over his chest, watching as Don presumably stuffed his belongings into his bag. Humiliated, for herself and for Don, Grace choked back a fresh sob and silently shut her door, then sank to her bedroom floor. It felt as though her heart were actually breaking in two as she heard the men's footsteps thud down the hall and the stairs and out of the house. She watched as the car started in the garage, backed out of the driveway, then drove its lonely way down Henry Avenue; she wondered if Don was looking up at her; it was too dark for her to see.

The stage might not be the so-called real world, she screamed at her father in her mind as the tears came again, *but it's the only world I want to be in.* How could it be otherwise when the world she'd come from had driven her to the theater, and it had taken her into its open arms?

CHAPTER 4

"Darling Grace," cooed Uncle George, enveloping his niece in a tight and understanding hug, "tell me all about it."

It was a hot May afternoon, and Grace had been reading Arthur Miller's *All My Sons* under the shade of an enormous umbrella beside the club's glittering blue pool. Uncle George was a welcome sight for her wrung-dry eyes.

"I can't imagine things being any worse," said Grace, setting aside the play and curling into a ball with her knees tucked under her chin.

"I can," said her uncle. If she didn't love and trust him so much, his amused and vaguely patronizing tone would have sent her around the bend. Instead, she was curious.

"You can't be serious," she countered.

George looked up at the umbrella, appearing to gather his thoughts. He was like an oasis in the desert. Though he shared some of his good looks with his brother, Jack, George's unblemished skin hadn't been ravaged by years of barking orders to construction workers under the summer sun. His dark hair was just long enough to show its wave, and he kept it combed gently back from his face. In his short-sleeved white linen shirt and pressed chino pants, George Kelly was the epitome of summer elegance.

"Well, for one thing," he said, "you did graduate from the Academy. With flying colors, I might add."

"But I couldn't attend the ceremony," she pointed out.

"Your curriculum vitae will not say whether you attended the ceremony or not," he countered. "And no director will ever ask."

"And no director asked me to audition for his next play, either."

"Sometimes those invitations don't come until later," he said. "And you're young. You need to pay your dues."

"I didn't pay my dues at the Academy?!" Grace whined indignantly, feeling hopeless and put-upon once more.

Uncle George chuckled. "Whoa there. Some of the best actors I know had to take small roles in smaller theaters first. They worked their way up. Adjust your expectations down."

Grace ground her teeth. Not only was it irritating to know her uncle was right, it was even more irritating to know that her impatience came from her win-at-any-costs father, who was — as she sat there licking her wounds — on the Schuylkill River mercilessly goading Kell toward his second Henley.

"I'd be willing to sweep the damn floor of a theater, Uncle George, if you could just get me out of here." If she had to go to one more luncheon or garden party with her mother, she was going to go insane.

"As it happens, I might have your ticket out of here," he said, smirking at the way she lurched forward to grab his arm in anticipation. "Don't get too excited," he warned. "I can't get you back to New York just yet. But I can get you into the Bucks County Playhouse this summer. They're doing *The Torch-Bearers,* and since I think you'd make a marvelous Florence McCrickett, I can put in a good word for you. Of course, you'll have to audition."

"Oh!" Grace said, grasping her uncle's arms. "Truly, George? Do you think Mom and Dad will let me?"

George gave her an exaggeratedly reproving look. "Do you honestly think I'd come and taunt you with this suggestion if I hadn't already spoken to them first?"

At this, Grace flung her arms around her uncle and squealed with delight. "You're the best!"

"I am, aren't I?" His voice was airy and devil-may-care, and she wished she knew how he did it.

"When do I go?"

"Now, now, hold your horses. You'll be commuting from home all summer, and that's only *if* you get a part. About an hour and a half each way. It'll mean a lot of late nights and early mornings. But I couldn't convince your parents to let you stay with the company."

For a moment, Grace felt her heart take a plunge, but then, she realized that Fordie would make all that time in the car more than bearable. "I'll do anything it takes," she said.

"Excellent," said George. "You can thank me by getting a good part. I've told the director to look for you."

A week later, Grace celebrated landing the part of Florence McCrickett in both *The Torch-Bearers* and *The Doctor's Wife,* as well as the smaller role of Marian Almond in *The Heiress,* which meant more to Grace in some ways than the leading parts in her uncle's plays, because it indicated that the company valued her for more than just her family relationship to a prizewinning playwright. To celebrate, Uncle George took her for champagne, then to the Mask and Wig, Philadelphia's oldest college musical venue, which her uncle had loved since he snuck into it as a local high school student, and they laughed themselves off their chairs at a troupe performing excerpts from *The Mikado*. Grace felt expansive, grateful, *excited* for the first time in ages. She couldn't wait to see what would come next.

She worked hard that summer, always tumbling onto the leather seat of her family's comfortable black sedan sweaty, exhausted, and rapturous from the day's exertions. As Fordie drove south on the dark highway, their headlights the only illumination for miles, she'd relive the day she'd spent in the gristmill-turned-theater, a big red barn of a building where Helen Hayes and Lillian Gish had starred before her.

"Fordie!" she'd exclaim, her new voice a real voice now; she could modulate it at any volume. "It's like nothing else. We rehearse lines outside in the morning in the shade. It's like we're Puck and Bottom, except of course we're not. We're the McCricketts, but that's what it *feels* like. Then, in the afternoon, we go inside and work on the stage, and it's so *hot,* you wouldn't believe it. They set fans on us, and they're either so loud, we can't hear each other, or too quiet to make anything cooler. But no one cares. It's all part of the charm of the place. They only turn on the air-conditioning for audiences — it's part of what they're paying for," she laughed.

"Have to keep those customers happy," Fordie agreed, smiling over at Grace, for she always took the passenger seat beside him those nights. She hated the formality of sitting in the backseat with him driving her around. And he didn't mind if she didn't want to talk, and instead closed her eyes while the sultry night air billowed in from the open window and she composed letters to Don in her mind that she never actually wrote but once. Most nights, she was so tired, she fell asleep by the time they reached Henry Avenue, and there wasn't any time for letter writing during the rehearsal days, and on Sundays her mother made sure she attended church, then showed her off during lunch at the club. Sunday afternoon was her one time to herself, and she usually napped or caught a movie with Lizanne, or met with Uncle George to talk about the plays.

Don sent a few letters, always to the playhouse so her mother couldn't get her hands on them, and though they were amorous and full of support for her summer endeavors, as well as his hope that they might be reunited in New York soon, he felt very far away. Summer stock was proving more all consuming than any other theater experience she'd had before. The players and set designers, musicians, and everyone involved with the production became her world, and anything and anyone outside Bucks County . . . well, it simply didn't exist. Those Sunday excursions with her family even felt like visiting another planet, false somehow, not the real world. It didn't hurt that she'd been carrying on an increasingly less platonic flirtation with Paul Valle, the dead-handsome lead set designer who was also a painter with his first gallery show in New York coming in the winter.

She arranged for Fordie to see the dress rehearsal for *The Doctor's Wife,* because, maddeningly, her parents would never approve of him sitting in the audience for opening night. "So you can see it before they do," she told him, with a mischievous, shushing finger at her lips, "with Uncle

84

George and William." When the small, motley audience leapt to their feet in applause, Grace's heart was beating so fast, she could hardly breathe. Her fingers linked with the other actors' in relieved solidarity while they raised their arms above their heads, then let them drop. As they bowed, she felt exhilarated and happy in a way that was completely new. In fact, had she ever been happy before? Somehow, all her previous happinesses seemed trivial now. This explosion of heat and energy in her chest was the real thing, what she knew she'd spend the rest of her life in quest of.

With a kiss on the cheek, Fordie gave her a bouquet of pink and blue hydrangea blooms, and said, "You were amazing, Gracie. You've got the gift."

"You did my script proud, Grace," said Uncle George. "I think this will put you back on the Yellow Brick Road."

William handed her a large wrapped box, beaming with pride and excitement, and said, "It's from both of us." It was her certificate from the Academy in a lovely burnished-gold frame. Tears came to Grace's eyes as she said, "I can't wait to hang this in my next New York apartment."

Later, in a stolen moment after the cast party, Paul kissed her with such hunger, she was tempted to spend the night with him on the mattress that lay unceremoniously on the floor of his studio among his canvases. If it hadn't been for Fordie waiting to drive her home, she might have done it, since Paul's firm, strong body was exactly what her own felt it needed to settle its restless energy that night. But Fordie was indeed waiting for her, and she was still in Pennsylvania. Her father's territory.

But, her uncle had said, she was on her way. She'd make damn sure of that.

CHAPTER 5

"Which beaus are *these* from?" Prudy wondered aloud as she carried a box of roses from the door of their apartment into the kitchen. "I swear, Grace, we don't have enough vases!"

"We'll just have to get another one from Mr. Chin on the corner," Grace said, digging in her purse to find her favorite lipstick as she clicked in her new heels across the hardwood floor of their six-room flat. There were already two other vases of roses on their kitchen table.

She looked at all the red petals, and shook her head. "These men show no imagination," she lamented. Asmir Kazmi's far more impressive arrangement of exotic blooms — orchids and pink foliage she'd never seen before — had long since died off, and she hadn't seen him anywhere recently. Back in late September, he'd told her he had business in Paris, and would be back in New York soon. Now it was Halloween, *The Father* was going to open on Broadway in just over two weeks, and it looked as though he was going to miss her debut. She wasn't even sure why she cared — it wasn't like she was in love with the dark-haired, long-lashed playboy. His attentions were flattering, though, and a welcome break from the bond traders and lawyers she met when she went out with her girlfriends. For their first date, Asmir had taken her on a private boat ride up the Hudson, rather than to the Waldorf or the Plaza or one of the trendy restaurants popping up all over the Village that made the uptown men feel very au courant for patronizing with an actress on their arm.

After the debacle with Don, she'd sworn off actors for a while. When she arrived back in New York at the end of the summer, having just landed the role of Bertha in Strindberg's masterpiece, playing opposite the great Raymond Massey of all people, she'd seen Don on her first night back in town. It was a forbidden meeting, which made it all the sweeter. When Uncle George suggested she audition for *The Father* at the end of her run in Bucks County, she'd taken the train to New York without telling her parents and furiously knitted a scarf for Lizanne and baby boots for Peggy's little daughter while awaiting the results. She'd been just about to embark on an ambitious sweater project for herself, just to keep herself busy, when the director called. "We were quite impressed, Ms. Kelly, and look forward to seeing you in rehearsals," he'd said, and it had taken all her restraint not to shout, *Oh, thank you, thank you! You have made my day — my week — my year!*

As soon as she hung up, she rang Uncle George and demanded, "What are we going to tell Mom and Dad?"

"I've been thinking about just that," he said, sounding for all the world like an Agatha Christie detective as he explained his plan: Grace would share an apartment with her conservative friend Prudy Wise from the Barbizon, whom Grace's mother had met and loved. They would reside in a small building with a strict doorman — of course, Uncle George knew just the right one — and their place would have a guest room for any family member who cared to drop in and check on her virtue.

Breathless with nerves and hope, she explained it all to her parents one night after dinner at their place in Ocean City, where her father was always at his most relaxed and magnanimous.

"You'd better not see that Don Richardson fellow," he snarled nevertheless.

"Daddy," Grace lied in a light and dismissive tone, "I haven't seen him for months. And if there's one thing this summer's shown me, it's that I'll be too busy with the play to see anyone socially." Her mother raised a skeptical eyebrow, but she and her father let Grace go. The truth was, she had Kell to thank for her parents' permission. He'd won at Henley again in July, and her father had been in the best of moods ever since, floating high above everything and everyone. Anything that didn't have to do with sculling and his son happened so far beneath him, Grace's escape to New York hardly merited more than his warning.

She hadn't even unpacked her suitcase in her new place on Sixty-Sixth Street when Don knocked on her door and pulled her by the hand to one of their old haunts, and instead of spending her first nights in her new bed, she spent them in his old familiar one. The morning she readied herself for her first day of rehearsals, he'd zipped her dress and watched from the bed as she fastened her earrings and put on her glasses, then turned to him and said, "How do I look?"

"Like you're ready for a day at Bloomingdale's instead of hard work."

Ignoring the edgy feeling, she playfully stuck out her tongue at him before grabbing her purse, kissing him on the cheek, and setting out into the crisp September morning. She'd always known what to wear, and she refused to let Don make her feel differently. But the comment, from the mouth of a former teacher, put a damper on her sprits that day. She knew he was annoyed that she'd stayed away from New York for so long — he couldn't understand why she was willing to "do Daddy's bidding," as he'd put it. He just couldn't respect that she wanted her parents' approval.

And he kept at it. "I don't see why you go home to visit so often," and "To be a real actress, you're going to have to give up the country club," and "You're so successful as a model, you don't even need their money, so why bother?" She let his comments all go with a shrug, and occasionally a firm "They're my *parents*, Don."

Once when she said this, he replied, "Did you ever stop to think who you might be if you had different parents?"

"Whyever would I do that?" she replied, genuinely shocked. "I wouldn't be *me* without them. The good and the bad."

She could see the muscles in Don's jaw

tense as he shook his head. "I've been avoiding telling you this, but I think you should know it," he said, too aggressively, "but your brother's been calling me and telling me he'll beat me with a rowing oar if I don't stop seeing you."

"Why would you say something like that? Kell's not a thug." A tiny voice inside her — where was it? Her heart? Her belly? Her head? — said, *It might be true, you know.*

"You can take the boy out of Philly . . ."

"Shut up, Don," Grace snapped, her color and anger rising to silence the tiny voice. "It's one thing if you can't cope with my success, but don't . . ."

"Success?" Don laughed. "One Broadway play and you're a success? Let's just see what the reviews say, shall we?"

At that, Grace pressed her lips together, snatched her overnight bag, and slammed the door on her way out. *Wait!* called the tiny voice, and Grace shut a door on it as well.

Don had apologized with a phone call that night, and shown up to the theater with a box of her favorite French chocolates a few days later when he hadn't heard back from her — which was really a dirty trick, because he knew half the cast and she had to be nice to him in front of them all. He managed to get himself invited out to dinner with a group of them that night. Though she tried to avoid it, she still somehow got squished into a booth between Don and the director's secretary, a ruddy woman with flaking lipstick called Hannah Simpson. Grace made valiant conversation with Hannah all through dinner, and found out everything about the middle-aged woman's high school–age son and daughter, both of whom wanted to be actors themselves, and her aging father with dementia, who lived with them in Queens much to her husband's chagrin. Passing on all the wine offered to her, Grace felt particularly disgusted when Don slurred in her ear, "I'm real sorry, Grace. I'm sure you're going to get rave reviews. Are you going to punish me forever?"

She turned to him then and saw the drippy infatuation in his face, the same as all the boys she'd known growing up. And here she'd been thinking Don was different. But he was only older, which somehow made him all the more pathetic. One thing kept her from recoiling altogether, or making a cutting final remark in reply: that word he'd used, *punish*. Hadn't she thought the exact same thing about her own father, back in the spring, and so many times throughout her childhood: that his favorite punishment was the silent treatment? Wasn't she doing the exact same thing to Don? She might not have been willing to accept criticism of her family, but neither did she want to be like them. That was what her whole New York project was about, after all — *being* Grace Kelly. The Grace Kelly her parents could finally see, respect, and adore.

Curling her lips into an apologetic smile, she put her hand on his under the table and said, "I'm sorry I've been distracted lately. I've been so worried about the play, and . . . well, I've sort of forgotten myself."

Looking immensely relieved, Don said, "I understand completely. This is a big break for you, and nerves are good — they're healthy. But you're going to be terrific, Gracie. Just like you were in Bucks County. Better."

"Thanks, Don. That means a lot coming from you." And it did. But it didn't change anything.

That little exchange nicely paved the way for her to say, when he tried to tug her toward a cab to his place, "Not tonight, Don. I'm exhausted and need to sleep tonight or I'll never get through rehearsal tomorrow."

She only had to put him off a few more

times before he took the hint. It helped that when he showed up one last time at her place unannounced, he'd seen Asmir's impressive vase of flowers prominently centered on her dining room table. Lesson learned: involvement with another actor was hazardous. Proceed with caution.

It was a good thing her theater career was taking off, or she'd have been far more disappointed. But there was a perfect and complete consolation in getting off the subway at Forty-Ninth and Broadway every evening for rehearsal, when the white lights of the theaters were just shining on in the autumn twilight. Every day throughout October, the set came together piece by piece as she and Raymond Massey and Mady Christians, who played her mother, brought the play to life on the drafty stage. It was the largest stage she'd ever been on — it seemed they kept increasing in size and stature just as she had planned in her daydreams — and initially she'd felt tiny standing upon it. But as the play took shape and she felt her character bond to Raymond's and Mady's, felt the rooms of the set taking up space behind and around her, Grace began to feel larger herself on the stage.

Four days before the play opened, Grace

celebrated her twentieth birthday on November twelfth at Sardi's with Raymond and Mady, Uncle George, Prudy, Carolyn, and some of her other Barbizon friends who were still in town, and their boyfriends. Not wanting to complicate the evening, she'd gone stag to her own party and felt like a million dollars in her new black dress from Saks with its full chiffon skirt and ballet neck. Then, because she missed her mother — who, in any case, would be up with her father in a few days time, to see the play and celebrate a belated and more intimate birthday with the family — Grace added the pearl choker her mom had given her for her eighteenth birthday. It was a fizzy evening, with excitement mounting about opening night of *The Father,* and many toasts to Grace's health and promising career.

"Thank you, everyone," Grace said after she blew out the candles on the chocolate cake. "I feel like the luckiest girl in New York, which is to say *the world,* to be here with so many talented and thoughtful people tonight. I hope you'll all feel the same way about me in five days!"

As her friends jeered playfully at her self-deprecation, Grace raised her champagne coupe. "To the best of friends." And she felt her heart swell, knowing that these friends would love her even if the play — or she — failed. She felt the same way about all of them.

In the back of her mind, though, she heard someone sneer *cover girl,* and it put a lump of worry in her throat, as if everything she was enjoying that night were unfounded, stolen, not even hers for the taking.

Brooks Atkinson of the *New York Times* said that Grace "gives a charming, pliable performance" in her Broadway debut.

"That's fabulous, Grace," said her childhood friend Maree Frisby over Cokes and cheeseburgers at a busy midtown diner the day after the play opened. Grace had been up all night with the rest of the cast awaiting the review in the papers; then she hadn't been able to sleep a wink when she tumbled into bed at six in the morning. By eleven, she was starving, so she'd phoned her friend at work to see if she could meet for lunch.

"Pliable," said Grace with a frown. "What does that even mean?"

"It means flexible, Grace. It's a compliment."

"I think I'd rather be bold. Like Katharine Hepburn. Or Marlene Dietrich."

"You'll have to change your look, then, I

think," said Maree.

"Why? Why can't I be myself and still be bold?"

"Because you look like a ballet dancer, not a pantsuit-wearing broad, that's why."

Grace thought about this paradox while she munched on a French fry. "Ballet dancers are some of the toughest women working today."

Maree rolled her eyes. "Boy, are you in a contrary mood today. Be happy with the review, Grace! It's good! And for your first time on the Great White Way, I'd say it was fantastic."

That night, Grace arrived in her dressing room feeling somewhat revived after three hours of deep, post-cheeseburger sleep, to find an enormous bouquet of autumnal dahlias, roses, and Chinese lanterns, with a note in Asmir's own hand saying, "Break a leg. I made us reservations at Delmonico's after."

No "Please join me" or "Could you come to dinner?" Asmir didn't fool around with propriety, and his confidence was extremely appealing.

From the wings of the stage before she went on for her first scene, she glimpsed him sitting in a private box, gazing down appraisingly. Thankfully the lights were too bright and her eyesight too poor for her to see him while she said her lines; but nevertheless, she felt his eyes on her as she moved about the stage, and the connection between them felt intimate and illicit; she thought perhaps her performance was a little bolder because of it.

Later, as she was tugging on her gloves and wondering if she should go to Delmonico's at all — maybe it was best to treat Asmir as distantly as possible, and just enjoy the admiration from afar — one of the crew members knocked on her door and put her head inside and said, "Miss Kelly? There's a car waiting for you at the back entrance." Beneath the protective folds of her coat and dress, her body gave an immediate and powerful physical response to this announcement and all it implied. She wanted handsome, mysterious Asmir. And he appeared to know exactly how to seduce her.

He was not in the car but waiting for her at a secluded booth in the back of the restaurant. He stood when she arrived and the maître d' took her coat. "I am so glad you could join me," he said, kissing the fingers of her gloved hand.

"Well, you didn't give me much choice, did you," she said, though not as a question.

"With me, you will always have a choice," he said, sitting down and placing the white napkin on his lap. "But I will always make my preferences known."

"And what are your preferences, Mr. Kazmi?"

"That the most beautiful and talented young actress in New York should have dinner with me tonight," he smiled, and it was only when he smiled that she saw how young he really was, for the gesture was just a tad too eager. She'd read somewhere that he was twenty-six, but his black hair and equally dark eyes gave him an almost ageless look. It was his smile that gave him away.

"What a ridiculous thing to say with Vivien Leigh and Gene Tierney in plays right now," she said, though she took the seat offered her, and gently laid a napkin on her lap.

Asmir dismissed her modesty with a gentle wave of his hand. "You must learn to own yourself, Miss Kelly. You were excellent in the play tonight. Know your worth. Such confidence is very attractive in a woman."

Not to all men, she thought to herself. And anyway, she had a feeling Asmir only found those qualities attractive in his mistresses;

he'd want a very different kind of woman as a wife.

But that's hardly what I'm here to become, she thought as she ordered herself a glass of champagne and began to relax. Curiously, though, Asmir did not try to make her his mistress. She saw him twice more before he left New York again, and both times their dinners were quite chaste, ending only in a kiss before she took a cab home. To her own surprise, she was relieved. She had a feeling that if he'd wanted more from her, she'd have given it, and it would have led to problems. She could see herself falling for him, see herself getting pulled into his orbit and left wanting more and wondering why he couldn't give it to her. Even as it was, he left her wanting more — not from him exactly, but from a man like him, someone unafraid of her looks or her ambition, who could still appreciate both and make her forget all her doubts about herself.

The night her parents and Lizanne and Kell were in the audience for *The Father,* Grace was tied in knots. She half wanted Don backstage to make her feel better, since he was the only other actor she knew who had met her family and could maybe understand the particular brand of nerves she was

101

experiencing. For the first time in years, she actually threw up before the curtain call.

Get ahold of yourself, Kelly, she told herself. *Show 'em what you've got.*

But it was hard when she felt like so much was at stake. If she choked onstage, not only would it sink her chances of future roles, it would prove to her father that she was exactly what he'd always said: the weakling younger sister of Perfect Peggy, his darling Ba. And as a bonus, it would prove to her less-kind classmates from the Academy that maybe she was just a cover girl after all.

Grateful again for her blindness onstage, she managed to get through the play, though she had little idea how. She knew she'd said all the right lines, made all the correct moves. In the wings and at intermission, Raymond Massey and other fellow players told her it was her best performance yet. She'd always thought she'd be able to tell when she was giving her best, but that night it felt as though she'd entered some sort of dreamlike dimension, in which she spoke and moved, but heard her own words and those of others from far away.

When the audience roared its approval, the dream dissolved, and suddenly she was very present and hearing everything at full volume. The applause hurt her ears. People in the audience were standing and whistling. She held the hands of her castmates on her left and right, lifting their clasped fists into the air. As she stood and waited for the director to come out and take a bow, she squinted into the audience and couldn't find her parents anywhere. Everything was a fuzzy silver-and-black blur. Still, she felt the applause vibrate up her legs and all through her chest, and she smiled so hard, her cheeks ached.

In her dressing room after, her family crowded around her. "You were terrific!" exclaimed Lizanne, and Kell even said, "I'm impressed, Gracie. Nice job." Her mother gave her a tight hug perfumed with Chanel No. 5, and said in her ear, "Beautiful, just beautiful," before holding her at arm's length and saying for everyone to hear, "Who'd have imagined little Grace Kelly of East Falls would find her way to Broadway!"

Her father said, quoting the *Times,* much to Grace's surprise, "*Charming, pliable* Grace Kelly. Not that anyone back home reads the New York papers." Her heart gave an angry spasm in silent protest, but she did not reply.

Raymond Massey passed by the open door to her room, and stopped when he saw all the people. "Grace! I'm hurt," he said jestingly, his hand clutching his heart. "You didn't invite me to your party?" Grateful for the distraction, Grace said breathlessly, "Raymond! This is my family, up from Philadelphia." And she introduced them all around.

When he and her father shook hands, her fellow actor said jovially, "Jack! I haven't seen you in ages. I didn't know Grace was *your* Kelly. How the hell are you?"

Grace's eyes widened as she asked, "You two know each other?"

"Army golf tournament after the war. Of course your father beat us all," Raymond replied with knowing good humor. Then, directly to Jack, he said, "You must be so proud of young Grace here."

"I'm proud of *all* my children, Raymond. Did you hear Kell won his *second* Henley this summer?"

Raymond raised his eyebrows in surprise as Grace and Lizanne exchanged indulgent *Well, what're you going to do? Daddy's just being Daddy* expressions. Her mother smiled as if to echo *I'm so proud of all my children.* Behind the stiff stays of her corset, Grace felt her father's slight as a dagger's jab in her stomach. *I have a long way to go.* This thought was both maddening and comforting at the same time, a slip back into childhood, into a world without the confusing and often conflicting sentiments of men like Asmir or Don, or fellow players like Faye and Raymond. At home, she'd mastered the rules and known how to behave to get what she wanted — within reason, of course, always within reason and decorum, the dual tyrants of the world that had made her.

CHAPTER 6

1951

She was beginning to feel like a complete fraud. In fact, she was tempted to call her theater agent, Edith Van Cleve, and demand, "Why do you bother with me? You represent Marlon Brando, for heaven's sake, and I haven't managed to get a part worth a damn since nineteen forty-nine!" Instead, she said something like it to Sally Parrish, a fellow model and friend from the Barbizon, and now her new roommate on Sixty-Sixth Street.

"What are you talking about, Grace? You work all the time!" Her friend handed her a cold soda. It was a stiflingly hot Saturday in late May, the kind that filled the air with the scent of garbage and made anything you wore stick to your back all day long. All their windows were open and fans were whirring, but still the perspiration trickled down her limbs.

"Oh, television work, sure. But that's hardly *theater*," said Grace.

"But it's not nothing, either. And there was the movie, too, don't forget."

Filming *14 Hours* for two whirlwind days in sunny Hollywood when she would have otherwise been shivering on the streets of late-fall New York, then going to the film's premiere in a new Christian Dior dress, *had* been fun. But she was tired of everyone trotting it out as some sort of proof of her success. It was a bit part, and it hadn't exactly gone anywhere. Anyway, for a star to rise in Hollywood, you had to sign a contract with one of the studios, and then they owned you. How could she keep the door open for New York theater if she became a slave to Hollywood?

"You make more, and work longer hours, than anyone I know, including most of the doctors and lawyers," Sally went on. "*It'll happen,* Gracie. You just need to relax. A watched pot and all that."

Grace sipped the cool, fizzy soda and felt it crackle down her throat.

She felt sorry for herself; that was all there was to it. And since she hated self-pity, she was angry at herself on top of it.

It had been almost two years since *The Father,* and she hadn't gotten any other

Broadway parts. Oh, the summer stock companies she joined July after July were wonderful, like becoming part of a big, raucous family for a few glorious and sultry weeks. In fact, she was off to another one in Denver, at the well-regarded Elitch Theater, very soon.

But in New York, Edith sent her to all sorts of auditions, and she even got a few callbacks, but never the part. *Always the bridesmaid . . .* Every time, she'd learn her lines and dress carefully to go to the theater to deliver them, hope beating a drum in her chest. Then she'd be cautiously happy for a day or two, while she knitted and read novels in her apartment, leaving only to take a long walk in the park and collect a few groceries early in the morning, since she didn't want to miss the call. Then she'd find out the part had gone to someone else, and she'd try to soothe herself with a night out on the town. The champagne and flirtation made her feel better temporarily, but she'd always wake the next morning feeling as heavy as the bed she was lying on. After the first dozen rejections, Grace took to just staying in bed for a day, her hair stringy and her limbs mushy.

There were always reasons — "notes," Edith called them — though Grace couldn't do anything about most of them because they were more related to who she was than how she acted. Too pretty. Too quiet. Too cold. Too tall. Not curvy enough. Not experienced enough. Not old enough. Or her favorite, "She's a great actress, but she's just not right for this part." What was she supposed to do with that?

Utterly useless.

Had she peaked too soon? And what a peak: some summer stock and one short Broadway run. It was more like a foothill than a mountain.

Meanwhile, offers for television work poured in. She knew she should be happier about this, as it paid very well and the live dramas were even a bit like theater. The players rehearsed on a stage, the sets and costumes were always well designed, and they acted out the drama in one long take, interrupted by a few commercial breaks. There were no do-overs as in the advertisements she was also hired for, or as there were in the one movie she'd done. As in the theater, there was a do-or-die mentality among the TV actors: they had one shot to get it right, to use their voices and bodies to reach out and touch the hearts of the thousands of viewers watching them on their screens that night.

The thought of those viewers, a far bigger audience than could fit in even the largest theater, was some solace. But the paltry applause of the cameramen, wardrobe and makeup stylists, and other workers around the set when the director shouted, "And that's a wrap!" just wasn't the same. And — she'd admit this snobbery only to herself — there was something cheap and Cracker Jacks about television dramas, especially because of the commercials for detergents and toothpastes that interrupted the shows, a few of which she was even in! She wondered what viewers thought about watching her in costume as a princess, or a thirties housewife, or a Tudor courtesan, only to see her hawking the latest dish soap in a frilly apron at the break — if television viewers even noticed such details! No, much as they had in common, television just wasn't the theater; it could never have the same gravitas, the same lineage of Aristophanes, Shakespeare, and even Noël Coward.

Peggy and Lizanne were very sweet, and watched all the programs she appeared in, and in kind, sisterly fashion, they always called the next day to tell her how much they liked the show and Grace's performance in it. Uncle George caught most of them and also called with his congratulations. She had the impression her mother was watching most of them, for she always had something to say when they spoke on the phone: "That was such a sad story you were in the other night, Gracie. I don't know how you do it without getting depressed." Or: "I wasn't sure if it was our television or you, but I could barely hear you last night. Maybe you should speak up a bit?" And once in a while, she'd drop a precious gem of a compliment into Grace's ear: "I loved the program last night, Gracie. And you looked absolutely beautiful."

Once, Grace made the mistake of asking her father if he'd seen any of the shows she'd been in, and he said, distractedly, "The only thing I turn on that damn machine for is baseball." A Broadway play her father couldn't ignore. He had to show up at some point, if only not to look like a jerk to his cronies.

Ironically, though, it was her father who put her onto the idea that gave her the most hope. She was down in East Falls for a short visit before going to Denver, and he was grousing at dinner about losing a contract for a building to another firm with better connections on the hallowed Main Line.

Connections, Grace thought. Maybe it wasn't an accident that she'd won her best part when she'd just finished with the Academy, when her name was freshly off their graduate rolls and on the tips of her well-connected teachers' tongues. *Maybe I need more lessons . . . and connections.*

Apart from the thought that a well-known teacher could open new doors for her, she quite liked the idea of being a student again. Surely there was more to learn, and maybe a mentor could help her decode Edith's notes and make them into meaningful instructions to follow.

Luckily, New York had many choices. Lee Strasberg was making quite a splash with his Group Theater, though Grace didn't think she could abide his so-called method. She'd heard that Strasberg and his colleagues Harold Clurman and Cheryl Crawford entreated their students to tap into their own reservoirs of pain and suffering to play afflicted characters. With the exception of playing Tracy Lord in *Philadelphia Story* at the Academy — which, after all, was a comedy, and not some soul-searching tragedy — acting had always felt like an *escape* from her own pains, not an excuse to indulge them. And look where the method seemed to be getting poor Marilyn Monroe, that absurdly talented stunner who, Grace had heard, could barely show up to work.

But there were other teachers, splinters from the Group Theater, like Stella Adler and Sanford Meisner, who might be better suited to her.

She had just enough time in New York before going to Denver to secure a spot somewhere for fall, but she'd have to move quickly. Washing the night's sticky, nervous film off her skin with a cool shower, she slipped into a linen dress and took the subway to the Academy, where she knocked on Don's office door. Slowly and unexpectedly, after seeing each other at this party and that club around town, the two of them had found their way to friendship after the end of their romance. Grace had the sense that Don would have fallen right back into the sack if she said the word — he regarded all her other dates with jealous eyes — but she'd made it clear that their relationship was now strictly platonic. For the past few months, he'd been going out with Judy, an eccentric and gorgeous young sculptor who lived in SoHo and whom Grace enjoyed seeing when they all went out.

"Well, isn't this a nice surprise?" He beamed when he opened his door and saw her standing there.

"I need some advice about finding a new teacher."

They went to a pastry shop around the corner and ordered Danish and coffee, and Grace told Don that she felt she needed more instruction.

"I thought you'd never ask."

"Not *you,* Don. I've learned all I can from you," she said lightly, a tease.

"You haven't," he said firmly, "but I agree you need someone else."

She felt stung by his affirmation that she needed more training, but then — this was Don, and . . . well, she *did* need help.

"Don't say Strasberg," said Grace.

Holding up his hands, palms to her, he said, "Give me some credit for knowing you better than that."

She broke into a huge grin. This was exactly why she'd come to him. Even better, he added, "I was actually just having a conversation with Artie and Greg about this very subject." Arthur Miller and Gregory Peck, Grace had to assume. She'd read in her alumni bulletin that both men had come to the Academy recently to teach short workshops.

And off they went on a conversation about the relative merits of Strasberg's, Adler's, and Meisner's schools of acting, comparing them to Uta Hagen's ideas, which had largely been the foundation of the Academy's courses. In the end, Don said he'd call Sanford Meisner and put in a good word, and Grace floated onto the bustling sidewalk, feeling like life had meaning and purpose again.

With Sandy Meisner's tutorials to look forward to in the fall, for he'd accepted her into his atelier on Don's recommendation, Grace allowed herself to marinate in the blue skies of Denver by day and the hotbed of talent in the Elitch Theater every night. In the first week, she became involved with fellow player Gene Lyons. Almost as soon as they met, he said to her, "Who'd've thought two kids from Pennsylvania would be headlining summer stock at the Elitch out west, eh?"

Their shared mid-Atlantic childhood — he from Pittsburgh and she from East Falls — made him feel like home right away. Blond and tan from long hikes in the mountains, Gene was rough around the edges even when he was trying valiantly to fit in with a more genteel crowd, and like her father, he had a chip on his shoulders about not belonging in that crowd. Grace was aware that her fine nose, meticulously refined posture, and corrected voice allowed her to blend into the most rarefied circles;

people were always surprised to discover she was one of *those* Kellys, and if they didn't know her family, they were shocked to discover she was Catholic, and of Irish descent; she rarely mentioned that in fact her mother's family was from Germany, since she hardly remembered it herself, so thoroughly had Margaret Majer become Margaret Kelly. Being with Gene tapped into some vein she hadn't realized ran through her, and she began to revel in her outsider status.

"The arts might be full of certain kinds of outcasts, but they form their own mafia, the intelligentsia," Gene said derisively. "What about us folks from meat-and-potatoes America? We'll show them, Grace."

Had her father said this, Grace would have wanted to throw her own potato at him. But after all the rejections in New York, she found Gene's attitude viscerally appealing. *Yes,* she thought, *let's show them.* And anyway, she understood that what Gene meant was not that he wanted to beat the intelligentsia, but rather to be treated as an equal by them — which was all she'd ever wanted herself.

Gene was the exact opposite of Asmir and the other wealthy men who courted her in the city, but he was also so completely unlike Don and the other actors she'd known that she gave up her no-actors vow to be with him. In bed, he was thrillingly red-blooded, with no airs. His kisses were long and deep, and he kept his eyes closed except to look at her body as his hands roamed appreciatively over her small breasts and slim thighs. With corsets and hourglass figures all the rage, Grace was always nervous about her naked body, that free of the padding and cinching of her carefully selected wardrobe, her lack of curves would be disappointing to a man. But Gene groaned with pleasure at the sight and feel of her. He handled her a little roughly and wasn't afraid to use his teeth, as if he knew she wasn't a china doll; he knew she could take it, wanted it, that somewhere in her was the femme fatale she'd never be cast as. It was exhilarating to play that role in bed with him.

They had to keep it on the q.t. because he was still married, though he was awaiting an annulment. The secrecy made him simultaneously more safe and more dangerous. Safe because she wouldn't have to deal with the inevitable questions from theater gossips about their relationship, and dangerous because of the risk of being caught, and because of what a future with him would mean. She wasn't eager to repeat the anguish of her affair with Don and her family; even though Gene was at least Catholic, she knew she would have to fess up to the fact that he'd been married before.

One lazy Friday morning, as she was sleeping off a particularly late night with the company, Edith woke Grace with a phone call. "Edith," Grace said groggily, looking at her clock and seeing it wasn't even eight, "it's two hours earlier out here."

"I didn't want to run the risk of you going out for the day and missing you. I've got Jay Kanter on the line, and he has an important opportunity for you. Hear him out." Though Grace had only spoken to Jay Kanter once before, very briefly before she did *14 Hours,* she knew that Edith and Jay each represented Marlon Brando for theater and film, respectively.

Her interest piqued, Grace sat up in bed and patted her sheets down around her legs, relieved that Gene was sleeping off the party at his own place.

"Grace?" said Jay, eagerly and effusively. She'd forgotten how impossibly young he sounded, so much younger than no-nonsense Edith, who talked to Grace more like a thrice-married aunt who knew exactly what Grace needed to hear and never

118

pussyfooted around. Brando had signed with this *boy*? She supposed the other actor's and her own theater agent's faith in Jay merited him some time, so she tried to listen carefully, though it was challenging before she'd had any coffee and still felt exhausted from the drinking and singing and dancing of the night before.

"Grace, it's such a pleasure to speak to you again. I wish I could get out to Denver to see your work this summer." *Typical flattery,* Grace thought, waiting for him to go on. "And even though I know your heart is in the theater, I have a movie opportunity for you that I think you'll find appealing. Now, before you protest, I want to tell you I completely understand your position on studio contracts, and I respect it," Jay said with surprising conviction. "And for this picture, you wouldn't have to sign one." Grace heard the implied threat that this wouldn't be true the next time, but she held her tongue.

Instead, she said gently, "I'm listening."

"Good, good. So you'd star opposite Gary Cooper, in a picture directed by Fred Zinnemann. Now, you might not have heard of Zinnemann yet, but he's making quite a name for himself in town, does a terrific mix of avant-garde and more commercial work. He wants this picture to have a theatrical quality, and so of course Edith and I both thought of you, as did he after seeing that screen test you did a few years ago. And anyway, if Coop's going to be in it, I don't think you can go wrong."

Grace felt her pulse increase, her cheeks flush. Gary Cooper was one of her father's favorites. And Jay had said the word *star* — which seemed unlikely as this would only be her second movie, a ploy to lure her away from New York, but still . . . "What's it about?" she asked calmly, trying to betray nothing of her rising excitement.

Jay cleared his throat. "Well, now, it's a Western. But as I said, Zinnemann wants it to be more than just that. It's a real dark-night-of-the-soul sort of picture, if you get my meaning."

Jay was giving her the hard sell. It made her wonder if Zinnemann had lost his first choice of leading lady, and they were hard up for a second choice. But did it matter? Careers were built on that sort of opportunity.

But a film career — was that what she wanted?

No.

And yet. "Sounds intriguing," Grace replied.

"I'll have the script airmailed and messengered to you," replied Jay. "I'll need your answer by Wednesday, I'm afraid."

Oh, yes, another actress had definitely bowed out. She wondered whom. "I look forward to reading it," said Grace.

"Swell, swell," said Jay, seeming relieved. "I think you'll like it, Grace. I really think you will."

Grace laughed, because how did young Jay Kanter know anything about her tastes? But she tried to make herself sound indulgent, like they were at a party and he'd just cracked the most marvelous joke.

The thing was, though, she did like the script. Very much. She read it all in one sitting, drinking a pitcher of iced tea with her feet up on the couch. She could see herself as Amy Kane, and — she had to admit to herself — the thought of her name on a marquee and on the posters that would go up all over the subways and movie theaters of New York made her a little breathless. Gary Cooper and Grace Kelly. *We'll show them.*

Jay had been right about the script having a theatrical quality, and of it plumbing the depths of a man's soul — a woman's, too, it turned out, but no one ever mentioned the woman. It was her character, Amy Kane, who would save Gary Cooper's in the end, after an internal struggle with the demons of her own past. This appealed to Grace. She began considering different ways to play the role of Amy Kane as she read.

When she called Jay to tell him she liked the script and ask about the production schedule, his voice in reply was like a tightly wound coil ready to spring. "I'm so glad you liked it. I had a feeling you would. I appreciate your getting to it so quickly. You're going to be amazing in this picture, Grace. It's the perfect next step for you, and will position you to work with only the best directors and actors going forward. I can meet you at the airport the last weekend in July. You'll meet Fred and get fitted for costumes and such."

"So soon?!" Her mind was suddenly reeling. Had she even agreed to *do* the picture?

"Just for a day or two."

"Yes, well, but . . . when does filming start? How long will it take?" She was thinking now about Sanford Meisner and the classes she was supposed to start in the fall. And Gene. They had been talking around the subject of their continued involvement for the past week. He'd mentioned a possible move to New York. And now she was going to be in California.

"A few weeks, tops, starting right after Labor Day," replied Jay.

Not forever. Of course. Nothing to worry about. "I need to be back in New York by the end of September to start my studies with Sanford Meisner," she said.

"I'm sure that won't be a problem," said Jay, though she had the sense he'd say anything to get her on that plane. And she was committed now, even in her heart.

The next day, Grace showed up at Gene's place with some blueberry muffins and coffee, and even a beer. "Hair of the dog," she said as she plunked it down in front of him. There hadn't been time before their evening performance the previous night to tell him her news, and then everyone had gone out again and there hadn't been a good time. Plus, Gene had gotten drunk again, which peeved her.

"You're the best, Grace," he said with a yawn, as he popped the bottle open with a clink and a hiss.

He revived quickly, and before she could broach the subject, he was kissing her and taking her to bed. She let him, relieved for the temporary distraction.

You have to tell him, she told herself as

they lay in bed, her head resting on his chest, their legs languidly tangled together. She liked this better with Gene, in the morning, when he wasn't intoxicated and about to pass out.

"I got a call about doing a picture," she said. It came out as sort of a question.

"And?"

"Well, I did a screen test . . . gosh, ages ago for a movie called *Taxi*. That was how Henry Hathaway found me for *Fourteen Hours*, and now apparently Fred Zinnemann's seen it. He wants me in a Western with Gary Cooper next month."

"Well, dagnabbit, Grace, that sure is the most terrific news," Gene said in mock cowboy drawl.

She giggled. Gene could be very sweet. "So you think I should do it?" She wasn't even sure why she was asking, since she'd already said yes. But she needed . . . What did she need? His approval? His permission? Validation?

"I don't see's how it's up to me, little filly," he said, staying in cowboy character.

Grace sat up and laughed, though she gently nudged him with her foot. "Be serious, Gene."

"I am," he said, returning his voice to normal. "It's your opportunity. I'd never stand in your way."

Something in her gut wanted him to, though, which seemed insane.

"It *is* a good opportunity," she said.

"Then why the long face?" He smiled up at her, his face so open and kind. She thought she was in love with that face. She didn't want to leave him.

"It's just that I'll have to go to California right away," she said, "and on-site pictures always take ages to shoot — at least that's what I've heard. And I'm nervous about getting back to New York in time to start with Sanford Meisner." All of which was perfectly true, but she also hoped that mentioning New York would call to his mind their tentative plans to be there together.

"If it were me, I'd skip the lessons to do a picture with Gary Cooper. I mean, it's Gary Cooper. Coop."

He said it with incredible confidence. As if there was no question. She envied him that. And she also felt disappointed. Was he not even going to mention the next time he'd see her?

"Right," she said, nodding and agreeing with what he said. "So . . ." How could she put this? *Oh, just ask him.* "I don't suppose you want to come to California for a little while?"

Gene's eyes widened; then he shut them tight and rubbed both hands on his face as if he was just then waking up. Then he looked over at Grace. "I do love it here out west," he said. "I feel freer here."

Is that all you love?

"But," he said emphatically, "I have my annulment and other things to sort out. I'll have to see."

She must have looked crestfallen — she certainly felt it, literally, as if she were falling off a high precipice, her stomach high above her — because when he glanced up at her, he said, "Hey, don't be sad. You'll be doing a movie with a living legend, and I'll be in purgatory."

Laughing a little in spite of herself, she said, "When you put it *that* way . . ."

Then Gene studied her in earnest and took her right hand in both of his and said, "If I can get to California, I will. I promise. I'd like nothing more than to sponge off the purdiest girl I ever seen."

"Stop," she said, but she really wanted him to go on like that forever. It slowed the falling feeling.

"The most talented, too," he added. "How would a cowboy say *talented*?"

Grace slid back down on the bed so that her toes met Gene's, then she reached up

126

and ran her fingers through his messy blond hair. "I don't care how they say it," she whispered before she kissed him, then reveled in the immediate response his body made to her touch, the hungry way he kissed her back and pulled her on top of him, his hands on her hips, fingers digging into the soft flesh of her backside. Like this, she always knew how much he wanted her, and she found enormous pleasure in that power.

CHAPTER 7

United Artists, who was producing the film, put Grace up in the Chateau Marmont on Sunset Boulevard. The long-necked, chinless bellboy handed her the key and said reverentially, but also as a dare, "Bogart stayed here last week." *And who are you, lady?*

She might have been green in Hollywood, but Grace knew enough to know that the Chateau Marmont had been home to all the major stars at one time or another. In fact, when Jay told her this was where she'd be staying, a flutter of excitement made her breath catch in her throat. In contrast to most of the low stucco or angular wood buildings in the Hollywood hills, the Chateau was a white building that looked like a genuine château, or maybe even a small castle. Inside were dark wood beams and paneling, among other heavy Renaissance decor, like the iron chandeliers, fleur-de-lis drapery, and pointed archways. Her room was spacious, with a large bed and a separate sitting area, and a picture window that had a tremendous view of the surrounding area — when she lifted her eyes, they roamed over the piney green hills colonized by houses in a riot of styles: pink Spanish, white Greek, flat modern. At street level were the ubiquitous palm trees lining all the main roads, the streets loud with motors and shiny with brightly painted cars at every hour.

Above it all was that remarkable California sky, which she'd marveled at the last time she was out here. It simply seemed bigger here, which of course she knew was ridiculous — the sky was the sky. But in California, the pale hydrangea blue seemed absolutely limitless.

But it was not calming. She stood at her window, looking into its abyss her first morning after a rotten night's sleep, feeling completely wrecked, clutching at the lapels of her terry cloth robe. She ought to eat something and try to sleep some more, but she knew she'd never drift off. The only things she had any appetite for were coffee and juice, the combination of which would be hell on her stomach even if the juice was squeezed from oranges grown on these very hills. California was surreal.

She wished Gene were there, but he was sorting things out in New York. They'd had dinner together just two nights ago, and already it seemed a month. He had said he'd be "out west" soon — how she loved the way he said this, the way he referred to this land of sun and oranges and strange faux châteaus as one large, puzzling expanse.

On her way to the studio for read throughs, she'd tried knitting in the car sent to fetch her, but she couldn't concentrate on the fuchsia yarn. A bad sign. Knitting usually relaxed her. Then she felt like a real bumpkin arriving on the partially built set with her tapestry bag of knitting supplies, wearing her glasses — even if she was dressed in a crisp white blouse with navy culottes and espadrilles, an outfit she'd meticulously re-created from the pages of *Vogue*'s recent "California Style" spread.

Gary Cooper's hand was callused like she imagined his character Marshal Kane's must have been, and his grip was firm but not too tight. His sun-stained skin was deeply creased above his brow and around his mouth, and he greeted her with a ready smile and a "Pleased to meet you at last, Miss Kelly."

"Likewise, Mr. Cooper," she replied, amazed she could make her voice work at all. She hoped she didn't sound as nervous as she felt.

"Please. Call me Coop." He looked kind. And as old as her father. And yet she was supposed to be playing his wife.

She smiled and nodded. "And please call me Grace."

And with that, they got to work. Curly-haired Fred Zinnemann sat in his director's chair opposite a lineup of Grace and Coop, Thomas Mitchell, Lloyd Bridges, and Katy Jurado, and asked each of the actors to explain in a few sentences who their characters were and what they wanted. Grace appreciated this icebreaker, especially because it gave her an opportunity to understand not just each character better, but how each actor intended to play the character — and also how Fred wanted the character played. He even counseled Gary not to play the marshal with too much confidence, saying, in his light Austrian accent, "Will Kane is a man at the end of his tether. I don't want to see Gary Cooper in front of the camera, but a man who's ready to die to save the town, even though the town has turned its back on him."

This correction made Grace feel better

when it was her turn, and she said, slowly and unsurely — for she thought it would be too presumptuous to say what she really felt, which was that Amy was the ultimate hero of the picture — "Amy Kane's a young bride who wants to start over with her new husband, to escape the violence of her youth. So when she finds that she can't escape it, she's devastated."

"Devastated, yes," said Fred, looking into Grace's face and intensely holding her gaze, "but she also finds her strength when she realizes what she must do to help her husband. She cannot run. She must fight."

"Yes," breathed Grace, relieved that the director shared something of her vision of Amy. *Strength* was a word most people would apply to Katy Jurado's character, the capable and seductive saloon owner Helen Ramírez, but when Fred used it to describe Amy, Grace felt her stomach settle down — at least partially. She still had to figure out how to play Amy opposite a man so much older and more experienced than she was, in a medium with which she was not trained and far from familiar. Her television work had taught her to modulate her facial expressions and voice for the camera — everything had to be bigger and louder for the stage — but the big screen was another beast entirely. She hoped Zinnemann and Cooper would be able to give her good direction. At least she seemed off to a positive start.

The Hollywood machine managed to link her to virtually every actor in town except Gene, the one she was actually involved with, chewing her up and spitting her out in gossip columns everywhere. If she so much as greeted another actor with a kiss at a party — or, even more tamely, at a restaurant when they were seated at separate tables! — some stealthy photographer captured the moment and printed it with a headline. *What's going on with Grace Kelly and Gary Cooper? Marlon Brando! Gregory Peck!*

Some of the gossip hit closer to home, though. Obviously, some of her old Academy compatriots had decided to sell lascivious stories about her to the press. One recent column speculated about Grace's willingness to sleep her way to the top, citing a relationship with "one of her teachers at the American Academy," and quoting an unnamed former peer who said, "It's well-known that Grace would do anything to land a role. When she got in line for a part, the rest of us didn't stand a chance." This barb made Grace irate, flooding her with all the anger she thought she'd left behind when she boarded the plane for California. Don had been *one teacher,* and she'd *loved* him. He was the first person in her life other than Uncle George with whom she'd been able to discuss the subjects closest to her heart — of course she'd been attracted to him! And she'd lost many, many more roles than she'd won. All those wasted mornings in bed nursing her bruised ego. These articles made it sound like she was a ruthless harpy who'd never suffered a day in her life.

"It's insane," she said to Uncle George as they sat in air-conditioned splendor in his very square white house on a golf course in Palm Springs, where he'd recently decamped with William. "It's like the papers and their sources just make things up!"

"If you signed with a studio, they would manage the press much more closely," George said.

"You can't seriously be suggesting I give up that much power to one of the studios? They might control what goes into the press, but I'll have no say over what they do tell reporters."

"They're a necessary evil in the business, I'm afraid," he replied with a shrug.

"There must be another way," said Grace, shaking her head, then taking a sip of pink lemonade.

"The old Kelly obstinacy," George laughed. "I like it. See what you can do."

"I get it from both sides," Grace pointed out. "The Majers are hardly fainthearted."

"Too true," agreed George. "But do be careful, Grace. Many actors have tried to fight the studios and lost. I'm not sure it's worth it."

"I know, I know, Bette Davis, blah blah," Grace said, rolling her eyes.

"Grace," said George firmly, "Bette Davis was extremely valuable when she tried to get out of her contract, and she lost. She was nearly ruined."

"I'm planning to avoid that fate by never signing one of those blasted contracts," said Grace, straightening her back in her seat and refolding her napkin in her lap. "And anyway, at the end of this picture, I'm returning to New York to work with Sanford Meisner and get myself back on Broadway. Hollywood isn't for me. For one thing, I can't stand the heat." It had been miserable to dress as Amy Kane on location: she'd spent the past week in layers of thick cotton, bonnet and all, shooting scenes in the dust. The pipes that connected her nose to her throat felt rubbed raw and made it a chore to speak properly. Worse, she felt like she was doing poor work. Fred kept shooting her scenes over again, and even when he said, "Cut. That's good," she felt he wasn't thrilled. At first, she asked for his advice, but he was so absorbed with the cameraman and the set, he didn't seem to have much time for Grace.

"Ah, the determination of youth," Uncle George said airily. "I'd love to have you in California more, Grace. People are much more . . . accepting here. I find I fit in better. Certainly better than in provincially minded Philadelphia, and better even than in New York, which purports to be so cosmopolitan."

"Wouldn't you have better luck with the younger crowd in New York? You're always with the Edith Wharton set."

"I'm too old for the Arthur Millers and Tennessee Williamses, I'm afraid. Edith Wharton's New York is what I know, where I'm accepted as much as I can be. To you youngsters, I'm irrelevant. Out here, I can remake myself."

Grace felt unsettled by her uncle's uncharacteristic melancholy. "Where's William?" she asked. "He always puts a spring in your step."

"Oh, he's off indulging his newfound passion for golf," said George. "Hence our new location." He gestured at the expanse of rolling green out the massive windows behind him.

"I see," said Grace. "Do you play as well?"

"Occasionally. Mostly I appreciate the time to myself."

"Any projects marinating?" Grace asked enthusiastically, wanting to hear but also wanting to shake her uncle out of his mood.

No such luck.

"Wouldn't you like to know?" he said, getting up from the divan and putting an end to the conversation for now. "I'm starving, and Maria said she'd make her famous crab-and-avocado salad for lunch."

The bad press about Grace and her romantic exploits was so noisy and far-reaching that it actually infiltrated the Philadelphia papers, and the next thing she knew, Lizanne had been dispatched to stay with her at the Chateau Marmont as a chaperone. The Kelly sisters had a couple of fun nights out on Sunset Boulevard before Grace had to depart for more on-site filming in the arid California wilderness.

"You won't get in trouble while I'm away?" Grace asked her sister with a knowing smile on her lips. Lizanne had been flirting with a busboy at the Chateau's patio restaurant the night before. She'd lately realized that the Chateau, with its decidedly understated entrance and complete enclosure by high walls and dense oleander and bougainvillea, was one of the few places where the press was banished. Perhaps United Artists had been doing her a favor putting her up here. It was a vault of sorts. And so she'd started taking more of her meals there.

"I promise to go to church every morning, and read the Bible every night," joked Lizanne.

Grace opened her mouth to say something about how mad her parents would be if they thought she'd corrupted her little sister, too, when Lizanne cut her off to say, "Relax, Grace. I'll be fine. Anyway, no one here knows who I am. I can do what I want and not worry about the papers."

She had a point. And Grace found herself jealous of her sister's anonymity.

Back under the relentless sunshine, Grace worked hard to bring Amy to life in front of the camera, to infuse every word and gesture with the young woman's frustration and bravery. But it was hard. Fred kept saying things like "Too much" or "Not enough," and she couldn't make heads or tails of any of it. Coop and Katy made it look so effortless. Oh, how she envied Katy's sultry nonchalance. Her posture was pole straight but her gestures fluid and soft; her low, accented voice could move from confident to come-hither on a dime.

At the end of a particularly grueling day, once Grace had showered the dusty grime off her face and out of her hair, she was about ready to collapse in bed without bothering to eat dinner when there was a knock on her hotel room door. Wrapping her dressing gown tighter around her, she opened the door and found Katy dressed in a formfitting navy dress, hair done and lipstick on. "Let's have a drink," she said to Grace.

"That's a very nice offer, but . . . ," Grace croaked, her voice having been scoured yet again by the dry heat.

"No excuses," said Katy, wagging a finger. "Meet me downstairs in ten minutes."

And off she went, leaving Grace to wonder why the other woman would bother getting so gussied up for the backwater hotel's saloon. The place they were staying resembled the Old West buildings on the Warner Bros. lot, where they filmed other scenes, which had felt charming at first. Now Grace found herself wanting to escape into something luxuriously modern at the end of each day. What she wouldn't have given for a slick, air-conditioned restaurant and a gin and tonic in a crystal glass. As if in protest, Grace put on her dungarees with flats and a short-sleeved sweater, not caring that the outfit showed her figure to be the string bean it truly was — flat where it should be curved, slim where it should be voluptuous. Then she topped it all off with her cat's-eye tortoiseshell glasses.

Katy was waiting for her on a round leather barstool. Many of the crew members were also in the bar and restaurant, but none of the other lead actors were around, and Grace was grateful for that. Sitting on the stool to Katy's right, Grace ordered a gin and tonic and was buoyed a bit when it was served to her quickly in an attractive, heavy tumbler. Katy was drinking a clear liquid on the rocks, and Grace tried to guess what liquor it might have been but realized she didn't know Katy well enough to have any clue.

"You look nice in glasses," Katy commented. "Too bad you can't wear them during filming."

"You're telling me," said Grace, though being half-blind while working had become second nature to her. It was easier on a film set than on a stage, because everything was closer to her. Small favors.

"Maybe if you could see better, you'd relax more," said Katy.

Grace sighed. "Is it so obvious I'm not relaxed?"

Katy smiled sympathetically. "Sorry. But that's why I wanted you to come out with me tonight, such as this place is," she said, moving her eyes around the wood-paneled room that smelled of old smoke and whiskey. "I thought maybe you just needed to unwind a little."

Grace bristled at the implications of Katy's statement. She'd been hearing versions of this critique more and more lately — in the papers, during summer stock, and even in Edith's notes, she was starting to realize. Comments about her appearing icy or uptight or, the kinder version, being classy or patrician — how funny *that* was, considering where she'd come from! Her dad might have made a substantial fortune in the building business, but nothing could take the Irish Catholic out of their blood.

No matter how it came out, she didn't like being pigeonholed any more than she liked being called a cover girl at the Academy. All the labels boiled her down to something she fundamentally wasn't. She liked to think that with the right dress and the right script, she could play a role like Katy's in *High Noon.* That was what it meant to be a versatile actress.

"I am relaxed. Thank you," said Grace, knowing she sounded anything but. Then, more softly, she added, "I'm just very tired."

"I used to say I was tired whenever things weren't working out, too," said Katy, and Grace would have liked to get mad at the other woman, but she spoke matter-of-factly, without malice. She wanted to help.

"Well," Grace began, "I *am* tired, but you're right that it's also a convenient excuse. I'm not even sure what I'm doing here, to be honest." Her words sped up as she went on. "Coop's character is far too old for mine, I've only been in one other movie, and here I am thrown in with a director who doesn't have any time for me, and what I really want is to be back in New York auditioning for stage plays and wearing a goddamn jacket in the evening. It's September, for Pete's sake. It's unnatural to feel this hot all the time."

Katy laughed. "Now, there's the real Grace Kelly. *This* is a girl I could get to know. And I agree that your character is too young for Coop's, but doesn't it happen all the time? Pairing the beautiful young girl with the older, more experienced man? As if we need guiding, shaping."

"I hadn't thought about it like that," said Grace. But it was true. Humphrey Bogart and Lauren Bacall — and Ingrid Bergman, for that matter. Vivien Leigh and Clark Gable. "But it's not like Coop or Fred have any interest in shaping me," Grace pointed out.

"Stop asking. Shape yourself."

"That sounds very empowering," Grace sighed, "but I still just feel like I have a lot to learn." Inside, she felt sloshy, as if everything on the other side of her skin was water and unable to hold her up. Katy looked like she had a finely wrought skeleton beneath her much thicker skin.

"Doesn't one of your famous American acting teachers say that everything you need to play every part is in here?" Katy tapped her heart.

"Lee Strasberg," said Grace. "But not everyone agrees with him. I don't. I like to play people who are different from me. I like to pretend to be other people." Saying this, she felt five years old again, the little girl who'd made her bedroom into magic fairy lands, or kingdoms with dragons, using puppets and dolls and cardboard boxes.

Katy shrugged. "You can play people who are different from you while still finding their heart inside your heart. What can Grace Kelly give Amy Kane?"

"That's a very good question."

"What's stopping you?"

"Expectation." The word was out of Grace's mouth before she'd even thought it. "I'm in this movie with a legend. Gary Cooper. People will expect me to . . . I don't know. . . ."

"Shine like a star?"

"Something like that."

Katy finished her mysterious drink and signaled to the bartender for another.

"What are you drinking?" asked Grace.

"Tequila. They have a good one from my province of Mexico here."

Grace had never tasted plain tequila on ice before. It sounded exotic and sophisticated. When Katy's fresh glass arrived, Grace realized it had a large wedge of lime also squeezed into it. Katy pushed it to Grace. "Try it."

Ice clinked in the glass as Grace tipped it to her lips. The clear liquid had a fire to it that felt especially harsh on her dry throat, and the lime stung her lips. "You're a stronger woman than I am, Katy Jurado," Grace said with a cough as she placed the

144

glass in front of her new friend.

"Not stronger," said Katy. "Just . . . harder."

Grace wasn't exactly sure of the difference, but wasn't about to admit it. And anyway, she was glad of the company, glad not to be in bed already with her hair in rollers, wondering idly and nervously what tomorrow would bring. As they continued talking, they found more common ground in the movies they'd loved as girls (*Gaslight* was a particular favorite), and funny stories about actors offstage and off set. Katy had a hilarious one about seeing Cary Grant doing some sort of clown act, complete with juggling, at a party in the hills. "You'd never have known he was the same man in *Notorious* or *Philadelphia Story.*"

Their laughter was interrupted when Coop sidled up to them, hair wet and smelling of aftershave, and said, "I hate to interrupt, ladies, but I think it's time I finally bought you both drinks."

"Why, Coop," said Grace, feeling flirty and relaxed after her drink and with Katy at her side, "I thought you'd never ask."

Within an hour, the three of them were sitting at a table with other members of the cast and crew, laughing and trading quips, drinking tequila and eating steak and baked potatoes and wedges of lettuce doused with Roquefort dressing. *This* was what she'd been missing in Hollywood — the camaraderie, the sense that they were all part of the same family, if only for a short time, which was so common and usually instantaneous on the set of a play, especially the summer stock companies.

Though she stopped drinking after the one gin and tonic followed by a cold cerveza with her steak, Grace felt emboldened to do one of the impersonations that had entertained her Barbizon and Academy friends. It started with Coop teasing her that when she showed up on the set with her glasses and bag of knitting supplies, "I turned to Tom here and said, 'Oh, boy, we've got a school marm in model's clothing on our hands.' " In response, Grace launched into her well-practiced imitation of Eve Arden's Miss Brooks, everyone's favorite sarcastic English teacher on CBS Radio; in short order, Grace had the table in stitches with her routine about needing glasses.

Tumbling into bed far too late, Grace felt content for the first time in ages. Maybe Uncle George was onto something. Maybe she could learn to like Hollywood after all.

CHAPTER 8

"You seem happy this morning," Grace said cheerfully.

"*You* seem happy this morning," Sanford Meisner — Sandy — said back to her, putting on his gruff Brooklyn accent, and giving her a nod and a smile.

"You seem happy this morning," Grace said again, letting doubt creep into her still-upbeat tone.

"You seem happy this morning," Sandy said with a touch of sarcasm, turning away from her.

"You seem happy this morning," said Grace, inquiringly.

"You seem happy this morning," Sandy said, hands on hips, openly hostile.

"You seem happy this morning." Grace took a step toward Sandy, reached out her hand, then snatched it back. She was feeling genuine doubt now in her own body, like panic ballooning in her chest.

"You seem happy this morning." Sandy looked at the ceiling, impatient.

"You seem happy this morning." Quieter now, a plea.

"You seem happy this morning." Sandy rounded on her, yelling.

Without thinking, Grace took a step back, opening her mouth to say the line but not able to get the words out except as a whisper. "You seem happy this morning."

Sandy waited a beat . . . two . . . three . . . then hung his head, sighed, and ventured hesitantly forward. Awkwardly patting Grace's back, he said apologetically, "You seem happy this morning."

Grace raised her eyes to his, her heart thumping in her throat. "You seem happy this morning."

Sandy didn't reply this time, let at least two full minutes tick by as they held each other's gaze. Grace looked at him searchingly, lips pressed together, chin very nearly trembling. All the emotion of the scene coursed through her — which was precisely the point at this stage of her training, for the words to be virtually irrelevant compared to the authentic emotional connection between the actors.

Then, on a dime, Sandy broke into a hearty, appreciative laugh. "Well done,

148

Grace. Well done. *That's* what I want you to remember when you get in front of the camera this week."

But how, Sandy? she wanted to ask. In a short period of time, Grace had come to love bespectacled Sandy Meisner — for such a leading light in the acting community, he was utterly unaffected. His lessons were fascinating and challenging, but Grace was having trouble figuring out how to actually apply "You seem happy this morning" to her script for *The Cricket on the Hearth,* her next television drama. Her sessions weren't long enough for her to waste time asking, and she didn't want to appear hopeless in any case. Don told her she'd get the hang of it with practice, and so she forged on, ruminating while she did dishes or took walks under the autumn leaves in Central Park, on how to use Sandy's lessons in her TV work and in the few auditions for plays Edith managed to get for her.

It helped to have Gene in town. His annulment had come through, and so he was a free man, but they continued to keep things quiet because, as Grace explained to him over soda and pizza one night around the corner from Meisner's Neighborhood Playhouse, where she went for her lessons,

"I can't run the risk of my parents sending me home again."

"How can they possibly do that? You're a grown woman."

She knew he was right, and yet the fear was real. As was the uncomfortable knowledge that her relationship with Don had started to unravel at this very conversation. "They'll never see me that way," she said.

"Make them, Grace. You're free of them financially. What could they possibly say or do to sabotage your life?"

She picked at the crust left on her paper plate. "Maybe you're right," she said. In fact, she'd had this confrontation with her parents many, many times in her imagination — the conversation in which they tried to stand in the way of her new life and she told them, finally, "No." The scene always filled her whole body with a powerful energy, making her want to burst outside and run. Sometimes Sandy's exercises tapped into that energy, and she'd noticed that those were the ones she was most praised for. Not the ones where she felt compelled to simper, whine, or grovel. Those exercises she always had to do over.

"I *am* right," said Gene. "You just have to flip the switch in that beautiful brain of yours and realize that you *are* independent, and stop giving them any power over you." Gene was so much better when he hadn't been drinking, and this sober pep talk was also kinder than any of Don's had ever been. She'd met him at this dive tonight specifically because they didn't serve alcohol. After a few drinks, Gene would have just slurred, "Don't worry. I'll tell your dad where to put his Catholic ideals of womanhood," before changing the subject altogether. His drinking made it easier for her to put off the conversation with her parents, because she wasn't entirely sure the relationship with Gene would last, though she wasn't yet ready to admit that out loud, and certainly not to him.

"Easier said than done, but . . . you *are* right," she said. "I know you are."

He put his forehead to hers. "It's hard, Gracie. I know that. I think we Catholic kids who were raised with all that guilt find it extra hard to stand up for ourselves and what we want. That's the reason I stayed married too long. Guilt and expectations."

"What's the opposite? I wonder," said Grace. "The opposite of guilt is innocence, and I don't want that, either."

"Better to think of the antidote, not the opposite," suggested Gene. "Pride and independence?"

"*Poise* and independence."

"I like that for you. You are poised, Gracie. That's what makes you a natural actress." He kissed her over their paper plates, and she felt lucky and happy until he suggested they meet some friends at a bar downtown. She wanted to end their evening now, when it was perfect, not hours later with Gene so drunk he could barely hail a taxi home.

"How about we go back to my place and have an early night?" she countered, sliding her arms around his waist and hooking her thumbs into his belt as suggestively as she dared in public.

They were standing on the sidewalk now, and they kissed as the evening traffic blared by.

"Just one drink," he said.

There's no such thing with you. "I can't," she said, pressing against him. "I have to be up for Sandy and a rehearsal tomorrow."

"You're too good," he said, and she knew he meant it as a compliment, but it was also the start of his rejection. The good time with friends was more alluring than the tumble and early bedtime with her. It stabbed at her heart.

"The early bird and all that," she said, unhooking her thumbs and stepping away. "But if you have a later day, I understand."

She didn't, but she also knew she couldn't say that. *Silence.*

He caught her hand, squeezed it, then kissed her again. "You're the best. You know that? I'll call you tomorrow."

She'd always remember that as the moment she knew she'd never risk her relationship with her parents for Gene. Though she wasn't ready to end things, either, not just yet.

Nineteen fifty-one bled seamlessly into nineteen fifty-two. Grace was comfortably settled into her New York life, seeing Sandy every week and working constantly — Edith had lined up close to a dozen television dramas before the summer! *High Noon* seemed to be stalled forever in editing, and wouldn't be released till July, and so any breaks that might come from her role in that were in the unseen future. Still, she won a part in a comedy scheduled for the Booth Theatre in April, *To Be Continued.* Grace knew from the start that it wasn't destined for greatness, but she accepted the part just to get up on that stage. "Good for you, Grace," said Uncle George. "Every part counts."

As winter wore doggedly on, she found herself making more and more excuses not to stay out with Gene, and socialize with her girlfriends instead. One of her nights on the town with Sally and Prudy and Carolyn found the four of them at the Copacabana, eating, listening to jazz, and laughing riotously about their Barbizon days.

"What were we *thinking*?" Carolyn demanded, slamming her open palm on the table with conviction, demanding to know why they had dutifully followed all the rules of the strict boardinghouse.

"I was worried about having to go home," said Grace, to the agreeing nods of the other three.

"It was the only place for girls like us in those days," added Prudy.

"In those days?" Sally said mockingly. "It was only three years ago!"

"Was it really?" Prudy asked dreamily.

Grace nodded. "It seems like much longer ago to me, too." And it did, though Grace was very aware of the ways in which her life was precisely the same.

"Don't look now" — Carolyn leaned forward, bare elbows on the white tablecloth, and said in a low, conspiratorial voice — "but Dean Martin just came in."

"You can't just say that and not expect us to look," snapped Prudy, whose head and eyes went straight to the entrance. Grace didn't have to move her body in order to see in that direction, and she admired the dark-haired crooner in his dinner jacket; on his arm was a gorgeous woman with platinum blond hair and a sparkling black dress.

But Grace's eyes didn't follow him to his table as those of her friends did; instead, she immediately recognized the woman who'd been standing behind him: Josephine Baker, the singer, who looked resplendent in a peacock blue evening gown and a headband embellished with real peacock feathers. She was with a handsome young man in a tuxedo whom Grace did not recognize. On Uncle George's suggestion, Grace had started listening to Baker years ago, and her records were among Grace's favorites. To her, this legend's appearance was far more thrilling than Dean Martin's. After all, the singer and actress had had to overcome so much to become who she was. Fed up with the intolerance and prejudice in her own country, she'd expatriated to France, where she'd been one of Paris's most sought-after cabaret stars, then — as if that wasn't enough — she had been instrumental in the resistance during the war. Grace admired much more than the woman's voice.

Though her friends continued gossiping

about Dean Martin and their recent dates and job opportunities, Grace felt distracted by the presence of Josephine Baker. Rarely had she wanted so much to introduce herself to a star, and yet she felt incredibly shy. Who was she to talk to the great Josephine Baker? Sure, she'd been in *High Noon* with Gary Cooper, but that picture hadn't come out yet, and the television work she was somewhat known for was such small potatoes compared to what the other woman had done in her career.

"Grace." Prudy sang her name and waved a hand in front of her face to snap her out of it.

"Are you dreaming of Dean?" giggled Carolyn.

"Hardly," said Grace. "I want to introduce myself to Josephine Baker, but I don't know how."

"You?" Carolyn asked, genuinely shocked. "Grace Outgoing Kelly?"

"Am I?" Grace asked, surprised that anyone would use that word to describe her.

"You can talk to anyone," agreed Prudy.

Sally nodded. "And those impressions you do! They take guts."

Buoyed a bit by her friends' faith in her and the idea of herself as outgoing, she swallowed the last of her wine and stood up. "All right, then," she said. "Wish me luck."

Legs wobbling, she squared her shoulders and walked over to Ms. Baker's table, feeling the soft layers of tulle from her petticoat swish around her calves. Suddenly she was at the singer's table, and words were coming out of her mouth. "Excuse me," she said, trying to make eye contact with Ms. Baker and her date, both of whom looked at her in surprise, "but I just couldn't let tonight go by without introducing myself and telling you how much your music has meant to me since I was a little girl. My name is Grace Kelly."

Ms. Baker smiled graciously, thrust out her hand, and said in her richly textured voice, "Pleased to make your acquaintance, Miss Kelly. You look familiar." Narrowing her eyes and concentrating on Grace's face, she asked, "Do you sing?"

Grace laughed, blushing. "Hardly. I think the lowest marks I received at the Academy were for singing. No, I do a bit of television and modeling work. I was on Broadway once, and I keep trying for more. And please call me Grace."

Ms. Baker snapped her fingers and said, "That's it! I saw you in a television version of Molnár's *Swan*! Didn't you play the princess?"

Blushing hotter, Grace nodded and said, "That was me."

"You were excellent!"

"I can't tell you how much that means to me," Grace said. In fact, it was probably the single best compliment she'd ever received; she could hardly believe her ears.

"Why don't you join us?"

"Oh, thank you, Ms. Baker," stammered Grace, feeling more flustered by the attentions of this woman than she had by those of any man. "But I'm here with a few friends tonight, and I couldn't leave them."

"Well, bring them over," she said, "and call me Josephine."

"Truly?"

"Truly," said Josephine with a firm nod.

Suddenly light on her feet and dizzy with excitement, Grace went back to her table to ask if her friends wanted to join Josephine Baker. Of course they did, and the Copacabana staff genially moved chairs and place settings to accommodate the request. Introductions were made all around, and they learned that the singer's good-looking friend was Carlos Rodriguez, lately from Havana.

Josephine insisted on buying them all drinks and raised her glass to all of theirs, saying, "To new friends," while she looked directly at Grace.

While Josephine was in New York, she and Grace went out a few more times. Though the singer was old enough to be her mother, she was so youthful and effusive about the latest and most controversial jazz and film and theater, Grace found it challenging to keep up with her; it seemed every moment of her day and night was scheduled with performances and dinners and drinks, and Grace beamed with pride anytime Josephine introduced her as her friend. And it seemed they really were friends. Grace even opened up to her about Gene in a way she'd never dream of doing with anyone else.

"Tell me more about this Gene character," Josephine said one night as they nursed martinis at the 21 Club. "If you don't mind me saying so, you seem too young to be intent on just one man. Not when you are so beautiful, and everywhere we go, men stop talking to their wives and dates as you walk by."

"They do not," Grace protested, genuinely embarrassed by this flattery.

"You must notice," Josephine said.

Grace shook her head. "I try to be with the people I'm with. And I suspect that when you and I are together, people are looking at *you*. You're Josephine Baker, for heaven's sake!"

The other woman frowned. "My name doesn't mean what it once did," she replied. "In some ways, the twenties were more tolerant than today. And at least in the thirties and forties, we were all united against a clear evil. First poverty, then Hitler." With a faraway look in her glimmering kohled eyes, Josephine took the last olive off the toothpick from her glass with her teeth and chewed. Grace wondered what she was thinking, but didn't dare ask.

After a moment of private reverie, Josephine refocused on Grace and said, "So. Gene Lyons. Tell me."

"Oh, Josephine, I don't think I can be with him anymore. And here we are about to do *The Rich Boy* together for television. It's based on an F. Scott Fitzgerald story about a drunk and the girl who loves him, and it's just awful because it's basically about me and Gene."

"I can't remember that one," said Josephine, "though I always thought Scott was a bit of a self-absorbed prick. Remind me how the story ends?"

Grace couldn't help laughing at the casual way her new friend had skewered one of their country's most famous writers, as if he were nothing more than a boy down the street. "How does any Fitzgerald story end?" she lamented, trying to sound as worldly as she could. "Tragically. The only good thing about it is that Sandy's instruction to think about my character's own emotional history is coming quite easily to me for this role. I don't have to think so far outside my own head!" She didn't bother adding that she hated these roles that trapped her inside her own mind.

Josephine studied Grace for a moment, then replied, "Is Gene what you really want?"

It was such a simple question. And yet . . . Grace had never thought about Gene or anyone else in such terms.

"I . . . I . . . ," she stammered. "I don't know."

Josephine lightly tapped her right index finger on Grace's nose and replied, "That, *ma chérie,* is what you need to figure out."

When *To Be Continued* closed after a dozen performances in May, Gene was precisely what Grace wanted, for he knew better than anyone how to forget troubles. Especially with Josephine back in Paris.

"Even though I knew it wasn't a masterpiece," Grace said in the cab on their way to the Copa, "I still just wish it had played a bit longer."

"Just wait till *High Noon* comes out," said Gene consolingly.

"I'm tired of waiting, Gene! I'm twenty-two and I've been at this since I was seventeen."

Gene laughed gently. "That's only five years, you know. And twenty-two is *young.*"

"You say that like you're so old. You're only thirty-one!"

"And thank God for that," he said. "I'm not exactly getting the big break, either. You've got to remember why you're in this, Grace."

"Why am I in it, Gene? Tell me because I can't remember."

"You're in it because you love the stale-smoke smell of the dressing rooms and the frigid air onstage that only the lights heat up. The way your footsteps echo on the wood before there are any sets up."

She did — she loved all those things. And she loved the applause: that precious appreciation that all the best actors craved but never admitted out loud they wanted, and some went so far as to decry. But all that felt out of reach. "Oh, Gene, what if I never make it?"

Gene laughed and put his arm around

her, and she set her head on his shoulder. "You have to think more about what making it really means to you, Grace. And in the meantime, find a way to enjoy *getting* there."

At the Copa, she and Gene danced for hours to the bright blaring of the brass band, and even stayed for the late-night comedy act. Then, in the early-morning taxi back to Gene's place, as he snored lightly next to her, she asked herself what it would mean to follow Gene's advice — to focus more on *getting* where she was going rather than feeling rotten all the time about not being there already. She did enjoy working with Sandy, and she liked the television work well enough. Even when she didn't love the script, she enjoyed working with the other actors toward a common goal. She liked waking up every morning knowing she had work to do, for which she'd be paid well. Still, as much as she loved all that, something was missing. Whatever it was, it sent her into her habitual daydream of standing onstage at the end of a great performance, knowing she'd been seen at last.

CHAPTER 9

Seeing herself in *High Noon* was surreal. She rarely saw herself in the television dramas because they aired live, and she preferred to think of them as plays — ephemeral, each performance a moment in time that was over when the last line was said. Occasionally, she watched a reel of one with the other players but she'd learned this was usually an ego-stroking opportunity to criticize one's own performance in a way designed to elicit the praise of the other actors: *Oh, I did that scene so poorly! Just look at my face!* To which someone would inevitably reply, *I think you're convincing. And your body conveys just enough anguish.*

Sitting in the dark movie theater in her gauzy new off-the-shoulder Balmain gown — very *un–*Amy Kane — Grace held her breath through the opening credits, knowing she was in one of the first scenes, getting married to Coop's Marshal Kane.

Stealing a sideways glance at Coop, who was sitting to her left in a fine tuxedo, she saw that his eyes were unwaveringly fixed on the screen, so that was what she did, too. But seeing her pale skin and hair practically glowing with naïveté was jarring. She knew her appearance was supposed to provide an innocent counterpoint to the vengeful, murderous plot underfoot, but she couldn't help thinking she'd played it all wrong — too sweet, then too bitter. And she was so *big* on the screen. There was no hiding her performance.

And yet Katy Jurado, who sat on her right, gently squeezed Grace's hand at the end of her first scene. Grace looked down to see her own fingers clenched over the end of the armrest. Katy's touch was such a surprise, she looked at the other woman, who smiled as if to say, "It's rough, I know."

Katy's presence at her side made the rest of it easier to watch. In fact, after the initial shock wore off, Grace found herself completely absorbed in the film. The metronomic clip-clop in the sound track, which suggested both horses and the ticking of a clock toward noon, had a hypnotic effect on the black-and-white action. Coop was perfection itself, and for a few minutes, she was so absorbed, she actually forgot how the story ended. When she saw herself as Amy Kane enter the shoot-out in the final scenes, it was like watching someone else entirely. That bonneted blond couldn't possibly be her — she was Marshal Kane's wife, and Grace was proud of her.

When the curtain swished to hide the screen and the lights went on, everyone applauded, and Grace looked around her feeling light-headed and disoriented. The rest of the cast clapped and nodded at one another, so she joined in, trading heartfelt compliments about performances. When Fred went to the stage, everyone stood up and whistled and clapped louder than Grace had heard in any theater — though maybe that was because she was *in* the audience, not in front of it.

It wasn't the applause of her daydreams, but it was deeply moving. She felt an intoxicating mixture of pride, camaraderie, and gratitude fizzing like bubbles in her chest. She couldn't wait for everyone she loved to see the film. And she found herself hungry for another experience like it.

"Did you like it, Mother? *High Noon?*" asked Grace, unable to resist but also on edge that her mother hadn't brought it up immediately. The buoyant mood from the premiere had worn off, and now she felt nervy about what all her friends, and especially her family, would say about the movie and her performance.

She and her mother were having lunch in Philadelphia on a Monday; Fordie had picked Grace up from her little flat near the Bucks County Playhouse, where she was doing *Accent on Youth* before heading back to New York. She knew her parents had gone to see *High Noon* the night before, and from the moment she'd gotten into the car till Fordie had dropped her off and she and her mother ordered Waldorf chicken salads for lunch, all Grace and Margaret Kelly had spoken about had been Peggy's children and Kell's work.

By contrast, Fordie — who had seen the movie on opening night the week before — had telephoned Grace the next morning to tell her how much he loved it. He'd whistled in appreciation and said, "You added some class to that picture, Gracie. Without you, it would have been a dreary movie indeed. I can't wait to see what you do next." Tears of appreciation had rushed to Grace's eyes as she held the phone to her ear and gushed her thanks to Fordie for seeing it right away.

"It was very good, Grace," her mother replied in measured tones. "Of course, I don't see many Westerns, but your father was quite impressed by the direction. He said it was unusual, the way the story was about the town turning on the marshal. But I'm afraid I didn't understand the meaning of that music and the sound of the horses."

Forget the score, Mother! Did you like my performance? But Grace replied, "I think Zinnemann was trying to convey the passing of time."

"Yes, yes, I understood that," said her mother impatiently. Then finally: "It was wonderful to see you in such a big picture, Grace. Your father and I were very proud. And everyone in town has seen it and told us how marvelous you were, how *amazing* that little Grace Kelly is in a picture with Gary Cooper!"

"Thank you, Mother," said Grace, grasping this thread of praise, but also feeling its meagerness. She was quite certain it was the amassed opinions of family friends that pleased her mother most.

"Do you think you'll do more movies?" Grace could hear the undercurrent in her mother's question: *Because I could get used to being the mother of a movie star.*

"We'll see what they offer me." Grace shrugged, not wanting to give her mother the satisfaction.

"Your father says there's much more money in film than in theater."

"I'm not doing it for the money." She also didn't want to get into the issue of studio contracts with her mother.

"No." Her mother frowned. "But you do seem to be making enough of it. That's a lovely dress you have on."

Grace looked down at the linen shirtdress with the wide belt she was wearing. She loved its cheerful salmon color; as soon as she'd put it on at Bonwit Teller, her mood had lifted. "Thank you."

"Are you seeing anyone special?" her mother asked, stuffing a mouthful of chicken and walnuts into her mouth and chewing.

Of course you'd rather talk about that, Mom.

"No one special," Grace replied, which was unfortunately true these days. Her relationship with Gene was hanging on by a thread, especially after a fight they'd had in June after a cast party in Philadelphia where she'd been working with the Playhouse in the Park. She'd hoped Gene might be able to charm the producers into getting his own work with them. But he'd spent the whole night getting so sloshed that he didn't impress anyone with his off-key rendition of "The Surrey with the Fringe on Top."

"This is *not* my idea of fun, Gene!" she'd yelled at him back at her flat.

"You wouldn't know fun if it bonked you on the head!" he'd shouted before slamming the door behind him and walking barefoot to the nearest hotel because he was too proud — or too drunk — to come back for his loafers.

"Well, I do hope you'll find someone soon," said her mother. "You need someone to take care of you, Grace. And you've always said you wanted children."

"I have," Grace agreed, about the children at least. She chafed at the notion that she needed someone to take care of her. Weren't all her lovers constantly telling her how independent she was? What an irony. Still. Making sandcastles and reading *Madeline* with Peggy's mischievous little blond tots at Ocean City earlier in the summer had given her a dull ache in her womb.

Irritated, Grace pointed out, "Mother, you didn't get married until you were twenty-six. And you took care of yourself quite well before that. You were coach of women's teams at Penn! Dad always said you turned him down a few times before you accepted him." Though her mother's initial refusals were all part of her father's shtick about how hard he'd tried to win the prize that was Margaret Majer, Grace had always been more impressed by her mother's determination than her father's.

Grace's mother crunched another mouthful of salad, then dabbed her mouth with a napkin before replying dismissively, "I was just biding my time. And I *did* enjoy having someone to take care of things once we got married. Your father . . . likes to do things himself, and I have found my life is easier when I let him."

Somehow that didn't sound like a man taking care of his wife. "All right, Mother," Grace said lightly, glancing down at her watch. Another half an hour and it wouldn't be rude for her to excuse herself to get back to New York.

"I watched a repeat airing of *The Rich Boy* on television last night," said Sandy at the start of their second year of classes together. "And I was impressed all over again, Grace. Your work there was exceptional. Do you know why?"

"Because I felt so connected to the character," she replied — knowing the answer would please her teacher both because it was the truth (he was uncannily good at sensing a lie) and because it was the core of all his lessons: How does your character

171

feel? What does she want? How well do you understand her?

"Exactly," he said, leaning toward her and looking intently into her face through his chunky black-rimmed glasses. They magnified his eyes slightly, and Grace always felt a bit like he was looking at her through a microscope. Sometimes she felt like her own glasses provided a shield from his probing, though he rarely let her wear them during their sessions. "You must practice as you'll be in front of the camera and onstage," he told her.

"Right, *blind*," she only half-jested in reply.

"How can we get you to connect with all your characters as deeply as you connected with Paula?" He blinked, and it was the only move he made; the rest of him was like a statue as he waited for her answer.

Grace wished she had a great answer. Even a passable answer. But the truth — that she understood Paula because in so many ways she *was* Paula, and she wasn't yet sure how to *be* anyone else — was certainly not a good answer. Unable to tell the truth, she paraphrased his advice: "I need to find my common ground with my other characters. I need to try to understand what makes them tick."

"Precisely," he said, not letting up his

intensity. "The key is making the director believe you can play the role. And you will, Grace. You will. It's a matter of time and experience, and word getting out that not only are you a very fine actress, you're dependable as well. Rarely have I worked with an actress as punctual and thoughtful as you." *Thoughtful. Punctual. Pliable.* Better compliments for a housewife than for an actress.

There were times she wished she were a wounded bird like Marilyn, or a tough broad like Katharine — a personality that would force people to take notice of her. Her height was her most commanding feature, and it *cost* her roles. Instead, she was a well-mannered girl from Philadelphia who sent her teachers boxes of homemade fudge for their birthdays, which she assumed was part of what Sandy was referring to now when he described her as *thoughtful.* Nothing at all to do with her talent.

She tried to be grateful that the television work continued to come in, and she had another chance at playing a woman of the Wild West in *The Kill.* Sandy and Don both said she seemed more relaxed in that program than she had in *High Noon,* and she could feel it in the way the lines and gestures

173

came to her with so much more fluidity. Even Katy Jurado called her up when she saw it and said, "Nice work, Grace."

She couldn't have been more surprised when Jay Kanter telephoned her at the very end of September. "Grace? That screen test you did at that dump studio back in forty-nine is still paying dividends. John Ford wants you to come out to California for a color test this week. Get this: he's doing a remake of *Red Dust* with none other than the original star, Clark Gable. And he wants to shoot on location in Africa."

"No," Grace breathed. *Clark Gable? Africa?* She couldn't imagine a better opportunity that didn't combine the words *Elia Kazan* and *Broadway.*

"Yes," laughed Jay, "yes, yes, yes, Graciebird." Grace liked this nickname for her and had taken to calling him Jaybird in reply.

"My goodness! I must admit I'm speechless." And her heart was thudding in her throat.

"You only need to say one word, and I'll book your flight out."

"Yes!" she said.

John Ford did the test himself. "He doesn't want to waste any time," Jay had told her on the phone the morning before she headed to the studio.

It was impossible to read the director's expression, though, as his round glasses had tinted lenses, and his soft face was inscrutable beneath his high forehead and receding hairline. "Thank you, Miss Kelly," he said after she'd read for the part of Linda Nordley. She'd thought a great deal about the part on the flight from New York to Los Angeles, and she couldn't help it — her best way to understand Linda was to admit that the two of them shared the same goal: to impress Clark Gable.

Apparently, it was enough. The next day as she swam at the pool of the Hotel Bel-Air, where MGM had put her up, she was interrupted by a bellhop who handed her a red telephone connected to an extremely long cord, setting it on a chaise by the pool and indicating she should take the call. Wrapping a towel around her torso, she sat and put the sun-warmed receiver to her ear. "Hello?"

"You did it, Grace! Ford wants you for the picture. This time, you will have to sign a contract, but don't worry — I'll make sure it's good enough for you and leaves you time to work in New York. Congratulations, Graciebird! This is a big break. You're on your way."

It was all so exciting, she didn't even mind about the contract — not that day. She called her uncle George right away and suggested they meet at Musso & Frank. In one of the smooth red booths, she and George and William toasted her success with goblets of red wine and rare steaks.

"Hard to believe this wine is made just a hundred miles north of here," commented William, looking into the deep ruby liquid in his glass.

"When I was your age," said George to Grace, "all California wine was considered swill. Amazing how times change."

"This is just one step up from swill," William said, squinting into his glass. "Maybe two steps. But sometimes a rough red is just what you need." He winked at George, who smirked back, and Grace blushed to know they were sharing an intimate joke.

Clearing his voice and raising his glass, William declared, "To Grace!" George and Grace clinked their glasses to his.

"We are so proud of you," said Uncle George.

"And we can't wait for the gossip on Clark Gable!" said William wickedly.

Grace laughed and drank the wine, which was deliciously rough. It suited her mood. She'd be in Africa for her twenty-third birthday! With Clark Gable and Ava Gardner. She wondered if Ava would bring her husband, Frank Sinatra. Miraculously, she felt no nerves, just excitement like champagne bubbles in her veins.

While she and her uncle and William ate with gusto, Spencer Tracy and Katharine Hepburn came in, arm in arm. Grace was the first to see them, and she put her hand on her uncle's forearm and squeezed gleefully.

His eyes, and William's, and every other eyeball in the place followed the couple to their seats at a table in the center of the restaurant. Kate and Spencer didn't seem to notice, and they laughed and chatted with the maître d' like old friends. Before they'd even ordered, two cocktails arrived for them. It looked like an old-fashioned for Spencer and a gimlet for Kate. Once they were left alone at the table and their eyes fell to their menus, the rest of the Musso & Frank patrons went back to their own meals.

"That'll be you someday," said Uncle George.

Grace laughed. "Hardly. You flatter me."

"You're ten times the beauty she is," said William.

"That's entirely in the eye of the beholder," said Grace, "and I know I'm not ten times the talent."

"Don't let your charming innate modesty get in the way of proving yourself wrong, niece," said George warningly.

"I'll do my best," she said, sensing for the first time in her whole life that it just might be possible.

Two weeks later the contract arrived by courier at her apartment in New York. Jay and his boss, Lew Wasserman, had promised to make it more favorable to Grace, but she couldn't see how on earth she'd ever get back to New York if she was promising to do three pictures a year for MGM for seven years! Blood really boiling, she called Jay.

"I want every other year off from movies," she told her agent. "Otherwise, I'll never be able to get anything done in theater."

Jay hesitated.

"And you can tell them," added Grace, "that more money won't sway me, since I make much more money as a model and television actress than they're offering or even likely to come up to. Anyway, it's not about the money," she said, remembering she'd said the exact same thing to her mother a few months before. Saying it again to Jay made her feel stronger, bolder, truer. "It's about time to be the actress I've trained to be."

"I'll try, Graciebird," said Jay.

Grace hadn't been encouraged by Jay's tone, but the next day he told her they'd agreed. "MGM really wants you, Grace. I've never seen Dore Schary agree to anything like this before."

It was pretty nice to feel wanted, to feel seen, Grace had to admit with a satisfied grin as she hung up the phone. *I could get used to this,* she thought as she went to pack her bags.

CHAPTER 10

Under a benevolent May sun, Grace stood
with Frank Sinatra and her old Hollywood
roommate and fellow actress, Rita Gam,
and felt the heat reflecting up from the
white Carrara marble of the wide, curved
staircase where they stood surveying the
hundreds of people in the stone palace
courtyard. Behind them were the Renaissance arches of the Hercule Gallery, one of
Grace's favorite parts of the palace with its
pleasingly regular columns, graceful arcades,
and colorful frescoes of myths and heroes.
Much of the stone of the courtyard had
been covered with green grassy sod in honor
of the Texas barbecue picnic theme of the
event, Rainier's Silver Jubilee.

"I still don't get what roast pork has to do
with Monaco," said Frank, holding up a
sandwich dripping with spicy brown gravy,
"but this is the best slop I've had outside

the Lone Star State."

Grace laughed, pleased not just that her friends were enjoying themselves, but that the Monégasques who were eating and laughing, whose children were playing throw the horseshoe and riding ponies, all glowed with surprised delight. She finally — *finally* — felt accepted by them, in this eighteenth year as their Princess. This past Christmas, when she and Rainier had sat in this very courtyard handing out presents to every small child who lived in Monaco, as they had done from the earliest years of their marriage, she'd noticed that even the grandparents had begun to thank her. For many years, they had held back or greeted her stiffly and Rainier warmly. But last year, as today, even the oldest Monégasques approached her with wide smiles and enthusiastic embraces. *"Merci, votre Altesse Sérénissime. Nous sommes si heureux que vous soyez ici." Thank you, most Serene Highness. We are so glad you are here.*

Secure in their love and respect, Grace had felt comfortable taking a risk with the theme of Rainier's twenty-fifth-anniversary celebration. "I wanted us to do something different," she explained to Frank and Rita. "One of the best vacations Rainier and I ever took was to a ranch in Texas a few years ago. We wanted to share some of that joy with Monaco." Even after all this time, it felt embarrassing to say *our subjects,* especially in the company of old friends, and she found herself avoiding it. When she woke up in the morning and felt the pillow under her head, her fingers in the folds of her soft cotton nightgown, she was just Grace Kelly of Philadelphia. The idea that she had subjects was absurd.

But there they were, basking in the mild spring warmth. She caught Rainier's eyes — he was below, helping a little boy aim a toy gun at a tin bull. He winked at her, and for a moment she was twenty-six again, seeing her prince and seeing him see her. He was dark and handsome, with the most impeccable social graces of any man she'd ever met. The best compliments she'd ever received. *Your intelligence shows in all your pictures. It's what makes you so beautiful. . . . You have a keen eye, the best ability to distinguish between true fashion and mere trends, of any woman I've met. . . . I can't imagine what you see in me. . . .* So much of his courtly flattery had been in the letters they'd written to each other at the end of nineteen fifty-five. She wondered where they were, those letters. So much had gotten misplaced in the many waves of palace renovations and restorations. And the compliments seemed to have been lost with them. She'd learned that fleeting moments like his wink a moment ago weren't much more than a performance of love for any audience member that might be watching. They weren't binding, nor were they enduring.

Grace turned her attention back to the palace, which she'd come to think of as her own Globe Theatre. Open to the elements and quite intimate in scale (*How small the palace seemed when I first saw it!*), each of its set pieces helped the members of the Grimaldi family play their roles. From the Hercule Gallery, Serene Highnesses could look down on their subjects to wave beneficently, present new heirs, or lead Monaco in times of trial and hardship. But they were not as far removed from their people as were the kings and queens of England at Buckingham Palace, and Grace preferred this closeness with the people who left their work behind to pay homage to their rulers. Slowly, Grace had come to understand that her role was to soften the effect of the medieval ramparts, the harsh climb of the ancient fortress walls from the craggy rock on which it sat. How ironic that her demeanor, once labeled icy and untouchable, was now valued for its accessibility and authenticity.

And like a theater, the palace was amazingly versatile. This courtyard had been transformed many times since she'd arrived. Though underneath it would always be a European castle built by conquerors and princes, today it was a convincing Texas ranch, complete with split-rail fences, bales of hay, and even a small brown barn with shaded games for the children. Every male citizen of Monaco had given up his beret for a cowboy hat, every woman traded her silk scarf for a red bandanna. Everyone was a player today, shedding their real selves and real troubles, and escaping into the fantasy of another place and people. Grace sensed they found the release as marvelous as she always had.

Grace excused herself, and let Rita and Frank catch up while she rejoined her husband. She passed around trays of watermelon and helped Albert while he gave square-dancing lessons. Even Caroline was having a good time, smiling and talking and eating with her friends. Stéphie ran ebulliently from one activity to the next, a bright pinwheel in her tight little fist, trying everything and munching a thousand ears of corn, with Cary Grant's little girl, Jennifer, trailing enthusiastically behind. Grace smiled. After all of Cary's tumultuous years in psychoanalysis, little Jennifer had turned out to be his savior. His love for her was palpable.

She hoped Cary and his family, as well as Josephine Baker and her children, among her many other friends, were enjoying themselves; she'd hardly had a chance to do more than greet them. Well, she consoled herself, they would all have a more intimate supper together the next day at Roc Agel, their blessed escape just half an hour up the road toward the little town of La Turbie.

At one point, it seemed like half the guests were on the stage at the far end of the courtyard. Shoulder to shoulder, scores of sun-browned Monégasques were learning the two-step. Rainier found Grace there, sweating and laughing in a group of older women, and he took her by the hand to the hoots and hollers of all surrounding them, then surprised everyone by stomping her expertly around the stage. They had practiced this dance for weeks, for exactly this moment, and after a few nearly broken toes — his *and* hers — they had finally gotten the hang of it.

As everyone clapped, Rainier kissed Grace on the cheek, and she closed her eyes for little more than a blink, but it was like time slowed down, allowing her to soak in the warmth and joy of the moment. She wished, so much, that it was enough.

"It was a triumph, darling," proclaimed her mother as they put their sore feet up on ottomans in the cozy living room in the family wing of the palace. A tray with a pot of herbal tea sat on a glass table between them, steaming into the cooler evening air. They would have to change clothes and make another appearance for the fireworks in a few hours' time, and this was a welcome and much-needed respite.

"And I must admit," Margaret went on, "I had my doubts. A *barbecue*? But it was wonderful, just wonderful. I heard people everywhere raving about the food, and the entertainment, everything! Nicely done, Grace."

"Thank you, Mom." Grace basked in her mother's compliments. Though their relationship was hardly perfect, something important had shifted between them in recent years and softened her mother toward her. Grace had suddenly become the easiest Kelly child, certainly easier than Peggy, who drank far too much no matter how often she swore she wouldn't, and Kell, whose philandering had effectively ended his marriage. No doubt Margaret found it more relaxing to spend time with her second daughter. For her part, Grace had begun to understand and appreciate her mother better, what with the challenges of raising Caroline and Stéphanie with Rainier, under the hungry lens of the paparazzi.

A few minutes of contented silence passed between Grace and her mother as they sipped their tea. Caroline and Albert, she knew, were napping before their official obligations at the fireworks, after which they had permission to go out for a night on the town. They rarely left the house before ten on a party night, and Grace had begun to make peace with this; she especially liked it when they went out together, as she felt that Albie had a steadying influence on Caroline. Stéphanie was in the theater watching a movie with some of her little friends, unwinding after the merry chaos of the day.

Rainier was visiting his zoo animals, which always put him in a more tranquil frame of mind. She still didn't understand how all that cawing and clawing could possibly help him unwind — after all, monkeys and macaws were nothing like the warm, sanguine body of a loving dog on your lap. One of her caramel poodles was nestled under her legs right now, snoozing away contentedly. But even though she didn't understand it, she respected that Rainier's zoo was necessary to him. And honestly, she was relieved he had something that had nothing to do with her to bring his blood pressure down.

"Have you decided what to do about Caroline and her *baccalauréat?*" Her mother's question about this high-stakes test for which her daughter would need to enroll in a special program of study was casual enough, but the piercing reality of it fractured the rare calm of the moment.

"Rainier and I are still discussing that," Grace said evasively, regretting the phone call from a month ago in which she had tearfully poured out to her mother so many of her fears and frustrations about Caroline going to study in Paris, especially after four years of sanctuary while she attended St. Mary's School Ascot in England. But her oldest child wanted to study politics at the *École Libre des Sciences Politiques* in Paris, and for that she'd need high marks on a *baccalauréat,* which St. Mary's didn't offer. Caroline had been accepted into the *Dames de St.-Maur Lycée* in Paris, and now the question was where she should live.

It was one thing to stay out late in Monaco, where the teenage princess was known and beloved and relatively protected. Anytime she went out in another city, however, the vultures descended with their cameras and lies. In the hopes of protecting and maybe even guiding Caroline to stay out of the parties and related trouble she'd lately gotten into, Grace wanted to live with her during the week in Paris, and bring Stéphanie with them and enroll her in a nearby school. The very thought of raising her girls in one of her favorite cities thrilled her — for, despite the comfort she felt in Monaco, she also felt restless here, bored with the duties she'd mastered. She needed new challenges, new stimulations.

But Rainier thought Grace was being overprotective, as usual. "She chafes under your mothering," he was always telling her, though she often felt the critique was unfair. She let Caroline go clubbing in Monte Carlo, for heaven's sake — and she wasn't even eighteen yet! She couldn't help feeling that much of Caroline's behavior could be attributed more to Rainier's spoiling her; from the moment she'd arrived, she'd had everything she ever wanted and asked for more.

"You know you are right," Margaret said pointedly, interrupting Grace's train of thought. "Don't let him change your mind."

"Mother, please, let's not talk about it now," said Grace, but her mother's words, and everything they called to mind, had set her stomach churning. A few more minutes ticked by and sheer exhaustion helped Grace forget her mother's words by sending her into a light sleep on the couch.

The next thing she knew, Rainier was picking up her feet and putting them on his lap as he sat down beside her, smelling of hay and the sea wind and faintly of the droppings of many animals, the domesticated ones of their party as well as the more exotic breeds in his zoo. He had a glass of brandy in his hand. She wished he would rub her feet, but it had been many years since he'd touched her like that.

"I thought it went well. Didn't you?" he asked his wife and mother-in-law.

Groggily, Grace opened her eyes and sat up a bit so that her feet slid off Rainier and burrowed under his hip. He seemed in good humor.

"It's not even a question," replied Margaret robustly. "The day was a wild success."

"Everyone did seem to have a good time," he said musingly. Then he patted his soft belly and said, "I don't think all the spice

190

agreed with me, though."

"I forgot to eat," said Grace. Her stomach growled as she thought of this. "In fact, I'm starving."

"You don't think the different chilis were a bit much?" Rainier asked. Grace heard the shift in his tone, the neediness, and she knew why — she and her mother hadn't immediately flattered him about the role he'd played in the proceedings, and so now he was going to pick something apart. Her toes curled. It was almost better when he fell asleep at an event and had less to say. Grace had been horrified years ago when she realized Rainier did this on purpose. Dozing off at the opera once in a while she could understand, but closing your eyes during Hamlet's monologue — in the state box, no less! — was the height of rudeness. When she'd tried to suggest he stay awake at important events so as not to offend their hosts, Rainier had only replied, indifferently, "They should try harder to keep me awake." She'd become so practiced at delivering the lie — *"My poor Rainier, so tired from everything he does for the people of Monaco, he can't even stay awake at the theater!"* — that she nearly forgot the truth these days. It was much easier to believe her own words.

"I loved the chilis!" Margaret exclaimed,

which Grace knew would not endear the pots of red, white, and green chili to her husband. Grace wasn't sure if her mother made comments like this to rile him on purpose or because she was simply done placating husbands.

"Let's not fret about any details when overall it was a grand day," said Grace silkily. The last thing she needed was tension before the next wave of appearances, so she went on. "The pork sandwiches and barbecued chicken were popular, and I think everyone in Monaco could do a respectable do-si-do when they left. You led me expertly around the dance floor, darling," she cooed, putting a hand on his arm. Her mother stood up and looked out the window, her back to her daughter and son-in-law.

"I did manage not to step on your toes," said Rainier, clearly angling for a bigger compliment.

"You did better than that," said Grace with a warm smile, feeling as she said the words that *having* to say them bled all the joy out of the memory.

"The fresh ice cream was also a hit," added Margaret, still at the window. "The children couldn't get enough."

Grace laughed, grateful for the added praise. "I'm glad Rainier told the kitchen to double the amount they were planning to make!" It was actually she who'd told the kitchen to increase the order, but what did the truth matter if peace reigned in the palace?

Rainier smiled as if recalling this small gallantry in the kitchen, and he patted Grace's foot absentmindedly. The three of them were silent a few moments before Rainier asked, "Margaret, how is Kell's bid for mayor coming?"

Grace's mother pulled in a sharp breath, and turned away from the window to face them on the couch. In a tight voice, she replied, "Oh, it's just in its early stages."

Grace tried to give Rainier a look that said, *I'll fill you in when we're alone,* which he heeded since he let the subject drop — and Grace was glad again that she'd successfully stroked his ego about the jubilee. Had she not, the conversation with her mother could have taken an ugly turn.

Much later, after the deafening but spectacular fireworks and a few required turns on the dance floor — all waltzes, and much more subdued than their do-si-do — Rainier asked, "Why did your mother seem so angry about Kell?"

Unfastening her favorite feather-shaped pearl-and-diamond earrings and clinking them into the little porcelain dish where she kept her most loved jewelry, she replied, "Well, you know that since his separation Kell's been running around Philadelphia like a madman." It had been five years since Kell's wife, Mary, had understandably kicked him out, and everyone hoped his philandering would calm down. But Peggy had told Grace on the phone after a few too many mimosas at a christening that it had actually gotten worse. *And there are rumors that the latest one is actually a man dressed as a woman.* Grace had no intention of getting into *that* with Rainier tonight, so she said, "And Mother is beside herself that he hasn't pulled himself together, even with his political career on the line. She wished maintaining the good Kelly name was enough to curb his behavior, but since it isn't, she hopes that if the stakes are higher, he will fall in line. But he hasn't. Yet."

Grace's heart went out to her brother. If Kell were gay, what a confusing time of life he must be in — already married once with six children and a bitter, exiled wife. Better to have chosen the other path early in life, like Uncle George, than to have confused matters by pretending to be something he wasn't. But then, so many men felt they had to get married and do what was expected of them, even in Hollywood, where differences were tolerated in ways they were not in Philadelphia.

Kell had spent his whole life living up to their father's expectations — Henley, the Olympics, running Kelly for Brickwork — and nothing was ever quite good enough for John B. Kelly Sr. Certainly not the bronze medal, but not even the two Henley wins. For so long, Grace had been jealous of the praise her father heaped on his son, until she'd come to realize the heavy price her brother paid for it — the constant striving for more, more, more. It dawned on her now that she and her brother weren't so different in the relentlessness with which they pursued their goals, in the hopes of their father admiring them. She wondered, then, what the difference was between them: why was Kell coming apart at the seams, so outwardly and publicly, while Grace came undone in ways no one could see?

As she rubbed a thick salve of shea butter into her hands, Rainier approached her from behind, and set a black velvet box on the table in front of her. She was sitting before her vanity mirror, and so she looked up at him standing behind her and said, "You shouldn't have."

"But I should," he said.

Her breath caught, wet, in her throat. And there she'd been, thinking unkind thoughts about him all day. She opened her mouth to say something, and Rainier interrupted, leaning over and tapping the box. "Open it."

With a muffled *pop!* the box opened, and inside there was a thin silver bracelet with two charms on it, one in the shape of a cowboy boot and the other with the number *25*. Turning to face him, she said, "It's perfect, Rainier. Thank you."

"You know you can go to Cartier anytime you like," he said, "but I didn't think you'd make yourself something of real Texas silver."

Grace shook her head and swallowed down the rising emotion. Occasions like these felt so confusing — she couldn't feel pure joy in the gift, because it was such an isolated moment. Then she felt guilty for constantly, inwardly criticizing. There was also the familiar despairing question: which was the real Rainier? The one who knew how to bestow compliments and gifts? Or the one for whom nothing was good enough? It seemed impossible that they were one and the same.

She plucked the bracelet out of the box and slid it over her hand. The two charms jingled together merrily. She put her hand on Rainier's cheek and kissed him. "Thank you. I can't imagine a more perfect gift."

He kissed her back, and it was warm but dry. He retired to their large bed, with its stacks of books and magazines and half-drunk glasses of water on each side, and Grace wondered if she was really going to live the rest of her life in this marriage with a man who seemed to think a bracelet was a substitute for love, real love. Grace craved the kind of understanding he had seemed capable of so many years ago. She wanted to hear him say, knowing he meant every word, "I love you, my darling Grace. I want you to be happy. What would make you happy?"

She was forty-four years old, and she *felt* young. When she saw a handsome man on the street, she felt the tug of desire inside her — but only the suggestion of it, nothing close to the release. When she saw a movie, especially one of Hitch's, or one with Audrey Hepburn, who was a mere six months older than she was, she felt such a mounting tension of jealousy in her chest it seemed as though her ribs might actually crack from the pressure.

As she got into bed, where Rainier lay reading a magazine about sports cars, Grace observed the expanse of white-sheeted space between them. Could passion fix the rest of what ailed their marriage? What would happen if she crossed to his side of the bed, if she pulled her cotton nightgown over her head and kissed him, first on the cheek, to gauge his interest? She sighed, remembering the last time she'd tried something like that — what, a year or so ago? *Not tonight,* he'd said without looking up from his magazine. To some it might have seemed like a small rejection, but she remembered it — and felt it again that night — as a blow to the center of her body. It might have been one moment, but it was in keeping with so many other small moments, that it had the effect of a final sucker punch that left her winded.

So she picked up her own magazine from the top of the stack on her side of the bed and stared unseeingly at the words and pictures, formulating in her mind a list of tasks to accomplish the following day. Ticking each item off the list would at least bring her a sense of peace, and for now, that seemed to be the best she could hope for.

CHAPTER 11

The first thing Grace did on their "ladies' weekend" in Paris was take Caroline and Stéphie to see a movie. "But we must go incognito!" she announced. To her daughters' amusement, Grace opened a chest full of old sweaters, skirts, and trousers from the days before her every move outside her residence was photographed. Her friends had always teased her for her pack-rat tendencies, and also her formerly frumpy taste in clothes.

"We'll be retro girls today," said Grace. Despite the eight-year age difference between them — seventeen and nine — both Caroline and Stéphie appeared equally tickled by their mother's determined game, and threw themselves into it with the same gusto they'd had playing dress-up as little children. Grace tied a scarf that smelled faintly of old perfume around her head and knotted it under her chin, then put on a

199

thin wool-felt coat she remembered buying at Saks shortly after she graduated from the Academy. The faded scent and the light weight of the coat flooded Grace with memories — Don's kisses, Carnegie Hall on damp New York mornings, and steaming coffee from Chock Full o'Nuts. Shaking her head, she tried to clear her mind and be present in this moment with her girls.

"Well?" she asked her daughters, twirling in the hopes of getting their approval.

"Mom, wear these," said Stéphanie, sliding a pair of her own pink plastic sunglasses onto Grace's face.

"Perfect!" squealed Caroline, who looked more like herself than ever, scrubbed of all makeup with her dark hair scraped back into a ponytail. Grace's two daughters looked gorgeous, but totally unlike their usual overdone selves. Caroline had on a cashmere sweater in cotton candy pink, a polo shirt's collar popped up from underneath. With some of Grace's round sunglasses, she was the picture of preppy American clean; Grace would never say so, but her daughter looked a bit like a tourist, a California girl in the City of Light. Stéphie chose a jaunty beret and a black skirt, then her sister's denim jacket, which was too large for her preadolescent frame but served to disguise her well.

"All right, phase one of Operation *Great Gatsby* is complete," said Grace.

Next, they giggled in the elevator as Stéphie babbled excitedly to the attendant, Monsieur Dubois, what they were up to.

"*Bonne chance,*" he said with a tip of his hat as they exited the lift and turned their backs on the marble lobby and the two paparazzi stationed just outside the door — there always seemed to be a pair standing sentry — to wend their way through the service hallways and out the back entrance. They emerged onto the wide sidewalk in the crisp spring air, and Stéphie and Caroline high-fived each other, then Grace. Her heart swelled in her chest. She loved it when she managed to choreograph something like this. They were rare, these moments when all three princesses of Monaco could unite around a single fun project. Grace wanted to savor every second. Offering a hand to each daughter, she was amazed when they laced their fingers through hers, and she felt tears rush to her eyes. *Don't be silly,* she told herself, swallowing back the rising emotion.

We're off to see the Wizard . . . , whistled Stéphie.

They managed to get all the way into their red velvet seats in the center of the movie theater, with a bag of candy each. Only then did Grace remove the scarf around her head and say, "We did it!"

"Can we do it again tomorrow?" asked Stéphanie, regret that their adventure was already partly over creeping into her voice. Grace understood the feeling, but was determined to wring every moment of happiness out of this glorious afternoon.

"Maybe," replied Grace. "But let's not worry about tomorrow. Let's enjoy today."

And they did. Robert Redford and Mia Farrow were marvelous as Jay Gatsby and Daisy Buchanan. Caroline had recently read Fitzgerald's novel for an American literature class at St. Mary's, and even though much of what the characters were living through went right over Stéphie's head, Grace could tell her younger daughter was drinking in the well-staged spectacle of Prohibition-era parties and costumes.

"That was *so good,*" Stéphie breathed as the credits rolled.

"It was a really great adaptation of the book," agreed Caroline judiciously.

"Yes, it's a much better production than the one that came out when I was your age," said Grace, remembering Alan Ladd and Betty Field in the main roles. She recalled feeling that picture was serviceable, but not more. Who'd she seen it with? Don? Maree? Prudy? It seemed impossible she couldn't remember. She'd never forget seeing this one with her girls.

As soon as the time came to discuss school with Caroline, the spell was broken. She waited until the following afternoon to bring it up, and proceeded with the utmost caution.

"Wouldn't it be fun," Grace began, "if the three of us could have more adventures like yesterday?"

Caroline didn't answer right away. They were sitting in the living room with the rosy combination of antiques and comfortable, deep sofas. Caroline was lying on one of those now, one foot up and the other flat on the Persian rug on the floor. Flipping through *Marie Claire,* she didn't look at Grace as she spoke.

"Mom, you know as well as I do that yesterday was an exception and not the rule."

Undeterred, Grace said, "I don't see why that has to be the case."

"I know what this is about. You want to live here when I go to the *lycée* in the fall. But I'm seventeen, the same age you were when you left for New York."

"When I left for New York, I was nobody,"

Grace said. "There weren't photographers outside the Barbizon waiting for me to make a mistake."

"Lucky you." Flip, flip. Her daughter couldn't be *reading* anything so quickly. Was she even seeing the pictures?

"I was lucky. It's true. I feel terrible that this is your life, Caroline. I really do. Let me help make it up to you by protecting you."

"I don't need protection, Mom."

Oh, but you do. "I did at your age." Grace hoped reframing the discussion to make it about her would help. "My parents used to send Peggy or Lizanne to chaperone me all the time, and I liked it." This was partially true, at least. She *had* liked the sisterly company. She had *not* liked the parental insistence that she needed help, which made it all the harder to try to take this position with her daughter now. She understood what it felt like to want freedom and feel perfectly capable of living freely. The problem was, her parents had continued to baby her even after she'd proved she could live independently — earning her own wages and paying for her rent, clothes, and everything else. She didn't intend to make that mistake with her girls, but Caroline was nowhere near independent yet.

When she looked at Caroline, Grace saw a little girl. Someone who still slouched at the table, simpered to get her way, and spent too much money on the Champs-Élysées. Perhaps it was her fault that Caroline had become that way, with money at least — heaven only knew, she hadn't been as frugal a parent as Margaret or John Kelly, since shopping was one of the few ways she had of accessing her daughter's softer side. But the point was, she couldn't see Caroline living alone as she'd done at her age.

Oh, how she wished for a situation like the one at the Barbizon, complete with firm regulations about gentleman callers and curfews. At St. Mary's, the nuns and strict teachers were the perfect scapegoats. Cowardly as she knew it was to hide behind their rules, Grace had been grateful for them. When she'd suggested to Rainier that they find a similar boarding situation to the Barbizon in Paris, he'd scoffed, "Caroline's not some middle-class girl getting a secretarial degree, Grace."

"Neither was I," Grace had snapped back. That had been a particularly nasty fight, and all the togetherness of the Silver Jubilee was forgotten.

"I've warned you again and again," he'd said, "and you've never taken any of my advice. If she goes off the rails, you'll have only yourself to blame. You must do what I've done with Albert. Be firm and consistent, and all will be well."

Grace had felt anger explode, hot and mutinous, in her chest. "Thank you, Dr. Spock," she couldn't help saying.

"You always do this," said Rainier, his tone becoming clipped and irascible. "You're never able to take criticism of any kind, and then you shoot down anyone who has an opinion different from yours."

She'd nearly rolled her eyes. She'd taken instructions and criticism her whole life, from acting teachers, directors, even her costars, and she *enjoyed* feedback, when it was helpful. What she didn't like was when her husband, who was supposed to be her partner, her equal, treated her as something . . . less. But of course to him, she *was* less. She hadn't been born a princess or even a duchess or a countess. She was a bricklayer's daughter from Philadelphia.

Think about that later, Grace told herself. *Your daughter's in front of you now.*

"I'm *ready*, Mom," said Caroline, dropping the magazine on the floor and sitting up. She leaned forward, elbows on knees, and said, "Dad thinks I'm old enough. *He* has faith in me."

Grace's breath caught in her throat. It would be just like Rainier to comfort Caroline by saying how much *he* loved and believed in her, always the first-person singular. It had taken Grace too long to realize the difference, and the profound effect of one little pronoun. *J'adore, je te fais confiance,* not *nous adorons, on te fais confiance.* As if he were the only one who loved his children. Grace always tried to present a united front. *We, us, our.* Grace was furious that he had delegated this uncomfortable conversation to her because "It's what *you* want."

"Your father and I have discussed this at some length, and we agree that you should not live completely on your own," Grace said to Caroline in measured tones, because that much was entirely true. He didn't want Caroline to live alone. "The question is *whom* you will live with. Me and Stéphie, here in this house, or in . . . another arrangement." And therein was the problem. What arrangement? Rainier had suggested Caroline live with their friends the Corvettos, who had a lovely home very close to the *lycée.*

Grace suspected the reason he didn't like the idea of his wife and daughters living together in Paris had more to do with her than with Caroline. "How will this look?" he'd asked Grace. "My wife deserting her subjects and her husband for Paris?" Grace had assured him that she and the girls would return to the palace every weekend. He said he'd think about it, and Grace couldn't quite believe she was waiting for her husband's permission to do something. It brought back so many claustrophobic feelings from her youth, all the many times she'd needed permission to do something important to her, like work at the Chatterbox in Ocean City, study at the Academy, go back to New York after Don. Even after her parents didn't need to give permission, there had been MGM to contend with. Had she *ever* not needed permission to do as she liked?

The question stunned her.

"No more convents," pleaded her daughter.

"No," Grace agreed with a nod. She heard her own desperation in her daughter's voice, and felt a momentary pang of jealousy that teenage Caroline was allowed to express her vexation this way while an adult woman like Grace was not.

"You seem to have enjoyed St. Mary's, convent though it was," she ventured with an encouraging smile. "You made good friends there, and you've become a marvelous horsewoman. And who'd have thought that London would have made you such a fashion plate!" She hoped that by invoking the lighthearted London–Paris sartorial rivalry between them, Grace would lighten the mood.

Caroline did smile, wistfully, as if she was looking back on events from years ago, not merely months. "Please, Mom, I just want to feel free."

Grace crossed the short distance between their two couches to sit next to her daughter, and put her hand on Caroline's. "I know you do, darling. I know that feeling perfectly. I promise to help." She just needed to figure out a way to help that would limit Rainier's hostility and bring her closer to her daughter. No small challenge. But she felt equal to it, and ready for more. It was spring, after all, and once upon a time, good things had happened to her in the spring.

Chapter 12

"Did you really just order our meal in Swahili?" Clark Gable asked. Grace blushed and giggled. He sounded exactly like he did in the movies, with that pat-on-the-back attitude in the slightly nasal tone. Not many men could speak like that and still be sexy. But this was Clark Gable: dark hair, tan face, trim mustache, and all. And his shoulders were huge, Grace was pleased to note. Quite a specimen, even though he was old enough to be her father.

"I had quite a lot of time to study on the plane," she said, smoothing the napkin in her lap.

"Grace is a master of impressions, so it's not at all surprising to me that she's a natural with languages, too," added Ava Gardner, whom Grace had met once or twice at parties in Hollywood. It was good to see her again, and in such fine humor with her husband, Frank Sinatra, along. "Couldn't pass up a chance to see Africa on a boondoggle," Frank told Clark when the older actor had greeted him with surprise in the lobby of their hotel.

"This I have to see," said Clark, now fastening his famous eyes right on Grace. Mortified, she blushed again and looked down at her napkin. Was she really here, in Africa, shooting a John Ford movie with Clark Gable and having dinner with Ava Gardner and Frank Sinatra?

"Oh, no," she said, shaking her head and looking down at her plate as her cheeks burned. "I need much more wine before I can attempt *that.*"

"Well, fill her glass, then, fellas!" Clark said, grabbing the neck of the bottle on the table and filling her mostly full goblet to the brim.

"Mr. Gable, back home we have a name for men like you who try to get the ladies drunk," Grace said with a coy reprimand in her most ladylike lilt.

"My dear, you can call me anything you like if you do an impression of Gary Cooper for me tonight."

Grace swallowed. "We'll see," she said.

Frank raised his bottle of beer and said, "Nice work, Clark."

The evening proceeded at the same joyful pace under the most starlit night sky Grace had ever seen — zillions of little white twinkles competed for space in the blackness above. Their party reclined in woven cane chairs on the patio, enjoying the sultry November night. It was impossible to believe snow flurries had been falling in New York when she left, and here she was sitting in a linen dress. Harder to believe she'd be twenty-three in a few days. In some ways, she felt like a girl — eager for Clark Gable's approval and yet nervous about getting it or, worse, not getting it — and in other ways she felt ancient, as if she'd like nothing better than to take her leave and get a good night's sleep in preparation for the challenges ahead. She knew it was essential for her to play the former and not the latter, so she drank just enough wine to feel loose and hid her yawns behind her fingers.

Before dessert's end, she rose to Clark's challenge, doing an almost silent spoof of Gary Cooper's Marshal Kane that had everyone in stitches.

"Yes!" exclaimed Frank, as he clapped appreciatively. "I thought he looked exactly like that."

"Constipated?" laughed Ava.

"You said it, not me, sweetie." And he

212

kissed his wife hungrily on the mouth.

The immediate repartee of the cast made for a great environment on the set. Though most scenes required many takes, as John Ford was as much a perfectionist as Zinnemann, no one minded, since it was so much fun to chat in the shade of the Meru oak trees, or visit the animals and learn about elephants and monkeys and even a lion cub from the skinny men who tended them. Their skin was so black, Grace reflected, Fordie and Josephine's complexions seemed closer to her own than to theirs.

Though a few of their equally dark countrymen were employed to help John Ford on the set, Grace felt uncomfortable with the way they were treated — when one of the men who always showed up in a freshly pressed white shirt and khakis asked one of the cameramen a question, Grace noted that the cameraman brushed him off, saying, "If I have time, I'll show you later." Grace doubted later would ever show up.

All the fine restaurants where they ate were populated entirely by white foreigners like her and serviced entirely by black locals, who silently filled water glasses, cleared plates, and fetched coats. She wondered what Josephine might have to say about Africa.

Grace liked it best when the cast stayed the night in hotels, as the beds and room temperatures were far more comfortable than those of the so-called luxury cabins in which they slept down the river. At least the huts had the benefit of putting Grace and her fellow cast members in more authentic frames of mind to play characters who were out of their element in the wilds of Africa — except for Clark, of course, who frequently played men who could rough it with the best of them, then clean up nicer than the tidy intellectual who had no hope of winning the girl.

Grace wondered if she'd ever get to play a part like the one Ava was playing — sultry and wisecracking, just wanton enough in her capris and blouses unbuttoned just so, her short hair revealing the kind of neck any man would want to kiss down to the collarbone. Only on Broadway could she pull it off, Grace suspected, where typecasting wasn't as prevalent and actors could even break out of time-worn ruts. Her breasts weren't big enough to play that kind of role on celluloid, even if she could drop her voice to sound like she smoked a pack a day. *That's just not you, Gracie. Stop being silly.* There seemed to be a chorus of people telling her that in her head.

Mogambo's good times — days of productive work and nights of food, drink, jokes, cards, and charades — lasted through her birthday, Thanksgiving, and Christmas, with the additional treat of Ava's birthday on Christmas Eve. Around New Year's, though, the novelty had started to wear off. The truth was, the script was only so-so, and everyone had grown weary and started pining for the comforts of their American homes. Grace herself had started to dream about hot baths in her claw-foot tub. They all wondered if Ford's direction and Gable's star power would be able to carry the film, aided in some small way by the rest of their contributions.

It was hot and everyone was soothing insect bites or upset tummies, mistrusting certain foods or not taking their cocktails with ice unless the poor waiter could guarantee the water had been triple boiled. Frank started drinking too much beer because he didn't have enough to do, and Ava was getting annoyed that he wanted to be with her all the time she wasn't on set. "I need some time to myself, you know?" she said to Grace in the ladies' room of the hotel, where she was meticulously applying cherry red lipstick to her full lips, and adjusting her wide neckline for maximum effect. Grace touched up her own coral lipstick, then smoothed down her lace pencil skirt, and reflected jadedly that these parallel colors and fashions said it all about the differences between them — on-screen and off.

On one of the first nights of 1953, Grace and Clark were the only ones left at their table, the rubble of another dinner strewn over the white tablecloth. Clark was smoking one of his cigars, and the mulchy-clovey scent perfumed the air around them.

"How are you faring, Kelly?" he asked, looking not at her two seats down the table but at the curl of white smoke he'd blown into the night.

"I'm doing well. Thank you." She paused, suddenly feeling a butterfly flit against the walls of her stomach. It wouldn't do to reveal to Clark Gable that she still had to pinch herself some mornings to remind herself that she wasn't dreaming, that she really was where she was, in the company she was in. "I'm enjoying the picture and everyone in it, and I learn something new every day. Did you know that elephants can recognize themselves in a mirror, and they avoid eating the leaves of certain trees because they don't like the ants that live there?"

Clark sniffed and bobbed his back. "Your enthusiasm is wonderful to behold, Kelly."

He sounded so . . . It wasn't patronizing exactly. It was more nostalgic.

"What about you, Clark? Are you enjoying yourself?" she asked.

"I prefer the company to the picture," he said, looking over at her with a bittersweet half smile. "You remember, I've already done this movie. More than twenty years ago. You know you're a dinosaur when you start doing the same movie a second time around. And they have to make you look younger by picking girls the same age they were the first time around."

"I think it shows your staying power," Grace disagreed. "And isn't it a compliment to think that men everywhere who are your age wish they could be you?"

Clark laughed, and looked up at the sky. "Oh, but they don't. Not really. I'm a fantasy, same as you. The ladies want to be *with* me, and the gentlemen want to *be* me. But only for the two hours it takes to watch the picture. In the end, they're happy to go home to their spouses and meat loaf."

Grace raised an eyebrow. "Do you mean *you'd* like to go home to meat loaf?"

"Maybe," he said. Then, with a laugh that was clearly at himself, he said, "Don't listen to me, Kelly. I'm just an old rambler."

Feeling emboldened by their sudden intimacy, Grace asked, "What kind of fantasy do you think I am?"

"That's easy. You're the untouchable society girl. Too beautiful to actually go after, but men will think the most vile things about you in their private moments."

"I thought they were happy with meat loaf?"

"You got me, Kelly. Yes, they are. But when they get unhappy with it, they can dial up their fantasy of icy Grace Kelly and what they could do to defrost you."

"Defrost me? How terrible. Is that really how I come across?"

"It's a good thing, Kelly. Not many girls can do what you do. Vivien could, but her version was more hot-blooded, like she could scald you if you got too close." He said this with such admiration Grace ached to understand why.

"Do you think I could ever play a part like the one Ava's playing?"

"See now, you're not asking the right question. You should be asking why you'd even want to bother. You're the untouch-able, the prize. Why be the girl next door?"

"The challenge," she said in earnest. "I want to be a versatile actress."

At this, Clark really had a good laugh, and Grace felt twelve years old, stupid.

"We all have our limitations," he said. "And someday you'll realize that what you've got isn't worth trading." He took a long drag on his cigar. They sat in silence for a few minutes, Grace feeling frustrated that she couldn't figure out anything to say that wouldn't make her appear even younger and more naïve.

When he finished his cigar, he stubbed it out with hearty satisfaction and turned to her to say, "Time for bed."

His eyes lingered on her for just a moment too long, and Grace felt her skin, every inch of it, flame up. What would it be like to feel those shoulders moving above hers? Feeling suddenly beautiful, wanted, powerful, she returned his gaze with what she hoped was sufficient invitation. An onset romance with Clark Gable? What girl would turn that down?

But he stood up with a yawn, put his large, warm hand on her shoulder, and said, "Good night, Kelly." Then, without looking at her again, he headed to his room, leaving Grace to wonder what on earth had just happened between them.

Clark was more distant after that, as if their

moment of solitude and closeness — which he made sure never happened again — had flipped some sort of switch inside him. He was rigorously avuncular after that, giving unsolicited advice, patting her on the shoulder or hair, taking advantage of opportunities to tease her. She made sure to tease him right back, but it was exhausting. And if she was being honest, it was also discouraging. She'd hardly seen a future for herself and the movie star, but the idea of a fling, the possibility of tousled sheets as the sun rose over the savannah, had been so alluring and validating that Grace felt she was actually grieving the end of an affair that had never even begun. *Your imagination will get you into trouble someday,* her father had once told her. *Get my heart broken is more like it,* thought Grace, as she flew with the cast and crew from Nairobi to London to complete shooting.

By drizzly mid-March, she was back in New York, and for the first time, she wasn't thrilled about that. Settling back into her routine of lessons with Sandy, television dramas, Broadway auditions — and their inevitable stinging rejections — and rotting memories of Don and Gene, not to mention other crushes and dates that had gone nowhere, made Grace feel blue. She found herself craving the thrilling ride of the past few months: being swept off her feet by a Hollywood dream of John Ford, Clark Gable, and Africa, complete with MGM wanting her badly enough to modify their precious contract just to nab her before another studio could.

She kept herself afloat with fantasies of *Mogambo*'s premiere in the fall, when she'd be reunited with the cast. In the meantime, she kept telling herself to stop wishing Jay would call with a great new script. Because why would he? He was surely too busy for his difficult client who kept saying no to Hollywood for a chance to audition for New York directors who wouldn't even have her. Plus, he was getting married. *Another wedding,* Grace thought with an irritation she knew was unbecoming, so she never uttered a word of it to anyone. Adding insult to injury was the fact that the girl Jay was marrying — Judy Balaban, whose father, Barney, was president of Paramount Pictures — was three years younger than Grace. For Pete's sake. Was she destined to be a spinster as well as a failed Broadway actress?

Grace was not usually prone to self-pity, but in the early spring of fifty-three, she'd take long walks through Central Park, willing the pink and white blossoms and green leaves to hurry up and unfurl from their branches, asking herself, *Why not me? What's wrong with me?*

Why can't you be more like Peggy? came the unbidden answer in her father's voice. Occasionally she heard it in Clark Gable's voice, which was so absurd, she made herself laugh. The question itself was absurd — more so now than it had been when she was a child and it seemed plausible, if not irrefutably true. Back then, her older sister was gorgeous, the belle of every ball, the star of every play and sporting team she joined. Her dresser was a jumble of trophies and ribbons that their father would pick up from time to time, then sit holding on Peggy's bed, for the excuse of reminiscing about how proud he'd been of his Ba when she'd won this race or that award for service at school.

Now, though, Grace asked herself, *What's Peggy today?* A Philadelphia society wife and mother of darling twins, Meg and Mary, who was so busy playing tennis and ferrying the girls around to their activities and lessons, then entertaining George's colleagues and their country club friends, she hardly even had time to write her own sister. And, Grace told herself, *Peggy* hadn't just returned from Africa.

And yet . . .

Why should she still be jealous of her sister?

The grass only looks greener, Grace. Cut it out.

So she soldiered on, attending Jay's wedding and discovering that she adored Judy, a loud and joyful blonde who was hilarious, and hilariously pragmatic, about "the industry" she'd grown up in. Because she'd known famous people since before she'd understood they were famous, she wasn't fazed when Montgomery Clift or Lucille Ball stopped by expecting tea and sympathy, or something stronger. To her, they were just people. If Jay wasn't so clearly smitten with her, Grace could see the practical, mercenary appeal of marrying such a well-trained friend to the stars, but Jay looked at Judy with such a dopey expression in his eyes that Grace knew he'd found the real thing.

Grace appreciated that Judy was a dyed-in-the-wool New Yorker who loved nothing more than cocktails at the Plaza, where she kept watch for Kay Thompson, or catching a Wednesday matinee of the latest show on Broadway. "I hope Jay doesn't move me to the Left Coast," she'd told Grace the first time they met. "I don't think I could bear to leave the Bemelmans Bar. Anytime I was sad, I'd say to my mother, let's go talk to Madeline, and she'd take me to the Carlyle, even though of course Madeline isn't anywhere *in* the murals — but it looks like she could make an appearance at any moment! Anyway, Mother would have a martini, and I'd have a hot chocolate that the bartender *swore* was the very same chocolate Madeline herself drank in Paris. I sometimes still order the hot chocolate. After my martini, of course," she laughed, and Grace laughed along with her, as the Carlyle was one of her favorite spots as well, for much the same reason: the murals by Ludwig Bemelmans were so like the pictures in her favorite children's book, that Grace couldn't help thinking of mischievous little Madeline, who liked to walk out of line and make trouble for Miss Clavel. Sitting among Bemelmans's whimsical drawings, Grace never felt alone or lonely.

They quickly began calling each other Judybird and Graciebird, and their new friendship was a bright spot that season, as the city slowly, finally blossomed into spring. By May, the cherry trees had flowered along Riverside Park, and Grace was just in from a windy walk along the island's western promenade, feeling that fresh, new things were possible, when the phone rang.

"Graciebird?"

"Hello, Jaybird. How are you this fine spring day?"

Jay laughed. "Nice to hear you so cheerful."

"Well, I'm shaking pink petals out of my hair, and my agent's just called with good news, I hope, so I've decided to put on my happy face."

"I do have good news, as it happens. You know of Alfred Hitchcock, right?"

Grace's pulse quickened. "I know his work, of course. I loved *Notorious.* Anyone who loves Ingrid Bergman as I do also knows the director who used her so artfully."

"Well, he's asked for *you* to do a screen test for his next movie, an adaptation of the play *Dial M For Murder.* MGM would have to loan you to Warner Brothers to do it, but I don't think that will be a problem. Hitchcock saw your old *Taxi* test and seems to think you could be his next Ingrid."

"No," she said breathlessly, her legs suddenly gelatinous.

"Yes. You are quite like her, you know. You're both —"

"If you say 'icy blondes,' I'll kill you, Jaybird."

"I was going to say nothing of the sort. I was going to say 'high-class blond dames.' "

Grace laughed, even though she wasn't sure how much better that was. "When do I leave?"

CHAPTER 13

Grace met Alfred Hitchcock for the first time in one of the many nondescript buildings on the Warner Bros. sprawling studio lot in June. She had heard he was odd, though no one had ever been able to quite describe *how* he was odd, except that he was pudgy and had a dirty sense of humor — and neither of those traits were odd unto themselves — so she wasn't sure what to expect. Not wanting to trip or do something else to embarrass herself, Grace wore her glasses with her teal blue Dior day dress, so the first thing Mr. Hitchcock said to her in his peculiar twangy English accent was "No one told me you wore glasses."

She immediately took them off, and everything behind him blurred. "I don't have to wear them," she said apologetically.

He frowned appraisingly, then said, "You've read the script?"

"Oh, yes, and I saw the play last year. It

227

was marvelous."

"Indeed," he said, turning his back on her. His chubby hands were clasped behind his wide back, and his gray hair was clipped so short, he didn't even need pomade. She could tell from his neatly pressed brown wool trousers and old-fashioned waistcoat over a bespoke shirt that he was fastidious about his appearance. She wondered how that jibed with what she'd also heard about him, that he was a man of appetites.

He walked onto the sparsely decorated set, which looked like someone's living room before they'd acquired enough furniture, and he looked up at the large cameras set upon cranes and tripods, then complained, "They want me to shoot it in Three-D. As if I am a monster matinee maker." He sniffed.

"Which you are clearly not," Grace assured him. "The studios do ask for strange things from their best talents. I suppose they want to sell more tickets to keep us making movies."

"That is rather an optimistic view from an actress who resisted signing her own studio contract."

He knows about that? Somehow, though, Grace already had the sense that Alfred Hitchcock knew every detail about all the people in his orbit. Nothing would escape him. *Remember that, Grace.* Demurring, she replied, "Perhaps. But in the end I decided it was the lesser of the evils."

"Hmm," he mumbled noncommittally. "And you are comfortable with the scene in which you will be murdered?"

There was the faintest hint of lasciviousness in his voice. She was glad he wasn't looking at her as he said it, though. She wondered if disorienting her was part of this test. "Well, I don't actually get murdered, though, do I?" she replied.

He turned and faced her, smiling, his small teeth bared between his lush lips. "No, Miss Kelly, you do not. But the scene is grotesque, and I plan to shoot it in all its barbarity. People will talk about the way I direct it."

Grace's skin immediately erupted in goose bumps. She'd never have imagined that such a short, squat man with such soft, round features could so much resemble a wolf. And yet she wasn't afraid. She was drawn in, deeply curious about the inner workings of this director who'd so brilliantly commanded the best talents of the past twenty years. Ingrid, of course, but also Cary Grant, Laurence Olivier, Joan Fontaine, and Marlene Dietrich. If she got this part, she'd star alongside Ray Milland and Robert Cummings.

"If you're trying to scare me, Mr. Hitchcock," she replied, straightening her back, "I'm afraid that doing my job — which is to say, rising to the challenge of difficult scripts and scenes — will not frighten me in the least."

Clearly surprised at her boldness, Hitchcock raised his eyebrows and nodded his head with . . . was that *appreciation*? "Then let's begin. Ray!" Then, turning to look her directly in the eyes, he said, "And please, call me Hitch."

She was grateful that he didn't ask her to do the screen test with the murder scene he'd just described. In the partially furnished apartment set, he asked her and Ray Milland to do the opening scene. Then he asked her to read the phone scene when she is surreptitiously talking to her lover. Robert Cummings wasn't there to read it with her, so she had to say his lines in her head at a pace that seemed correct before making her replies.

Second to the paradoxes of the director, the biggest surprise of the day was the electric current that sparked between her and Ray Milland the moment they shook hands. He had black hair and long, sharp features, and he carried his tall frame with an elegant ease. In his gray flannels and crisp white shirtsleeves, he was the picture of the debonair Englishman, with the perfect baritone voice and accent to boot. He was two decades older than Grace, but he hardly looked it, as he'd taken good care of himself. It was also plain to Grace that Hitchcock saw the attraction, too — he gave them an unmistakable knowing look, the sort you give a child you've caught stealing a cookie to say, *I won't tell.* Unfortunately, Ray was married, Grace reminded herself. For quite some time, in fact, to a woman named Muriel Weber. Theirs was one of the few long marriages in the industry, and she had no intention of toying with that.

She just wished she didn't catch him looking at her so appreciatively. His gaze warmed her arms and neck and that telltale place below her navel, the core of her that was never wrong when it told her she wanted someone and he wanted her, too. She found herself pushing away thoughts of him the whole plane ride back to New York.

When she returned to Hollywood at the end of July to begin filming, it was clear he'd been thinking about her as well. Only three days of torturous attraction on set went by before he invited her for a drink and told her that he and Muriel had "an arrangement."

Grace was perched cross-legged on a round barstool at the Formosa, nursing a glass of white wine while Ray leaned sideways against the bar, scotch in hand, the silver buckle of his black leather belt millimeters from her knees.

"An arrangement?" Grace swallowed, her throat parched. "I must tell you, that makes me feel like a mere notch on your bedpost." If only it also lessened her craving for him.

He leaned in closer, and his buckle pressed on her kneecap. "I love my wife, Grace. And our children, and the life we've made together. This is not an arrangement I call on often. Only when I feel it will be worth it."

He was so close to her. He smelled of tobacco, peppermint, and a spicy cologne she couldn't place. She hadn't wanted anyone like this since Gable in Africa, and as with Gable, she was aware that this must be a passing fancy. It wouldn't put her any closer to what Peggy had: the domestic life Grace wanted so much when she wasn't wishing for a part on Broadway. But both theaters and brick houses with sprawling lawns seemed a million miles away from the Formosa and this man, whose physical

232

proximity made her feel reckless with desire. She didn't care about those things when Ray Milland was close to her, and so she brought him to her room at the mercifully discreet Chateau Marmont.

Sharing her bed with the leading man on the picture gave her a shiny secret to ponder in her quiet moments. Milland's smooth, gentle hands were a revelation, obliterating her lingering nostalgia for Gene's rougher touch. Though she was sure no one else knew about their trysts, she was equally sure that Hitch knew full well. Thankfully, he seemed as determined to keep her secret as she was.

"My *God,* he was sexy. I kept wishing he'd throw a glance my way, but he was all business," Rita Gam said of Ray Milland as they sat on Rita's little patio, eating summer tomatoes on toasted sourdough bread. It was a Sunday afternoon, and Ray was home with his wife and children. Grace and Rita had been introduced at a party earlier in the summer, and hit it off right away. Rita had costarred with Ray the previous year in *The Thief.*

Grace was extremely relieved to discover that Ray's *arrangement* had not included Rita, whose persona on- and offscreen was more hot-blooded and brash than that of

Grace Kelly. Though Grace sensed that Rita's marriage to Sidney Lumet, a young director and intellectual on the scene, was not altogether happy, Grace also didn't think she'd cheat on him.

"He is sexy," Grace agreed, guarding her secret even with Rita. It wouldn't do to have people knowing. She and Rita were new friends in any case. It always took a while before Grace knew if she could trust someone.

"Are you blushing?" asked Rita, eyes wide and voice playfully prying.

Oh no. It was just like her body to give her away in Ray Milland's case. "Maybe," Grace admitted, taking a sip of water for something to do.

"Well, if there's anyone who can take care of herself, it's you," said Rita, getting up to pour herself another glass of cold white wine. She held out the bottle for Grace, who shook her head. "See? You hardly even drink."

"I like to keep my wits about me," Grace replied, "and wake up fresh in the morning." She remembered Gene and how she'd drunk more with him for a while just to be social, then regretted it every morning. Even when she hadn't been truly hungover, she'd felt fuzzy and sluggish.

"See? That's what I mean," said Rita. "Not many girls our age have made that connection. Look at poor Marilyn, and she's older."

"I don't get the sense that wine is her problem," said Grace. She'd met the famous blonde only twice, at parties, in particular a small gathering at Jay and Judy's place in New York. She had a very sweet way about her, like she was a rescue kitten that needed constant stroking. She actually snuggled next to Judy on the couch, barefoot, while she had every man in the place listening with rapt attention as she told some story about Bette Davis from the set of *All About Eve.* What really struck Grace, though, was the way she apologized for everything, from how tired she felt to having to use the ladies' room, to even her performance in *How to Marry a Millionaire,* which was supposed to come out later that year and had already garnered phenomenal buzz.

Grace was so glad the Academy had broken her of the apologizing habit, and wondered if Marilyn had been taught the same essential lesson in the Actors Lab, where the other actress had taken classes. Perhaps she had been taught, but hadn't been able to stop the compulsion. Or perhaps — and Grace sensed this was the most likely answer — all the apologizing won her the attention she needed; it was *part* of the act.

"I think Marilyn's kind of lost," added Grace.

Rita shrugged. She wasn't a gossip, and this was one of the things Grace liked about her. Maybe she *could* confide in her about Ray Milland. But not tonight. Then Rita changed the subject: "So what do you think about Elizabeth's party tonight?"

Grace sighed. Elizabeth Taylor's party. It was a big deal to be invited. But this was one of the problems with Hollywood. There was always a party — or five. And because everyone had houses or stayed in hotels all over a rather sprawling geographical area, you had to really commit to going: you had to get all done up, hire a car (well, most people hired cars, but Grace drank so little, she could probably drive herself, but then there was the problem of getting parked in on a lawn with no one else sober enough to part the sea and let her out — she'd made this mistake more than once already), and then you were *there.* If you were bored, decorum dictated that you were stuck for at least a few hours. If the crowd you were with wanted to move on, you had the same car problem all over again, then the drive to get to the next location and the fear of what press monsters might be lying in wait to find out whom you were party hopping with. It was exhausting. And people wondered why she didn't go out more. Nights in with a lover were far more enticing.

"Oh, I don't know," Grace said, fingering her stringy hair to ascertain how much work it would need before a party. A fair bit, unfortunately. "What about you?"

"I need the work, so I'll be going," said Rita. "And Sidney wants to go."

So there was the truth. Grace wondered if Ray and his wife, Muriel, would be there, and if it would matter. Elizabeth Taylor's place was probably massive. It was easy to get lost in an LA mansion. "I think I'll sit this one out," said Grace.

Rita shrugged. "Suit yourself," she said. Then she sighed. "I wish Sidney didn't want to go."

"He could go by himself," Grace said.

Rita gave a *he should* look, with an eye roll to the heavens, then said, "Wait till you're married, Grace. Then the capable man you thought you were marrying will turn into a little boy, expecting a mother as much as a wife."

Grace went back to her hotel room and took a long bath, then sat up in bed with a novel. Pretty soon it was close to midnight, and she was yawning and switching off the light. Had she been at the party with Rita, she'd no doubt be deep in negotiations about whether to stay or go, which party was sizzling hottest that night. Hollywood could do without her. It would rage on, sending its euphoric laughter into the night, where it would echo between the golden hills to infinity.

"I hoped to see you last night at Liz's place," Ray Milland growled in her ear at the table with coffee and Danish the following morning on the set.

Grace laughed, never more glad that she didn't have after-party circles under her eyes. "I'm not a mind reader, Ray," she said, setting a bear claw pastry on a paper plate. "And anyway, if you *wanted* to see me so badly, maybe it wouldn't have been a good idea?"

"Muriel wasn't there," he replied to her implication.

"But other people might have seen us," she hissed before walking away, now annoyed. Why couldn't she just find a nice, unmarried man and not have to deal with all this subterfuge?

That day, they were shooting the scene right before the attempted murder, in which

Ray's character, Grace's husband, called her in the middle of the night to rouse her from bed so that Anthony Dawson's character, Charles Swann, could sneak up on her and murder her. Grace had read this scene many times, and some of the director's notes were bothering her. She was glad she was well rested, because before shooting began, she screwed up her courage and approached Hitch to talk to him about it. Standing patiently while he finished talking to one of the cameramen, she felt rattled from her exchange with Ray and now nervous about waiting to offer a suggestion to Alfred Bloody Hitchcock. Strangely, she realized that she hadn't even really *decided* she was going to make this suggestion until Ray had hassled her about the party. But for once, she'd had enough of these *men* not understanding things. And here was a detail in a movie she might actually be able to do something about. So she was going to forgo her usual silence and say something.

When he finished with the cameraman, Hitch turned to face her and said, "Good morning, Grace. I trust you are well this morning? None the worse for wear?"

"If you're referring to parties, Hitch, you'll be glad to know I was in bed with a book most of last night."

"Glad?" he said with a tut. "I'm *most* disappointed to hear it."

"Hitch," she said in mock horror, "you mean you'd rather have me gallivanting around Hollywood than getting a good night's sleep to work on your picture?"

"Only because the image of you gallivanting pleases me, my dear," he said with the wolfish — but somehow avuncular — grin.

Only Hitch.

"Well, you can imagine it all you like. Isn't that the point of fantasy? That it need not ever happen?"

"Well said, Grace, well said." Though it irritated her to admit, Hitch's approval of her quips made her heart swell with pride. She liked winning his rarely given praise and occasionally his surprise that Grace Kelly could call on her upbringing and swear like a bricklayer. She knew she intrigued him, and that was deeply satisfying — she hoped it was enough to get him to respect her ideas as well.

"I wanted to talk to you about something in the script," she said with as much confidence as she could muster.

"Yes?"

"It's about this scene where the phone call wakes me up."

"And?"

240

"Well, the script says I should get up and put on my robe."

"Would you prefer to appear before the camera in your knickers?"

He was trying to unbalance her with flippancy, and she wasn't about to let him. "Of course not."

"I thought so. And I would never dream of putting a fellow Catholic, a *lady,* such as yourself, in that sort of compromising position."

Somehow she doubted that, but she pressed her position. "But a lady like Margot wouldn't be asleep in her underwear, either. Nor would she go to the bother of putting on a robe before picking up the phone in the other room. It's the middle of the night. And remember, she assumes she's alone in the apartment."

"What are you suggesting?" he asked, a subtle note of impatience creeping in.

"That I wear a lovely and modest enough nightgown to bed, then get up from the bed and answer the phone wearing that."

Hitch regarded her with his nose definitively raised in the air so that he could gaze downward at her ever so slightly — for in the flats she was wearing, she was nearly his height. She noticed that a few crew members were watching them carefully, and she wondered — too late, she realized — what had happened to other actors who attempted to improve upon Hitch's direction. From the tension she sensed in the air, she guessed it hadn't ended well. But he did appear to be considering what she'd said, so she added, "It's just that the movie is going to be perfect under your direction, Hitch. I wouldn't want any lady in any movie theater wondering why Margot bothered to put on her robe, because wondering would take them out of the story."

Never lowering his nose, Hitch let a few beats pass, then said with timing that Sanford Meisner himself would have praised, "Well . . . I certainly wouldn't want any of the ladies who have dragged their husbands and beaux away from the television to have reason to regret their choice. We shall see how the scene *looks* the way you suggest, Grace. And there is the timing to think of, you know. Let's also see how long it takes you to get out of bed without fastening a robe."

Then he turned on his heels and summoned a cameraman with two fingers.

Grace exhaled and felt her heart beat again.

She'd done it. And after shooting the scene and examining its aesthetics and pacing, Hitch never asked her to put on the robe. She couldn't remember the last time she'd felt so proud of herself. For the rest of the day, she felt as though she was walking on a cloud.

When she and Ray Milland were in bed together the next night, he said to her, "That was quite a coup you pulled off, you know. Hitch never listens to anyone. Either he really respects you, or he really wants to sleep with you."

With her head still resting casually on his chest, she said, "I resent both the notion that respect and sexual relations are mutually exclusive and the notion that he would only listen to me if he wanted to sleep with me."

"Easy now, tiger."

"If you were a woman, you'd hear your words very differently."

"Good thing I'm not, then," he said. And then with that infuriating way he had, he pulled her up to kiss him long and deep. "And I for one," he breathed, "have nothing but respect for you *and* a bottomless desire for sexual relations with you."

She thought now was as good a time as any to stay silent and enjoy herself.

CHAPTER 14

As Grace had assumed from the start, the affair with Ray Milland was specific to the time and place. His desires were not as bottomless as he'd proclaimed, which suited Grace fine, if she was being honest. As summer drew to a close and she knew she'd be returning to New York and an audition for the part of Roxane in *Cyrano de Bergerac,* the stress of hiding her comings and goings with her married costar in Hollywood was beginning to wear on her. She let him break it to her gently over champagne and oysters — *Muriel has been so good to me and the children. . . . I've had the most marvelous time working on this picture with you* — because she enjoyed watching this debonair gentleman get uncomfortable. She put him out of his misery with generous understanding, and their last night together was memorable enough to make her regret it was their last.

In the sultry late-summer weeks, as she

was preparing for the *Cyrano* audition and doing a few TV dramas, she went to a party and met Oleg Cassini, a fashion designer whose dresses she'd admired in *Vogue*. With his slim mustache and wavy hair swept back from his tan face, he looked something like a gambling playboy, the sort who'd be cast as a race-car-driving distraction from the heroine's true love with Tom, Dick, or Harry. Add to that his easy laugh, dreamy Continental accent — originally Russian, but after Oleg had lived so long in the fashion capitals of the West, it had softened into something more pan-European — and wicked sense of humor, and he was the opposite of Ray Milland, who now seemed stuffy in comparison. And although he was sixteen years older than Grace, he was six years younger than Ray, which made him seem positively boyish by comparison.

She was getting used to older men. Because she had been cast with them so often, it felt natural to have romantic feelings for them, much more so than for men her own age, who seemed rather juvenile. Moody, intellectual Marlon Brando was a special case, as he seemed much older than his years. But young men like that very nice and quite talented Paul Newman, whom she'd met on the sets of a few television dramas? No, thank you. When other girls — girls only a few years younger than she was now, who lived at places like the Barbizon — talked about their dates with these young actors, they twittered about pizza and Chinese food eaten out of cartons on floors that needed sweeping. None of that sounded appealing to Grace. She preferred an established man.

Over tea at the Plaza, her old friend Maree Frisby mentioned to her none too casually that she'd read in *Reader's Digest* that some girls who went for older men might have unnatural feelings about their fathers.

"My penchant for older men isn't . . . *oedipal*, Maree," Grace replied. "I hardly have an Electra complex."

"Oh, I'm not suggesting you have any feelings like *that* for your father," said Maree. "But your dad's always been, well, a big deal in your life. Someone you feel like you need to impress."

"I don't see what you're getting at," said Grace, her skin prickling with irritation and also the uncomfortable recollection of how much Hitch's praise pleased her — though the director had never been her lover, his appreciation was in some ways more potent than Ray Milland's because of his stature. Had either of them been her age, Grace knew their approval wouldn't have meant nearly as much.

But to Maree, she protested, "Well, my father would *not* be impressed by Oleg. He'd hate his 'European ways.' " Grace put two-fingered rabbit ears around the last two words and dropped her voice an octave to mock her father. "To say nothing of Oleg's *two* divorces."

Maree giggled. "It's nothing, Grace. Just something I read that I thought you'd find interesting. Don't worry about it. If you're happy, I'm happy."

"I'm happy," Grace said, and she was happier still to discover that she meant it. Her life felt full of possibility again, and she sensed that something exciting was just around the corner. Still, the conversation with her friend made her hold back from Oleg and resist his advances. Even when he began sending her flowers, Grace said no to dinner with him, though she thoroughly enjoyed his lavish attempts at getting her attention. Her apartment looked like a florist shop! As Asmir's had been years ago, Oleg's flowers were not standard issue. He sent a fuchsia orchid with an almost obscene green center, birds-of-paradise, rare cherry blossom branches flown up from South America.

Then, a few days before her audition for *Cyrano,* she woke up with a nasty cold, and no matter what she did — and she tried everything, including hot baths every night, metallic-tasting medicine, cups and cups of hot water with lemon and honey, and even a wretched little contraption called a neti pot that Don swore by but made her gag and splutter as vile goop poured from her sinuses — her voice still was not right the day of her audition. Plus she was even more blind than usual from the lack of sleep. She didn't even get a callback.

Was God punishing her for her wayward behavior? Her Catholic upbringing suddenly made her feel abjectly guilty. Was it possible she wasn't getting Broadway parts because of the way she was conducting her personal life? But that was ridiculous, she countered inside her own head. Look how morally bankrupt half the leading lights on Broadway were! By comparison, her limited dalliances with married men seemed positively innocent; besides, she told herself for the umpteenth time, once *she* was married, she'd never cheat. So what was the problem? Why couldn't she just get a damn part?

While she was in this low mood, Oleg — handsome, single (if formerly married), artistic Oleg — sent her another heavy vase of fragrant blooms, and this time he included a funny poem: "Roses are red, violets are blue, please, Grace Kelly, do give me a clue." And below it he wrote, "Hope you're feeling better and that we can have dinner soon." Doubled over, Grace laughed until she coughed and had to sit down. Goodness, she liked him. More than she'd liked anyone in a long time. And perhaps God was sending her a man instead of a part on Broadway for a reason.

She planned to proceed with caution. This was not some on-set fling. Oleg's star was rising in the fashion world, and his movements were carefully monitored by New York socialites and artists alike. And she was gaining fame, too, what with *Mogambo* movie posters with her face plastered everywhere she looked. New York reporters weren't as intrusive as their Hollywood counterparts, but they *would* have a field day with a relationship between a fashion designer and a movie actress.

So she said yes to dinner with Oleg, but — enjoying the sense that she held all the cards for once — she wrote him a note explaining that their date would have to wait until she felt better and until after the *Mogambo* premiere.

Then she was presented with the most

wonderful choice of her career — it was so wonderful, Grace couldn't help but feel that God must not only have forgiven her sins but entirely approved of her choices.

Jaybird called to tell her she'd been offered two parts, and she had to choose one or the other because the filming for each would happen at the same time: Edie Doyle opposite Marlon Brando in a screen adaptation of *On the Waterfront,* which Elia Kazan was shooting himself in New York City. Or Lisa Fremont opposite James Stewart in Hitch's next movie, a thriller called *Rear Window,* which would take place in New York but be filmed in a Hollywood studio. Hitch was planning to build the largest set ever created just to make an authentic facsimile of the backs of two apartment buildings with a shared courtyard.

What a decision! She couldn't sleep or eat for thinking about it. Her heart was not a reliable source of information, as it beat faster when she thought of *both* films.

She discussed it with everyone — Don, Rita, Sandy, Josephine, Judy, Jay, Maree, and even Peggy while she sizzled pork chops for her family on the other end of the line. There was a fifty-fifty split vote on which movie she should do. Actually, Jay and Sandy refused to vote — they told her to take the part that spoke to her most. Initially, that was impossible to discern. So she read and reread the scripts, and began to feel a stronger affinity for Lisa Fremont in Hitch's movie.

This surprised her. She was certain that had Jay given her this choice a year ago, she'd have chosen *On the Waterfront* in a heartbeat. Without even thinking. It was based on a successful Broadway play, after all, and she'd get to study with the legendary Elia Kazan. And it would also give her the opportunity to play a hardscrabble working-class girl, against type.

However, the role was much smaller than that of Lisa Fremont. And when she read Hitch's script, she actually heard her own voice speaking Lisa's words. It came naturally. Though the challenge of playing Edie appealed to her, Grace couldn't quite see herself playing the part. Plus, she could see her performance getting utterly eclipsed by Marlon's. If she was going to pick a movie to further her career, Hitch's was the right choice.

She'd just about made the final decision when Hitch tipped the scales by calling her directly.

"This is *your part,* Grace," he said, his low voice carrying all the way across the country.

"No one else can play it but you. I know you have another opportunity with Elia, and I can't say a word against him, as I have nothing but the utmost respect for his talent. But you *are* Lisa Fremont."

Everyone, including Jay and Sandy, was so pleased when she took the part in *Rear Window,* it was like they'd all been holding their breath, hoping she'd make that very choice. Judybird and Jaybird toasted her in their cozy apartment a few days before she left to go back to Hollywood, and Jay said, "Hitch is going to make you a star, Grace. I'm glad you didn't take the risk with Kazan."

"Don't say that, Jay. She'd have been terrific." Judy waved her husband's comment away.

"She would have, of course," Jay agreed, and Grace could tell he meant it. "But I think audiences would have been confused. They would have asked, *Who is Grace Kelly?* Hitch will make it easy for them to answer that question."

Not too easy, Grace hoped, for there was something in Jay's excitement about Alfred Hitchcock making her into *Grace Kelly* that made her grind her teeth and want to change her mind.

But the part of Edie Doyle had already

252

been accepted by Eva Marie Saint, and it was gone.

On the red carpet for *Mogambo* on a chilly autumn night, Clark Gable was effusive in his praise of Grace to the press, and Ava wrapped her in a tight hug. For once the photographers were restrained and complimentary, and Grace felt glamorous and desired. "Can you believe we started filming a year ago?" she remarked to Ava, as they sipped champagne from gold-rimmed coupes.

"I know. Can you believe we were in *Africa*?" Ava replied.

"From Africa to King Arthur's court for you," laughed Grace. "I can't wait to see you play Guinevere." Ava's next movie, *Knights of the Round Table,* would be out by the end of the year.

"And back into Hitchcock's den for you," said Ava. "I heard you're going to do a second one with him?"

The two of them chatted excitedly about their upcoming projects. Ava even said to Grace, "You know, I'm a bit jealous. Hitchcock hasn't had a muse since Ingrid Bergman. And look what he did for her career."

Grace blushed and felt hot inside her head and chest. She hadn't thought of Ingrid

Bergman when she was making her choice, but Ava was right, which only reinforced her decision.

Then Frank came over and put his arm around Ava, planting a warm kiss on her cheek. But Ava didn't break eye contact with Grace, and appeared annoyed at the sudden affectionate appearance of her husband. The three of them made some small talk; then it was time to see the movie. Clark, Grace noticed, continued to keep his distance from her. After his initial greeting and kiss on the cheek, he'd steered clear of her. Inwardly, she shrugged. She saw now that his avoidance was a confirmation that something had sparked between them.

As the lights dimmed in the theater and the jibber-jabber of the audience dwindled to silence, Grace felt excitement rise in her chest. She had to admit she enjoyed being part of an audience viewing her work, as she could never be onstage. Not only could she experience the part as an actress; she could enjoy the other performances as an audience member.

Watching herself in her third feature film, on-screen with Clark and Ava, stirred something in Grace. *There I am.* And her performance was good. Though she could remember what had been going through her mind right before and after each and every scene, she could also remember how her mind had cleared while the camera spun its celluloid from one reel to another, how she'd become Linda Nordley in those moments. And the results of that discipline were clear: the audience was rapt. Even her father would have to admit that this time, Grace had done well. Surely.

Cyrano and the stage seemed very far away from the comfortable movie theater seat in which she watched herself that night. And her first date with Oleg was in just a few days' time. Then another movie with Hitch was just around the corner. Was that happiness she felt flutter inside her? Butterflies hatching from cocoons they'd been trapped inside too long.

CHAPTER 15

Edith Head was Grace's new favorite person in Hollywood — maybe anywhere. The designer with the thick black glasses, severe bangs, and dark hair was nearly the only person Hitch trusted with his costumes, and Grace could see why. Edith was practical and no-nonsense, and she had an impeccable eye. Over lunch at Musso & Frank, they discussed the upcoming scene in *Rear Window* in which Grace's Lisa Fremont would inform Jim Stewart's Jeff Jefferies that she'd be spending the night in his tiny apartment, and what the sartorial needs of the scene were: Lisa had to be seductive but ladylike, cosmopolitan but girlish. The Mark Cross overnight bag that Edith had found was a stroke of genius in Grace's opinion. It gave Grace's character the opportunity to show her practical side in precisely the superficial way her boyfriend could not abide, which made him even more skeptical of Lisa's ability to tag along while he took prizewinning photos around the world because, as his character put it, "You don't sleep much, you bathe even less, and you'd have to eat things that you wouldn't want to look at while they were alive."

Grace and Edith had a good laugh about that over steak and salad at lunch.

"Why is the poor son of a bitch going out with Lisa anyway?" Edith mused.

"Lust," said Grace.

They both laughed.

"Maybe the better question is why Lisa wants to be with Jeff," said Edith. "What does he offer her, besides a bohemian life she doesn't really want? And he's constantly putting off her advances — he hardly seems like a man consumed by lust."

"Oh, that much I can understand," said Grace. "Haven't you ever wanted someone who keeps you at arm's length? It can be a very effective method of seduction." She thought of Don and Gene. Clark.

"No," said Edith emphatically.

"Well, then, maybe I should be taking more than clothing lessons from you."

In truth, though, Edith took a few cues from Grace, and Hitch let the two of them create Lisa Fremont together. Grace encouraged Edith to make Lisa's dress as frothy as possible for her first scene in the movie, and so she'd designed a stunning black-and-white dress with a gorgeous bell of a skirt that swirled like fairy dust around her legs, and rustled just so, then wrapped tightly around her waist and shoulders and gave her the stature of a ballet dancer. Grace added her own pearl choker and earrings, and "Voilà!" Edith exclaimed. "Lisa Fremont. In this dress, no one will even notice how flat-chested you are."

"Well, you added just the right amount of padding, magician that you are," said Grace, feeling curvy and sultry in Edith's concoction.

"No magic here," said Edith. "I prefer to think of myself as a sartorial surgeon."

Grace shivered. "I don't like scalpels," she said. "I prefer to think of you as my fairy godmother."

"You won't call me that out loud if you value your career," said Edith, pointing her shiny stainless steel scissors at Grace.

"Bibbidi-bobbidi-boo," teased Grace.

"You! No one would guess what a little insubordinate you are, Grace Kelly," Edith said, and though her surface tone was irritated, beneath that were musical notes of respect and surprise, and Grace beamed inside.

She also took an apartment with Rita on Sweetzer Avenue in West Hollywood, and the two of them spent many hours between Grace's shoots and Rita's work and auditions taking long walks through the hills around the nearby Chateau Marmont, sweating out the industry tension that permeated their skin. In the simple flat, one of hundreds of similar apartments in low, square buildings on a street lined with purple flowering jacarandas and miniature palm trees, they took turns cooking simple meals and taking each other's telephone messages on a yellow pad of paper in a red pen that they kept by the phone in the kitchen. They'd draw little happy faces and dancing stick figures for people they liked, and angry faces and pots of wet noodles for people they didn't. Rita didn't discuss it, and Grace didn't pry, but Sidney was living in New York. She rarely took messages from Rita's husband on their pad. But there was an increasing number from Oleg Cassini for Grace.

In addition to writing letters once or twice a week, he also called and entertained her with tales about the Persian Room and the Copa, ice-skaters in Central Park, and the Christmas windows at Macy's. Every time they hung up, she felt a tightness in her body that rarely loosened on its own — she always had to *do* something, like take a walk or read a consuming novel or go to work. Though she recognized the feeling as longing, she wasn't entirely sure what it was she wanted: Oleg or New York.

She'd signed the lease for Sweetzer on something of a whim, in a fit of pique, fed up with living in a hotel all the time and anxious to make her own coffee and oatmeal every morning, to keep a few photos and personal items she wouldn't have to schlep coast to coast every time she had a job. But once she had actually brought her suitcases to the bedroom and unpacked them into the dresser she'd gotten at an antique store in the Valley, Grace felt suddenly winded, and had a hard time catching her breath. Sinking down on the bed, she felt the fear and sadness build in her chest.

She told herself she was being silly. An apartment in Los Angeles was a practical decision. It didn't mean she wasn't going back to New York. In fact, she was *lucky* that she had the means to make her life more comfortable this way. What did it matter how much time she would actually spend in this apartment? What mattered was that it would make her happier to shoot movies if she knew she had a place with a friend that felt a little more like home.

And she did love working with Hitch. Every day on the set was an affirmation of that; she was learning as much from him about craft as she had at the Academy or from Sandy. Hitch taught her about restraint, about the power of silence in a scene and in a movie overall, and how to show just enough — never too much — emotion for the camera. But their relationship wasn't merely a teacher-student one; Hitch treated her if not as an equal (for he considered no one his equal, and in a strange way, this was part of his charm), then at least as a trusted professional whose ideas mattered to him. They'd also developed a ritual of trading Catholic jokes when they greeted each other in the morning. Hitch was always delighted when she delivered one he'd never heard. His favorite was "The Mother Superior went to the corner market and asked for a hundred ten bananas for herself and the other nuns, and the salesman told her it would be more economical to buy a hundred twenty-five. The Mother Superior replied, 'Ah well, I suppose we could *eat* the other fifteen.' " Then, when he told her the one about two nuns cycling down a cobbled street, and she replied, "Oh, Hitch, I went to a girls' convent school. You'll have

261

to try harder than that," he laughed so hard, she thought maybe he would choke.

Grace reveled in reliving these details with Uncle George on her days off. Now that Grace had moments of her own to offer, their conversations felt more balanced instead of sounding like a dialogue between an instructor and his protégée. "Oh, Grace," Uncle George said one cool November day over Thanksgiving leftovers at his Palm Springs house while William took a nap, "I am so glad you've finally found someone who appreciates your considerable talents."

"You mean someone other than *you*," she said.

"Well, yes. One never believes one's family in the same way as a stranger. Correction," he quickly added. "We never believe the good our family says of us. We're only too quick to believe the bad things they say."

"Mmmm." Grace nodded, feeling warm with bread stuffing and understanding. *Too bad you're not my father,* she almost said. Instead, she wondered, "Maybe those bad things they say about us are what make us want to be different from them."

"I know that's true for me," said George, "but I always thought in your case it was different."

"How?"

"You still want their approval."

"How could I not?" she asked. "They're my parents, my sisters and brother."

"Perhaps it was my . . . *other* choices that helped me shut out their voices in my head," George mused. "Perhaps it's different for you because you're a woman who wants the things women have been told to want."

Grace sighed, glancing down at her hands, her naked ring finger. "Sometimes I wish I didn't."

"Never wish away your truth," he said. Then, without waiting for her to reply, he picked up the bottle of white wine and refilled their glasses. "This goes well with the last of the pumpkin pie. And I want to hear more about Jimmy Stewart."

Another happy surprise on the picture was that her relationship with Jim was mercifully drama free. He'd been extremely professional from the start, shaking her hand and telling her how much he'd enjoyed her performances in *High Noon* and *Mogambo.*

"If you thought she was good in those, wait till you see *Dial M,*" Hitch had interjected, for that film still hadn't been released.

Grace wasn't sure if it was because Jim

was so engrossed in the acting, and his character did indeed hold hers at arm's length, or if it was because he was such a gentleman, but he never once suggested the two of them be anything other than colleagues. He had been married to Gloria McLean since 1949, but that hardly meant anything — Grace had to look no further than Don, Gene, or Ray Milland for proof of that. And yet, when Gloria visited the set and Jim greeted her with an affectionate kiss on the cheek, Grace had the sense that this couple had found the real thing in each other, a love and companionship that would endure.

And then Grace also had the sense that she was falling in love with Oleg. She saw him during the holidays on a week she spent on the East Coast seeing family and checking on things in New York. After dinner they went dancing, and Oleg held her tightly, murmuring in her ear, "When will I have you to myself, *ma chérie*? I am pining for you." For the first time in she didn't know how long, she felt a long velvet ribbon of *romance* unwinding slowly between herself and a man, and she loved that Oleg was not also an actor. He was a professional artist in his own right, and so he understood that ambitious, creative side of her, but the fact that he was not part of her industry made a relationship with him more appealing and also more promising.

That promise told Grace to wait before giving herself to Oleg, however. She didn't want to jeopardize the stride she'd hit in *Rear Window* with what promised to be a passionate entanglement with the fashion designer. By the same token, she didn't want to jeopardize a possible future with Oleg by being distracted by *Rear Window*. She found him so attractive, reveled in his intellect and his wit — she found herself thinking of him in nearly all her private moments, of all the conversations and kissing she wanted to experience with him. *Wait,* she told herself as her body began to buzz with desire. *Wait. Do things differently this time, and maybe they will proceed differently. End differently.*

Maybe they won't end at all.

She tried to focus instead on caring for herself, organizing her life so that when the time came to be fully distracted by Oleg, she wouldn't get as derailed as she had in the past. The Los Angeles apartment was a good first step, as was throwing herself into her second movie with her favorite auteur. She also hired a man to manage her money in New York, and drew up a budget that allowed for a possibly larger, finer place in Manhattan as well. After spending the afternoon at a bookstore in Los Feliz, she brought home a few books of poetry she'd found herself entranced by, as well as the latest editions of the *Betty Crocker Cookbook* and *The Joy of Cooking.* The following morning, she whipped up a batch of blueberry muffins for herself and Rita.

"Jesus, Grace, these are amazing," Rita said as she reached for another fluffy, sweet muffin.

"They are good, aren't they? Mother never made these kinds of things for breakfast," Grace said, deciding to enjoy a third muffin herself with another cup of coffee. "I think I had oatmeal every morning of my childhood. Except at Christmas." The idea that she could care for herself like this — without a corner bakery or someone else to run the errand — was something of a revelation.

Hitch wrapped shooting in January of 1954, and Grace couldn't wait to see the finished product. She had the sense that something very special had happened in the making of that movie — not because of parties or drunken camaraderie, but because everyone working on the picture regarded it as a job they were determined to do well, with all the skills they possessed. The whole experience had erased the regret she'd felt in not taking the part of Edie Doyle in *On the Waterfront*. Even more, *Rear Window* began to soften the hard edges of her resentment about Broadway. In the company of Hitch and Jim and Edith, Grace felt seen and appreciated in ways she never had on the stage, even in her early days at the Academy when Don couldn't say enough good things to her.

In a few precious moments of unadulterated optimism, Grace thought that *Rear Window* might be a work that would actually last. Much as she loved theater, Grace knew that great movies enjoyed long lives in a way that plays could not, even plays with very long runs. True, a picture could get remade, like *Red Dust* redone as *Mogambo,* but others were never made again because their magic could never be replicated: *The Wizard of Oz, Gone with the Wind, Gaslight.* Instead, those pictures were shown again and again all over the world, and thus the actors who were in them enjoyed the longest careers of any in the business.

Perhaps *Rear Window* would be one of those. Only time would tell.

In the meantime, Jay told her she had to do one small part for a Paramount picture

MGM actually wanted her to do before returning to New York, and she agreed without a fuss because *The Bridges at Toko-Ri* offered her a rare opportunity to make MGM happy with a small, easily managed role that would also give her top billing right beneath household name William Holden. A war movie made for the veterans who wanted to relive their World War II or Korean War glory, it was no *Rear Window,* but Grace tried to see it as fulfilling some sort of patriotic duty. And as a nice bonus, it made her father happy. "At least that's a movie I can see and understand, instead of that artsy nonsense you've been doing with that pansy Hitchcock," he'd said when she rung her parents to tell them of the new role.

His comment stirred the rebellious girl inside her, the one who'd packed her life into suitcases to move to New York at seventeen. As she slammed down the phone's receiver, she thought, *What do you know about art, you intolerant philistine?* But a few days later, the fury wore off, and her nerves started jangling in that familiar way, making her feel restless and disoriented, unable to just look on the bright side as she so much wanted to do.

Returning to New York that winter was a

welcome distraction, especially with the promise of a consuming romance with Oleg Cassini, with whom that rebellious girl inside her had decided to fall fully in love — likely parental disapproval of his divorces and Russian heritage be damned.

It began swimmingly, with a few nights of dinners and dancing, and then the clincher: the most unexpected and unusual date she'd ever gone on. After instructing her to wear blue jeans, not an evening dress, Oleg whisked her into a cab "for a true surprise," which turned out to be a dive bar in Brooklyn where they ordered beer and watched a wiry young man with black hair named Lenny Bruce take the microphone on a small stage, and do a comedy routine that had the entire place gasping for air and clutching their sides. She hadn't had this much pure fun in an audience since she was a little girl and Uncle George would take her to puppet shows and other small theater productions around Philadelphia — just the two of them, escaping the disapproving eyes of her athletic parents.

"How did you *know* about him?" Grace asked Oleg, her eyes wide with surprise and admiration that this sophisticated man who knew everything about French wine and Coco Chanel could also know about underground comedy in the outer boroughs.

"I like to talk to the people who work for me, the men and women who cut the fabric and sew the seams. They have told me about some of the very best food and entertainment in the city. And look! No photographers." He gestured around the smoky bar, likely a former speakeasy, now a standing-room-only crowd of bohemians who didn't give a fig about Madison Avenue.

Not one of them was looking at her or Oleg, let alone jostling for a photograph. Exhilarated and grateful, she seized on something else Oleg had just mentioned: "What kind of food do your seamstresses recommend? I'm starving."

He took her by the hand and led her into another taxi, whispering a location to the driver and refusing to say a word about where they were going no matter how much she begged. It was a long drive, and she started getting nervous — where *was* he taking her? But then the famous Ferris wheel and Cyclone roller coaster became visible in the distance, and she turned to him and said, "Coney Island? In February?"

"I thought you wanted to be surprised," he replied.

"I'm amazed," she breathed.

When they emerged from the cab in front

of Totonno's Pizzeria, a bitingly cold wind howled in her ears and she heard the sounds of waves crashing on the nearby beach. This was the last place she'd expected to be tonight. Inside, though, the aromas of herby tomato sauce and yeast and cheese and coal fire that greeted them were otherworldly. The air was moist and hot, and her cheeks prickled as they thawed. They sat and ordered more beer, and Oleg said something in Italian to the waiter, which promptly produced a basket of warm, oily breadsticks.

"This might be the most delicious thing I've ever eaten," said Grace with her mouth full, unable to stop herself from eating most of the basket, and then her half of the sublime pizza when it arrived.

Oleg laughed. "I like a girl with an appetite," he said admiringly, lighting a cigarette and leaning back against his chair, sated and smirking.

Grace wiped her hands and mouth with the hundredth little paper napkin, and sighed with the kind of relief that only comes after great pleasure. "But I don't think I can move now," she laughed.

"What a shame," said Oleg, flicking cigarette ash into the glass tray, then leaning forward to say, low and smooth, "because I did have one more surprise in mind for later."

Given how full she felt, Grace considered it a sign from God that her body responded so forcefully to his suggestion. They kissed deeply the whole long taxi ride back into Manhattan, their fingers tracing lips and necks and lacing into hair, and all the way up the deserted elevator and into Oleg's luxurious apartment, where they fell to the floor as soon as he shut the door.

CHAPTER 16

"I want this part, Jay," she said firmly. She'd invited him over for tea without Judy so that he would know this wasn't a social call and see that she was dead serious about playing Georgie Elgin in the upcoming movie version of *The Country Girl,* the part Uta Hagen had won a Tony for in the Broadway production. She'd be playing a very different kind of character — no glamour, no shopping at Magnin's or Saks, even though Edith Head would be doing the costume work, thank goodness. But unlike with Edie Doyle in *On the Waterfront,* Grace could see herself as Georgie Elgin.

It would mean leaving New York for Hollywood again, just as things with Oleg were getting off the ground, but she knew in her bones that this part in this movie would be worth it — and it wasn't because it was more likely to get her a break on Broadway. She wanted to do this *movie,* as a movie. It stunned her to realize that her old Broadway dream didn't grip her in the same way anymore. Perhaps it was more mature to want the things that seemed to want you back.

"I know you want it, Graciebird, and I think you'd be terrific, but MGM doesn't want to keep lending you to other studios," Jay said before taking another linzer cookie from the delicately flowered porcelain plate.

"Then tell them to send me a script worth considering," she replied.

"They believe they have."

"They send me rubbish, Jay, and you know it. *Toko-Ri* was painless enough but *Green Fire*? Please. It's little more than a dime-store adventure novel."

"Grace, none of the movies you've done with Hitchcock have released yet, so the movies in which you're getting top billing haven't reached their audience. You're getting to be better known, but it's all buzz and speculation until your performances are seen and reviewed. You don't have enough clout to call the shots. Not yet."

"Well, that was certainly honest," she said, a bit taken aback. Jay still looked like a blond kid who ought to be playing tennis with his buddies. But he was rapidly becoming an important player in Hollywood. He knew what he was talking about, and she chafed at his bluntness.

"I know you wouldn't expect anything less from me," he said, smiling with sandy crumbs on his lips.

"Actually, I'm more accustomed to you flattering me to get me to do what you think I should do next," she said, without malice — it was true, after all, and she'd followed his guidance willingly enough.

He smiled and said, "Then we appear to have reached a new place in our relationship."

Grace sighed, exasperated. Then she said, "Can you at least try to get me the part?"

"I'll do my best," he vowed, and she believed him.

Two days later, though, he called to say, "No dice. They want you to do *Green Fire* and more MGM pictures."

"But that's ridiculous! They just loaned me to Paramount for *Toko*!"

"Between you and me, they're also worried about your image. Georgie Elgin is a dumpy part. No glamour."

"That's absurd. As you just pointed out, I've only been in three movies that people have actually seen. I don't *have* an image yet."

"You know as well as I do that you do,

Grace. *And* they know how Hitch cast you. They've seen the promotional reels and the posters."

"I don't want to be pigeonholed. I'm only twenty-four. If the only roles anyone's seen me play are the fashion plates, what will I do when I'm forty?"

"You're not the first actress to ask that question."

"Stop talking like a fortune cookie, Jay, and be my *agent.*"

"I am, Graciebird. It's my job to keep you working, which means keeping you realistic. This business is a stinker for women over the age of thirty, but we'll cross that bridge when we come to it."

"I'll show you realistic," she said, heat rising from her belly into her cheeks. She'd had just about enough of people — *men,* it always seemed to be — telling her who she was and what to do. Maybe she should try being a little more like her father for once; he hadn't gotten where he was by being bullied. "You can tell Dore Schary to change my address in his book. I'll give up the lease on Sweetzer Avenue if I can't do *Country Girl.* I have my eye on a bigger place here in Manhattan anyway, where I make far more money in television. I'll accept their Christmas cards here."

"You certain about that, Graciebird?"

"Dead," she said, her blood throbbing briskly through her body.

"All right," he said, betraying no emotion. "I'll let you know what he says."

After seeing a tremendous production of the *Sleeping Beauty* ballet, Oleg and Grace took a quiet back table at the Persian Room, and he listened raptly as Grace told the story of her phone calls with Jay. As soon as she finished, he kissed her on the lips, then summoned the waiter and said, "Two glasses of Pol Roger, *s'il vous plaît,* so we may toast the Viking princess, Grace Kelly."

Grace giggled. *"Stop."*

"What? I admire your nerve, even if it does mean I'm going to have to fly to Los Angeles to see you." He shuddered in mock horror at the mention of their mutual least favorite city.

"Would you?" Grace's pulse quickened at the idea of her and Oleg at some of her favorite Hollywood haunts, then ending their nights on Sweetzer. Oh, she'd have to get some nicer sheets and furniture now.

"I meant what I said about finding a bigger place in New York, too," she said, hoping he'd catch the implication.

"A larger place would certainly suit the

starlet on the move who wants to come home to her stylish pied-à-terre between award-winning films."

"You sound like a magazine."

He sighed suddenly and forlornly. "Forgive me. I did just spend the day with the editorial staff at *Vogue.*"

"But that sounds like a marvelous opportunity!"

"It is," Oleg agreed. "But exhausting. In particular because I was up until dawn putting the finishing touches on the summer line."

"How do you think about summer when it's snowing and the air smells like chestnuts?"

"Imagination," he said, tapping his index finger to his temple. "I've always been particularly skilled at shutting out the world around me and indulging my fantasies."

Recognizing herself in his description only made Grace love Oleg more. She felt drawn to him with her mind as well as with her body; she hadn't truly felt that way since Don, so she knew how rare it was. Leaning toward him with her elbows and forearms on the white tablecloth in a most unmannerly posture, she cooed, "What sort of fantasies, Mr. Cassini?"

Slowly, he moved to mirror her hunch so

that their noses were inches apart across the intimate dinner table. "I'd be more than happy to show you later, Viking princess."

The rest of the dinner passed in a heightened state of anticipation, every touch and flirtation fizzing between them. When at last they were in his apartment, he kissed her passionately, then pulled away almost teasingly and said, "You wanted to see some fantasies, I believe."

Grace opened her mouth to reply, but found that desire had drained her of wit. Oleg laughed and clasped her hand, pulling her gently into his home studio, a corner room with windows that overlooked the city. It was a picturesque winter night: streetlights and home lamps shone in a random smattering, and the sky was a deep purple, bruised with clouds that promised snow before morning.

Oleg switched on a chandelier that cast a pinkish glow on the room. He gestured for her to sit on the chaise along one wall, while he went to his desk and picked up the stiff papers on top. He handed them to Grace and she saw a long, lean sketch of herself, attired in a white day suit with a dramatic collar on one page, then a revealing two-piece swimsuit that made her blush. On the last page, she was in a spectacular blue strapless gown, and he'd labeled it "Oscars."

She was about to open her mouth to say the Academy Awards were a bit of a stretch, but he beat her to it by saying firmly and huskily, "Next year." It was entirely new, this sense of being appreciated for what she did, what she'd worked so hard to achieve, and she felt tears needle her eyes.

Blinking them back, she whispered, "Thank you," and he took the papers and set them gently on the floor as he climbed onto the chaise and kissed her with such tenderness, Grace felt one of those tears escape down her cheek, adding a tang of salt to the sweetness of his touch.

"What if you said you'd do *Green Fire* in order to get *Country Girl*?" Jay asked on the phone.

The price. There was always a price. But she'd pay it. She'd been expecting worse.

"Done," she said, and in less than a week she was sitting with Rita in their kitchen on Sweetzer, having just spent a whirlwind few days shopping and sprucing up their apartment for the promised arrival of Oleg. She was already regretting it, though. She wanted to see him, *almost* more than anything — anything being focusing all her energy on *The Country Girl*. She'd figure it out, how to balance love with work, with *art,* she thought with a thumbed nose to her father, whom she'd not bothered to call to tell she was on her way back to Hollywood.

"Apparently Bing Crosby didn't want me to get the part," Grace said to Rita. "He thinks I'm too young and inexperienced."

"You're too pretty for the part as well. But what do you care? You'll prove him wrong."

"The problem is, I'm worried he's right. What if I am too inexperienced?"

"Elizabeth Taylor was only twelve in *National Velvet,* and Judy Garland was only seventeen in *Wizard of Oz.*"

"But they were child actors; it's totally different."

"Why should it be different? It just goes to show that great performances can be given at any age or level of experience."

Grace rotated her glass of iced tea on the table, making a pleasant, rhythmic whirring sound accompanied by ice cubes chiming merrily inside.

But it must have driven Rita nuts, because she clasped her hand on Grace's to stop her, then added, "You don't think Liz and Judy thought they were out of their league, too, when they stepped onto those sets?"

Grace raised a knowing eyebrow at Rita.

"All right, all right, probably not Elizabeth Taylor. But that's only because she's . . ."

"Elizabeth Taylor."

Rita growled with impatience. "You know what I'm trying to say."

"I do, and I appreciate it," sighed Grace. "It's just that I pushed so hard for this role, and for the studio to let me do it. I don't want to let anyone down."

"Forget about them," said Rita emphatically. "The only person you have to please is yourself. Give a performance *you* can be proud of, and forget the rest of them."

If only it were that simple. But she didn't want to argue. Her friend was trying hard to bolster her up. "You're right," Grace said. "What does Bing Crosby know anyway?"

A lot, Grace assumed. Plus he had more riding on this movie than she did. The part he was playing was — as many of the less delicate industry news sources had blatantly put it — uncomfortably close to his own life: he would be playing Frank Elgin, a once successful stage actor and singer who'd let alcohol get the better of him. Then he got one last shot at a comeback in a play whose director, Bernie Dodd, might be the only person in New York who believed in him. Dodd, who would be played by William Holden, whom Grace was happy to see again after *Toko-Ri,* thought that Elgin's problem was actually his seemingly overprotective wife, Georgie. By the end of the movie, Frank was forced to fess up to his own shortcomings, and Dodd reluctantly saw the light about Georgie.

Bing, whose career had foundered in recent years with too many parties and women, didn't want anything getting in the way of his own comeback — let alone "the Main Line princess," Jay had reported the singer had deemed Grace, which just went to show how little he actually knew about Grace. Had she actually *been* a Main Line princess, maybe her parents would have been more apt to see and appreciate her.

Grace hoped Rita was right, and Bing would come around quickly and see the beautiful irony that both of them would be playing against type — because even though Bing's private life had much in common with Frank Elgin's, his public persona was still that of the smooth, handsome crooner, the man whose songs had the Midas touch. What appealed to Grace most about Georgie — what made her believe she could play her well, in spite of her youth, which would be aged with makeup and appropriate costuming by her beloved Edith — was how misunderstood she was. For years, she unwaveringly loved and supported her husband, suffering mistreatment from him and men like Dodd, just like Cordelia in *King Lear,* Grace's old favorite. So Georgie withdrew into herself, and emerged from her cocoon of sadness when she was at last seen for the steadfast woman she truly was.

She was also drawn to the setting. *The Country Girl* was about the theater, her first love. "There's nothing quite so mysterious and silent as a dark theater, a night without a star," Georgie Elgin said to Bernie Dodd on an empty stage. The line reached inside Grace and clutched something at her very core. She might not be playing this part in a stage play, but it was as close as film got to theater without being a cinematic interpretation of Shakespeare or Chekhov. And in the unexpectedly happy ending of the movie, it was the theater itself — the work and inspiration of it — that redeemed Frank Elgin, and by extension Georgie. Grace hoped that it would serve to bring her and Bing together, too.

Rehearsals didn't exactly get off on the right foot, though. Bing was fidgety and nervous. Grace tried to excuse it as method acting, telling herself he was getting deeply immersed in his character. But when he barely shook her hand when they were introduced, William Holden raised his eyebrows and shot Grace a look that said, *Is that the best he can do?*

Grace tried to remain professional, to say her lines and take direction from George Seaton, who seemed downright mute after Alfred Hitchcock. But he had an unassuming quality and spoke to the actors of the power of the script more than anything else — which Grace thought wasn't surprising, given the fact that Seaton was a writer himself, as well as a director; in fact, he'd adapted Clifford Odets' script of *The Country Girl* for the screen.

After the first week, once the read throughs had graduated to shooting, Bing brought his lunch over to where Grace sat eating and reading a *New Yorker* with her glasses on — which was something else she liked about this role. She got to wear glasses, so she could see perfectly well everywhere she went.

His plate was a mirror image of hers: a hamburger with American cheese, tomato, and mustard, with a green salad on the side.

As soon as Grace saw it, she smiled and said, "I see you like hamburgers as well."

"Oh, I love them," said Bing, but with longing, putting a hand on his heart. "But they aren't so good for me anymore. Still . . .

when I saw them on the lunch line today, I had to have one."

Grace smirked conspiratorially and said, "I won't tell, I promise."

Bing smiled, looked down at his plate, then back up at Grace. He was wearing what could be described only as puppy-dog eyes. The expression made him look ten years younger. "I'm sorry," he said, "for being the cliché of a difficult old-man actor. I never should have doubted your talents."

Grace exhaled with relief. "I appreciate that very much, Bing. Of course, I never for a moment doubted *your* talents," she said with a laugh so he'd know it was a compliment and not a reprimand.

He reciprocated with a chuckle. "I hope to prove myself worthy of your belief in me."

"It would seem this movie is a risk for both of us," she said.

"For you because people might not see you as a cover girl anymore?" He was genuinely curious, she could tell, and he meant no harm in his question, but that term *cover girl* got under her skin, just as it had that day at the Academy when her classmate had used it to explain why she'd never be a real actress. She didn't want to ruin this fresh start with Bing by explaining why his comment was patronizing, though.

286

But she did want to be honest, so she replied, "No, that would be the best possible result. The risk is more that people won't be able to see me as anything *other* than a cover girl."

"Ah," he said, appearing to get lost for a moment in his own thoughts. Then, suddenly snapping out of them, he said sheepishly, "I wish I wasn't so aware of the risks I'm taking in this picture."

"Then we'd better make sure this is the best movie it can be," said Grace, "so you can sleep at night."

"I admit I'm sleeping better knowing you're playing Georgie."

It was a warm moment, and Grace was very grateful for it. She enjoyed another week of productive rehearsals, during which she felt she was doing Georgie justice and not disappointing herself or Bing or anyone else. She was also having fun with Edith, who remarked wryly, "It's not as much fun to dress you for this part, Grace. Where's the challenge if I can't make your string bean form into an hourglass? It's depressing to make a beautiful woman look forlorn."

"Cheer up, Edith. Hitch has been writing me letters about a possible film in France. Something *frothy,* he wrote. Won't that be fun?"

"Hitch? Frothy? He must be in love!"

"Not with me, I hope," Grace laughed, but Edith gave her a warning look, and Grace threw one of Georgie Elgin's dowdy sweaters at her. Then she picked up one of the sensible brown shoes she had to wear, and joked, "Maybe I'll wear these next time I see Hitch. That would certainly cure him of any attraction he might be harboring."

Edith snorted. "Or he'll ask you to dress in a habit and recite your dirtiest nun jokes."

At this, they both dissolved in laughter.

Oleg came and visited at the end of the week, and Grace picked him up from the airport in a warm pink twilight, driving a sporty red convertible and wearing her favorite round sunglasses and an Hermès scarf he liked tied around her head. After settling his suitcase in the backseat and kissing her on the cheek, he put on his own sunglasses, laced his fingers behind his head, and said, "Maybe I could learn to like it here. It was blowing a gale in New York when I left."

"Oleg, darling, the weather is part of New York's character," she crooned. "Don't malign it." Though even she had to admit that soaking up the Southern California sunshine in the dead of winter was a treat she was getting used to.

The next day she had off, so they spent it zipping around in her car, driving into the hills with a picnic of cold chicken and white wine, then spending a lazy afternoon in her redecorated apartment, mostly in the privacy of her bedroom, and later on the patio with Rita and Sidney, who'd come out a few days before. The other couple was getting on well, and they made such a merry foursome drinking spiked lemonade that Sidney had prepared, and trading stories about their New York acquaintances, that Grace and Oleg nearly missed their reservation at the Cocoanut Grove Club in the Ambassador Hotel.

Over a dinner of oysters and then New York strip steaks — how could they resist, when they saw them on the menu? — they talked about Oleg's upcoming designs and shows and eventually wound their way to her work.

"What's it like working with Bing Crosby?" Oleg asked, setting down his knife and fork, then tapping a cigarette out of his silver case.

"It was a little bumpy at first," said Grace, "but we're old friends now." She told him about Bing's concerns, then how he'd come around.

Oleg lit his cigarette and inhaled deeply,

then blew the smoke away from Grace as he knew she didn't love this habit of his.

"That was fast," Oleg said curtly.

"What was?"

"How fast he changed his mind."

Grace felt the skin on the back of her neck tingle a warning. Oleg seemed to be hinting at something, but she couldn't figure out what. Normally, he was so supportive, she'd expected him to say, *Well, of course! How could he have had any doubt?*

"He must have taken one look at you and known how lucky he was, that's all," he added, but without his usual complimentary tone.

"I feel like you're trying to tell me something. . . ."

"Oh, come now, Grace. I'm sure Bing knows as well as I do your penchant for the older men you costar with."

The tingling at her neck began to feel like a full-blown rash on her whole body. She wasn't sure how much Oleg knew about her romantic past, and she resented the judgmental way he was bringing it up. After all, his own record with women was hardly squeaky-clean. "Oleg, you can't possibly believe what you read in the papers," she said.

He inhaled his cigarette again and flicked

ash off of it into a silver dish on the table, without replying.

"Darling," she said in her most soothing voice, "everyone knows I'm in love with you."

"That doesn't matter in this town of make-believe."

"I thought you said you could get used to it here," Grace said, wondering if hives had actually erupted on her skin, she was so itchy for this conversation to be over. Again, he didn't reply, but his silence was as aggressive as any slur or slap.

"Oleg, people are going to write about me," she went on, "and it's all *lies.* Please, please, tell me you can ignore them. I only want to be with you," she said, putting a hand suggestively on his leg and looking into his eyes and trying to convey the depth of her affection.

It took him longer than she would have liked, but he finally put his hand on hers, squeezed it affectionately, exhaled apologetically, and said, "Forgive me, Grace. I haven't felt this strongly about anyone . . . in a very long time."

Grace sighed with relief. "Nor have I." She kissed him gently on the lips. *Poor man,* she thought. *I must be careful with his fragile heart.*

He smiled in surprise. "What a lovely thought." And he kissed her in return. *I hope he's as careful with mine.*

CHAPTER 17

Grace flew straight from Los Angeles to Bogotá, Colombia, for *Green Fire*. She wished that she could be as excited about traveling in South America as she had been about going to Africa for *Mogambo,* but this picture had none of the promise and the cast had none of the chemistry of that earlier picture. Oleg had offered to come with her, and she'd said no — a delicate conversation if ever she'd had one. But he seem preoccupied with his work in New York and comfortable enough in her affections that he did not argue or — worse — try to make her feel guilty about going. Colombia was hot and buggy, the set incredibly dusty. She had to soap up twice in her evening shower before the water would run clear into the drain.

Every day, she told herself it was her penance for getting to do *The Country Girl.* Sometimes she'd think wryly, *Dore Schary should be glad I was raised Catholic and think in such terms.* And mercifully, she only had to suffer through ten days before she could return to Hollywood to complete the filming.

"One silver lining in all this," Grace told Rita as they sat with their feet up, on their unspeakably lovely mosquito-free patio, "is that I was actually *thrilled* to come back to California. I couldn't wait for the plane to land and to come here and see you and go to the Bar Marmont."

"Cheers to that," Rita said, clinking her glass of iced tea — a Long Island in honor of Grace's homecoming — to her friend's.

What made finishing *Green Fire* even more exciting was the promise of heading to France at the end of May to begin filming Hitchcock's next movie, *To Catch a Thief*, with Cary Grant of all people.

"Wild horses couldn't keep me from you in the south of France, my darling," said Oleg when she told him where she was headed next. Grace laughed and didn't even try to stop him. In fact, she'd been planning to invite him; the thought of Oleg, Hitch, Cary, and spring on the Riviera made her feel combustible with joy.

At the *Dial M* premiere she attended before she left, Ray Milland was a complete gentleman, and their affair seemed so far in the past that he and Grace were able to greet each other with Continental kisses and mildly suggestive poses for the press cameras without so much as a spark flying between them. *I must really be in love with Oleg,* thought Grace.

The attention paid to her on the red carpet had a different feel from previous premieres. As the flashes popped, journalists thrust microphones into her face and fired questions at her: "Can we expect a ring from Mr. Cassini?" "Excited to be working with Cary Grant next?" "Are you planning to sell your New York place yet?" She tried to be gracious but vague: "I'm too busy to think about moving." "Mr. Cassini is a lovely man, but we have only just begun!" "I feel incredibly lucky that Mr. Hitchcock has paired me with the finest leading men," she said, lightly touching Ray Milland's nearby arm. By the time she sat in the theater to watch the movie, she was exhausted.

But any tiredness she felt quickly dispersed as the opening credits rolled to the tune of the drum- and harp-heavy orchestration by Dimitri Tiomkin, with her name and Ray's and everyone else's in wobbly gold capital letters before the circular dial of a black, white, and suggestively red telephone. For the first time, she didn't cringe and instinctively look away when her own image first appeared on the screen. Edith hadn't done the costumes for *M,* but Moss Mabry's ensembles looked absolutely perfect on the screen, playing beautifully against the rather staid London apartment decor — Grace's red lace dress in particular was an impeccable counterpoint to the interior scene, speaking volumes about the passions bubbling under the coiffed surfaces of the characters. She chanced a look at Hitch down the aisle of seats during the scene when her character rises from bed to answer the phone *without* her robe, and was delighted to see him look briefly back at her and wink.

By the end, Grace felt breathless. If *M* was this good, she could only imagine how *Rear Window* would turn out.

And then, practically in the blink of an eye, she was in France, sitting with Oleg; Hitch; Cary Grant and his wife, Betsy Drake; John Williams; and Brigitte Auber, at a restaurant in the medieval hilltop town of Saint-Paul-de-Vence. A kingly spread of pâté, olives, oysters, baguettes, rosé, and champagne was on the table before them — and it was only the first course! Hitch had told everyone to plan to spend the afternoon celebrating their good fortune.

"This place is a perfect jewel, Hitch," said Cary, who was already deeply tan for his role as John Robie, formerly the Cat, who was trying to put his life as a renowned jewel thief behind him. "However did you find it?"

"André Bazin mentioned it to me," Hitch replied.

It was indeed fabulous, Grace silently agreed, and quite out of the way from the hullabaloo of the towns right on the brilliantly blue Mediterranean coast. It was not the sort of restaurant to be reviewed in so gauche a place as a travel magazine. Saint-Paul-de-Vence itself was a cobblestone treasure, its narrow stone buildings nestled into the side of a peak high enough to afford spectacular views of the surrounding hills and towns. Grace took in the panorama as hungrily as she ate the delicacies on the table: the vines of grapes climbing olive-hued hills in the distance, small cottage farms with goats and sheep grazing, palatial resorts and sandy beaches at the water's level, and creamy châteaus dotting the hills among clusters of shady trees. Here she felt like she was in the true France — unlike in Cannes or Nice, which with their palm trees and fancy shops felt a bit like Hollywood, a likeness that had greatly surprised her; even the residential streets in those cities with their houses behind gated fences, all higgledy-piggledy set into the sun-seared coastal hills, reminded her of the miles ringing Sweetzer and the Chateau Marmont.

She took a sip of cold wine and enjoyed its tang as it cleansed her palate and cooled her throat.

"I wanted to appropriately thank you for coming out of retirement," Hitch added directly to Cary, his voice dripping with good-natured sarcasm; he pronounced *retirement* as if it was some sort of long-standing joke between him and the actor.

Cary raised his glass to Hitch and said, "How could I say no to this combination? My favorite director, Provence, and the chance to play a reformed villain opposite the incomparable Miss Kelly here."

"You flatter me," said Grace, feeling color warm her cheeks.

"Cary has taken it upon himself to work with all the most important leading ladies," said Hitch. "It's a sort of baptism, my dear."

"Maybe we should get you a collar," said Betsy, looking at her husband with a sideways smirk.

"I always thought a collar would suit me,"

said Cary, unruffled.

There was something a bit too suave about her costar, Grace thought. Not nefarious, exactly, but as if he was so practiced at the art of being debonair, sophisticated Cary Grant, there was no longer anything of substance beneath the veneer; if that cracked, the lovely statue of him would crumble. When he smiled at her, she felt his warmth but no depth. Grace found it difficult to explain, even to herself, but it gave her a haunted feeling, even a warning, about the effect of living too long as a movie star. But then, she hadn't gotten the same impression from Clark or Ray or Coop — all of whom had been in the business as long as Cary. She wondered what it was about Mr. Grant.

She checked Oleg for signs of the troubling jealousy he'd shown a few months before, but he looked perfectly at ease as Hitch asked him about his atelier and if he would be doing work while in France or merely doting on Grace.

"I'll be back and forth to Paris," Oleg explained. "In fact, I should thank you for the excuse to come and do some business here I've been neglecting."

Lunch continued in this complimentary vein until the shade from the building overtook the patio and everyone was stuffed. Edith Head arrived the following day with trunks of dresses she'd pulled from the best couturiers in Paris, and when Grace had trouble fastening one with the narrowest waist, Edith remarked, "May I suggest waiting until *after* shooting's complete to have another one of Hitch's all-day repasts?" Grace knew Edith was right, and not just because a few dresses were too tight — the heavy meal and copious wine had made her feel sluggish, though she'd never once felt drunk the day before. She'd eaten little other than fruit and coffee since that morning. Grace wanted to be worthy of Edith's costumes. They were the most exquisite yet, and her role as spoiled socialite Frances Stevens demanded quite a number of outfits. She wanted to enjoy wearing every single spectacular one, so she instructed herself to choose every mouthful of tempting cuisine carefully.

The following days and weeks unfolded with a chimerical perfection. Everything from the shoots to the meals with the cast, picnics with Oleg, long walks through nearby orchards and along beaches, swims in the early morning and late evening so as to keep her skin from turning the same color as Cary's (not that it would, Grace reflected, because first she'd turn the color of a boiled lobster) — everything had the quality of a dream conjured from the elegance and luxury of their surroundings. And even though they were not home per se, Grace and Oleg settled into a comfortable routine that balanced work and love with surprising ease.

Shooting scenes every day with Hitch and Cary, Grace relished every second of the witty, lighthearted movie they were making, while Oleg would work in Paris for a day or two, or more locally in Cannes and Nice. Then they would meet at the end of the day for dinner, and sometimes for dancing or a show. On their days off, they would rent bicycles and pack a picnic and explore the countryside. Once they skinny-dipped in a frigid pond encircled by wild lavender. And though he was no longer religious, Oleg took her to the town of Vence one Sunday for mass in the Chapelle du Rosaire, where the lush blue, green, and yellow stained-glass windows designed by Henri Matisse rained brilliant light on their heads as the priest murmured mysteriously in Latin. When they knelt for the Lord's Prayer, each of them reciting the words in the ancient language they'd learned in childhoods thousands of miles from each other, Oleg took her hand and Grace felt truly blessed. This was the life she was meant to lead, and when she prayed, she thanked God for showing it to her.

At a late supper toward the end of filming, Grace and Oleg dined privately in a small restaurant famed for its cassoulet, and Grace sighed, saying, "Do we have to go back?"

"I've been wondering the same thing," Oleg said. "This month in France has been one of the best times of my life — I've never felt so creative and productive, and," he said, squeezing her hand beneath the table, "so in love."

Grace sighed and said, "Too bad I can't work from here."

"Why can't you? Our primary residence could be in Nice, and we'd keep apartments in New York and California."

"Our?" she said, unable to contain the unabashed hope in her voice, even as the thought of keeping a *primary residence* with Oleg in the south of France, of all places, made her shoulders clench with anticipatory excitement.

"You want it, too?" he asked, his earnestness rising to meet hers.

"More than anything," said Grace. *But did she?* She wanted to be with Oleg, wanted her days of searching and feeling unsettled to end, which was why she added, "But I don't think I'd be very good at living life in three different locations."

"We can figure that out later," said Oleg soothingly. "Tonight, it's enough to know we want the same thing."

"We do?"

"We do." He leaned over and kissed her softly on the mouth, and she felt in his kiss all the promises she'd ever believed possible.

CHAPTER 18

When they returned to the States and attended the premiere of *Rear Window* together in Hollywood, anyone who didn't already know about Grace and Oleg certainly knew after August of 1954. To echo the black-and-white dress her character, Lisa Fremont, wore in her first scene, Grace and Edith chose another gown of the same colors, but in reverse, with a wide wrap collar in white exposing just enough collarbone and décolletage, with the rest stiff black satin — fitted at the top with a loose, long skirt. Her arms and shoulders were tan from her time in the south of France, and she liked the way her white gloves contrasted so sharply against the warm hue of her skin. She felt nothing but excitement about the evening — about seeing the film at last, about appearing with her arm laced through Oleg's, even about posing for the cameras because she was so proud of this moment.

The movie did not disappoint. It was as tense and taut and thrilling a mystery as Grace had suspected it would be during filming. She was secretly impressed by her sometimes saucy performance, and thought she might even succeed in changing a few minds about "Grace Kelly." *Ingénue no more.* When the lights in the theater broke the spell, everyone in the audience leapt to their feet in applause. Kisses and heartfelt congratulations were exchanged all around, and Grace felt buoyant with joy. "You were brilliant," Oleg whispered in her ear.

The next day, though, while Grace was floating dreamily about her Sweetzer kitchen, preparing a simple supper for herself and Rita, Peggy called.

"Have you told Mom and Dad about Oleg?" her sister asked, cutting to the chase.

"I've mentioned him, yes," Grace said, a sick feeling taking the edge off her appetite.

"Well, when they read the papers this morning and saw you two splashed all over them, Mom called me and asked what was going on."

Grace sighed, and she was amazed at how calm the air sounded escaping from her lips when inside she felt anything but calm. She'd been dreading this. In fact, she'd mentioned Oleg to her mother only once, very briefly, before she left for France. Not wanting to spoil her burgeoning affections with her mother's inevitable questions, Grace hadn't let on that he was anything special. Fearing she'd made a serious error in judgment, she asked Peggy, "What did Mom say?"

"First, she asked if he was another Jew."

Grace groaned. "And what did you say?"

"I said I didn't know."

"Peggy!"

"What? I don't."

"The truth is, he's not especially religious. He was raised in an orthodox Russian religion that's a lot like Catholicism."

"Oh, yeah, and Dad said he's heard he's Russian. A Commie."

Grace dropped her head heavily into her hands. Clearly, she should have groomed her parents better, not let them form so many ridiculous ideas that would be impossible to undo.

After a steadying cup of coffee, Grace took a deep breath and called her mother.

"Mother! I have missed you so much. I just can't wait for you to see *Rear Window.*"

"Your father wants to know when the war film with William Holden is coming out."

"December, I think," she replied, discouraged by her mother's evasive question. "I'm also very excited to introduce you to someone," she said, not seeing any reason to drag things out. They both knew why she was really calling.

"Mr. Cassini?"

"Mom, he's wonderful. So intelligent and successful, and kind. He —"

"Is he Russian?"

"By birth, yes." Grace felt like the very blood in her veins had expanded and was squeezing her from the inside out. "But, Mother, his family had to flee Russia. He grew up in Italy and came to America two decades ago."

Her mother was silent, considering. "I do love his designs," she said. "I saw a few of his dresses in a magazine a few months ago. But your father is —"

This fissure of light, this tiny opening of hope, cooled Grace with relief, so she interrupted her mother before she could go on about her father. "Come up to New York, Mom. We'll go shopping, and I'll introduce you to Oleg." She hoped her meaning was clear: *without Daddy.* "I'm also looking at new apartments, and I'd love your input."

"Well," said Margaret, and Grace could hear her mind working on the other end of the line, already putting a plan in motion, "let me look at the calendar and talk to your father and call you in a few days."

Oleg stood and gallantly kissed Margaret Kelly's gloved hand when she and Grace arrived at their reserved table at the Palm Court for tea. "I see where Grace has learned her charming habit of always wearing white gloves," he said, holding out a chair for her.

Grace could hardly breathe. Though she and her mother had passed a nice enough day in and out of Bonwit Teller, Saks, and Bergdorf's, Grace had felt fidgety and nervous the whole time.

"It's essential for a lady to hold herself in reserve," Margaret opined to Oleg. "How she treats her hands is an excellent indication of the respect she has for herself."

Grace remembered this lesson from her childhood. It was strange to hear it again. When she wore gloves now, she wore them out of habit, without even thinking. She selected them as an essential accessory to every outfit, though she had lately become aware that her ever-present gloves had become a topic of conversation in fashion magazines.

"I should think," continued her mother, "that a fashion designer would know that."

Grace cringed inside, but smiled.

Unfazed, Oleg said effusively, "I do, of course, Mrs. Kelly. I think a great deal on the reserve of ladies, and how to appropriately and elegantly attire them in every moment of their lives."

Margaret, unsure of how to react to someone who had not bristled at one of her barbs, held her menu in front of her face and busied herself with the items on it. The rest of the hour was a strained one, in which they moved quickly from topic to topic — recent movies, none of which Grace was in; the weather; what sort of dog Grace should get (her mother was staunchly in favor of a bloodhound, and Oleg thought she should take in a stray); and at last they resorted to discussing their favorite treats on the five-tier stand of lemon curd and scones and sandwiches without crusts. By the end, Grace just wanted to leave her mother and get drunk in the Oak Room down the hall. Instead, they had an appointment with a real estate agent to see an apartment on Seventy-Fourth Street.

"He's not right for you," her mother said at the first private opportunity, when they were at last back in her regular apartment. Grace looked around at the furniture there, all simple and monochromatic, and realized that nothing in it said *Grace* Kelly. In fact, it was full of castoffs from Henry Avenue: side tables and chairs her mother had been getting rid of when she'd redecorated a few years before. Grace made a mental note to decorate her new place so that it looked like her.

"Mother, do we have to talk about this now? I'm exhausted," said Grace, kicking off her pumps and putting her feet up on the couch.

"You need to hear this, Grace," said Margaret. "He's not manly enough for you. He thinks about ladies' dresses all day."

"Don't you mean he's not manly enough for Daddy?" Grace asked. "I should have thought that Oleg's occupation would seem wonderful to any woman."

"That comment about the gloves," her mother said, making a face as if she'd tasted something unexpectedly off.

"What on earth was wrong with that?"

"He's a *flatterer,* Grace. He's not *real.*"

"I disagree," said Grace, aware that her voice was not firm but pleading — and she was unable to change it. "You've only met him once. You haven't given him a real chance."

Margaret shook her head. "I know after I've met someone once. I knew with that Don Richardson, and I know about *Oleg*

310

Cassini."

Grace didn't reply. She felt like crying, but refused to do so in front of her mother.

"But" — Margaret heaved a sigh — "you're not eighteen anymore. You'll have to discover I'm right for yourself."

It didn't help that Oleg didn't give two hoots about Margaret Majer Kelly. "I know she didn't like me," he said two nights later in a taxi on the way to the opera. "And I'm sure that's very disappointing to you. But what does it really matter? We're adults. You're an independent woman."

Am I? Grace wondered.

She felt a modicum of independence when she signed the papers for a new apartment on Fifth Avenue, then hired a decorator and clipped pictures of rooms she liked from magazines. Time passed, and even as she garnered rave reviews for *The Country Girl,* Grace couldn't help but feel distracted by the dilemma of her parents' disapproval of Oleg, and Oleg's reciprocal disdain for her parents.

In midwinter, she finally adopted a puppy, and somehow, being the helpless little poodle's sudden mother brought all her fears to the surface. The tiny, curly black lump — whom she'd named Oliver — had shivered and cried the whole first night on

311

his bed in her kitchen, and so Grace had curled up with him on her old couch, and the two of them had slept fitfully together till morning.

Foggy and befuddled from lack of sleep, Grace stood on Madison Avenue with a paper bag of bagels, which she barely remembered procuring. Oliver looked up at her inquiringly from the other end of the leash. Grace met his eyes and began to cry. Scooping him up, she rushed back into her building and up the stairs, burst into her old apartment — for the new one wouldn't be ready for months — and sobbed. What had she done? She couldn't take care of this little creature. She was a failure as a Broadway actress, and she couldn't — *couldn't* — marry someone her parents didn't like. It would make her life a misery. *I'm not so independent after all.*

Oliver licked her toes while she cried; then she picked him up and let him lick her damp cheeks. She took a sip of lukewarm coffee with a bite of bagel, then got up and filled his dishes: one with water, and the other with puppy food. The sound of the kibble clinking against the ceramic dish was cheerful, and he wagged his tail in anticipation. Watching him dive into the bowl brought a smile to her face. But her heart felt inflamed and heavy, and taking a deep breath was difficult.

Sitting at her kitchen table, she picked up the phone and called a few of her favorite New York friends — Judy and Jaybird; Prudy; Don; and Ava and Frank, who were in town — telling each of them to bring a take-out dish and some wine, and come ready for charades, her favorite game. It made for a festive impromptu party, and everyone took turns petting Oliver, and taking him out for his business while a serious game of charades took shape. Mercifully, no one asked where Oleg was. When she tumbled into bed that night, Oliver snoozed contentedly at her feet, and she thought that maybe things would be okay after all.

But the next day when she was walking through Central Park with Oleg, with Oliver trotting along beside them, he said with a sharp edge to his voice, "I heard you had a party last night."

"It didn't start as a party, but I suppose it rather felt like one," said Grace, her intestines beginning to roil from guilt over not inviting Oleg. Worse, she couldn't even explain to him the real reason for the gathering — she'd needed a happy taste of life without him. "I thought you were busy with work last night," she added quickly by way of excuse, as it was at least partly true.

"I was," he said, "but I might have been able to finish early."

Grace kissed him on the cheek, hoping to sweep it all away quickly. "I'm sorry, darling. I'll be sure to check with you next time. You know there's nothing I like better than to be with you."

"Did *Don* have a good time?" he persisted.

Uh-oh, thought Grace, her insides now churning and gurgling at this familiar jealousy in Oleg. She hadn't seen it in a while, but here it was again, unmistakably. "Oleg, there is nothing to be alarmed about where Don is concerned. He's just an old friend." She also wondered how Oleg had even found out about the party.

"He'd bed you in a heartbeat."

"That's irrelevant, though, because I'm not interested in him that way."

"Oh? Do you know what he said to me at the do at the Met, when I saw him? He leaned very close to me so no one else could hear and asked if you still liked to have the backs of your knees tickled."

"What?" The word escaped Grace's lips as a gasp before she could think better of it.

"He's a jealous man, Grace. I don't like that you continue to invite him to events, particularly small parties in your own home.

It sends the wrong message."

Don is jealous? It takes one to know one, she wanted to shout. "Don is only a friend who's been very kind and helpful to me for many years. I can't just cut him out of my life," said Grace, struggling to keep her voice even. "He's more of a mentor now, like Sandy or Hitch. You don't feel jealous of *them,* do you?"

"I'm not crazy about the way Hitch leers at you when you're not looking, but he's too important for your career to jettison."

"Jettison?" This conversation was fast going off the rails.

"And you never slept with Hitch or Sandy," said Oleg brusquely, "at least not that I know of."

"What's that supposed to mean?" Her face felt hot even in the chilly air, and her arms were shaking. Grace regretted letting Oleg know anything about her former lovers. But he'd been so supportive and accepting at the start. She never had any idea he'd use the information against her later. She'd certainly never make *that* mistake again.

"It means that I don't really know what you've done with all the men on your various sets. And now you've invited Howell Conant to photograph you while you're in Jamaica? In a swimming suit? Come now,

Grace. What am I supposed to think?"

"You're supposed to trust me, Oleg." Oliver was pulling on the leash, trying to move them down the path, but Grace felt rooted to the spot.

"How can I trust you when you want to pose like a pinup girl?"

Grace rolled her eyes. "How can you say that, Oleg? Of course Howell's pictures won't be like that! I want to do something *different*."

"You want to show the public you're not an ice queen. Fine. But you don't have to be a whore to do it."

Grace's whole body went rigid. "What did you call me?" she whispered.

She could see the instant regret on his face, and something else that resembled panic. "I'm sorry, Grace. That was the wrong choice of words."

Oliver chose that moment to throw himself on a patch of grass and whine. Oleg frowned down at the puppy, then reached a hand out to touch Grace's arm, which she pulled out of his reach.

She wanted to turn and walk away, but she couldn't, and her heart was thudding so fast and loud, she could hardly think. Even though a part of her feared he was right — something in her had always chafed and

316

rebelled at the rules of her childhood — she couldn't bring herself to feel bad about it, not the way he wanted her to.

"Grace," he pleaded quietly.

She refused to meet his eyes again and kept hers fixed on Oliver. How could she love Oleg this much, despite what he'd just said? How could she still want to let herself be folded in his arms, as she had been the night he'd shown her his sketch of the Oscar dress?

He must have been thinking the same thing, because he said, "Academy Award nominations will be announced soon, and I have a feeling you'll get one for *The Country Girl*. I recognize that's who you really are, Grace. The most talented woman I know."

At last lifting her eyes to his, she said, "You can't cover what you said with flattery."

"Give me an opportunity to make it up to you. *Please.*"

Overcome with a need to get away, Grace bent over and scooped Oliver into her arms, holding him like a baby. He yawned, baring his tiny pointed teeth, his tongue curling out of his mouth. Cuddling him settled her a bit.

"Let's get him home," Oleg said, reaching out and waggling the puppy's ears with an affectionate pat on his soft head.

"*I'll* get him home," Grace corrected him. Then, nearly choking on the sudden rush of wet emotion rising into her throat, she added, "I'll call you when I get back from Jamaica."

CHAPTER 19

1975

The envelope didn't look like it would contain anything of import, but as soon as Grace read the typewritten letter from an English journalist named Gwen Robyns, she had a prickly sense that she was holding an opportunity in her hands. Gwen had contacted Grace to let her know that she was writing a biography focusing on her film years, and she wondered if it might be possible to interview her. She explained her credentials and the publisher of the book, all of which recommended her highly to Grace even though she wasn't familiar with the writer's work.

This wasn't the first request of this nature that she'd received, but because so much of the press about their family was either lurid or only shallowly grounded in reality, Grace and Rainier had become wary of all requests for interviews. Still, not all writers were opportunists. Just recently, Grace had spoken with young Donald Spoto, an earnest American film historian who was fascinated by Hitchcock's oeuvre, and she'd been deeply impressed by the depth and breadth of his knowledge, the intelligence of his questions about the director. She'd even offered to write the introduction to his book.

Grace held the crisp A4 paper, folded three times to fit in its envelope, and felt a curious pull toward the woman who'd written it. There was something beseeching in her tone, even self-effacing. "I want to make sure I have my facts straight," she'd written. "Only you know the truth. . . . I have no interest in writing an exposé. I despise the sorts of writers who camp outside your residences."

She didn't reply right away. But the next day, Grace found a little time to return to her desk and compose an invitation for Gwen to send a draft of her manuscript to Grace. She wasn't sure what she was getting into, and she felt nervous. At worst, she'd learned over the years, she could simply not respond further. But when the few hundred pages of the book arrived, photocopied typewritten pages neatly stacked in a manuscript box, Grace dove into them with gusto.

Gwen had a friendly, conversational style, the sort many women would like to read. The book felt like sitting down to lunch with a good friend — and the author had clearly done her homework. Her description of Henry Avenue was so precise, Grace wondered if she'd flown all the way from London to see it. Gwen's appraisal of her film performances made Grace laugh — this was no critic. But then she was glad that Gwen wasn't a Hollywood insider, because when she came to the parts about Don and Ray Milland and Gene and Oleg, Grace paused. Gwen herself might not have been an insider, but she'd obviously talked to a few. Grace wondered who'd betrayed her to the woman. Likely Don, she thought with regret; he'd become something of a crotchety blabbermouth in his older years, and Grace had the sense that he took the end of Grace's acting career personally and badly. After a few letters arguing about why she refused to return to acting, Grace had had to take a step back from Don, letting their correspondence dwindle.

Whom else had Gwen interviewed? It didn't matter. There were just enough people who knew what had happened in those early years of the 1950s whose stories and threadbare loyalty could fill a book. As for Gwen, she was only trying to do her job. That much was clear to Grace.

Grace was worried about Rainier, however. He would never forgive her if a book describing her premarital love affairs were to be published — especially if it got out that she'd read the draft and done nothing about it. This felt markedly different from the series of interviews her own mother had sprung on her, which appeared in every major newspaper in America during her engagement. Then, since he was still courting her, Rainier had said, "You cannot control what your mother says about you" and "Truly, Grace, they may be in bad taste, but she hardly says anything lascivious. These interviews are not tell-alls."

Now, Grace felt sure he would demand, "How does this make you look? How does it make *me* look?" All he'd be able to see was the past he'd banished from their principality along with her movies when they got married. And despite how the writer had described her project, Gwen's book *was* a tell-all. It laid bare some uncomfortable truths about her romantic life that her mother had had the good sense to obfuscate.

Grace was surprised to discover that she also wanted to change the book for herself.

After all, she'd given up everything she'd once loved to be a princess. What a waste that would be if the most complicated parts of her past as Grace Kelly were to come back and eclipse all the good she'd done as Grace de Monaco or, worse, to give her daughters license to behave as she had! "You had affairs with married men?" Caroline would say, and Grace could just see the mixed expression of accusation, disappointment, and relief that would come over her elder daughter's face. No, she couldn't let that happen.

As she went about her duties for the next few days, Grace thought about what to do about Gwen. She wished so much she could ask Uncle George what to do. Poor, misunderstood, and unfairly maligned Uncle George. And poor William Weagley, who hadn't even been invited to George's funeral the year before, who'd stolen in and stood at the back of the church, only to sneak out before the end like a thief giving back a stolen jewel. Grace made a mental note to write to him and invite him to stay at Roc Agel this summer.

Nerves wound tight, she avoided the subject with Rainier and wished she'd never replied to Gwen's letter, never gotten herself into this mess to begin with. On her third morning of dry toast and tea because she couldn't stomach anything else, Grace decided the only thing she could try would be to appeal to Gwen woman to woman.

She sent Gwen an invitation to Monaco, which the writer promptly accepted. In the week before her arrival, Grace met Maree for lunch in Paris, as her old friend happened to be on a holiday there with family, and found herself going on and on over the first two courses about how worried she was about her daughters, Gwen's book, Rainier's possible reactions, and a smattering of other problems with her work in the principality.

Maree set down her fork and said, brightly and abruptly, "You need something for *you*, Gracie. Something to do that will help you remember who you really are. It's like you've disappeared into everyone around you."

"I know who I am, Maree," she said, trying to laugh off the truth so that she didn't cry instead. In those exhausted bones of hers, the ones that wanted to lay themselves somewhere plush and comforting, she knew exactly who she was. Who she'd been.

"Maybe *remember* is the wrong word," Maree said, thinking out loud, "because people change. I know you're not a Hollywood star anymore. But could you be more than Princess of Monaco?"

Grace burst out laughing. "*More* than a princess?"

"I think you know exactly what I mean." Her friend looked at her sternly this time, eyebrows raised and lips pressed into a thin line.

"I do," said Grace. Because she did, exactly. She still pined for her acting career, and in two decades there had been no real substitute: not patronizing the arts, not giving her time to worthy causes. Not even motherhood, which she could never admit aloud, because who on earth could possibly understand that even though she loved her children — indeed, her love for them was the most powerful force in her life — the work of mothering had never given her what acting had?

Maree was right, though. Grace had all but disappeared into her roles as mother, princess, wife. She didn't think she'd survive another twenty years if she didn't find — and soon — a new part to play, beyond that of a forty-five-year-old woman from Philadelphia who was married with three children, whose husband just happened to be a prince.

"I'll give it some thought," she said, and it was as much a promise to herself as to her childhood friend, one of the few people she trusted because she'd known Grace Kelly before everything.

Over tea and cakes on a cloudy day when Rainier was away on business, Grace sat down with Gwen Robyns. She was about ten years older than Grace, aging attractively into her mid-fifties, with gray hair lacing its way through thick brown locks and warm dark eyes beneath heavy, thoughtful brows.

"Thank you so much for meeting with me," Gwen said right away, holding out her hand to shake Grace's.

"No, thank *you* for thinking to ask me about your biography," Grace replied. "It's very good." *This is an important role. Don't blow it.*

Gwen looked surprised. "That means a great deal to me."

Grace gestured for Gwen to sit. They were in the more casual living space, where the children had played with cars and dolls when they were small. Grace wore slim wool trousers and a simple sweater with her glasses, far less formal than Gwen, who was wearing a knee-length navy shift dress — a perfect choice for someone who had no idea what to wear. Grace was relieved to see that Gwen was just the tiniest bit off-balance, not knowing what to expect. This should help Grace with her plan.

While she poured tea and offered Gwen a plate of scones and sandwiches, Grace explained all the things she had admired — genuinely — about the writer's book, and Gwen blushed with grateful embarrassment and thanked Grace and said how delicious the currant scones were, the best she'd had outside Fortnum & Mason in London.

Then Grace got to the point. "But there is one thing that troubles me about the book." She paused and saw all the tension that had melted out of Gwen refreeze into her shoulders. "You see, I'm worried about my daughters. I would lose all authority with them if they were to discover . . . certain things about my past. Gene Lyons and Ray Milland, for instance. What happened between us, really, is private, and I wouldn't share it with any biographer — indeed, I haven't even confessed the essentials to my closest friends, as ladies didn't do that in our day, did they? But I digress. The point is, how can I ask my daughters to stay away from certain kinds of men if they see that I made a habit of being with them myself? I'd like to save them from the kinds of heartaches I endured."

"Is that ever really possible? Saving our

children from mistakes?" Gwen asked this question with authentic curiosity.

"Maybe not," admitted Grace. "But I can certainly save them from embarrassment. And save Rainier and Ray Milland, while I'm at it. Mr. Milland and his wife reside in France, you know, not far from here, and we see them socially on occasion. It would put us in a most uncomfortable situation if Mr. Milland's and my earlier . . . *misguided* liaison were to come out. I'm sure you understand, Gwen. *You* have the luxury of a private life, which I'm sure you value all the more for being a writer of imagination who is able to so accurately portray the lives of those of us unlucky enough to have so little privacy." *Stop talking,* Grace told herself. She had more to say, but sensed that she'd said enough, for now. She needed to let what she'd already spoken soak in.

Gwen sipped her tea pensively, holding the saucer aloft just below the cup. Grace had used the Silver Jubilee porcelain just for this occasion. Though Gwen was not now looking at the silver *25*s painted onto the delicate cups, with Grace's husband's profile suggested in the pattern, Grace felt sure the other woman had noticed what she was drinking from. At that moment, Gwen was staring inscrutably at one of the roses in the pattern of the couch on which Grace sat with her legs crossed at the ankles, her fingers folded on one another, resting on her bent right knee.

"I can understand that," said the writer, clinking her cup back into its saucer.

"I'm so glad," Grace said with a smile.

"It must be . . . so difficult," said Gwen, obviously casting about for the right words. "I've watched journalism devolve recently. Lose all decorum."

"Not all journalists," Grace said judiciously, seeing her opening and rushing in, "only the wretched paparazzi and other opportunists."

Gwen nodded, and Grace felt increasingly that they were on the same side, wayward girls in the school lunchroom swapping halves of sandwiches and stories about teachers.

"The only problem is, I'm not sure how I'll fill the pages I'd have to cut," said Gwen.

"Well," said Grace, heaving an enormous sigh that cleared her lungs, "*that* I can help you with. I'll give you an exclusive interview, a look into my real life, in exchange for this great favor to me. I want people to read your book!"

Grace felt triumphant by the end of her two hours with Gwen. So encouraged and euphoric, in fact, that she decided to fill Rainier in on all the details the following night, on his return to Monaco. So after dinner, when he said he wanted to take a walk in his zoo, she volunteered to go with him.

He eyed her suspiciously, since she hadn't gone willingly into the zoo for years, but he didn't stand in the way of her coming. In the soft tangerine twilight, Rainier pointed to this macaw and that tamarin, and Grace feigned interest, just as she had early in their marriage; at least then, she'd *wanted* to be interested; now it was harder to pretend. As they strolled slowly toward the exit of the zoo, she said, "Guess who I had tea with yesterday."

And she told Rainier all about Gwen and the biography, feeling proud of herself and thus open about all the details. But she was discouraged not to see Rainier smiling as she continued with her story.

"How do we know we can trust her?" he asked when Grace had finished. He'd stopped walking, and so she did, too.

"I can tell," Grace said.

"Women's intuition," he remarked derisively, looking from Grace back out into the jungle leaves and water surrounding his hippos.

Something in Grace snapped, like a guitar string that had been overplayed. "You think all your precious animals have anything other than intuition, Rainier? You accord them more respect than you do me, your own wife."

He sighed, sounding so unbelievably long-suffering. She couldn't stand it. "Fine," he said reluctantly. "If you trust her, I am willing to play along."

And if I'm wrong . . . Well, I'm just not going to think about that.

With that thought, something inside Grace shifted. It felt a bit like her old confidence, the daring that had led her to the Academy, to Hollywood and Jamaica, and even to Monaco. Was this what Maree had been talking about? *Could you be more than Princess of Monaco?* Could the woman she'd been, whom she'd been ignoring so long, remake herself once more?

CHAPTER 20

1955

The pictures Howell Conant had taken of her couldn't come out fast enough, but *Collier's* had delayed their publication until June. When she returned from Jamaica to her spacious, newly decorated New York apartment on Fifth Avenue, Grace couldn't believe how lonely she felt despite the many bouquets of flowers in every room, all sent by Oleg in apology for the jealous tirade she'd been mulling over for weeks. Oliver trotted up to her and licked her ankles, and she sat down on one of the fine Persian carpets, leaning against a velvet sofa and fondling his soft ears, kissing the top of his curly head. She surveyed the room, all richly colored and textured choices befitting a movie star, which her decorator had assured her that magazine editors all over would want to photograph. Oliver sat on her outstretched legs and enjoyed the affection.

"I missed you, too, sweet boy," said Grace, feeling tears rush to her eyes. What did it mean that she'd missed her dog more than any person in New York?

Her phone began to ring, on receivers in no fewer than four rooms — she couldn't ever remember how many telephones she now had. Fearing it was Oleg, she let her maid answer it, and a minute later, Greta came in to quietly announce that Edith Head was on the phone for her.

Gratefully, Grace picked up the receiver, then held it between her ear and shoulder while she continued to pet Oliver. "I'm so glad it's you," she said to Edith.

"Dore is a bastard," said Edith. "I heard they won't even dress you for the Oscars."

Grace sighed. "Yes, well, they've put me on suspension."

"Because you're doing *good* movies instead of the trash they send you?" Edith muttered a few choice epithets, then said, "It's a good thing my sewing machine is off-site, then. And I have a perfect dress for you."

Grace almost didn't trust herself to speak. "Oh, Edith," she choked out. "Thank you."

"Don't let them get to you, Grace. You've been very strong. When you win the award for a movie they nearly didn't let you do, they'll have to eat their contract."

"I'm not going to win, Edith," said Grace. "Judy's going to win. Everyone knows that."

"You never know in this town, Grace. You never know. Look at Audrey, who won last year for *Roman Holiday,* and Georgie Elgin's a far more impressive role than a princess. Listen. The big night's in just a week. When can you get here?"

Bolstered by Edith's friendship, Grace kept Oliver on her lap while she called for plane reservations, then rang some friends, inviting them over for a dinner party in her new place before heading west. She'd need a party after her next engagement: meeting Oleg at Bemelmans Bar that night.

Even the cheerful murals of Madeline's creator couldn't do anything to lift her spirits, though. She and Oleg sat across from each other at a corner table, and she said, "I thought and thought while I was away, and I just can't do this anymore."

Oleg rubbed his lips together, then thrust out his lower lip and blew air upward. Then he took out his silver cigarette case and lit one and took a drag before responding, "I made you the dress."

Instantly, her eyes were blurry with tears. "I can't wear it. . . . It would make me too sad," she whispered hoarsely, thanking heaven again for Edith, the only other designer whose dress could possibly take her mind off Oleg's.

As if experiencing a sudden jolt of inspiration, Oleg stubbed out his cigarette and said, "Then don't be sad. Be *happy*, with me. I love you, Grace."

"I know that, Oleg," she said, her resolve tightening in her chest. She didn't want to remind him of the real reasons this was happening, because she didn't want to go over it all again. The fact that she was true to him, that she'd never so much as looked at another man since committing to him in France, hadn't mattered to him — not enough, anyway. She might have been with other men in the past, but she'd *chosen* each and every one of them, and she'd been faithful to them while she was with them. She hadn't let her own father make her feel bad about the choices she'd made, so she wasn't about to let Oleg Cassini.

"I hate to think of you with someone your parents might choose for you," Oleg went on, "the sort of man who'd make you give up your career to be barefoot and pregnant, wearing a frumpy apron."

Grace laughed. "I'd never agree to that, Oleg. You must know me better than that."

"That's the problem, Grace — I know you

too well."

Grace simmered silently in her seat. Where was her damn drink?

Ah, there it was. As soon as the waiter left, she took a long sip of the tequila on ice she'd ordered, thinking of Katy Jurado. What was it the other actress had said to her about the difference between being hard and being strong? Grace couldn't remember, but ordering the tequila made her feel both, and that was what she needed tonight.

"Who *is* going to dress you for the awards? *Edith,* I assume?"

That's it, Grace thought, as if she even needed reminding. *That's why this is ending.* Oleg couldn't stand Edith's presence in her life any more than he could her male costars or her romantic past. He wanted to be the only one who had dressed her and bedded her, ever.

"I'm not your doll, Oleg," Grace said.

Oleg lit a new cigarette and inhaled deeply. "True enough. You're not my doll," he said at last. "And I hope you'll never be anyone else's, either."

Just as she opened her mouth to say that his jealousy knew no bounds, he put up a finger to stop her, and added, "Not because I want you to myself — although I do, that's now beside the point — but because in spite

336

of myself, I admire you, Grace. It pains me to no end that you won't be wearing my dress on March thirtieth, but I respect your reasons. And the reasons behind your reasons, even if you don't even realize what all those are."

This response, which Grace felt to be both a dignified admission of loss and an infuriatingly patronizing put-down, reminded Grace of Jeff Jefferies in *Rear Window*. And Bernie Dodd in *The Country Girl*. Hell, he reminded Grace of most of the lead male characters in most of the movies she'd been in or seen her whole life. Surely there was something better out there.

Not wanting to have the same old argument with this man to whom she had devoted her heart for more than a year, whom she still loved in spite of it all, Grace plastered a sad smile onto her face and replied, "Thank you, Oleg." She couldn't wait to get home to Oliver, to sit on the kitchen floor with him on her lap while her heart bled from all the places it was broken. But she ordered a second drink and made strained small talk about Oleg's summer line, before both of them bade each other adieu with Continental kisses and glassy eyes, almost as if they'd never been anything more than close friends.

■ ■ ■ ■

The sunshine and routines of life in Los Angeles began to stitch together her shattered heart. There were hours in New York when she had to leave her apartment and walk Oliver just to avoid picking up the phone and calling Oleg. *It wouldn't do any good,* she kept telling herself. After an initial rush of relief and romance — both of which she craved like a woman dying of thirst craved water — getting back together would only land the two of them in the same unhappy positions.

Sunglasses on, Grace took time to have a few meals with her favorite people and take long swims in the sparkling teal water of the Chateau's pool. She was feeling happy and even excited when she arrived for her fitting with Edith, but the carnation-pink dress the designer had set aside for her was strangely garish. "I can't believe it," said Edith, standing back and observing Grace in amazed frustration.

"This would be better on Rita," agreed Grace, panic rising in her throat. "But what *am* I going to wear, then?"

"The blue dress," said Edith without hesitation.

"The duchess satin one I wore to the premiere?" Grace asked. She loved that gown. It was probably her favorite of Edith's fairy-godmother concoctions.

"Wear it with these," said Edith, handing Grace opera-length white gloves. "And those drop pearl earrings of yours. No necklace," she said, tapping her lips with a pen. "We want to show off those milky shoulders and collarbones. And we'll sweep your hair up and back."

"Bibbidi-bobbidi-boo," said Grace.

Edith frowned. "Do you think that sugar-plum grew up eating pickled herring and bagels for breakfast? I doubt it very much."

"Magic is magic, Edith," said Grace.

Edith pointed a bony finger at Grace and said, "No parties before the big night. Drink plenty of fresh-squeezed orange juice and water. Get some sleep. You look like you need it. Is everything okay?"

"Oleg and I are done," Grace said glumly, suddenly aware of her tender heart.

"Good," said Edith, who was on her second marriage, to Wiard Ihnen, and had never cared for Oleg. "You weren't his muse, and yet he was possessive of you." Tutting with her tongue, Edith shook her head. "Let him find another girl to dress. Someone more compliant."

"Will I ever find someone who will under-stand me, Edith?"

"Perhaps," she said cautiously, and Grace could hear the doubt in the designer's voice. "But first you must understand yourself."

"I do," Grace insisted.

Edith ran her right hand gently up and down Grace's left arm. "You're too young to really understand," she said kindly. "But don't worry about any of that now. Sleep and juice. That's all you need for the next two days." Grace tried to take Edith's advice, adding in a few more swims and a long walk through the hills, plus a steak-and-salad dinner at Musso & Frank with Rita.

"We're eating with the blue hairs," complained Rita.

"Six in the evening is a perfectly reason-able time to eat dinner," said Grace, cutting herself a bite of tenderloin.

"If you're sixty," said Rita, pushing salad around on her plate.

"I have to get to bed early tonight," said Grace. "I don't want to look a fright tomor-row."

"You could never look a fright, Grace," said Rita.

"Be real, Rita."

"All right, all right," Rita said. "I can't

believe Judy's not even going to be there," she said. "What a badly timed baby."

"I heard there's going to be a whole camera crew in her hospital room," said Grace. "Can you imagine? How awful. I'd rather just issue a statement after the fact if I couldn't float down the aisle in one of Edith's designs."

"Maybe she's trying to show she's a real person, not always a fashion plate," said Rita.

Grace gave her friend a *you know better than that* look.

"What? I try to give people credit," said Rita. "Besides, I feel bad for her. She's had a tough time of it."

"She has," agreed Grace. "Do you think Judy's problem was her early fame? Or would she have been troubled no matter what life she found herself in?"

"Destiny or free will? I always come down on the side of free will," said Rita.

"I'm not so sure," said Grace, thinking about her parents. They had *made* her of themselves, from their own clay. But they had also raised her. It was hard to untangle the two.

Grace yawned.

"Maybe you should get to bed now," her friend observed. "Sometimes the moment passes me by, and even though I could have hit the pillow before eight, I wind up awake at midnight."

"Good idea," said Grace, yawning again and covering her mouth with the back of her hand, feeling completely exhausted.

When she lay in bed, however, she couldn't sleep, puzzling over the unanswered questions from her conversations with Edith and Rita. She *did* know herself, didn't she? And she *was* distinguishing herself from her parents, wasn't she? She was Grace Kelly, in spite of everything John and Margaret Kelly thought of their third child. Or was she Grace Kelly *because* of what they thought, how they'd made her?

Unexpectedly, the most consoling image, the one that finally sent her to sleep, was of Judy Garland accepting the Best Actress award from her hospital bed, her newborn baby cradled in her arms.

CHAPTER 21

William Holden, who'd won Best Actor the previous year for *Stalag 17,* and with whom she'd costarred along with Bing in *The Country Girl,* smiled with pure pleasure as he read, "Grace Kelly!" off the little white card. Grace froze — for a moment, it seemed she couldn't breathe, and her heart had actually stopped beating. Then, as the applause and congratulations from all around the theater filled her ears, she realized she had to move. Slipping her little blue satin purse up her gloved forearm, she walked the short distance to the stage and took the golden statue from William, smiling and stupefied. She'd prepared nothing to say.

As she looked out on the blurry audience full of other actors and actresses, directors, producers, and cameramen — Bing and Cary and Hitch, Frank and Ava, Katy, Rita, Clark, and Audrey, who'd won the year before — all clapping with genuine appreciation, what she felt most of all was gratitude. She was here because of their support. And Don and Sandy and Jaybird. And Fordie. And Uncle George. She so hoped he was watching. (*What on earth is Judy Garland saying in her hospital room right now?* Grace was glad for the other actress, that she was off camera so she could say any damn thing she liked.)

Names and images and phrases whirled in her mind, but she couldn't grasp the right ones, couldn't put the names or words in the right order. She didn't want to disappoint anyone by not thanking them! The press was cruel to actors who accidentally left out their mothers or spouses.

Mercifully, just as the applause died down, a few words came to her mind. "The thrill of this moment keeps me from saying what I really feel," she said, wondering how her voice sounded to the theater full of people and the viewers at home watching on the television. In her own ears, she sounded strained, winded. "I can only say thank you with all my heart to all who made this possible for me." Perhaps most of all in that moment, she was grateful to Edith for putting her in a dress that held her up.

Everything after that was a hazy whirlwind. Offstage, she was hugged and kissed by dozens of people, and before she knew it, she was being posed with Marlon, who had won for *On the Waterfront.* "We just made Jay the biggest man in Hollywood," he whispered in Grace's ear, and she giggled with him about their agent. She couldn't wait to hug him and Judybird. But that was hours in the future. First, there were photos, photos, and more photos, interminable chats with reporters, and then clapping so hard her hands hurt when *Waterfront* won Best Picture.

Of all the nice things anyone said to her that night, the nicest came from Bing: "I couldn't have asked for a more beautiful and gutsy costar, Grace. I owe the rest of my career to you."

"No," Grace said earnestly, her fingers cold and shaky on his warm hands, "I'm the lucky one, Bing. You took a chance on me, and I'll always be grateful for that."

"We'll just have to agree to disagree, kid," he said. "But we may get to do another picture together. Schary wants to do a remake of *Philadelphia Story,* but with singing. I told him you should do Kate's part."

"But I can't sing!" she protested. And Oscar or not, she couldn't imagine stepping into Katharine Hepburn's shoes on-screen.

What was Bing thinking?

"Nothin' to it," he said. "Don't worry your pretty head about it tonight. We'll talk soon." And he kissed her on the cheek and left her standing alone at the MGM party, until the next person accosted her with flattery and plans.

She was relieved when she and Ava and Frank sat down to a plate of fried chicken, and Ava said, "Congrats, Gracie. Poor Judy, eh?" She was the first to mention Garland all night, and Grace was so relieved.

"I know!" she exclaimed. "I feel terrible for her."

"Don't do that," said Frank. "You dames always do that. You won fair and square, Grace. Don't let anyone tell you you weren't as good as Judy."

"He would know," said Ava, and Grace couldn't quite tell if she was being sarcastic or not about Frank's Supporting Actor win from a year before, for *From Here to Eternity.*

"I would know. Thank you very much," Frank said with an edge to his voice; Grace decided it was wise to leave that subject alone.

"Well, I'm glad at least you said something," said Grace to Ava. "Everyone else is studiously avoiding the entire subject of Judy Garland."

"Well, enjoy it now," said Frank, " 'cause the papers tomorrow sure as hell won't ignore her."

Ava waved off her husband's doom and gloom, and focused her heavily kohled eyes on Grace. "So, doll, what's next for this Oscar-winning actress?"

"Nothing, unless MGM takes me off suspension," said Grace. "They wouldn't even get me a new dress for tonight, which shows how much confidence they have in me."

Frank smiled, and it was a little evil. "Now you can tell them what to do with their contract."

"We'll see," said Grace, who had a feeling her best hope with Schary was probably Bing. Man to man and all that rubbish.

But as it turned out, Dore Schary sent Grace a lovely arrangement of flowers the next morning with a note saying, "Congratulations. Let's talk soon."

Grace floated around on a cloud of congratulations, with invitations from directors and producers and other actors pouring in like never before — in both Los Angeles and New York, though it was all for film work. It appeared her Broadway dreams were as out of reach as ever. She'd once thought that Hollywood could help her get roles on the stage, that Broadway was a higher peak on the same mountain. Now she saw that theater was a separate range altogether, and it was shrouded in fog, harder than ever to see. But the view from where she was standing at the moment looked pretty spectacular, she had to admit.

She should have known it wouldn't last. Just a day or two later, while waiting for a dental appointment, Grace flipped through a recent issue of *McCall's,* stopping to skim an article about the Oscar contenders. Of all people, her father had been quoted: "I always thought it would be Peggy whose name would be up in lights one day."

She wanted to crawl under the covers of her large new bed in her perfectly appointed Fifth Avenue apartment — a bed and apartment she'd always assumed she'd be sharing with Oleg, whom she suddenly missed as wretchedly as she had in those first days after their breakup.

Grace wondered if her mother knew her husband had said this so publicly — it was one thing for it to be a family joke that her father preferred Peggy, and another for him to say it to a national magazine. Grace had spoken to her mother several times since winning the Oscar, and she was never anything less than effusively proud: "Your performance really was superior to Garland's, dear"; "The ladies at the club are planning a luncheon in your honor, so be sure to reserve Memorial Day Sunday"; "I always knew those years at the Academy would pay off, and look!"; "What's next, darling? The sky's the limit now!" Even her father had said to her face, or at least into her ear down the long-distance phone line, "Congratulations, Gracie. I'm impressed." *The two-faced . . . bastard.*

Inevitably, a few reporters called Grace to ask what she thought about her father's comment in *McCall's,* and she'd never been more glad of her training so she could pull off an elegant laugh and an "Oh, that's just Daddy" without so much as a crack in her voice.

And as Frank Sinatra had predicted, she eventually had to contend with a deluge of reporting and opinion pieces voicing outrage that Judy Garland hadn't won instead. Judy herself graciously sent an arrangement of pink peonies as a token of her own congratulations. Grace had immediately sent a handwritten note of thanks along with the finest baby blanket she could purchase. She tried to shut out the chatter surrounding her, but it was hard — she'd never thought she'd win, hadn't even prepared to win. The widespread critical opinion that she *shouldn't* have won — maybe they, too, thought it should have been Peggy if not Judy, Grace reflected bitterly — conspired to make her feel lower than she had in years. Even Hitch's very kind note — "Don't let the naysayers get to you. You're my most sacred cow" — only made her feel better for about an hour. Why, then, was he working with Doris bloody Day on his next picture?

Worst of all was putting on a cheerful face to help Lizanne plan her June wedding while Oleg was photographed all over Manhattan with a different beauty every night. Her younger sister was getting married while her father still preferred her older sister. And Kell was as ever the untouchable golden boy.

Only her old friend Maree saw the chinks in her armor that spring. She and Grace stood in the large church garden in East Falls as scores of children in pastel clothes scampered about finding Easter eggs. "It's not as picture-perfect as it might seem," Maree said, her tone dry. "In about two minutes there will be tears about which siblings have the most eggs, and in two hours, every single one of them will be beside themselves when the sugar wears off, and the mothers will have to do the thing we all swore we'd never do, and let the television be the nanny while we take naps because we were up too late hiding eggs around the house. And the husbands will have left to play golf."

Grace laughed. "You always did know just what I needed to hear."

"Oh, and did I mention the ham that'll be getting ever drier in the oven, waiting for said husbands to return, smelling of whiskey and cigars?" Maree added.

Grace laughed harder.

"But of course the daddies will be the children's heroes, because they will return from the golf course with more chocolate to ruin their appetites for the ham," said Maree.

"Sounds lovely," said Grace, wiping a tear of laughter from her cheek.

"Dreamy," deadpanned Maree, and for just a moment, Grace felt grateful for the trials of her own life, which she had a feeling Maree would have accepted in a heartbeat if Grace offered to trade.

Grace hadn't planned to go back to the south of France just a year after filming *To Catch a Thief,* especially as she knew memories of the best of her romance with Oleg would be lurking in every bottle of wine, every sidewalk bistro and cobblestone street, but the first of May found her in a first-class seat flying over the Atlantic as the sun descended in an obscenely pink-and-orange sky. She was heading to the Cannes Film Festival, where *The Country Girl* would be prominently featured.

In the weeks since Easter, however, her life had begun to feel a little less shaky, with her MGM contract back in place so she could star in *The Swan,* the Molnár play she'd done on television years ago that was being made into a movie and produced by Dore Schary himself. And there was the musical version of *Philadelphia Story* that Bing had mentioned that was being scripted and set to music as she sat on the plane, as well as the promise of playing Maggie in a film adaptation of *Cat on a Hot Tin Roof,* just as soon as it was done with its Broadway run. Grace felt she was getting a kind of satisfying revenge on Broadway in becoming a sought-after actress for movie versions of great stage plays. *The Country Girl* had been the beginning, and with *Swan* and *Cat* lined up next, who knew what else was possible?

And the mending of her heart had been unexpectedly sped up by the secret but extremely satisfying attention of darkly handsome Jean-Pierre Aumont, who would also be in Cannes. He'd phoned her out of the blue to congratulate her on her Oscar, and they'd fallen into a comfortable, often laugh-out-loud-funny conversation that continued over dinner and drinks about poodles and pastries and the television work they'd done together years ago and lately given up for the bigger screen. "Let's keep this on the q.t.," Grace had said in his rumpled bed the morning before they left for France in separate airplanes. He'd agreed. Grace had the sense that both she and Jean-Pierre knew and accepted the temporary nature of their affair. He was the first man she'd made love to without a care for a future, and she found surprising freedom and satisfaction in this kind of affection. It was something to enjoy in passing, like a sandcastle before the tide carried it away.

On the train from Paris to Cannes, imagining her private liaison with Jean-Pierre that night, Grace hoped no one would notice how flushed with desire she felt as she knitted an afghan for Lizanne as a bridal shower gift. She imagined her little sister and her new husband sharing it on cold nights before a fire as they read or watched a favorite television program. But her mind kept wandering over to the much more risqué evening she and Jean-Pierre had planned.

Grace was startled out of her reverie when Gladys, the Baroness de Segonzac, whom Grace had met on the set of *To Catch a Thief,* suggested they have lunch in the dining car. Suddenly ravenous at the suggestion of food, Grace agreed and set aside her knitting. The dining car was a clinking, buzzing hive of actors and studio personnel heading to the festival, and she and Gladys joined Olivia de Havilland and her husband, Pierre Galante, an editor at *Paris Match* magazine. They began with crunchy carrot-and-radish salads and conversation about what movies they were most excited to see, and gossip about slighted couturiers and illicit dalliances. To Grace's relief, no one looked at her askance or asked any sort of leading question, and she felt safe in thinking that her affair with Aumont was as confidential as they both wanted.

When their main courses arrived and Gladys and Olivia began chatting about an upcoming project, Pierre turned to Grace and said, "I'm glad I ran into you, as it saves me trying to track you down on the infernal phone lines that will be tied up all week."

"Oh?" Grace said warily. She could tell he wanted something, and her schedule was already jammed with promotional interviews and photographs and dinners. She wanted to preserve the precious few hours she had to herself, especially to share a few of them with Jean-Pierre.

"I know, I know," Pierre said, as if reading her mind. "You don't have time for anything else. I respect that. But this isn't just any old idea. Have you heard of Monaco?"

Grace nodded. "I have. In fact," she said, "I just read an interview with its crown prince in *Collier's*. Prince Raynor? Am I remembering that correctly?"

"Prince Rainier," Pierre corrected her lightly. "He's a young man, very witty, and the most eligible bachelor in Europe, as you can imagine."

Grace laughed. "I can only imagine the duchesses who beset him with their aristocratic daughters."

Pierre chuckled. "Indeed. Well, our French readership is quite taken with him, and we've been searching for a way to make this film festival more accessible to those same readers. And I thought what better way than to have Hollywood royalty meet local royalty?"

Grace found this flattery so hilarious, she

nearly spit out her mouthful of steak tartare. "You must be joking," she said when she recovered her composure. "Hollywood *royalty,* as you call it, is a lot of bricklayers' children and former circus performers. What would a genuine prince want with one of us? And furthermore, if you were going to pick a grande dame of Hollywood, you'd be better off asking your wife to talk to her *Gone with the Wind* costar. Vivien won her second Oscar three years ago."

Undeterred, a look of open amusement and determination on his face, Pierre replied, "Miss Leigh is a wonder, it's true. But she'd be the expected choice. *You* are the woman of the hour, the most recent winner of the statue, and — forgive me for being so crass as to point this out — *you* are the one most often described as a princess."

"An ice princess, you mean." Grace frowned.

"No," said Pierre firmly. "That went away with *Country Girl.* People see you differently now."

Grace was aware that Pierre was using flattery to get what he wanted, and at the moment, she wasn't sure if she cared. He also seemed to understand how she wished to be portrayed to the public, which was an appealing notion since he was the editor of a large magazine. And the idea of stepping off the usual junket was pretty enticing as well.

"I'm not saying yes," Grace warned, "but tell me more about what you're thinking."

CHAPTER 22

Prince Rainier was close to an hour late. And she was wearing everyone's least favorite dress — a floral taffeta number that Judybird had said made her look like a pear — since the beautiful rose-colored ensemble she'd planned to wear was a rumpled mess that couldn't be ironed because the electrical workers were on strike that day, which meant no electricity to press dresses or fix hair. Gladys told her not to worry. "It's one article in a gossip magazine no one reads outside France," she reasoned. "It will be off the shelves and a distant memory by July."

But Grace was worried now, having already toured the gardens of the palace with Prince Rainier's assistant and a flock of photographers, because everything seemed to be going wrong. She'd practically lost her breakfast on the hairpin turns to the palace. It had been so harrowing, she hadn't been able to enjoy the stunning coastal beauty of the little country — *Excusez-moi, principauté!* At first, she'd actually been glad the Prince was late, as it gave her a chance to steady herself.

Then, as time ticked by, only one person had apologized for the Prince's incredible tardiness. Grace couldn't see why his lunch in Cap Ferrat couldn't have been as properly scheduled as her own crowded agenda. *She* hadn't been late. Well, she had a dinner to get to, and she wouldn't be late for that, either, even if it meant leaving Monaco before the Prince arrived.

Anyway, she thought irritably, the palace wasn't even that grand. Compared to Buckingham Palace or Versailles, it was a positive cottage. The best thing about it was the setting — atop a steep wall of rock jutting straight up from the Mediterranean, the stone fortress was imposing enough to have given pirates pause in the eighteenth century. But the rooms inside were dreary and small. The dark Throne Room, where she sat now, hardly lived up to its name.

Just as she was consulting her watch for the umpteenth time, about to say she'd had enough, Prince Rainier was walking briskly toward her, hand outstretched, a look of genuine embarrassment and apology on his face. When they shook hands, he gushed, "I am terribly sorry, Miss Kelly. I have been trying to break away for an hour, but . . ." He shook his head. "I won't bore you with the details, especially as you have so little time left here. Please, accept my deepest apologies and allow me to escort you."

His unaffected, apologetic demeanor was so unexpected, it caught Grace by surprise. And his voice was so musical, layered like a finely played cello, complemented by a British-leaning accent — which was also unexpected, as she'd assumed he would sound French. Disarmed, and suddenly finding herself a touch off-balance, Grace replied, "Thank you, Your Serene Highness," as she'd been coached to address the Prince, dropping her head and bending her knees in a curtsy the nuns from her childhood would have approved of. She heard the cameras snapping all around them. "I'd be delighted."

"I am relieved and grateful, Miss Kelly. And please, call me Rainier."

"Please call me Grace." *How odd. I'm on a first-name basis with a prince.*

He nodded with a smile and offered her his elbow. As she threaded her arm through his, Grace realized that she was slightly taller than he was in her pumps — or maybe, at best, the same height. Someone should have told her to wear flats! This day had been a sartorial disaster. Not for the Prince, however — in his dark suit, pastel tie, and sunglasses, he looked uncreased and fresh. Clearly no one was on strike in Monaco! She only wished he didn't have that slim mustache above his lips, as it reminded her too much of Oleg.

"Your gardens are just marvelous," Grace said, hoping a compliment would assure the Prince there were no hard feelings.

"I'm glad you like them," he said, and she detected a nervous eagerness in his voice. "Have you been on the wall? There are some lovely flowers there as well."

Grace shook her head, and he immediately steered her out of the gloomy Throne Room and into the colorfully frescoed Hercule Gallery, which was rather lovely, she thought on second glance. They descended the grand horseshoe staircase and went into the internal courtyard. "I must confess," he said in her ear, "I don't love the palace itself. It's so dark, and not full of the best memories for me. I do love the grounds, however. Monaco's sunshine is its greatest asset, and I like to enjoy it as much as I can."

She agreed, but she was startled by his readiness to critique his own palace and confess such a personal detail about his memories of it. "I quite agree about the sunshine," Grace replied, "which I first enjoyed last year when I filmed a movie not far from here —"

To Catch a Thief," said Rainier. "I've seen it. You were a pleasure to watch, if I may say so. The scene of your picnic with Cary Grant isn't far from here, you know. Less than half an hour's drive."

"Is it?!" Grace liked knowing this; it instantly made her feel more at ease, even at home, in this strange stone palace.

"And I live in a villa much more like John Robie's," said the Prince. "I wish I could have met you there. But even though I think it would have made much prettier pictures, the magazine wanted us to meet at the palace."

"You don't live here?" Grace asked in surprise.

"No, no," he said. "This is my office."

"Some office," Grace said, making a show of gesturing around them.

Appreciating her irony, Rainier chuckled. "That is precisely why I need what you Americans call a getaway. But I believe a movie set built by the great Alfred Hitchcock would seem just as daunting — or, should we say, unbelievable — to the person who doesn't go to it every day."

"An excellent point," said Grace. Then, suddenly remembering the first time she'd met Hitch, she laughed and said, "It's really amazing what a person can get used to. Alfred Hitchcock was so accustomed to sets and cinematography by the time he did *Dial M for Murder,* he was furious he had to shoot that film in Three-D. He couldn't see all that amazing equipment as anything other than a chore. And then he thought absolutely nothing of constructing the back side of *two* New York City apartment buildings for *Rear Window.*"

"The human animal always acclimatizes," said Rainier, and Grace found this self-assured and philosophical pronouncement unexpected and thrilling.

Rainier stopped walking, and Grace looked around. She'd been so absorbed in talking, she hadn't noticed the scenery they had passed on the way, but the place where he'd stopped was breathtaking. Behind them was a garden she hadn't yet seen, lush with roses of every shade of pink and red, and before them was a low stone wall covered in ivy, the top edge of a precipitous drop-off. If she looked straight down, her eyes fell on the tops of red roofs and narrow streets, laundry lines strung up between windows and a few donkeys and carts dotting the roads. If she lifted her eyes, she could fasten them on a blue horizon, the deep azure of the water meeting the pale periwinkle of the sky. At the edges of her vision was the coastal land — from where she stood, a Cézanne patchwork of green, yellow, and cream.

"It's beautiful," breathed Grace, resting a gloved hand on her brow to shade her eyes.

"It never gets old," agreed Rainier.

They stood, looking and appreciating, and Grace slowly became aware that the moment was being photographed by the posse of men with cameras who had followed her from the moment she'd set foot out of the car. Funny, but she'd forgotten they were there for a few minutes.

"I've heard," said Rainier, his lips curling into a wry smile, "that your next role is as Princess Alexandra in Molnár's *Swan*? I saw a theatrical production of it in London a few years ago, and I must admit I appreciated the writer's understanding of the absurdity and tragedy of royal life."

"Yes, poor Alexandra cannot be with the man she truly loves because her family stands in their way. But if I may say so, that problem is one many families have — not just royal families, which is why I think the script resonates with so many people."

"Touché," Rainier said, turning away from Grace and folding his hands behind his back as he looked out at the view. "However, the way everyone is abused by Alexandra's mother in the interest of securing the crown for her family is, I think, peculiarly royal."

So many possible replies sprang to Grace's mind — a reiteration of the fact that even laypeople behaved as the characters did, using family members in their own single-minded pursuits; a question about what, precisely, was "peculiarly royal" about it; an impertinent comment based on something Grace had read about Rainier's own mother being unfortunately like Alexandra's. But before she could say anything, she was spared the effort by one of the photographers saying, "It's nearly five, Miss Kelly. You said we should let you know."

"Yes, thank you so much," she replied, giving the photographer a courteous nod. To her surprise, she was disappointed that her time with Monaco's Prince was over. Turning back to him, she said, "Regretfully, I must get back to Cannes."

"Yes, your own kingdom awaits," he said, with the utmost respect, utterly devoid of irony.

She laughed off his flattery. "As does

yours, I assume," she replied.

"Only a principality. Monaco has no king," he corrected her good-naturedly. Then he smiled sadly, and she thought he also blushed as he glanced away — the modesty and melancholy of this gesture tugged at something in Grace. "But yes, nevertheless, it always seems to await," he replied, "at the most inconvenient times." He lifted his hands and clasped both of hers in his. They were warm and dry, with a firm grip, and when their eyes met, Grace felt an electric current of attraction run from their hands up and down her limbs, as a hot red blush colored her own cheeks.

A few days after returning to New York from France, Grace sat at her new desk with Oliver snoozing on her new carpet beside her bare feet. In contrast to the luxurious newness of her decor, she wore some of her oldest jeans and a soft wool sweater from her Barbizon days. She had a stack of stationery and envelopes at the ready and her trusty pen from Uncle George in her hand. There were so many people to write to — Josephine and Maree and Rita, all of whom she could tell about her brief and bittersweet affair with Jean-Pierre, which they had agreed together should end as they shared a last basket of croissants on her hotel suite balcony. She also owed letters to Uncle George and Hitch. Thank goodness Jay- and Judybird were having a party that night so she could simply see and fill in most of her New York friends and gather their news in kind.

But she found herself turning first to Prince Rainier. It didn't take her long to formulate the words because she'd been turning them over in her mind since getting on her plane to return to the States. She wrote:

Dear Prince Rainier,
Thank you for your hospitality in Monaco. I have found myself thinking of your gardens and vistas and company often since I left, and believe my visit to your principality will help me play Princess Alexandra. I didn't have a chance to mention it when we spoke, but I played her once before, five years ago in a television dramatization of the play. I fear that version of the princess was a tad immature, and I am glad of the opportunity to play her again with the experience of a bit more age — and now add to that meeting a prince who rules over a European country much like the

one her family wishes for her (complicated as those wishes are, as you so insightfully pointed out). I'm grateful to Pierre Galante for introducing us, and only wish we'd had more time to speak.

Best wishes for a sunny summer.

Sincerely yours,
Grace

To her surprise, a letter from the Prince arrived just a few days later, on long, crisp paper with two scripted Rs mirror-facing each other beneath a red crown:

Dear Grace,
It is I who should thank you for taking the time to visit my little principality during your very busy festival schedule. Since you left, I have finally seen *The Country Girl,* and understand completely why you have been so honored for that performance. The role of Georgie Elgin is so different from that of the roles you played for Mr. Hitchcock, and opposite Mr. Gable and Mr. Cooper, I admit I was quite amazed by the subtlety and sensitivity of your acting. I quite forgot I was watching Grace Kelly, and was utterly absorbed in the plight of Mrs. Elgin. Congratulations on your perfor-

mance — the accolades that have flowed from it are much deserved. I look forward to seeing what you do with the role of Princess Alexandra, and feel confident that everything you bring to that will be your own talent, and have little to do with visiting Monaco, however much I might like to flatter myself that you enjoyed your visit here.

As for talking more — I hope the same. In fact, I am planning a trip to the United States for the holidays. Yes, much as I love it, I find I need a break from the sun of Monaco from time to time and I suspect that a white Christmas is just what I need so that I can return to my principality with renewed appreciation for its merits. Perhaps we could meet again if that visit comes to pass? In the meantime, I would treasure another letter from you. Tell me, when does filming begin on *The Swan*? Do you have another production in the works?

Yours very sincerely,
(just) Rainier

His invitation to correspond was so bewildering as to be surreal. She recalled the frisson that had passed between them just before she left; she was sure he'd felt it, too, and she admired him for not referencing it in any way even as she wondered if he'd recalled it as many times as she had. Well, she decided, there certainly wasn't any harm in writing to Prince Rainier. The idea that they could be anything more than pen pals was laughable . . . and yet . . . why would he bother writing to her without some sort of intent? She knew enough of the world to know that men didn't spend time or money on women they didn't expect something from, and princes had even less time than most men.

Don't get ahead of yourself, Grace told herself. *Just be glad he's Catholic and never been married.* And with that, she picked up a pen to reply. Then she set it down. Best not to appear too eager. She'd write back soon enough.

CHAPTER 23

Dear Rainier,

I apologize for this late reply to your wonderful letter, but my younger sister, Lizanne, was just married and now I can breathe again. Goodness, there was so much to do! I was much younger when my older siblings were married and less was expected of me, so I was quite unprepared for the many responsibilities of sister-of-the-bride! Of course, I enjoyed every minute of it, and her husband is so solid and perfect for her in every respect, I couldn't be happier for her.

You ask if I have another production in the works — well, I have to say that I'm taking the summer off. Last year, my filming schedule was nothing short of manic, and I need a break. I plan to enjoy myself with my family on "the Jersey shore," as it's called here, and where I've been going every summer since I was a little girl. I do love building sandcastles and eating ice cream and going to sleep freshly bathed after a day of swimming and reading.

Then filming will start on *The Swan,* in both California and North Carolina. I am supposed to play Maggie in a movie of *Cat on a Hot Tin Roof,* but that cannot start until the Broadway run is over, and it's still such a hot ticket, who knows when that will be? MGM keeps sending me other scripts, and I keep politely declining, but I know I must be careful lest I anger them and they suspend my contract again. Fortunately, *The Swan* is Dore Schary's own picture (and he is the King of MGM), so he is happy with me for the moment. And Bing Crosby wants me to be in his next movie, which will also be for MGM. I'm not sure how much you might know about motion picture contracts, but they are dastardly things I wouldn't wish on my worst enemy.

I hope I haven't bored you with this more authentic letter about the after all mundane real life of Grace Kelly. But I would certainly welcome one in return about the real life of His Serene Highness the Prince of Monaco. What is it really like? And remember, it's research for me as I consider how to play Princess Alexandra.

Sincerely,
Grace

P.S. I would of course welcome the opportunity to see you if you come to the United States. New York is divine at the holidays. It's what all the songs sing about.

Dear Grace,
Your life sounds positively full and marvelous, and I am delighted you would share such details with me. I fear the life of a prince whose entire country is a fraction of the size of your Manhattan will pale in comparison to a screen princess whose dominion is as vast as the terrain she traverses to make her movies, and the many theaters in which those movies conquer their viewers.

But since you ask, I shall try. In the interest of research.

I spend most of my days in meetings or on the telephone. Sometimes with people whom your average newspaper reader would recognize as important, like René Coty or Aristotle Onassis. But most of the time I am meeting with the truly important people whose names few people know but whose influence in Europe is vast — advisors, magistrates, ambassadors. The central project of my reign is to bring this beautiful rock out of the Middle Ages and into the twentieth century.

Speaking of ancient places, I have begun to see the palace differently since seeing you photographed in it (have you read the *Match* story? It was rather good, I thought). I wonder if some sprucing up could breathe life into it the way you did? Someday I suppose I shall have to inhabit it year-round, and be the true prince who rules from his palace. But I put off that day, as it would mean admitting I am a grown man, like my father.

Congratulations and felicitations to your sister. I hope her union is blessed with happiness and children. Also, I have heard of this Jersey shore you mention and wonder how it compares to the beaches of France. Do report back, and let me see it through your eyes. More details on my trip as I have them.

Sincerely,
Rainier

Dear Peter Pan,

Are you really so afraid of growing up? I should think a crown prince who meets regularly with the president of France would fancy himself an adult, but I suppose small children have worn crowns, too, so that's really no test at all. Fortunately and unfortunately, I have felt the weight of adulthood since I first left home at seventeen. While I have always prized the freedom of that stage of life, I have often wondered what I might have missed by not extending my childhood as many of my friends did — living at home, playing at volunteer work, and never living alone but moving seamlessly from my parents' home to my husband's.

Goodness, but I do feel open with you. I don't discuss these sorts of things with even my closest friends, and here we are writing about them. I hope you don't think me inappropriate.

Let me dissertate instead on French versus New Jersey beaches to lighten the mood. I suppose the first difference is the presence on this side of the Atlantic of modest bathing costumes! And beer. And hot dogs. In New Jersey, you'd not see a single bared breast, nor a bottle of cold Sancerre, nor a baguette. More's the pity. Maybe I'll bring my own when I head down next week.

Ice cream is what we all have in common. Thank the good Lord.

Now very hungrily yours,
Grace

Dear Hungry,
Please don't stop writing your innermost feelings on my account. I find it helps to unburden myself in writing, and makes me feel less alone to be able to send those writings to another person who cares — and I do care, Grace. I hope those same things are true for you.

Furthermore, I admire your independence and determination, though I detect some sadness, some sense that you missed out on something precious other women your age enjoy — a carefree stage of life when you are no longer a child but not yet a wife and mother. Perhaps you might be able to find some of that later in your life, even now? I hope my own girl children might be able to enjoy a few years as such — what a marvelous time to travel and sample the treasures of the world, no? When one is old enough to read about history and nature with the intelligence of an adult, and also experience it with the wonder of a child.

I do understand what you mean about the weight of adulthood, however, and wish you hadn't felt it so soon. My own parents separated when I was very young and their feelings toward each other can only be described as hateful on a good day. On bad days, they were bitterly cruel to each other, and my sister and I have always been caught in the cross fire. Nothing makes a child grow up faster or more troubled than being made a pawn in his parents' games. This is another thing I hope to give my children: freedom from my own neuroses. But I cannot end my letter on that note!

Did you bring wine and baguette to the shore? I want to see photographic evidence in the European gossip columns. Perhaps you'll start a trend, though I must admit that a cold beer on a sandy beach actually sounds quite delicious.

Thirstily yours,
Rainier

Dear Thirsty,
It turns out beer is easier to keep cold on a scorching summer day. Smaller

bottles in the cooler. Maybe the truth is that the French are actually drinking lukewarm wine? I'm laughing at that thought as I write. Also, I love hamburgers — better than baguette and ham or even brie. My father grilled some last night and I ate TWO on the patio with sand between my toes, and my bathing suit still wet from the surf. No, I don't think I'll be starting trends in Europe anytime soon. I'm just too much a product of this part of the world.

Now I must give you a stern talking-to, Serene Highness. Why should only your girl children benefit from this halcyon time of life you described so eloquently in your last letter? I hate to think of a boy missing out because he was in line for a crown (and I use that word literally and metaphorically, since my own unprincely father burdened his son with his very secular and thorny crown). And surely such wanderings and wonderings would be an antidote to the sorts of parental cruelty you endured. I admire you for knowing that you want to give your own children a different sort of childhood from the one you had.

In fact, your words have set me thinking about the ways in which I, too, would like my children to grow up differently than I did. I would like them to grow up free of expectations — my own expectations, anyway. The world will always encroach, won't it? But it would be very nice to grow up feeling that one's own parents don't play favorites and will love you for who you are. I have the sense that neither of us grew up with this sort of security.

And yet here we are — maybe all the stronger for the trials of our childhoods. I wouldn't trade the strength I've gained for the comfort I wish I'd had.

I'll be heading back to New York soon, then jetting to North Carolina! I'm looking forward to meeting Alec Guinness. Have you seen him in any theater or English television? It's amazing that *The Swan* will be his first American movie. And I can't wait to work with Agnes Moorehead, and hear her stories about Orson Welles! I'm hardly sorry to leave the beach and get back to work.

Sincerely sunburned,
Grace

Dear Sunburned,
I hope this letter reaches you wherever you are, as I don't have an address for

you in North Carolina — and please do tell me about that state. I admit that the southern part of your country is a mystery to me, and seems much farther away from Europe than it is geographically. The pictures I have seen of plantations, and bayous, and trees that quite literally weep into grasses and streams, make for a very foreign mix indeed.

I have seen Alec Guinness in a number of English films — he was wonderful as Fagin in *Oliver Twist,* as well as another Dickensian character whose name escapes me in *Great Expectations.* What is it like to work with actors whose names are so well-known? Screen royalty though you are, do you ever get nervous? I sometimes feel anxious before certain important meetings, especially if there's something I want to get out of it and I know I must "perform" in a particular manner. I detest performing, and could never do what you do with such poise (I had been about to write "so gracefully," but realized it would be a cheap pun).

I have also taken to heart your words about girl children and boy children. In my world, they are treated differently as a matter of course. But of course you are right: boys and girls should both enjoy a childhood free of expectations and worry. They should both focus on building their characters and experiencing the world. Adversity always comes, but if parents can avoid adding to it, that is for the best. I am sorry that you had parents who couldn't do this for you, but as you say, it did make you who you are. And you are quite amazing.

I must also tell you that I found myself on a short beach holiday, and took beer instead of wine. It was a revelation! I think I shall find myself right at home in your part of the world, as you describe it. My plans to come to your side of the Atlantic are taking shape, and I might be able to see you in Los Angeles in a few weeks' time. Would that be possible? I think often of how nice it will be to discuss these matters in person.

Fondly,
Rainier

Dear Fondly,
Oh, the puns that have been made on my name! Grace under pressure. Amazing Grace. Gracefully done. Say Grace. Even God's Grace — which, as a Catholic, I find blasphemous. My parents have given a great gift to tabloid writers

everywhere with my name.

And yes, indeed, I do still get nervous! It was much worse when I was just starting out. I was a mess during *High Noon,* as you can imagine — a complete know-nothing acting with the great Gary Cooper! These days, though, the butterflies in my stomach are much more calm. But even if I had been a nervous Nellie, Alec and Agnes would have put me at my ease right away! They are both full of terrific stories, which are too many and hilarious to do justice to in a letter. I shall look forward to relaying them all to you in person when you visit.

Speaking of which — I can tell *The Swan* is going to take an age to shoot; we're already behind. So please don't think me a wretch for saying that I preferred your plan to visit at the holidays. The director, Charles Vidor, is something of a perfectionist, and if you come when I'm in California and I'm working on this movie, I don't think I'll be able to relax and spend time with you. But I should be able to take a proper break in late December in New York.

Hopefully yours,
Grace

CHAPTER 24

"You've been writing letters for six months?" Rita was clearly gobsmacked, to use one of Alec's marvelous English expressions.

"No one is more surprised than I am," said Grace, sipping some hot tea on this unusually chilly December morning in their Sweetzer apartment. Deliciously, she was still wearing her flannel nightgown, which she had tucked around her as she sat on their sofa; she was like a human tent. A little tree they had decorated with white lights and colorful glass balls twinkled in the corner of the room.

"And he's going to meet your family?" Rita repeated the other detail Grace had just shared. "At Christmas, of all times? Like Christmas isn't a strained enough time for most families? You're going to have a *prince* for dinner?"

"Technically, the Austins are having the

prince. Did I tell you that story?" Rita shook her head, eyes still wide and amazed by the recent news about Grace's life. Grace laughed, remembering the details. "Well, Edie and Russell Austin are old friends of my parents'. I grew up with them just down the street. Nice couple, nice children, though I was never close with their kids. They were always a bit funny about certain things, though. They always had to have the latest and greatest of everything, whereas my parents would wait to see if something had staying power before investing in it. And they love a good party. So when they went to France this summer, they got it in their heads that they wanted to go to the Red Cross do in Monaco —" Grace laughed out loud, remembering Peggy telling her this story, and how Grace had imagined plump, middle-aged Edie and cigar-smoking Russell hatching this plot on the golf course in East Falls. "And since they'd seen the pictures of me and Rainier in *Paris Match,* they actually wrote to Rainier saying that they were good friends of Grace Kelly's family and would like nothing more than to attend the Gala. Could they buy tickets?"

"No!" said Rita.

"Yes!" Grace howled with laughter. "Can you imagine the nerve? But even funnier, he said yes! Or this Father Tucker, whom Rainier trusts with his life, said yes. Didn't ask any questions! Just said any friend of Grace's is a friend of ours, and here are two tickets to the biggest party in Europe. Even *I* haven't been to that party."

"Sounds like you could go," said Rita with a whistle, "anytime you want."

Grace wiped a tear of laughter from her eye and said, "Maybe. But that's not the point. The point is that the Austins and His Serene Highness of Monaco are now the best of friends. And my mother cannot remember that it's *Monaco* to save her life. She keeps saying Morocco."

This time Rita laughed. "Sounds like Christmas will be more Frank Capra than Currier and Ives."

"Oh, I do hope so. Rainier needs to see what it's really like."

"Whhhyyyyy?" Rita asked coyly.

"No reason," Grace said, equally coy, touching her chin to her shoulder and batting her eyelashes.

"Grace Patricia Kelly, you cannot be serious," said Rita, genuinely scandalized.

"About what?"

"This Christmas dinner isn't a prelude to . . . to something more serious, is it?"

Grace shrugged and couldn't help grinning widely.

"You barely know the guy!"

"I feel I know him better from his letters than I ever knew Gene or Oleg. And on my side, I feel as if not being able to see him in person has given me some space to be more honest than I have been with other men in the past. And the . . . the physical side of things hasn't muddied everything up, as it so often does. It's strange, isn't it, that a person can actually be more honest in a letter than they can be face-to-face?"

"It's also easier to hide," observed Rita. "You're both given plenty of time to rehearse."

"Oh, Rita, I'm too old not to be able to tell the difference between real and performance. I haven't performed with him, and I believe the same of him."

"What do your parents say?"

"He's a prince! What *can* they say?"

In fact, while Margaret Kelly couldn't get Monaco right to save her life, she was absolutely aflutter with plans and excitement. And her father had said, "He's royal, he's Catholic, and he's never been married. If you don't go after him with all your feminine wiles, I might have to have your head checked." But she wasn't about to share that with Rita, who looked positively scandalized by this most chaste of romances.

Then Rita smiled, and shrugged. "At least you're not twenty-bloody-two, like I was when I met Sidney. *Babies*. And Rainier's only a few years older than you, unlike the other geezers you've been with," she joked.

"Thank you for finding the silver lining," Grace said good-naturedly. She knew Rita was only looking out for her; after all, her friend had seen up close how difficult the relationship with Oleg had been. Grace felt just as protective of Rita, having watched the toll her marriage to, then divorce from, Sidney had taken on her; she wasn't sure what to think of Rita's new romance with Thomas Guinzberg, other than to understand wholeheartedly the appeal of a man outside their industry. Eager to reestablish common ground with her friend, she said as much: "I also like him for one of the same reasons you like Tom: he's not an actor, director, or producer."

"But Tom's an editor. He works with creative types all day, so he kind of gets it, you know?"

Rita must have noticed the look of disappointment that began to make Grace frown, because she quickly added, "But yes, I agree. No more movie types for us." She raised her glass of iced tea, and proposed a toast. "To new adventures."

Grace took a great gulp of air into her lungs. "To new adventures." Exactly. She couldn't have said it better herself.

Shooting for *The Swan* ran so late, Grace had to postpone her singing lessons for the duet she was to record with Bing in the musical remake of *Philadelphia Story,* at last titled *High Society.* After Christmas in Philadelphia, she would have to rush to New York for those earlier than she'd like — but she decided not to warn Rainier about this and cast a dark cloud over the excitement they both felt about his visit. Who knew what would happen between them anyway? It might all go terribly wrong. She wasn't about to change her work schedule for him. Yet.

Because she'd been thinking — and thinking and thinking — about this very issue a great deal recently. Her acting had been a problem for Oleg. As proud as he'd been of her, and as understanding as he had been of her desire to express herself in this creative way because he was an artist, too, he had not liked the way her acting had taken her away from him: he had not liked the fact that she'd had to collaborate with other designers like Edith, or kiss other men in front of cameras, or spend late nights and long hours working with men she might have dallied with in the past.

She could see why this would unnerve a man — Kell had even said at Lizanne's wedding that if Grace didn't want to die the old spinster of the Kelly clan, she had better give up on Hollywood. "Men don't like to be shown up by their wives, and all the successful actors are runarounds as far as I can tell." And even more pointedly, her father had said to her as they waltzed across the parquet dance floor, "You're in your prime, Gracie, and your mother and I have been patient while you've had your fun. Isn't it time to settle down and forget this acting nonsense?" Grace had always been aware that her own mother, once an unusually successful woman in college sports, had given up work to be Mrs. John B. Kelly. Apparently without any regrets.

Rainier seemed like someone she could discuss her career with. They had discussed so much already, and the way he spoke of children moved something elemental deep inside her. After reading what he'd written about childhoods free of expectation and worry, she'd taken Oliver for a walk in Central Park and found herself choking back tears.

Still, despite all the flattery about her vast dominions, she had a feeling she knew what he'd say about her career. He was a man. She'd known so many men, starting with her father. And until very recently, all actresses were regarded as little more than whores — especially in Europe. A man like Rainier would want a wife who was more like Lisa Fremont or Frances Stevens than Grace Kelly, even though Grace Kelly could play those socialites with perfect pitch.

Rainier was also the first man whose attentions didn't make her feel nervous — which made no sense at all, even to her. He was a prince, for heaven's sake. Being with him would cause more of a storm, in their families and in the press, than a relationship with just about anyone else, including Clark Gable (or, these days, Marlon or Montgomery). But she had the sense that they could each be the other's sanctuary from that storm. His letters certainly had been — a warm, beating heart of a secret she carried with her in pockets and purses every day. Not only had their presence acted as a buffer between her and the rest of the world, Rainier had actually written recently, "I'd like to think I could protect you from some of the attention you so decry. Being a prince has given me certain tools to keep me distant from people I don't want to be close to. And there is also the wonder of escape. I'd love to show you some of the most private places I've seen and enjoyed, where I can be completely myself."

She wanted that so much, to be completely herself. And she felt she might have that prize with Rainier, who seemed to understand, as Oleg had not, how much she loved her parents even though they didn't always appear to return her affections in the way she would have liked; he understood, as Gene could not, her desire to live a balanced and temperate life and even to add more of her childhood religion back into her life; he showed compassion to her, as no one else could have because she'd never felt brave enough to share certain of her fears, except on paper. In one of her letters, she'd gone so far as to confess that she wasn't sure what sort of mother she could be, much as she wanted to be one, and Rainier had assured her, "Your heart is uniquely warm and capacious — and this is surely the foundation of motherhood." She wanted so much to believe his vision of her, and while she wondered how he could possibly know anything about her after some letters and one meeting, she squelched this question. *He's intuitive and sensitive. Isn't that what you've always wanted?*

With all these thoughts swirling in her mind and making her feel just queasy enough to lose her appetite, she arrived in Philadelphia on Christmas Eve. Fordie picked her up at the train station with a hug and kisses on both cheeks. "Well, if it isn't our Oscar winner," he said proudly and with such fondness, Grace felt wretched for not phoning him to chat in weeks.

"Fordie, you mustn't flatter me so," Grace objected.

"You deserve it, Gracie. You've worked hard to get where you are. I'm proud of you."

She sat next to him in the new Lincoln. "How are you, Fordie? Tell me about your wife and daughter." And she listened as he told her about his wife's work at the church and his daughter graduating from college in the spring — prompting Grace to open her agenda and quickly jot down "Fordie — graduation gift!" in May.

"She could be anything," he said of his daughter, "but she wants to be a teacher right here in Philadelphia. Wants to help the kinds of kids others think can't be helped," he said, his voice thick and warm with emotion. "But first she's determined to go to Montgomery and see what good she can do down there."

Grace's stomach fluttered with a different kind of nerves now, and she asked, "But is it safe down there?" Just a few weeks ago, a woman named Rosa Parks had refused to sit at the back of the bus, where the laws of Alabama said she must sit. Grace had called the Southern white lawmakers and so-called law-abiding citizens racist pigs at a recent party in Los Angeles, where feeling was overwhelmingly with Ms. Parks, but she knew she'd be very worried letting any child of hers go south to join another bus boycott. Ever since *Brown v. Board of Education* last year, things had been so unsettled in the Southern states, with violence erupting every other day, it seemed.

"I couldn't stop her if I wanted to," said Fordie. "And I don't want to. I'd go myself if I could." And Grace heard the underlying message: he couldn't afford to go; he had to keep driving her parents around Philadelphia, freeing his daughter to make her own choices.

"You're very brave," said Grace, surprised to find her own voice hoarse with admiration and sadness. She cleared her throat, wishing she could give Fordie what he needed: a nest egg that would allow him to retire and be with his daughter. She had sufficient funds, but her parents would kill her. Knowing she wasn't brave enough to defy her parents for Fordie gave Grace a burning feeling of shame inside.

Ever the diplomat, Fordie shifted the conversation to other things: new roads being paved throughout the city, and an exhibit of ancient Egyptian artifacts he'd seen at the museum recently. Then, before she was ready to face it, they had arrived at Henry Avenue.

Though her parents had always decorated festively at the holidays, this year the house was decked out as never before. The fragrance of pine was strong and fresh, and made Grace wonder if her mother had waited to get the tree and swags for the mantel until yesterday or if she'd recently replaced them with new ones. All the holly berries that dotted the room were plump and shiny, the plaid bows round and crisp. Her mother must have prevailed this year over her father and forbidden the "tacky" tinsel she'd never liked, and a few extra strings of white lights illuminated a tree that was at least a foot taller and wider than last year's, with copious presents professionally wrapped in shiny foil and grosgrain ribbons from only the nicest stores, which Margaret must have procured on an excursion to New

York: Bergdorf's, Saks, and Tiffany's. A new stereo cabinet softly played holiday tunes, a perfect auditory complement to the other elegantly jolly elements assaulting her senses.

"It's lovely in here," Grace said, overcome by the most intense craving for one of her mother's ginger cookies, the soft ones with the sparkly sugar on top and spicy bits of ginger throughout. Miraculously, she saw a plate of them sitting on the coffee table, and she bent over to pick one up. Taking a bite, she was immediately five years old again, filled with nothing but unabashed excitement for the holiday and its potential. "Delicious as always, Mother."

Margaret Kelly, wearing a dark green A-line dress and pearls, was wringing her hands at her waist. "I see you brought only two suitcases," she observed as Fordie carried them up the stairs to Grace's childhood room. "What are you planning to wear tomorrow?"

"Something appropriate, Mother. Don't worry," she said, though her casual tone was the opposite of how she felt inside every time she pictured her next meeting with the Prince. "Anyway, if the Prince liked me in that horrid taffeta dress, I think I could wear just about anything tomorrow."

Just then her father came in with a Waterford glass of whiskey in his right hand. He said, "We're not so impressed by royalty around here," then bent over to kiss Grace on the cheek. She wasn't sure if his nonchalance should make her relax or worry more. Thankfully, Rainier's breed of royalty was Catholic, not Protestant like the old boys of Henley, whom Jack still despised though his son had beaten them twice. "And what's this about you playing Kate Hepburn's role as a Main Liner? Old man Williams was ribbing me about it at the benefit the other night."

"Daddy," Grace said impatiently — she couldn't help it — "I told you about *High Society* ages ago."

"More than once," her mother added pointedly, and Grace was grateful for her mother's defense.

Her father drained the rest of his whiskey and said, "I guess I'm more excited to meet this prince than I am to see my daughter pretend to be something she's not."

At this, her mother actually rolled her eyes. What was going on in this house, with her mother showing such impatience with her father? Grace hoped the discord wouldn't be visible to anyone but her the next day, because despite what she'd said to

Rita about wanting to give Rainier an authentic look at her life, the truth was that if he were to really see what went on in the Kelly family, she was sure he'd want nothing to do with her. Her father would make sure of that.

Ironically, her main hope was the social climbing her parents had cultivated since she was a child. She'd always hated it, resented the ways it made her mother and father ride all their children for perfection, but if there was one thing the aspirational founder of Kelly for Brickwork would not do, it was ruffle the feathers of a prince.

At least, that was the hope she clung to.

CHAPTER 25

After presents and coffee with a slice of the same delicious stollen she'd been eating toasted with heaps of butter and cranberry jam since she was old enough to stuff the bites into her own mouth, Grace spent a few tedious hours being fussed over by her mother's hairdresser, Betsy. Margaret claimed to have paid her quadruple to work on Christmas morning. But Betsy, whose teased blond chignon didn't inspire confidence in Grace, seemed bubbly and happy to be there. Grace told her firmly that she wanted to look *natural.*

"Of course, honey," Betsy said in a Philly accent.

Grace calculated how much time it would take to undo whatever Betsy was about to do to her. But she was very pleased to discover that Betsy could achieve natural. In fact, Grace's stringy hair hadn't looked this full and bouncy in ages, and so she agreed to purchase an arsenal of products from the salon the next day in order to do it herself in the coming weeks. Betsy's Christmas was made.

Feeling pretty and festive, if still nauseous with overwrought nerves, Grace asked her mother if she needed any help. "Are you crazy? The last thing we need is that dress getting a stain before the Prince arrives." Margaret, wearing a red wool dress today, scrutinized her daughter and said, "Speaking of dresses, I like that one. Where did you get it?"

"Saks," said Grace, looking down at the full skirt of the creamy dress made of stiff silk brocade, which buttoned in pearls all the way down the back and had a Peter Pan collar and three-quarter-length sleeves. She'd fastened a glittering red wreath brooch above her right breast.

"It's very . . . pure," said her mother. Grace suspected that even her mother couldn't use the word *virginal* without laughing — or spitting.

"I'm glad you like it. Everything looks wonderful here, too." Glass bowls of nuts and toffee and other treats were all about the room, the decanters of wine and whiskey were full, and the detritus of the morning with all of Grace's nieces' and nephews' new toys was cleared away, as if nothing had happened — though now the tree looked a bit bare without its presents. Her mother had lamented that morning, as all the luxurious paper and ribbon was tossed unceremoniously into plastic bags, that she'd originally thought the Prince would be here on Christmas Eve. But the skirt that lined the tree was also beautiful, stitched by hand by Grace's grandmother.

"I can't believe I forgot," said Margaret now, casting nervous glances around the room, "to try to serve something they would have in his native country of Morocco."

"It's *Monaco,* Mother," Grace said for the millionth time.

"Yes, of course," she replied, and Grace could tell this would not be the last time she'd need to correct her. "Mother, maybe it's best if you don't mention the Prince's country when he's here," she suggested as gently as she could, but still Margaret Kelly darted her a sharp and disapproving look.

"Anyway," Grace added, "I don't think it's necessary to serve anything Monégasque. He's here for an American Christmas. Experiencing a holiday in another country is part of the fun."

Soon her siblings and their spouses arrived — without children, who were all apparently comatose in front of a television screen at Peggy's with a Jewish grandmother as a babysitter. "I like this version of Christmas dinner," said Peggy, the ice in her old-fashioned clinking brightly. "An adult meal and servants to do the dishes." Grace thought it had been a bit much, her mother hiring a whole army for the kitchen, but it seemed to make her feel more comfortable, so Grace hadn't argued.

As the hour of Rainier's arrival neared, Grace felt the knots in her shoulders tighten and even started to hear a buzzing in her ears, making it hard for her to listen to or focus on anything else. But the ring of the doorbell cut right through all that, and suddenly everything was too loud, her body almost too loose. Goodness, what was *wrong* with her?

Her father answered the door. Her brother, Kell, along with Lizanne and her husband, all of whom had been sitting, stood up; and so their whole party was awkwardly formal when Prince Rainier entered with Edie and Russell Austin, as well as a priest Grace knew to be Father Tucker, Rainier's most trusted advisor.

Showtime, thought Grace, taking a deep breath and holding it.

"Welcome!" said her father jovially, shaking Rainier's hand. "Merry Christmas!"

"Merry Christmas to you as well," said Rainier, a wide smile on his face as he shook her father's hand and clasped him on the forearm with his other. Her athletic father was several inches taller than the Prince, but it didn't seem to matter — Rainier had a warmth, a presence that filled the room. And she'd forgotten how musical his voice was, how seductive his vaguely English accent.

As everyone shook hands and made introductions, two girls on the staff Margaret had hired magically appeared in black dresses and white aprons, quietly tidying up coats and gloves and hats, and Grace was grateful for the wisdom of her mother's choice. She hung back near the fireplace and stepped forward once the rest of the group had met. "Hello, Rainier," she said shyly, and — natural as anything — they clasped hands and kissed on both cheeks. "So good of you to join us tonight." His touch sent shivers of anticipation through her, and he looked at her just a beat longer than he needed to, Christmas lights reflecting mischievously in his very dark eyes. So. She hadn't remembered wrong. There was something electric between them.

"I wouldn't have missed it," he said huskily.

Then, as if remembering where he was, he cleared his throat and said, "Allow me to introduce you to Father Francis Tucker, who is very glad to be back in his homeland for this birthday of our savior."

The gray-haired priest of about sixty came forward to shake Grace's hand. "Monaco is charming at Christmas, of course," he said in a low and kindly but gruff voice, "but I admit I did welcome the opportunity to come home again." Turning his attention to the mantel, he said to Grace's mother, "That is an absolutely beautiful crèche, Mrs. Kelly."

Beaming, she replied, "Why, thank you, Father. It's from Venice. John and I bought it on a trip to Italy after the war."

Examining the hand-painted baby Jesus and all the other players in the biblical drama through his horn-rimmed glasses, Father Tucker observed, "Simply marvelous craftsmanship."

"Can I get you a drink, Rainier?" Grace's father said, obviously relieved to have been instructed to call the Prince by his casual name. Rainier asked for a whiskey and soda.

And thus the party began. Soon the room was loud with talk and laughter, and Grace marveled at how completely normal it all felt. As she sipped less and less nervously at her lightly spiked ginger ale, she began to slowly enjoy herself. Amazingly, it was like Rainier had been a friend for years — he appeared relaxed and to be enjoying himself immensely. She purposely kept her distance during cocktails because she knew her mother had seated them next to each other at dinner. When the time came to sit for the first course, Grace was grateful for the support of the familiar upholstered seat. She breathed a sigh of relief as she laid the red linen napkin on her lap. Rainier, slipping his own napkin out of its gold ring, leaned over to say in her ear, "At last some time with the beautiful woman I came to see," and Grace smiled with private pleasure.

"It's wonderful to see you again," she said. "Merry Christmas."

He took her hand in his beneath the table, pressed it gently before releasing it, and said in those smooth, low tones that reminded her of a saxophone played in its lowest register, "Merry Christmas, my dear. I am grateful beyond words to be here."

Though they spoke to each other at dinner, it was always part of a larger conversation with others at the table. Grace was relieved that her father steered clear of subjects that might stir controversy, like the recent events in Alabama, James Dean's death, or Eisenhower's reelection campaign following his coronary in the fall. Instead, the conversation stayed with Disneyland's opening and Jack and Margaret's plans to take the grandchildren there, and the new polio vaccine that promised to rid the world of "that horrid disease," as Margaret called it. Jack and Kell were even happy to excoriate the Yankees and praise the Brooklyn Dodgers for beating them in the World Series. Remarkably, Rainier had something witty and knowledgeable to contribute about all these American topics.

Before they adjourned for a dessert buffet of cookies, cakes, and ice creams in the living room, Grace said to Rainier, "I'm amazed at how much you know about American sports and amusement parks."

"I read at least five newspapers a day," he replied. "And the *New York Times* is one of those, though I have to admit that after a certain American actress came to my attention, I began to read the entertainment sections more closely."

Grace felt soft and warm like the wax of a melted candle, and she hoped her smile and blush showed him her gratitude.

After dessert, Father Tucker excused

himself to bed, as did Grace's parents and the Austins, all of whom said they should retire but that "you youngsters should continue the party."

"What about a game of bridge?" suggested Peggy, and everyone agreed.

Her sisters set up her parents' trusty card tables, giving Grace and Rainier a moment alone. He took her hand, and again she felt the sparks run up her arm. "I hope that tomorrow we might have some time to ourselves," he said. "I thought, perhaps, a picnic? The weather looks surprisingly fine, and I do love the fresh air."

"Perfect," she said. "It will be wonderful to spend some time together alone. I'll pack us a lunch."

The next hours passed in friendly competition, and Grace was thrilled to see Rainier fit in like he'd grown up down the street. The eight of them traded coy quips about the cards in their hands, and Rainier had them all in stitches, telling stories about a few of the croupiers and dealers who worked in the casino in Monte Carlo, regular workaday Monégasques Rainier counted as friends.

"Goodness," said Peggy, "I'd never guess you grew up in a palace."

Rainier smiled widely and said, "That is

the highest compliment you could pay me. I have never wanted to be an inaccessible prince."

Grace felt the meaning of his words reverberate inside her, and she smiled at how well Rainier and her sisters were getting on.

By one in the morning, everyone was stifling yawns, and Rainier said he ought to get to bed. "Shall we call you a cab?" asked Grace, embarrassed she hadn't thought of this detail before. "Our chauffeur has gone home, and —"

"Not to worry," said Rainier. "I have someone waiting outside."

"All this time?" Peggy gasped.

"He's been well equipped." Rainier smiled.

Grace glanced outside and couldn't believe she hadn't noticed the large black Mercedes parked on the street near the driveway. She'd been entirely focused on what had been happening inside the house. Goodness. She couldn't imagine what equipment it would take to occupy a grown man for six hours inside a car.

"Next time," Grace said, "please invite him in. At the very least, he can stay in the kitchen where it's warm and there's plenty to eat."

Rainier smiled and said, "What a fine idea," though she had the vague sense that he didn't really care one way or the other. But the evening had been too great a success to fret over a detail like that.

Her siblings gave them one more moment alone, when he had shrugged into his soft, thick overcoat. Curling an arm around her waist, he moved closer to her and she could smell the faint, musky notes of an aftershave. It was a seductive scent, and Grace closed her eyes and breathed it in as she allowed herself to absorb the heat from his body. She could feel desire building inside her, and she thought for sure he would kiss her on the lips, but instead he gently, lingeringly, kissed her left cheek, then murmured in her ear, "Tomorrow cannot come soon enough."

The next day, Grace felt unnerved by two men in suits and heavy overcoats who settled down on a tartan blanket four or five yards from them to eat their own cartons of chicken and spaghetti from a local Italian restaurant. She was unpacking the basket she'd brought for herself and Rainier — a picnic of leftovers made from what appeared to have been his favorite dishes the night before, along with a bottle of white burgundy. Grace had to ask: "Are those the same men who were waiting for you last night?"

"Georges was. At least one man must come with me wherever I go," he said with that same air of nonchalant resignation. "Security, you see."

"Of course," she replied, feeling silly for not noticing them before.

"It's strange, but they are like family, and yet I hardly notice they're with me all the time. We rarely speak, and yet I trust them with my life."

"Does it ever feel like a peculiar way to live?"

"That is difficult for me to answer, as I have never lived any other way," he said. Then he frowned and added, "But many of my friends have felt it to be. Peculiar, that is."

Grace had the sense that the peculiarities had cost him friends and surely also lovers. She knew of his long and troubled relationship with a French actress named Gisèle Pascal, but didn't want to pry into that any more than she wanted him to ask about Oleg or Gene. "I'm sorry to hear that," she said. "Having experienced life before being in the public eye, I can tell you that the lives of entertainers are peculiar as well. And even though your average Joe or Joan would swear up and down they would love to be us, the truth is, they really wouldn't." *Listen to me. I sound as jaded as Clark Gable!* Well, she thought ruefully, it had just taken her a few years to realize he was right.

"And yet, even to you, my life seems peculiar?"

Grace felt hot with embarrassment at how her earlier question must have sounded. "No, I mean . . . ," she stammered, feeling flustered, then decided it was best to be honest. "Well, yes, I suppose. The *press* follows me around, but not security men."

"Do you think you could accept them as a presence in your life? If there were enough good things to balance them?"

This was not an idle question; Rainier was only choosing his words carefully to give her an out. She saw that clear as day. Hadn't this been what she was hoping for, somewhere in her recently mended heart? She was fearful of it being rent again, as it had by Oleg, which must have been why she heard that buzzing in her ears, felt that tightness in her chest. She swallowed, and replied, "I think I could, yes. I've adapted to many other circumstances in my life."

"Indeed, you have." Rainier smiled playfully and added, "With grace, I might add."

She giggled, and said, "Oh, Rainier, you'll have to try harder than that!"

This little joke, this reference to their correspondence, lightened things between them. As they shared the wine she'd brought in a Thermos with an assortment of cookies, they laughed and talked, and another hour sped by.

"I'm very glad we have met again, Grace Kelly," he said, the intensity of his eyes on her face making her look away, down at the odds and ends left from their picnic.

"As am I," she agreed.

"Your family has been very kind as well, very welcoming. I enjoyed speaking with your father last night."

Well, you must be the first of my boyfriends to say that! Though *boyfriend* felt entirely inadequate to the task of describing Rainier. "They had a ball," she assured him. "Mother was in a bit of a tizzy before you arrived, I don't mind telling you, but I could tell she relaxed as the evening wore on."

"She is a perfect hostess," Rainier said. "The food was delicious, the surroundings homey and unpretentious. I know from your letters that your home life has been . . . more . . . *complicated* than what I saw last night, but I can assure you that my own unhappy parents would never have been

411

able to accomplish an evening like that one without someone bursting into tears."

Her heart swelled for the boy this man must have been. Grace put her hand on his, and said, "It must have been very hard to grow up that way."

"My mother, Charlotte, was a bastard, you know. Her father, Prince Louis II, fell in love with the beautiful daughter of the family's laundress and together they had a child out of wedlock — which did him no favors with his own father, His Serene Highness Prince Albert. Albert did his best to avoid recognizing my mother, but when it became clear that Louis would never marry another woman and produce a legitimate heir, he had to acknowledge her or else Monaco would fall into French hands." Rainier paused here to gauge Grace's reaction.

"Go on," Grace said, relieved to be hearing this story from Rainier himself. "I've done a bit of reading about Monaco" — *in fact, I've read of this very situation* — "and I know that if the current Prince produces no heir, Monaco will become part of France."

Rainier smiled at her, clearly pleased by her research, and nodded. "And of course no Prince or Princess can ever allow this to happen. But my mother was never meant to be Her Serene Highness. When my great-grandfather Albert passed the crown to my grandfather Louis, it was with the understanding that Louis would pass the crown to me. Never my mother. And to make matters more complicated, I have an older sister who feels she would do a better job as crown Princess than I could ever do as Prince."

Grace gasped — *this* she hadn't read anywhere. "Has she tried to depose you?"

"There have been whispers of it, but no proof yet. She and I are not close." The terseness and hurt in his tone was unmistakable.

This put the petty jealousies of the Kelly clan to shame, Grace thought. At least on Henry Avenue, there was no country at stake.

Squeezing Rainier's hand, Grace said, "I can see all the more why you want to give your own children a carefree youth."

Rainier sat up a little straighter from his reclining position, and took his hand from hers in order to tuck a lock of her still-bouncy hair behind her ear.

"When I am with you, I feel . . . understood," he said, his hand lingering on her cheek. It felt warm and reassuring, and Grace closed her eyes and inhaled his cologne once again — though today it was brighter, a spicy mixture of pine and cardamom and citrus.

"As do I," she murmured.

It was strange, but even though they traded flirtatious compliments and she was undeniably drawn to him, their connection felt much more chaste than her relationships in the past had. She thought about this in the back of her mind as they walked and talked for another hour or so, their hands occasionally brushing against each other's. She purposely left off her gloves, even though it was chilly, because she'd been hoping for the frisson of skin-to-skin contact with this man so that she could figure out if the chemistry between them was real enough, strong enough. A few years ago, she'd have said that it wasn't, that this gentle tug of attraction was nothing compared to the lusty magnetic pull she'd felt toward Clark, or Ray, or Oleg. And why should she settle for less?

But passion had gotten her nowhere, earned her nothing except heartache. She *was* attracted to Rainier, especially his voice, and oh, how he made her laugh — not with the kinds of corny jokes so many men in her profession relied on for easy laughs, but with funny allusions to their shared knowledge and sometimes a hilarious observation about a person or a situation they passed, like when they saw a man wrestling playfully with his golden retriever in McMichael Park, and Rainier remarked wryly, "I think they would make lovely puppies together, don't you? Though I must admit I think the bitch could do better." Grace had laughed hard at this unexpected gallows humor, which reminded her of the side-street theater Uncle George had taken her to as soon as she was old enough. She was impressed that Rainier didn't seem to be a snob despite the circumstances of his birth.

As the day wore on, she wanted more and more for him to kiss her. She was surprised he had not yet, especially as there had been opportunities throughout the day, and she wondered what was holding him back. If he was trying to stir her desire, it was working, though what she felt for him was at bottom girlish, strangely pure in a way. The thought of the passion she'd shared with other men made her feel exhausted. There was something energizing, if not exactly enthralling, in what she felt for Rainier — she felt an excitement about being with him, having children with him, living with him until they grew old together. Surely passion fizzled anyway after a few years? None of the old married couples she knew seemed ready to carry each other off to bed at the drop of a hat. No, that wasn't what sustained a couple. Shared values and shared laughter were what bound two people for life.

She had a feeling she had found that with Rainier Grimaldi. *Prince of Monaco,* Grace thought incredulously. And if she got to be a princess into the bargain of a happy marriage — well, what was so bad about that? She could accept a bodyguard if it meant a husband, children, the whole picture of domestic contentment she'd wanted for so long.

Reflexively, she could just see the odious gossip columns, hear the malicious whispers at parties from which she'd been excluded, speculating on her choice: "Cover Girl to Princess"; "Hollywood Royalty Not Enough for Grace Kelly"; "Hitchcock's Princess Dumps Him for Another."

Stop it, she told herself. *You know there's no point in entertaining any of that nonsense.*

As she was mulling all of this over from the squishy comfort of her childhood bed, there was a knock at her door, and her father asked, "May I come in?"

"Of course," she replied, sitting up and swinging her bare feet to the floor.

Grace couldn't remember the last time — if ever — her father had crossed the threshold into her bedroom. She had a feeling she knew what had prompted this rare appearance, and the somber but not unhappy expression on his face confirmed it. He took the chair from her desk and flipped it so that sitting on it, he would be facing her. He was so tall, the chair looked ridiculously small.

"I raised you to be a smart girl," he began, looking at his hands between his knees, then at her. "So I guess you know what I'm about to say." He paused, as if waiting for *her* to say it.

"Is this about Rainier, Daddy?"

"You know it is."

"I love him," she said. How strange that she should say these words out loud for the first time to her father, of all people.

"Well, that's good, because that priest told me last night that Rainier plans to ask you to marry him."

"A girl might like to be surprised by her proposal, Daddy," she said, feeling both unsettled and annoyed by this conversation. She'd regularly dodged little lectures by her father in childhood by running to the bathroom with a stomachache or saying she was so tired, she needed to turn in early.

Then she'd escape into this very room to read, play with her dolls, and daydream about what life far away from Henry Avenue would be like.

"Under regular circumstances, I would agree with you," said her father. "But this is anything *but* regular. You mother and I talked about this, and we agreed I should ask you before I give any kind of . . . permission."

"Has he asked you for permission?"

"Not yet."

"But you want to make sure I'd say yes?"

Her father nodded, and Grace felt a sudden gush of gratitude for her father. He was giving her an out, if she wanted one. He was willing to be the one to deliver the bad news, man to man.

"It's very sweet of you to ask, Daddy," said Grace. She took a deep breath and exhaled slowly before saying, "But I plan to say yes."

Jack leaned back in the chair, which crackled under the pressure of his long, lean body. He studied his daughter, folded his arms across his chest, and said, "You're sure about this, Grace? How long have you known the guy?"

The guy, as if he were a basketball player who wanted to take her to prom. *Am I still failing your tests, Daddy?* "We've been corresponding, sometimes two letters a week, for more than six months," she reminded him. "Seeing him after all that writing has just confirmed the feeling that has been growing in my heart."

This time, Jack Kelly rubbed his chin with two fingers, and Grace could see him move his tongue over his teeth behind his closed lips. After a while, he said, "Well, I couldn't have designed a better husband for any of my daughters. Catholic, never married, close enough to your age, successful, smart, and — it's hard to ignore — royal. I never would have imagined that for one of you girls, but now that it's an option, I can't deny it's far better than a Main Liner, who'd be a WASP in any case."

"So you approve?" Grace's heart was thudding hard and loud in her chest and ears. She wanted her father's approval, very much.

"I do," he said, and without even thinking, Grace leapt up from her bed and hugged her father.

"Thank you, Daddy," she said.

He returned her embrace and said, "I wish you every happiness, Gracie. You've done this family proud." His hug was so tight and affectionate, a tear of relief rolled down

Grace's cheek, which she just had time to wipe away before he let her go.

CHAPTER 26

The following week was full of so many momentous events, Grace constantly had the sense that something was escaping her notice, that her life was slipping ever faster away from her. The fact that she wasn't sleeping more than a few hours a night didn't help; she made sure to carve out nine hours of rest every night, but she found herself lying awake, feeling a pendulum swing inside her between incandescently happy and vertiginously afraid.

The best of the happiness was in New York City, where Rainier accompanied her because she had to begin the singing lessons for her single with Bing — a previously looming concern that now seemed infinitesimal compared to her other cares. In her favorite city, Rainier finally kissed her, at the door to her apartment on Fifth Avenue, and she was very pleased to discover that he knew what he was doing, how to hold and stroke her face and back as his lips explored hers. They stood and kissed for quite some time, but she did not invite him in, much as her body hummed with desire and curiosity.

On their second night in Manhattan, he took her for dinner at the Waldorf Astoria, where he was staying, and he was jumpy and distracted all evening, then seemed deeply irritated when they bumped into a doctor acquaintance of Rainier's, and his nurse, who invited themselves along for their planned walk in Central Park. Grace had a feeling she knew why Rainier was in a mood — it had already been two days since her conversation with her father, and even she'd begun to wonder when (*or if!*) Rainier was going to get around to popping the question.

At last, he grabbed her wrist on Park Avenue and literally jumped around a horse-drawn carriage, stranding the doctor and the nurse at a red light. He led her into the southernmost piece of Central Park, and stood very close to her and took both her hands more gently in his and said, "My dear Grace, I am sorry I've been miserable company tonight. It's only that I've been so nervous because I want to ask you, the most intelligent, accomplished, and beautiful woman I've ever met, to be my wife. Will you marry me, Grace? Please say yes." His face was so hopeful, like a child asking Santa for a special toy, and Grace felt her love for him explode in her heart like firecrackers.

"Yes, Rainier. Yes! I will marry you!"

His kissed her then, for only the third time since they had met. Somehow the fact that they had kissed only a few times made this romance even more like the fairy tale she had been refusing to tell herself about their relationship — with her playing the screen "princess" to his prince from a land so gorgeous and far away, it was the stuff of a children's storybook. The chasteness of their love made this story feel true, and made her feel somehow new again, as if her past was so irrelevant as to have not existed.

The sense of their love erasing her past made the fact that she had to submit to a gynecological test all the more jarring. "You have nothing to fear," said Rainier the day after his proposal. "It's only to see if you can have children."

Grace looked down at her hands. On her left was the brilliant diamond-and-ruby band Rainier had slipped on her finger the night before, whispering in her ear, "The real ring isn't ready yet. I'm so sorry. But I hope you'll be pleased with this placeholder. I didn't want to wait another day to make you mine."

They were sitting in her apartment, sharing breakfast at the gleaming and hardly used dining room table, and Grace fiddled with the hem of her Dior jacket, as she wondered fleetingly if she'd be able to bring this table with her to Monaco. She'd agonized so long over choosing it. But more urgent emotions swirled in her like a hot, bubbly mixture in a witch's cauldron. Part of her felt that this test was absurd — if he loved her and wanted to marry her, that was that. It shouldn't matter if she could have children or not. But then — he *was* a prince. And he'd made it perfectly clear that the crown prince of Monaco must produce an heir in order for the principality to remain independent. She was a practical enough person to appreciate that for Rainier, marriage was more than a matter of the heart; much as she disliked it, it was also his most important matter of business.

The truth was, she was far less worried that they would find her to be barren (after all, her mother had produced four children, her older sister two, and she was almost positive Lizanne was pregnant as well) than that they would inform Rainier she was not a virgin. She was fairly sure he knew this already, just as she knew that after his many years with Gisèle Pascal he wasn't, either. But to have his doctor and priest know it about her as well — and potentially judge her for it, as Oleg had? No, she had to find a way of asking if this detail would matter.

"Are you sure that's all they want to know?" she asked him. "I can assure you and them I'm perfectly healthy." *Oh, just be honest. There's no use in starting your marriage with deceit.* "It's just that I'm . . ." *For heaven's sake, just say the words.*

Rainier smiled indulgently, and Grace sensed he was happy to see her struggle to say what she wanted to say. "I know, Grace," he said smoothly. "And to be perfectly honest, I'm glad. I love you for your independence, not to mention your allure, and you didn't come by those traits by being a good little girl all the time. I promise that's not what the doctor is looking for."

Thank goodness. Almost instantly, she felt awash with relief. "All right," she said.

The test itself was little more than a standard annual physical, with the addition of plenty of questions about the reproductive history of her family. The following morning, when she saw Rainier and Father

425

Tucker, no one mentioned it. She must have passed the test because almost immediately, the next order of business was on the table, and it had her father shouting at her on the phone.

"That son of a medieval bitch wants two million dollars for you! As if getting my daughter isn't enough, he wants a *dowry*. It's going to be nineteen fifty-six in a few days, for Christ's sake."

"Now, Daddy," she began, wishing Rainier had warned her that this was part of the marriage contract. He'd already told her that there would be a contract, and that she would have a copy later in the day. Did her father already have his copy? How did he know this about the dowry already? "Daddy, remember, Prince Rainier is European royalty, and they do things differently from us."

"And don't even get me started on your mother," he railed on. "She's beside herself that the wedding can't be in Philadelphia."

This, at least, Grace had been prepared for. She'd even broached the subject with her mother before she'd left Henry Avenue, but her mother had been so feverish with excitement about the impending engagement, Grace didn't think her mother had heard a word she'd said.

"Daddy, we're all going to have to make some compromises to make this work, and —"

"Two million dollars is *not* a compromise, Grace! It's highway robbery! Are you sure this guy has *any* money of his own? What's he need two million of ours for?"

It was too much. Grace managed to get off the phone quickly, begging off on account of rehearsals for *High Society,* which she really did need to get to. But what she *wanted* to do was crawl under the covers and cry. Or sleep. It was only *money.* What was money compared to a lifetime with a man who made her happy? When would she ever have an opportunity like this again? This one had taken so long to arrive. . . .

But she had no time to indulge her distress. She put on her winter gloves, and took some comfort in the familiar sight of her hands encased in soft brown leather, even in the way they covered the temporary engagement ring. She was still herself.

On a break from her singing lesson, she called Maree, who was mercifully free for lunch. Grace had already made a series of euphoric phone calls to inform her closest friends about the engagement, but she had yet to have a good long chat with one of them. And today, with the tears threatening at every moment, she needed someone to whom she could admit her fears and frustrations about the test and the contract, and now her father acting menacing about Rainier. They arranged to meet back at Grace's apartment, because she just couldn't cope with the idea of the press hounding her elsewhere. She had Chinese food from a few blocks away delivered, and opened a bottle of wine, and when her friend arrived, she hugged her tightly.

"How's the future Princess?" her old friend asked. "You've come a long way from the Barbizon."

"I miss those days," Grace said, though it wasn't exactly true. She missed some things about those days — the sense that everything and anything was possible, that she was young and had plenty of time.

"Are you all right, Gracie?" Maree asked, her voice full of concern.

Why had she called her friend in the first place? Was she really going to admit all her fears and frustrations now? Everything was dammed up below her throat, the stormy waters raging in her chest and arms, all the way down to her legs. She felt like she might drown from within. What a relief it would be to open the floodgates.

Grace smiled and swallowed. "Of course

I'm fine," she said. "Just exhausted." Then she proceeded to pummel her friend with questions about *her* life as they drank wine and ate chow mein and moo shu pork with chopsticks, to avoid saying anything but the bare minimum about her own life. When Maree asked questions, Grace sidestepped them. *Do your parents like Rainier?* How could they not? *You haven't even announced the engagement yet and the press is all over you — can I help?* Oh, it's not as bad as all that. Thank goodness for this fortress of a building and taxis! *Are you happy?* Happier than I've ever been.

While they were eating, a messenger arrived with a large envelope emblazoned with Rainier's crest, and Grace knew exactly what it was. Setting it aside, she finished her lunch with Maree, though she felt the envelope's contents taunting her the whole time.

"Grace, are you sure everything is okay?" asked Maree.

I could tell her. Maybe she'd understand. But who could ever understand my father? And what it's like to be engaged to a goddamn prince? "Truly, I'm fine," she replied, fiddling nervously with the hemstitched edge of her pale blue linen napkins. "I'm sorry if I've been distracted."

Grace knew that Maree could sense there was another truth below the surface of her words. Her friend cocked an eyebrow ever so slightly and seemed to be searching for the right things to say. "I'm here if you need me, Grace. For *anything.*"

"Thank you," said Grace, her voice clogged with emotion. She cleared it, and added, "I suppose I'm getting some hay fever on top of it all."

"Take care of yourself, Grace. I mean it. Get some sleep. Eat an apple. Call your friends."

"I'll try," Grace said, suddenly anxious to have this imploring friend gone. Maree was making her uncomfortable. "In fact, maybe I'll lie down for a nap now."

"Good idea," Maree said, stroking Grace's arm.

As soon as Maree was gone, however, Grace tore open the fat envelope that had arrived during lunch. The contract. Skimming, she quickly found the sections her father had objected to; then she skimmed the rest to see if there was any reference to her acting.

Nothing. But she couldn't sigh with relief, because there was a terrible surprise lurking instead: should the marriage end for any reason, their children would remain in

Monaco with Rainier. She'd be relinquishing all rights to them. Again, a tempest raged inside her.

She closed her eyes and breathed slowly and deliberately, the air inflating her chest. And she prayed, as she had not prayed since she was a much younger girl, the girl who believed that God guided all her footsteps down the right path. These days, she knew she alone put one foot in front of the other, but in that moment, she felt she needed all the help she could get. In her mind, she pictured herself and Rainier with their children, golden from the sun, sticky from ice-cream cones, enjoying that "carefree stage of life" she and Rainier had not experienced with their own families but were determined to share with their own children. The storm inside her quieted a bit.

That evening, before she met Rainier for dinner, she prepared to call her father back by putting on her best armor — a stunning green brocade design of Edith's, pearls at her neck, diamonds on her ears, and white gloves on her hands. He should have had at least one whiskey by now.

"Daddy," she said, cutting to the chase, "I'll pay the dowry."

"No," he said firmly. Then, after a beat, he added, "What would people say?"

"No one has to know," she said.

"You really have that much dough?"

She wanted to relish the surprise in his voice, which had the flavor of being more impressed than floored. But instead, she found she was full of anger. *Yes, Daddy, Mother taught me to be frugal — always having to accept Peggy's castoffs as my own wardrobe — at the same time you were teaching me I was never enough unless I was the best. I was listening. I learned.*

"I can take care of it," she said. *Then will you be proud of me?*

There was silence on the other end of the line, the tinkle of ice in a glass. A swallow. Then he cleared his throat and said, his tone softer, "As it happens, your mother and I were just talking about this when you called. We can pay the dowry if Rainier agrees to have the wedding in Philadelphia."

She almost laughed at her parents' provincial negotiating. There was no way the wedding could be anywhere other than Monaco — only Margaret Kelly didn't seem to understand that the world would expect to see this wedding in the faraway fairyland Grace would soon rule over with her husband. And both of her parents appeared oblivious to the fact that this was her wedding, not theirs. *Though I suppose that's hardly surprising,* she thought bitterly. With the same fierceness she'd felt talking to Jay about MGM, she knew this was true: she was offering to pay the money so they didn't get to make demands. Besides, there was something much bigger than a wedding location she wanted from that contract, and she wasn't going to waste her capital on something that would make only her parents happy.

"Daddy, the location is fixed," Grace replied as gently as her gritted teeth would allow. "The wedding must be in Monaco. Can you put Mother on?"

In a moment, her mother had picked up the other house line in their bedroom, but didn't greet her daughter with any words, only an audible huff. "Mother, think how gorgeous it will be to get married in a cathedral overlooking the Mediterranean, among paintings and sculptures older than the Liberty Bell. It will be so glamorous and exotic, and you'll be the mother of the bride! The most important woman present. What would the dowagers at the Merion say about that?"

She waited, breathless.

It was quiet for a while.

Then it was her father who spoke, irascibly. "Grace is right, Margaret. I was saying the same thing to you earlier."

Imagine that. It seemed the mere prospect of this wedding had turned everything in the world inside out.

"Fine," said Margaret, and Grace knew her lips were pursed. "I know when I'm outnumbered."

"Thank you for understanding, Mother," gushed Grace. "We'll arrange a time to look at the spring dress collections very soon. I want to get you the most wonderful ensembles for all the events!"

She heard her mother hang up the phone, and then it was just Grace and her father again.

"I can't let you pay this guy," her father said. "It just wouldn't be right. But neither is him asking for it."

Ignoring her father's argument, for she knew there was no way she'd convince him otherwise, Grace went to her plan B: "How about you contribute one million, and I contribute the other? I don't know how much you have, but I certainly don't want to endanger your and Mother's retirement. And that way, if you want to crab about the dowry to all your cronies, you won't be lying about paying Grace's husband a fortune to marry her off." She hoped it was time for a little humor. She even crossed the index and middle fingers of her left hand; the right one was tightly clutching the receiver. Oliver sat patiently at her feet, wagging his tail in the hopes that she might play kitchen fetch with him soon.

"Is this how you got your contract done with Dore?" her father asked.

"Something like it," she replied, removing one glove and bending down to pet Oliver's head and ear. He licked her wrist.

"Then you're more my daughter than I realized. Done, Gracie. I hope he's worth it."

He's shown me more understanding than you ever have.

"He is, Daddy. You'll see."

There. One down, one to go.

The champagne-and-oyster course done, glasses of a deep garnet red sat before them as they awaited their holiday roast — a rich meal Grace could hardly fathom even nibbling in a ladylike fashion after so many other festivities and so little sleep and exercise, none of her usual long walks outside in the fresh air because of the threat of reporters. There was a brief lull in her conversation with Rainier, and she knew that now was the time to broach the topic.

"I received the parcel today," she said as

lightly as she could.

Rainier gave her an apologetic smile. "I'm so sorry our happiness is being held up by meaningless paperwork."

Yes, yes, the meaningless paperwork that will determine the course of the rest of my life. "Thank you, darling," she said soothingly, "I agree. It's maddening. I want you to know that Daddy was quite put out about the dowry, but I helped him see sense."

"I knew you would," he said, and she detected significant relief in his tone. She'd saved him a great deal of unpleasantness, and she hoped that knowledge would put him in the right frame of mind for her request. "And I want *you* to know," he went on, "that if it was up to me, we would dispense with such arcane practices. But the principality demands it."

Grace nodded. "I understand completely, and I know how hard you are working to modernize Monaco." She put her hand on his, and he immediately laced his fingers through hers. She felt heat and promise there.

"I am so lucky to have found you," he said.

She leaned over and kissed him on the cheek — it was more than a peck, and she took her time to breathe softly and suggestively in his ear. She felt his body tighten.

Pulling away, she took a coquettish sip of wine and said, "I'm afraid my mother is still fuming about the wedding being in Monaco instead of Philadelphia, but I suspect it's nothing that a little shopping won't cure."

"I have also sent your mother a token," Rainier rushed to put in, "which she ought to have received today, that I hope will help her forgive me on that score."

"I'm sure it will," she cooed. "She just wants to feel recognized, I think. Thank you for thinking of it, Rainier."

"I also noticed that your father appreciates good whiskey, so I had a case of the best Irish sent to him as well, along with a gold flask, to prove that the dowry isn't because I'm broke." At this, he smiled as if he'd just made a joke, and Grace giggled on cue, but she did think it was curious that her father and Rainier had both thought so alike on this subject. She couldn't dwell on that now, however; she had to stay focused. So far, the conversation was going well.

"Perfect," she said, moving her hand to his forearm. "There was one other thing in the *parcel* I wanted to discuss with you, though."

"Of course," he said lavishly, entirely focused on her, as if every word she uttered was the most important he'd ever heard.

"It's more than a question, I'm afraid," she said, biting her lower lip and withdrawing her hand to fold it with the other in her lap. "It's about the children."

"The subject of the children is not negotiable," he said, not unkindly but firmly.

"Please try to see this from my perspective, Rainier. The way it's written now — if you were to die, I would have to stay in Monaco with the children."

He nodded. "Because you would be the sovereign Princess. You would have to help our son rule the principality until he came of age, and raise our daughters to be well-regarded Princesses."

She had to admit, she had not thought about that — the fact that *she* would be in charge of Monaco if Rainier were to die before their child was old enough to take over. Now instead of feeling anger and anxiety, she felt fear. She didn't want power like that. But at the same time, she felt certain she would be able to take on the mantle if it meant helping her child.

"I hate to discuss these matters," she went on, changing tactic slightly. "I especially hate it when all I want is for both of us to be happy. But I must think of myself in some respects. I've been in charge of my own life for so long, including reading contracts. And of course, I think the world of you and believe you have no intention of doing me any harm. But what if . . . what if you were to leave me? It would add horrible insult to injury if I was cast out of your home and I lost my children at the same time. I beg you to consider this now, while our love is strong."

Rainier was impossible to read. He was still listening to her intently, but his face betrayed no emotion. This, more than anything else in their extraordinary court-ship, gave her pause. Could she marry a man she didn't yet know inside and out?

Of course I can, she answered herself immediately. How dull to have already learned all of your spouse's quirks and foibles by the time you walked down the aisle. How much more exiting to be at the start of learning about each other, with so many wonderful surprises in store. Her father was a man of big, obvious moods, as were Don and Oleg. Rainier would be a challenge, and this excited her.

"You raise a good point," he finally said. "And I am sensitive to it because of the plight of my own mother." Grace had been counting on this and hoped she had calculated correctly.

"And so I agree with you on this — to a

point. But what if you leave me? Then you are effectively leaving the principality, because it and I, and my children, are one."

Again, her lack of royal training had made her unprepared to reply to this argument, which she could understand from a certain point of view. She wanted to argue, to say that he and his country were *not* the same thing, but she knew that this was a matter of perspective. To her, an American girl born and raised in the City of Brotherly Love, where the very Declaration of Independence *from monarchy* had been signed, Prince Rainier was not Monaco. He was a man who loved her, whom she loved in return. But to him, raised in a tradition of warriors and treacherous crown stealers, it *had* to be that the Prince *was* the Principality.

He continued. "But I do see that if I choose to leave you, it's not the same thing as you leaving Monaco. So," he said with a nod of resolve, "I will ask my lawyer to change the paragraph to say that if the Princess leaves the marriage and thus Monaco, she will also be forgoing the children. But if the marriage ends for other reasons, you will have rights to see the children."

She knew this was the best she was going

to get out of this conversation; she'd been prepared for the possibility that he would not budge at all. So she kissed him on the cheek, said, "I am very grateful to you for seeing my perspective, darling," then changed the subject.

There was still one more test left that evening — one *she* was to administer and was sure he didn't realize he was taking. Privately, though, she'd told herself that if he didn't pass, she'd consider backing out of the engagement altogether. Because how could she marry a man who had the power to take her children but not deliver any pleasure, who refused to break any rules for her? The decision, and promise to herself, made her feel powerful.

"Come home with me tonight," she murmured in his ear as the taxi back to his hotel sat in traffic overflowing from Carnegie Hall. It seemed a lifetime ago that she had gone there every morning for classes at the Academy. She put her hand as high on his leg as she dared, and felt him shift uncomfortably in his seat.

"We shouldn't," he said, but his voice was thick with lust, and she could tell he was considering it.

"We'll be married soon enough," she said, beginning to bite his ear very gently. "As

441

long as you don't mind wearing a —"

He stopped her talking by kissing her on the mouth with a hunger that completely took her by surprise. Soon they were in her bed on Fifth Avenue, their evening wear haphazardly strewn between the door and her room, popped buttons and all, and he was passing her unspoken test with flying colors. His lovemaking was a delicious mix of rough and gentle, his body firm and strong. He gloried in her long legs, cupped her small breasts in his hands as if they were abundant, all he'd ever need.

What were the chances she'd ever leave this man anyway? This intelligent, witty, thoughtful man who was also a marvelous lover. She fell asleep to a soothing reverie of Rainier and their adorable children — one girl and one boy — coming to visit her on the set of another Hitchcock movie. No, better, a Broadway play. She could show the children how the pulleys that controlled the curtains worked — children always loved that. Her life would be complete at last.

CHAPTER 27

Her parents' house on Henry Avenue was decked out like a movie studio. The bedrooms and bathrooms had been made into greenrooms and dressing rooms, and in the living room, all the wood had been polished to a ruddy gleam, the porcelain lamps and vases and assorted other knickknacks dusted and shiny — the curtains had been steamed and the pillows fluffed. A few side tables and other antiques had been rearranged by the photographer for "balance and maximum effect," much to her mother's chagrin. This aspersion on her decorating was the only thing that troubled Margaret Majer Kelly that chaotic day — she was otherwise happier and more full of purpose in preparation for this press conference than Grace had seen her at even her siblings' weddings. "Isn't this amazing?" Grace heard her say to her father. "Our house, our *family,* in little old East Falls will be broadcast around *the world."* Yes, thought Grace to herself wryly, her mother seemed to have embraced the international concept of her daughter's wedding pretty quickly.

Upstairs, Grace stole a few minutes to herself in her childhood bedroom, the place she'd shed so many tears about school friends, then boys — *Don!* That saga seemed like a lifetime ago. Her mother hadn't thrown out her precious dolls, the ones that had kept her company on so many lonely afternoons. *They took direction so well,* she laughed to herself, remembering the plays she'd staged with them. She'd toted them every summer to the shore so they could be her playmates there as well, and they showed all these signs of use in their lilting eyelids, the cracked paint on their lips. Grace felt her nose get stuffy and wet heat needle her eyes at the memory of these dolls' company.

Don't be silly, she told herself, using a tissue to dab her eyes and nose, taking care not to disturb the powder and mascara. Then Oliver trotted up to her and barked for attention, and she was glad to laugh as she crouched down to pet him as he wagged his tail, though he tried to jump on her when she wouldn't let him lick her face as she usually did. She was in this state of affectionate struggle with her dog when

Rainier put his head around the door, which was ajar.

"May I come in?" he asked.

"Please do," she said. "And would you close the door?"

He whistled for Oliver and led him out before shutting the door and muffling the noise of the house. Then he crossed to her and took her hands in his, and when she glanced down, she saw the remarkable diamond ring he'd given her the night before. It was so large and sparkly she wanted to spend all day gazing at it, and yet she felt a simultaneous embarrassment at its size. With all her other jewelry, Grace had taken such care to wear only what was large and beautiful enough to convey taste, avoiding ostentation at all costs. But then, she'd always been single, and in her mind, single girls wore pearls. Married women wore diamonds, whatever Marilyn's hit song might have said. Still, she wondered what Edith would say when she saw this Cartier diamond ring. Her mother had said, "It's a good thing you're tall enough to carry off something like that," the jealousy in her tone crystal clear.

"My darling," Rainier said, "I want nothing more than to kiss you, but I fear I will be beaten by the woman who applied the color to your lips."

Grace laughed. "I think you're probably right."

"Are you ready?" he asked.

Grace heaved a great breath in and out. "As I'll ever be. I'm much more excited to leave this circus behind and go with you to California." *Where I can work, and forget about some of this madness.*

"But surely another circus awaits us there?"

"Yes and no. We'll be photographed, of course, but there's no harm in that because our engagement is public. And this is our main press conference, as everyone's been told," she said, gesturing down the stairs, where they'd soon be answering a score of the public's most pressing questions, "so I hope everyone will be satisfied for a while."

"I hope so, too," he said, "though I miss Monaco, where I can put more controls on this . . . this insanity."

"That sounds heavenly," she agreed. To live in the palace — where they had agreed to live, officially, "as grown-ups at last," Rainier had joked to Grace — was nothing short of a dream come true. She couldn't wait for those thick fortress walls to insulate her and this man she loved from the hoopla that had plagued her since her film career had taken off.

"You will make the most wonderful Princess," he said, kissing her cheek lightly enough not to disturb her makeup; still, the heat of his breath and the scent of his fine cologne sent a shiver of longing right through her. "Girls everywhere will look up to you."

"I just hope our own daughters will," she said, blushing at his suggestion. It really was a marvel that nothing he'd said had been less than perfect, almost as though he were reading from a script.

He'd just opened his mouth to reply when someone from downstairs shouted "Showtime!" and someone else rapped purposefully on her bedroom door. "Gracie! It's time!" Peggy. Even though her older sister wasn't going to be part of the press conference, she was there to help direct traffic, and if necessary divert their father.

Grace and Rainier gave each other *Let's get this over with* looks, and sighed at precisely the same moment and in the same rhythm, and they both laughed. "Already we are growing alike," Rainier commented, and the truth of this warmed Grace in her core. Hand in hand, they descended the stairs and let the cameraman tell them where to sit, nestled on a couch surrounded by Grace's parents and Father Tucker. Then the reporters who'd been waiting outside came filing in and stood clustered around the lights and cameras, holding their pens and notepads at the ready.

Soon the camera was rolling, and the list of vetted and rehearsed questions and answers rolled off everyone's tongue, even her father's. "Miss Kelly, what will be your first act as Princess?" *I'm sure there won't be a single first act, but that my duties will be many. I'll discuss them with Prince Rainier, and we'll decide together what will take priority.* "Prince Rainier, aside from your beautiful bride here, what has been your favorite thing about America so far?" *I appreciate how open the people of this country are. I have felt so welcome in the Kelly home, and in the home of their good friends the Austins. Even in New York, I found people in shops and on the street to be helpful and kind.* "Mr. Kelly, how does it feel to have a son-in-law who's a prince?" *It's a relief to know Grace is finally marrying a prince of a guy!*

Then one of the reporters asked a question that was off script: "Miss Kelly, when will you return to Hollywood? Your contract with MGM is only half-complete. Am I right?" Grace felt the blood rush from her cheeks into her toes. When she'd received the list of possible questions, she and Rainier had both crossed out every single one that had to do with her career, though they'd never discussed their reasons. She couldn't imagine that discussing it now would do any good. After she produced an heir and a spare — she'd laughed to herself that she was in such a position at all — it would be an entirely different conversation. Silence was once again her best weapon.

Now that the question had been posed, she felt Rainier tense next to her, saw him narrow his eyes and put his lower lip out very slightly, not in a pout but in an expression of determination. She laughed as if someone had just given her the nicest compliment, and she opened her mouth to say something polite but evasive, *How kind of you to ask about my acting, but of course my wedding is foremost on my mind at the moment.*

But Rainier spoke first, his tone firm and annoyed: "The Princess of Monaco will have more important duties than moviemaking."

Grace kept her smile plastered on, though a terse reply rose into her throat: *Wasn't it moviemaking that brought me to you?* But she swallowed it down like a too-big bite of holiday stuffing. *Silence, Grace,* she told herself. *Arguing will get you nowhere.* Glancing down at her lap, away from Rainier and the reporters and everything else, she saw her ring glittering up at her, an enormous kaleidoscope of light and promise.

In the back of her mind, she made a note to pack up all her dolls and have them shipped to her new home in Monaco. She had a feeling she might need their stalwart company from time to time.

She let a day pass before she brought it up. How could she not, when every single friend who'd read the article had called to demand answers from her, none more vehemently than Rita, who said, "Grace, you've worked too hard to give up acting for any man."

"I don't think of it as giving it up for a man," said Grace, feeling she was making excuses just as she had her whole life about her father. *It's nothing! I'm fine. . . .* "I think of it as prioritizing family. And anyway, he can't be serious."

"You might want to consider the possibility that he is," Rita warned.

To tell the truth, what bothered her most of all was the memory of how her father had clapped Rainier on the back as soon as the director said, "That's a wrap!"

"Nice work, Rainier," her father had said

to her future husband. "Welcome to the family."

And her mother had said nothing at all about what had transpired during the interview.

"Rainier," Grace began hesitantly. They were in his room at the Waldorf Astoria, where he was packing a few things to take to Los Angeles.

"Yes, my love," he said distractedly, frowning down at his overfull briefcase. It was very like the Mark Cross bag from *Rear Window,* she thought piningly.

"I haven't wanted to mention this, but I feel . . . I must." She'd hoped this would get his attention, but he continued frowning into his case.

"I wasn't altogether happy with our answer to the question about my career yesterday." *Our* answer, rather than the accusatory *your.*

Rainier closed his eyes briefly as he sighed, then shut the case and came over to the bed, where she was reclining as casually as she could on her elbow. "My darling," he said, sinking down next to her, "I was dissatisfied as well. Of course, they never should have asked the question to begin with, and they must have known that to do so would only cause trouble."

"It doesn't *need* to cause trouble," Grace said hopefully. She sat up on the bed and crossed her legs, because she was wearing trousers on this chilly January day.

"The way I see it," he said, picking up her fingers gently in his, "is that we ought to both come to this marriage *clean.* Our subjects do not need to be burdened by either of our pasts. We are making something new, you and I. We want different lives and families from the ones we came from. What better way to do that than to wipe our slates clean?"

So many of these ideas appealed to her, and even echoed the very thoughts she'd been having about the pureness of her affection for him. And yet . . . she had the sense that the way he was using these ideas did not follow the same logic that she did. She felt suddenly befuddled, unsure what to say next.

"I agree," she said. Because after all, didn't she? "Except I don't want to make moviemaking sound completely unimportant. To do so would insult many people I hold dear."

"I would never want to insult those you love," he said earnestly. "You must know that."

"I'm sure you wouldn't but . . ." Good

Lord, what *was* she trying to say? She felt she couldn't say the essential thing, which was that she wanted to continue making movies because she knew he would not be able to agree to that now. She knew in her bones that she had to bide her time. He loved her so much, how could he ever stand in the way of her doing the very thing that made her who she was? She had to trust that love.

She did trust it.

She leaned over and kissed him on the lips and said, "Can you please just let me handle the answers to those questions from now on, should they come up? I'll know how to deliver the message in a way my colleagues and friends will understand."

He kissed her back, then pulled away. "Be my guest," he said. "I am more than happy to cede the floor to my beautiful bride."

They began kissing more deeply, and though she wasn't entirely reassured by their conversation, his trust in her was enough. For now. Was there ever anything else than now anyway? She let herself be pulled back down to the bed and into his arms, where she felt loved and admired, and full of a purring anticipation about his every next move.

■ ■ ■

The holidays over, the weather in the north-
east turned the iron gray and cold of midwinter. It was such a relief to wake up in
her Hollywood hotel suite, and open her
curtains to a blue sky that promised sunshine and warmth. Rainier had a room
down the hall, for show. They had breakfast
sent up every morning, and ate in compan-
ionable silence, buttering toast, pouring coffee, and trading newspaper sections until
she had to prepare to leave for the studio.
She felt positively bubbly with happiness,
and couldn't wait to get started on *High
Society,* couldn't wait to see Edith and Bing
and Frank.

All was hugs and kisses when she stepped
onto the set — everyone from Bing to the
makeup artists and seamstresses. Congratulations filled the air, and Bing even produced a bottle of Veuve Cliquot and popped
the cork to a round of excited murmurs. He
poured the fizz into flutes and topped each
one off with orange juice, and when everyone had a glass, he raised his and said in his
smooth crooner's voice, "To Grace Kelly,
the future Princess of Monaco. I hope you
know you've never been anything less than

a princess to us."

"Hear, hear!" everyone chimed in as they clinked their glasses together. The only thing missing from the moment was Edith. But maybe she wasn't on set yet. Frank caught Grace's left hand in his and gave the Cartier ring a long, hard look, then whistled. "Man alive, there's nothing like seeing another man's boulder on a woman's finger to make a guy feel like a schmuck."

Grace laughed and gave him a kiss on the cheek. "You're anything but a schmuck, Frank."

Not long after, Grace found Edith in her dressing room. "Edith!" she exclaimed, crossing the room to hug her friend. "You missed the champagne."

"It's not my favorite before noon," she said, unusually evasive, which put a hard lump into Grace's chest.

"Well," Grace said with a gusty breath of excitement to show Edith there were no hard feelings — though she did sense that a fairy-godmother reference right now would be met with worse than the usual snarl. "What have you got for me to wear today?"

All business, no bibbidi-bobbidi, Edith put Grace in a few possible outfits for Tracy Lord's first scene in the movie, and decided on the camel pants and shirt. "Casual and rich. Very Newport cottage. And you should wear that," she said, tapping a pencil on Grace's ring.

"You think?" The thought of wearing her engagement ring in the movie thrilled her.

"I was going to borrow one from Tiffany's, but they wouldn't let us borrow anything even half that size. And Tracy's supposed to be marrying something of a robber baron. Anyway, it will appear smaller on-screen."

The antipathy in her tone was unmistakable. Edith could get in a mood sometimes, like anyone else, but dressing her favorite actresses usually snapped her out of it. "Edith," Grace said cautiously, "is everything all right?"

Edith sighed and crossed her arms over her chest. She appeared to be mulling over her words carefully. The lump in Grace's chest began to throb.

"Is this really going to be your last movie, Grace?" Edith asked.

"Of course not," she replied.

"Prince Rainier seemed quite sure that it would be. I read the interview."

Grace had been assiduously avoiding all newspapers and magazines just so she wouldn't have to keep reading about that blasted interview. "Oh, come on, Edith. You know the papers make everything sound

456

worse than it is."

"I believe the words that came out of his mouth were 'The Princess of Monaco will have more important duties than moviemaking.' How could anyone make that sound worse?"

"He'll change his mind, Edith." *How could he not? He fell in love with a movie star, not a hausfrau or a country club dilettante.*

Edith scrutinized her with more canniness than she had for any outfit. Then she said, "Grace, most men are used to getting what they want, without any argument from a woman. But Rainier was raised a prince. He is more conditioned than most to getting . . . full cooperation."

"He's not like that, Edith, I promise. He listens to me. We want the same things."

"Does he listen to you when you want different things?"

"Yes, of course," Grace immediately replied, though once the words were out of her mouth, she realized how little they'd ever disagreed. Still . . . when they talked about the marriage contract, he'd listened to her. And he *had* said she could be the one to talk to the press about her career. And they wanted the same things, the important things, for the family they would make together, which was much more than she could say for the men in her past.

"Good," Edith replied. "So," she said, her tone shifting into its more familiar firm but friendly notes, "let's talk about your wedding dress. I already know it can't be by me, because Dore's going to order it for you and make MGM out to be the generous studio it's anything *but,* so let me give you some tips for what to tell whomever they do hire. I'm putting in a word for Helen Rose."

Bibbidi-bobbidi.

Everything felt right again. As Edith fussed over another batch of outfits, the strangest thought came to Grace's mind: who would play Maggie in *Cat on a Hot Tin Roof* once the Broadway run was over, as Grace would no longer be available? If she had one regret in all this, it was that she wouldn't be able to play Maggie in the movie; she'd wanted to play that role forever. *I've wanted to be a wife and mother just as much,* she told herself. *And to a prince, at that! You've always wanted too much,* she scolded herself. *Be happy with what you have.*

CHAPTER 28

If 1955 ended on the highest note possible, 1956 did not ring in well. In January, just as she was enjoying the making of her final film as Grace Kelly, and luxuriating in the warm sunshine and delicious West Coast meals with Rainier, her mother made the outrageous decision to give an exclusive five-part interview on "My Daughter Grace Kelly: Her Life and Romances" to the Hearst Corporation, which meant it would be printed in half the major newspapers in the country! Grace couldn't remember ever being so angry.

"Mother," she screamed into the phone when the final installment came out, because she couldn't contain her anger any longer, "you sound like an inexperienced psychologist! 'Having achieved so much fame, Grace could not perhaps have found happiness with the boy around the corner,' " she read to her mother from the first article.

"And you leave out the names of certain boyfriends out of respect for *their* privacy, but what about *my* privacy, Mother?!" She was practically choking on her own words now. Her entire body trembled with fury.

"I have no idea what you are so angry about," said Margaret blithely. "I didn't want all the vicious rumors about you to fester into facts that your prince might find believable. I thought it best to nip it all in the bud. I didn't say anything that wasn't true, did I? And I tried to cover up some of what I suspect also went on."

"Oh, yes, Mother, you talk about my name being 'linked' to famous actors, but you never come out and confirm or deny anything because *you don't actually know what happened*! But anyway, that's beside the point! You have no right to talk about *my life* in the press! You're my mother," she sobbed. "You're supposed to be my port in the storm."

"I'm your mother, and I'm supposed to do what's best for you. Your father agrees," Margaret replied.

I will be a different kind of mother, Grace vowed as she slammed down the phone, wondering, too, what role her father might have played in this little maneuver. Was it possible he'd put her mother up to the interviews? It was much more his style to malign her in the press. Miraculously, Rainier laughed when he saw the articles. "Mothers are not perfect," he said with remarkable calm, and even a note of amusement. "And after all, she was politely vague about what happened between you and Gable and the rest. And she did donate her interview fee to charity."

Then, as she started to cry, he ran his hand soothingly up and down her back and said, "I'm glad of the opportunity to help you distance yourself from this . . . unpleasantness. You don't have to do this alone anymore," he said.

Why did this make her want to cry all the more?

By the time she boarded the SS *Constitution* in New York on April 4, Grace was exhausted and almost ten pounds thinner from the stress of trying to make everyone else happy with *her* wedding. Life had been more than a whirlwind; it had been an absolute tornado. There were all the last-hurrah events to attend and long lists of musts to accomplish. Goodbye dinners all over New York and Hollywood. She'd packed up all of her essentials from Henry Avenue and her New York apartment — her beloved apartment, which she'd hardly gotten to live in at all. She'd filmed *High Society*, recorded the single for "True Love" with Bing, and attended the Academy Awards, where as last year's winner for Best Actress, she'd had the honor of giving the Best Actor award to Ernest Borgnine for *Marty*, then partying one last time with her Hollywood compatriots.

All the while she fantasized that the sea passage to Monaco would be a break of pure fun with only her best friends and family — dinners, dancing, shows, and shuffleboard — but somehow a murder of crows had been allowed on the ship. Scores of reporters set upon Grace and her most favorite people like hungry black birds upon corn. "Unless you want me to have a nervous breakdown, keep them away from me," she hissed at Morgan Hudgins, the MGM press agent who was on the ship with them. She made sure her voice was full of an edgy, nearly hysterical vehemence, and he actually listened and did his best.

It took some subterfuge and organizing of events in the larger of the private staterooms, but Grace did manage to relax and spend time with her friends on the eight-day journey across the Atlantic. *I deserve some fun,* Grace told herself after another late night of singing and charades. And she found that the presence of the press had its uses, specifically as a perfect excuse to avoid her parents, except to smile and link arms with them in the required photographs.

On one of the final days, she invited Judybird and Maree and Peggy, all of whom would be bridesmaids, to her room for lunch and manicures. Sandwiches and iced tea and petits fours were all sitting out, as well as a buffet of red and pink lacquers.

"You need to eat more than sandwiches and tea cakes, Graciebird," said Judy when she arrived, a little early.

Grace sighed. "I know. I've lost too much weight in the last few months."

"And you didn't have any to spare!" her friend exclaimed.

"I don't know what to do," said Grace, for this weight loss really did make her despair — on top of the despair that had caused it. "I blame my mother and those treacherous articles."

"Well, I agree that the articles were horrible and uncalled for. But . . . you can't blame her for not taking care of yourself. You'll be a mother yourself soon, and you'll have to set a good example."

Grace sighed and thought that Judy, who was already a mother, probably had a point.

Still, she said, "I hope I have at least a few months to just be married first. And I don't know how to eat when I'm too busy to eat, or when the thought of food is" — how to even describe the way even the thought of food had triggered a gag reflex for the last few weeks? — "worse than unappealing," she said inadequately.

"Poor Graciebird," Judy cooed, putting her arms around Grace, who felt impatient with herself for wanting to cry yet again. Oliver, who always seemed to know when she needed rescuing, trotted up to her and gave a little jump up her leg, and Grace scooped him up and let him lick her chin. *I love you, too,* she telepathed to her dog.

Soon enough a gaggle of girlfriends had gathered around, nibbling and laughing, each of them taking a turn to ask if Grace was excited or nervous. In the distracting comfort of their company, Grace managed to eat a whole sandwich and two cakes before Peggy expertly filed her nails and painted them a lush and shiny crimson.

That night, there was a formal dinner, and Grace grimaced when she saw that she'd been seated next to her mother amidst the gleaming silver and crystal. During the cocktail hour, she avoided her parents and focused on the friends she knew she wouldn't see again as soon as the ship docked in Monaco and she had to take up the mantle of princess-to-be. The thought of the schedule that awaited her made her dizzy, and she shoved it out of her mind as she talked about the upcoming Red Cross Gala in Monte Carlo, her honeymoon stops around the Mediterranean on Rainier's yacht, and her gratitude for the thirty-six women who had sewn Helen Rose's confection of a dress into being for its trip down the aisle of St. Nicholas Cathedral in just a week's time.

"It's all impossibly glamorous," rhapsodized Muriel Gaines, an old friend of her mother's, a bejeweled hand on her chest.

"It is, isn't it? I feel very lucky," Grace agreed with what she hoped was an effusive enough tone of breathless gratitude and anticipation. Because glamorous was how it appeared to everyone else, and the last thing she wanted was to disappoint all the kind people who'd spent so much money and time to help celebrate her marriage. In spite of the three-ring circus it had become, Grace occasionally caught breathless glimpses of how poignant and magical it all appeared.

When it was time for the first course, Grace found her seat and busied herself with her napkin and water glass.

"You can't avoid me forever," her mother said quietly, leaning over and speaking low so only Grace could hear. "I'm not even sure what you're so angry about. Haven't you gotten everything you wanted?"

Grace looked into her mother's eyes, searching for some note of irony, the tiniest recognition that maybe her second daughter wasn't entirely happy. If it was too much to admit that the interview she'd given was in bad taste, maybe her mother could at least see that Grace was suffering? And reach out to comfort her?

But Grace saw none of that sympathy there. *Am I too good an actress? Have I managed to fool even my mother into believing this is a fairy tale?*

"I'm not angry, Mother," said Grace, and she was surprised to find it was true. "I'm . . . . afraid." The truth of the word stunned her as soon as it was out of her mouth.

"You? Afraid?" her mother said, eyes wide with genuine surprise. "How can the only child of John Brendan Kelly who never did his bidding be afraid?"

Oh, my God, Grace thought, her mouth open not in reply but in utter shock. All the times she'd stood on stages, wishing and

466

hoping, and all along . . . her mother had seen?

And done nothing? Nothing to take the sting out of her father's words? Nothing to acknowledge how hard it had been for her to be Grace Kelly?

I'm sailing away from all this right now, she thought, and the relief that thought brought her was so great, it temporarily lifted the weight from her shoulders, allowed her to breathe air into her tightened chest.

"Yes, Mother, I'm afraid," Grace managed to whisper.

Her mother put her right hand on Grace's left, covering her engagement ring. "You'll get through it. You always do," Margaret said, and Grace heard the thickness in her mother's voice, saw the glassiness in her eyes. Grace felt her heart burst in her chest. Then, before she could respond, Margaret turned away and said, almost to the menu, "You'll have plenty of time to rest when you're a princess."

CHAPTER 29

When Grace stepped off the SS *Constitution* with Oliver cradled in one arm so the other was free to wave to the thousands of people who had gathered at the dock and in the streets to get a glimpse of their new Princess, Grace was overcome with an uncharacteristic bout of shyness. *These are my subjects,* she thought, and the idea was surreal. The sea of applauding, waving people looked more like an audience. She preferred to think of them in this familiar way; it helped her smile back at them from under the protective wide brim of her hat.

Moments later, she was by Rainier's side in his yacht, the *Deo Juvante II,* and the crowd cheered louder, which she'd never have thought possible. "Darling, I am so happy to see you," she said, leaning over to kiss him on the cheek. More frantic applause. It was beyond her wildest expectations. They were two people getting married, for heaven's sake! It wasn't like they'd just done the unabridged *Hamlet*.

He kissed her as well, though she could tell it was all performance and left her feeling unmoored. She wanted desperately to lean on him and whisper how much she wanted to escape. But before she could make another move, he waved jubilantly to the crowd and spun the yacht into a foamy circle. The sound of the motor, and the crowd, the sudden, choppy movements of the boat in the water, nearly made Grace double over and retch. "Please, Rainier," she said, and though she shouted it, she doubted anyone else heard, "steady the ship or I'll be sick."

He did as she asked, then said as he slipped an arm around her, "We'll have to limber up your sea legs, Princess. This is Monaco, after all."

Then he looked back out at the cheering audience with as much pride as if he *had* played Shakespeare's Danish prince, and said as he waved, "And see, they love you! We wouldn't want to disappoint them."

"No, of course not," she said, linking one arm through his and waving out at them by his side, thinking to herself that this was the most thunderous reception she'd ever received, and for work that had next to nothing to do with her.

And so began a week of such decadent lunches, dinners, dances, and shows that Grace reflected to Judybird and Jaybird that even the ancient Romans had nothing on Monaco. When her father remarked on the bottles of Cristal and enormous baskets of fruit and cheese and candy in every guest room of the opulent Hôtel de Paris, "Now I know where the dowry went," Grace couldn't help but laugh.

"See, Daddy," she teased back, "I told you Monaco was in the black."

She felt she must smile and compliment it all, even if the Irish Catholic part of her that had grown up wearing her sister's castoffs occasionally thought, *This is too much.* She genuinely loved the flowers. Her own guest quarters of the palace looked like the inside of her favorite New York florist, Max Schling — festive sprays of exotic blooms as well as more familiar ones in artful arrangements sat in gleaming bowls and vases on practically every surface. The colorful petals and leaves had the effect of enlivening the palace, which had seemed so dark and staid on her first visit. The flowers and the fact that every piece of silver, every bronze or gold statue and sconce, had been polished to within an inch of its life. And now that she knew it was to be her home, Grace was glad of the palace's modest scale. She remembered how uncharitably she'd thought of its size, comparing it unfairly to Versailles, on her first visit when she'd been annoyed at everything from the French workers' strike to Rainier's lateness (he'd never been late again!). She couldn't imagine living anywhere larger than the Palace of Monaco. Even its current size filled her with trepidation — she was to be mistress of all this?

At every event, Grace tried to do something personal, like breaking away from a group of well-wishers to accompany Judy to the relative calm of the ladies' lounge in order to wish her and Jay a happy anniversary and apologize profusely for not being able to do more than express her felicitations in words. Though Judy was quick to tell her that she was being ridiculous, that in her place she wouldn't have remembered what day it was at all let alone that it was someone else's wedding anniversary, Grace felt it necessary to hold on to such small moments or else she'd get utterly swept away by the high tide of emotion and extravagance. Even the cars in Monaco were extraordinary — only the finest Rolls-Royces, Mercedes, and Bentleys drove the streets. And the fashion! Even on Fifth Avenue, she'd never seen such a high concentration of couture. She knew from her previous visit, and from the reading she'd done about the principality, that it had long been a playground for the wealthiest people who had millions to throw away in the casino and jewelry stores, but the wedding had amplified the ostentation by a magnitude of at least one hundred. It was mind-boggling that she was supposed to be Rainier's partner here, ruling over this extraordinary place. If she let herself think about it too long, she started to feel shaky in the knees and light in the head. She clung to what felt real — her friends and their shared history.

The most real moment she shared with Rainier was their last Tuesday night as unmarried individuals; soon they would be one, a single unit. After another formal dinner, at which her stomach simply said no to every creamy, glistening item on her plate, he laced his fingers through hers and lifted her hand to his mouth to kiss her hand. "Meet me in the chapel in an hour," he said quietly, referring to the small church in honor of St. John the Baptist at the west end of the palace.

She changed into a simple cotton skirt and sweater with her horn-rimmed glasses because she was so tired, she could hardly see at all, and he arrived wearing khakis and a white shirt under a navy sweater. His dark hair was freshly washed, and a bit tousled and wet. He looked so handsome that way, and she looked forward to seeing him be more casual in the future. She'd had about enough of tuxedos and ball gowns. He kissed her hello, then took her hand and said quietly, "I want to show you something."

They got into his Mercedes convertible, with the top up for privacy, and he began driving. "Where are we going?" she asked.

"I want to show you La Turbie. It is a true kind of place, salt of the earth. No yachts and nonsense. It's where we might want to consider raising our children."

The headlights of his car lit the way up the precipitous climb out of Monaco. Within minutes, the principality was far below them, and they were in France. The road was narrow and harrowing. She wasn't even driving, and she didn't dare take her eyes off the road, knowing that if she looked out or down, she might actually faint from the unprotected height.

"I don't know how you drive these roads,"

she said, trying to breathe slowly to calm herself.

"I grew up doing it." He shrugged. "You'll get used to it in no time, I'm sure. Did you not actually drive that car in *To Catch a Thief?*"

"Goodness, no," she said. "That was all done in a studio with the scenery added in later. For the picnic scene, we were transported in very safe cars that drove like snails at my request."

"Am I driving slowly enough for you?"

"Yes," she lied, for even a walking pace might have been too much for her that night.

Fortunately, the drive to the charming medieval town of La Turbie was short. Rainier parked in front of a little bistro with a worn blue-and-white awning and led her inside. The man behind the tidy but aging wood bar, Guy, greeted him warmly, and they chatted in French, laughing and joking about what sounded like Guy's son and daughter. Rainier introduced Grace to Guy, who bid her welcome and congratulations in French. She replied as best she could with the high school French she'd lately revived with a few lessons in New York. She'd need more earnest tutoring soon.

They sat at the bar and drank espresso

and shared a piece of a delicious *tarte aux prunes* before Rainier took Grace's hand again. After he grabbed a flashlight out of the trunk of his car, they walked along the edge of the steep cobbled streets, past the town's church, until they reached an ancient and still ruined arch. The soft silence of the town was heaven after the hoopla of Monaco. The only sounds were the occasional clinks of dishes or a baby's cries in the distance.

It was night, but clear, and so the moon and stars lit up the town in a kind of glowing violet light. Rainier hadn't yet turned on the flashlight, so all she could see were the general contours of buildings, shrubs, and climbing flowers. At a grand arch, he finally switched it on and said quietly, reverentially, "This is the Trophée des Alpes. It was built to celebrate Emperor Augustus's conquering of the Alps six years before Christ. The stone came from eight hundred miles away. Can you imagine?"

Fingers still intertwined, she followed him and the beam of his light as it moved slowly over the craggy surface of the huge Roman monument. Her eyes traveled up and up, taking in the crumbling magnificence of the site. "Was it bombed in the war?" she asked.

"Miraculously, no. It was ruined over

centuries, of course, but some enterprising philanthropists in the twenties began restoring it. It's quite an important piece of history."

"I can see that," she said, taking in the grandeur of the columns far above her, the round shape atop the enormous stone base. There would have been an impressive dome there nearly two thousand years ago.

"I find it inspiring," said Rainier. "The cooperative labor of men to build something that would last far beyond their times. The Romans modernized Europe. They are my inspiration for Monaco, which sorely needs modernization."

"And large trophy buildings?" she joked.

"No," he said with a smile. "But I'm sure you've noticed that we do need new buildings. So many of the old ones are falling apart. Even the poorest Monégasques should have a decent place to live, with shutters or awnings to keep out the sun, fresh paint, and modern plumbing."

These noble wishes, unconcerned with the residents and visitors who drove the fancy cars and wore the couture, made Grace's heart expand with warmth and admiration. *I'm marrying this man,* she thought, and she kissed him on the lips. He responded, but the flashlight made it laughably difficult to embrace properly, and so they wound up in a fit of giggles. "Come," he said with a nod of his head toward the other side of the monument.

"Oh," she gasped when she saw the view. Spread out before her was a vast descent of dark land, dotted by twinkling yellow and white lights. Shadows of houses, trees, roads, and other swells and hollows varied the deepest greens and blacks on their way to the inky sea. She could just make out where the water met the coast, and she could even faintly hear the far-off rushing of the water as it lapped against the sandy, rocky earth. Lights from boats in the harbor illuminated the surface of the deep with glowing, rippling halos.

Rainier was standing very close to her. She could feel his whole body behind her, its heat and contours. He rested his chin on her shoulder, and they looked out together at the spectacular view. "It's yours, my love," he whispered in her ear, sending shivers of both desire and awe down her spine.

It can't be, she wanted to say. "It's the most beautiful thing I've ever seen," she said.

"I hope it proves worthy of the sacrifices you're making," he said.

This acknowledgment was too much; her

heart overflowed, and she felt tears make her eyes wet and hot. *Do not cry,* she told herself. To stanch the flow, she turned toward him without another word, took the flashlight from his hands and placed it on the ground, then set about kissing him with all the passion she had, enough to obliterate everything else in her mind and heart.

Legally, they were married the day before the mass at St. Nicholas Cathedral, which would be televised and broadcast around the globe. *My most watched live drama,* Grace joked to herself. But on April 18, 1956, she wore a tea-length pink brocade dress that was just the sort of thing Edith would have designed for her to wear on the occasion, and she met Prince Rainier in the Throne Room of the palace with only their family and closest friends, where they were married in an intimate but long ceremony before Marcel Portanier, President of the State Council, Director of Legal Services, and Civil Status Officer of the Princely Family.

Monsieur Portanier spoke of devotion and sacrifice, then read from the seemingly interminable Civil Code all their respective rights and duties as Prince and Princess, then the astounding one hundred forty-two titles that she now shared with His Serene Highness. Having already gone over these details in the marriage contract, Grace found herself tuning out and practicing a game she'd learned at the Academy, in a movement class. She sat perfectly still, as if she'd been turned to stone. As a statue, she heard a great many noises behind her, honking and blowing and sighing and sniffling. It was a great challenge not to laugh at the mucusy humanity all around her. But the sounds and the exercise made this public reading of law tolerable.

Her gloved hand shook as she signed her name in the register, her heart throbbing blood dangerously fast through her body and so loudly she could hear it in her ears. But as soon as she'd done it, she felt relieved. Her heart slowed as Rainier signed his name, and when he kissed her in front of everyone gathered, she felt lighter and happier. "Are you ready to let your subjects congratulate you?" he asked, eyebrows boyishly raised, voice expectant as a child's on his birthday morning.

She didn't dare speak, but nodded as eagerly as she could.

He led her out of the room and to the marble balustrades of the Hercule Gallery. Hand in hand, they looked down and out onto the thousands of people gathered in the courtyard, who erupted with ecstatic cheers when their Prince and new Princess waved at them. Grace beamed her best smile down at these people, who apparently loved her as their Princess, an extension of their love for their Prince, while she tried to draw strength from the people *she* loved standing behind her.

It's just like a theater, she kept telling herself as she waved and smiled. *You've finally gotten what you always wanted.*

When she looked back on her wedding, it would be that day she remembered most clearly and fondly. The next day — the day she wore the dress MGM had designed and paid for, the day heavy with jewels and symbolism, overtaken by prayer and photographs — was a complete blur. She was Catholic, and she wanted to feel that the religious ceremony was the most important. She expected to feel a kind of beatific joy enter her heart as Monseigneur Barthe of Monaco and Father Cartin of Philadelphia — a compromise measure Father Tucker had invented to appease her parents about the wedding location — married them beneath the gold-and-lapis mosaic of God the Father and His Son, in the dome high over their bent heads. But she was so nervy from all that had gone before, so anxious for the whole spectacle to be over, she found it difficult to treat the endeavor as anything more than a performance in the finest costume of her career.

She did remember feeling thankful for the cool spring morning as she knelt before the altar in her heavy, modest dress because St. Nicholas was a small cathedral, and with so many people in the pews, it felt too warm and close inside. The perfectly pitched music of the organ and the choir was nonetheless too loud for the space and made her feel almost claustrophobic. When at last she could rise from her knees, knowing the ceremony was nearly over, she felt enormous relief.

At last, Rainier could kiss her freely before God, and when he did, all their friends clapped and cheered and whistled, just as they would have done in an American wedding, and she was so glad for this familiar moment. When she turned to face all the people who were standing and looking at her and Rainier — her *husband* — she saw their tears and smiles and hands on their hearts. She held Rainier's hand as they walked down the nave, smiling and whispering thanks to family and friends in the pews. When the heavy doors of the cathedral opened with a boom and a creak, Grace caught a glorious blurry glimpse of the same blue sea she'd so loved that night with Rainier in La Turbie, perfectly framed by the rectangular doorway. Bright, sunlit color encased by darkness, shadow. And then their people and the press swarmed, and it was gone.

CHAPTER 30

1976

When Engelbert Humperdinck took the stage at the annual Red Cross Gala, his baritone voice smoothing over everything like a velvet cloth as he sang "Release Me," Grace felt that she could take full breaths for the first time in weeks.

First, there had been Caroline's threat to quit university, which Grace could only assume was linked to her budding romance with the mysterious Philippe Junot, whom Grace thought far too old for their nineteen-year-old daughter — seventeen years older!

Then there had been Jay Kanter's very sweet phone call about a movie called *The Turning Point,* which offered, as he put it, "that rare opportunity for a woman of a certain age to rebuild her career." In a rush, she had felt all the pain of her youthful folly in not listening to Rita and Edith, of hoping that even after Rainier had outlawed the showing of all her movies in Monaco, he might still see that she needed to act. The pain of realizing too late that she had vastly overestimated his love for her. She couldn't stand it. It wasn't worth feeling that way when there was nothing she could do to change the situation, so she'd called Jay back after a respectable day of "thinking" to politely decline.

And if she was being honest, which she felt she could be only within the confines of her own skull, she was sick to death of planning the Gala. She'd been doing it since '56, for two full decades. After Josephine's second appearance in '74, standing in for Sammy Davis Junior at the last minute, Grace had been tempted to hand the baton to someone else. How could it ever be the same, after dear Josephine sang "Lonesome Lovesick Blues" for one of the last times in her life?

"Why don't you join me onstage?" Josephine had asked Grace on the telephone before that memorable night. "I'll do Bing and we can sing 'True Love.' "

Grace laughed so hard at the image of the two of them doing this duet in their ball gowns, tears leaked from her eyes and she gave herself a stitch in her left side. She could hear Josephine cackling with abandon on the other end of the line.

When their belly laughs had subsided into giggles, Grace said, "Thank you, Josephine. You don't know how I needed that."

"I did know, Gracie girl," she replied tenderly.

Grace felt tears gum up her throat. Was it so obvious she was unhappy, or was it that Josephine knew her so well? She preferred to think it was the latter.

"Thank you, Josephine. For everything."

"Anytime. Any old time at all."

Humperdinck was a very fine singer, but he wasn't an old friend, and as she added years to her own age, what Grace craved most of all was the comfort and company of people who knew her well; what a terrible thought that this relatively small coterie would dwindle in the coming years.

Her fingers fell lightly on the jewels at her neck, and she thought nostalgically of the pearl choker she'd worn so often at Edith's behest. It was strange how she hardly even saw the enormous Cartier diamond on her ring finger anymore; it was simply part of her hand now, like the skin that was dappled brown from too many suntans and the knuckles that had begun to protrude. Had she really wanted such a ring so badly once?

When Rainier had first slipped it on her

finger and she'd felt its unexpected weight on her hand, she'd understood little of what such a ring actually meant or what she was bartering when she accepted it. Oh, she'd thought she'd known everything at twenty-six — she'd escaped Philadelphia and risen to stardom, after all, stood her ground with the studio to get what she wanted more than once, and bravely left more than a few other men when it became clear that they couldn't offer her what she thought she needed. She'd thought she'd seen herself and the world so clearly. How could she even begin to explain any of that to Caroline, who was heading down a perilous road with Philippe Junot, without also explaining what her own marriage really was?

As was required at the annual Gala, Rainier asked her to dance. With a light touch on her elbow, he interrupted a conversation she'd just struck up with a documentary filmmaker. Reluctantly, she excused herself from a conversation about film and art, and allowed her husband to take her in his arms. She was reminded of so many of their past turns across the floor: at the Waldorf Astoria right after they'd become engaged, at their wedding, at Rainier's Silver Jubilee, and once, about a decade ago — she blushed now even to remember it —

naked at Roc Agel when the power had gone out and after much tinkering Rainier had gotten an old wireless to work, which piped in a station playing fuzzy oldies. They'd drunk too much wine and made love; then — of all things — Grace's own number one hit had come on, "True Love." She'd felt so swept away that night. She couldn't remember the last time that had happened.

Rainier looked into her eyes now, as they moved together in their finery like the practiced couple that they were. This year, they had celebrated their twentieth anniversary. Wasn't that worth something, if not everything? She decided to believe it was, if only for that moment, and she smiled at him with an affection that felt like a warm hand on her heart.

After all, things had been all right between them lately. It helped that Gwen had made good on her promise — her book about Grace was a success despite all it had left out. Rainier had taken to buying it as a gift, ordering scores of copies with Gwen's signature. Though he never thanked Grace directly for her hand in directing the biography, Grace told herself that this touching act of support for Gwen was thanks enough.

It also helped, bizarrely enough, that she and Rainier agreed completely about Philippe Junot. "He's a typical cad, and I can't believe our Caroline has fallen for a man of this type," he'd said the other day. Grace kept bracing herself for him to blame her imperfect maternal influence for Caroline's attraction — or, worse, the romantic past she'd gotten Gwen to cut out of her book — but he hadn't done that yet. In fact, she might even have Gwen to thank for this: had Gwen printed the full truth, it would have been all too easy for Rainier to wave the book under her nose and say, "How's Caroline supposed to behave when she knows *this* is how her mother acted at her age?" But since Grace had taken action to prevent the truth from surfacing — truths Rainier only obliquely knew in any case, and might even have scalpeled out of his own memory and perception of her — surely he saw that Grace was as invested as he was in protecting the image of them as Monaco's two Serene Highnesses, happily and productively married.

The image that — at moments like this, as the music of the orchestra swirled around them, holding their elegant forms in its soft embrace — was intact, whole, and as enviously smooth as the ring on her finger, which took in every ray of light and reflected it back out again.

■ ■ ■ ■

"Don't you find it a bit — I don't know — morose?" Caroline bent over the rough wooden table and squinted down at the array of dried lavender, bougainvillea, roses, and other flowers and greenery that Grace had been carefully cutting and drying from her gardens in the past year. Though the flowers around the palace were showier, she found she preferred the wildflowers that grew around Roc Agel, where she stood with her daughter now in a back room she'd recently cleared of clutter and remade into a studio.

"Not at all," said Grace. "In fact, drying flowers is a way of prolonging their life and beauty."

"But they're *dead*," said Caroline.

"I like to think I'm giving them new life," said Grace, amused but also a bit disappointed that her daughter couldn't see the metaphors in her work. She'd taken to arranging the dried petals and stems and leaves in collages on fine handmade papers, affixing them with extreme care in abstract patterns and also sometimes in the form of words like *Love* or *Dream*.

Gwen at least loved this new project of

hers, and had even suggested the two of them do a book on flowers together that would feature Grace's creations. The thought thrilled her. Imagine, Grace de Monaco — an artist! Though she never mentioned it to anyone, even Gwen, she cherished a daydream of a small but successful gallery show in Paris.

Finally, she felt as though she had a creative pursuit. Coming to this room in Roc Agel felt like coming home.

"Did you know," she said brightly to her daughter, "that Vladimir Nabokov was a lepidopterist? He studied and drew butterflies."

"The guy who wrote the novel about an old man and a teenage girl?"

Grace restrained herself from rolling her eyes, and said, "*Lolita,* yes. Haven't you read it?"

"No," said Caroline, and Grace was surprised, not just by this fact but also because of her oldest child's prudishness about it.

Grace remembered reading the novel when it came out in 1955. So many people had been shocked by the brazenness of the title character, but she hadn't been. Lolita was young, yes, very young, but the age difference between her and Humbert Humbert hadn't been so different from that between Grace and most of her male co-stars. Why was anyone so surprised? As a mother, she might disapprove of her daughter going out with someone so much older than she was, but she was hardly *surprised.*

Anyway, that wasn't the point she was making now. "I like the idea that a great writer," she said to her daughter, "could have another fulfilling creative pursuit. I am sure his work with butterflies must have somehow informed his writing."

Who knows where my own work with nature will take me?

Caroline shrugged and said, "If it makes you happy, then great."

"Thank you, darling. It does."

The next day, Caroline picked two luscious handfuls of flowers on a hike through the hills. One she set in a vase on the kitchen table, and the other she sorted into types and left on Grace's worktable. The splashy orange poppies were very like her elder daughter: impossibly beautiful, wiry, and hearty. *Whatever happens with Junot,* Grace found herself thinking as relieved, wet emotion needled the backs of her eyes, *she will be okay.*

Chapter 31

"Will you take me rowing, Kell?" Grace asked her brother. It was a stunning spring morning — the green leaves had just unfurled on the branches of the towering maples and oaks all over Philadelphia. As Fordie drove her home from the airport, Grace had looked out her window at the length and breadth of the Schuylkill River, where her father and then her brother had both trained to be Olympians. After decades of looking at that water and seeing nothing but punishment and retribution, Grace felt the river call out to her for the first time.

Kell looked up from the coffee he'd been drinking at the kitchen table where they'd shared three decades of breakfasts and countless arguments over how the family would spend a gorgeous day like today. Grace's vote for a movie or an outside puppet show was always drowned out in favor

492

of a tennis match or a parade.

This morning, though, their father lay upstairs asleep once again from the heavy narcotic the hospice nurse gave him to blunt the pain — and everything else — caused by his cancer. "Goddamn parasite," her father had called it, "eating me alive."

"Seriously?" said Kell to his sister.

"Seriously," she said. "How about a canoe? We can take the children and a picnic."

Everyone else — Peggy, Lizanne, and their mother — declined their invitation to join them, and so it was just Grace, little Caroline and Albie, and Kell and his toddlers, John and Susan. Kell's wife, Mary, had a headache and seemed relieved to have some time to herself.

In the boat, Kell insisted on manning the oar single-handedly, and explained to the children the difference between them and the oars in scull and crew boats. He also explained what a crew boat was and all the positions a man could have on a crew team. Albie wanted to be the coxswain and immediately began barking orders in his high-pitched toddler voice: "Faster! Faster! Sit up straight! Eat your vegetables!" Grace and Kell exchanged highly amused glances and tried not to laugh.

As the canoe stopped wobbling and began

nosing its way purposefully down the river, Grace rested her elbows on her knees and closed her eyes. She tried to take it all in — the breeze on her face that ruffled her hair; the murky scent of water and the wet earth beneath, teeming with fragrant, swampy life; the sound of the wooden oars breaking the surface of the water, then pushing it — *rrrrruuuuush!* — with a ring against the metal sides of the boat. Though she knew she was not the one with the burning shoulders and arms, she began to understand the allure, the way in which she was simultaneously on her own and also part of the river, something larger and more powerful than herself. For a moment, she even forgot that the security men she was required to travel with were in a canoe just yards away.

When they got home and Kell devoured the cold chicken sandwiches he'd eschewed on their picnic, saying he didn't want to give himself a cramp as he paddled them back, he asked her what she thought about their ride. "It was marvelous," she said with a grateful smile. "Thank you for doing all the hard work."

"My pleasure," he said. Then, after washing down a mouthful of sandwich with some Coke, he asked, "Why today?"

Grace looked upstairs. "I thought maybe

it would help."

He nodded. "Did it?"

"A bit," she said.

But there was so much more a trip down the Schuylkill could never wash away.

"If you don't mind my asking," ventured Kell, and Grace could hear the apprehension in his voice, "why didn't Rainier come? I thought he and Dad always got along."

"They did," she sighed. "They do. But . . ." She had made so many excuses. Her whole life. It was probably her most useful and finely tuned skill, a cousin to the silence she'd perfected first. "But he had some meetings he had to attend. France, you know. The big bully next door." But Rainier hadn't even offered to come. "He's too young to go like this," he'd said huskily to Grace when she told him that she needed to make a final visit to see her father. She got the eerie sense he was talking less about Jack Kelly than his own father, Pierre, whom he'd loved more than all his other difficult family members — certainly more than his mother, who took no interest in him, or his sister, who'd tried more than once to overthrow him.

"Of course," Kell said, nodding. "I just wanted to make sure, you know, everything is okay. We all like Rainier."

Grace remembered Don's long-ago complaint that Kell had crank-called him, even threatened to beat him up if he didn't leave Grace alone. And now here was her brother checking to make sure she and Rainier were on solid ground.

If only they were.

In these first four years of their marriage, it had become clear to Grace that she was fatally flawed. That had to be the reason why her father constantly compared her to Peggy, and now her husband thought she was in dire need of instruction. It wasn't just the French lessons — which were coming along nicely, thanks to her mimic's ear, which her teachers at the Academy had always described as pitch-perfect, thank you very much — or even the tutorials with Father Tucker, in which they discussed the who's who of European royalty and politics so that Grace would know exactly who everyone was, where they hailed from, and what dramas their families had been party to, going back several generations. Yes, those she could see the necessity of.

But the tirades about using the wrong kinds of flowers or moving the furniture in their receiving room to better accommodate the number of guests? "You should know better, Grace," he always seemed to be saying. Or the constant questions about tasks she'd already completed, as if she knew nothing at all about etiquette: "Have you written the thank-you notes yet? I wouldn't want Ari or the Windsors wondering why we haven't thanked them yet"; or "Have you begun planning the Christmas festival yet? Best not to let anything linger too long."

And lately he'd started in on her appearance. "Have you thought about growing your hair? Short hair seems a bit dated these days, don't you think?" Or "Let's skip dessert this week, shall we?" a few weeks after she'd given birth to Albie and felt her whole body sloshy and hot and humming with a need for the only pleasure she could think to give it: chocolate cake.

There was something so familiar about his criticisms, they were almost comforting, as if they confirmed what she'd always known about herself: that she had so much to learn, always. Familiar, too, was the raw chafe these lessons produced, the way they rubbed against the sense that she knew more than she was given credit for, that she could be trusted to get things right. Rainier's complaints confirmed her sense that nothing she could ever do would be enough.

Maybe this was the reason she'd never been a Broadway star: she hadn't tried hard enough. She'd allowed herself to be distracted by Hollywood, by the easy glory of stardom.

But, oh, how wonderful and freeing that distraction sounded now. *We all have our limitations,* Clark Gable had said to her nearly a decade ago. *And someday you'll realize that what you've got isn't worth trading.*

I think I'm starting to see your point, she thought. *I just hope it's not too late.*

But it was like that whole part of her life had been erased when Rainier had outlawed all her movies in Monaco. Banned them from being shown in any theater.

"Why?" she'd asked nearly four years ago, bewildered and swollen with Caroline growing in her belly.

"I thought you understood about sacrifice. And wiping our slates clean," he'd replied.

What have you given up? What sins did you expunge?

"And look what you've gained," he said gently, laying a hand on her taught, round stomach. As if on cue, the little one inside kicked. "See?" he'd said with a warm, fatherly smile. "This is our new beginning."

What could she possibly say to that? It was true. In a way. Wasn't it?

The children went back to Monaco with

their nanny after a few days with their American family, and Grace stayed in East Falls with her dying father. Hugging little Caroline and Albie goodbye had been wrenching. She succeeded in not crying as they ran together down the gangway with their nanny, but as soon as they were gone, she had to bite down hard on her fist to keep herself from breaking down in the airport. *Those children,* she thought. She loved them so much, she felt naked with them, constantly caught off her guard. Sometimes, like on the canoe, it was joyful in the purest way, and she could enjoy the giddiness they inspired in her. Other times, like now, she felt like she'd fallen off a cliff and her hot, clenched heart had risen into her throat.

She'd been glad it was Fordie's day off and it was an anonymous taxi driver who'd had to listen to her choke on her sobs all the way back to Henry Avenue from the airport.

At least they were happy to be on their way home to see their father. Rainier was so sweet with them — verging on too sweet, Grace sometimes thought. He bought them anything they wanted, was always ready with his tickle-monster routine and a piggyback ride, even if Grace was trying to get them ready for bed and didn't want them wound up again. One ride around the nursery on his back as he whinnied like a horse would set bedtime back half an hour or more, and since their toddlers had never been able to sleep in, the next day they would be cranky and only Grace would have to cope. She'd once asked him to shift his silly play with them to mornings, and he'd just said, "Oh, lighten up, Grace. We're just having fun." But at least he was a demonstratively loving father. Unlike her own.

"Isn't it just like Daddy," said Peggy drunkenly one night, "to die in a way that makes all of us bite our fingernails while we wait? Just like he lived." It was so uncharacteristic of her older sister to be negative about their father, who'd lavished so much love and praise on his dear Ba over the years, that Grace wondered what other resentments simmered under the surface. But she didn't think she could cope with the answers, so she didn't ask.

On the plane ride to Philadelphia from France, Grace had been full of fantasies about sitting at her father's bedside, sponging his face and reading him the paper while he submitted to her care and finally, just once, said, "Thank you, Grace. I want you to know I'm proud of you. I know you've

500

tried hard all these years." Like Lear, who finally recognized Cordelia's loyalty and even mistook her for an angel in his fever.

But he didn't ask for anyone, and the nurse wouldn't let anyone else sponge his face. One night she went for a walk in Mc-Michael Park across the street from their house, and sat on one of the swings she'd enjoyed as a girl. Higher and higher she'd pump with her long, skinny legs, very nearly flying off each time she reached the top front of her upside-down arc; every time, her rear end caught a bit of air, separating at least an inch from the seat. If she hadn't been holding the chains so tight, she might have really hurt herself, but she'd learned well the art of swinging just high enough.

That night she twisted the chains of the swing and let them unwind a few times, which made her feel a little queasy. She was about to get up when Fordie of all people sat in the swing next to hers.

"Your entourage is wondering where you are," he said. It wasn't a reprimand; he sounded more amused than anything about the security men hanging around her childhood home.

"Oh, them," she said. "I sometimes pretend to forget they're there and that my life is still my own."

"Your life's always been your own, Gracie. You've proved that again and again."

"Have I?" she laughed. "Because it doesn't feel that way to me."

Fordie was quiet for a minute.

Then she realized something and said, "I'm sorry, Fordie. That must sound horribly spoiled. How is your daughter?"

Fordie smiled wide, and Grace saw a lightning bug buzz bright green behind him. Then another, and another. "She's doing great," he replied. "Teaching, marching. She's met a young man, and he's real nice. Her mother and I like him a lot."

Grace smiled. "I'm glad," she said. "If you like him, he must be a good man."

Did you like Rainier when you met him?

"He is a good man," agreed Fordie. " 'Course, he's no prince," he laughed.

She laughed, too, but without any real humor.

"I'm sorry you're unhappy, Gracie. And I'm sorry your daddy's on his way out. Nothing I can say to make that right for you."

Grace tried to blink back the tears that had immediately flooded her eyes at Fordie's words, the gentleness of his voice, but instead water leaked out and rolled down her cheeks. She sniffled and patted at her jeans pockets, but she didn't have any tissues.

Fordie handed her an immaculate, crisply folded hankie.

"Thank you," she said hoarsely, taking it and wiping her nose.

"For what it's worth, Gracie, I don't think you sound spoiled at all. You sound like a girl who loves her father and doesn't know how to make heads or tails out of what his loss will mean." He paused, and Grace sobbed silently, making a wet, wrinkled wreck of his hankie, which smelled so comfortingly of their car and the mint gum he always chewed.

"A lot goes unsaid in a life," he went on, "and sometimes what is said isn't the best. The only thing we can do is learn from the mistakes of the people we love, and do better. You're doing great, Gracie. I saw you with your boy and girl. They love you, and you treat them like the prince and princess they are. Keep that up. That's what'll heal the hurt you're feeling inside you now."

"You think?" she hiccoughed.

"I know," he said, and he sounded so sure, her belief in his words calmed her nerves. She stopped crying long enough to take a deep breath. And then a yawn rose up in her so strong, it lengthened her spine and pushed her arms in the air in a languorous stretch.

"Thank you," she whispered.

"Anytime," he said, and together they walked back to the dignified brick house Jack Kelly had built with his own hands three decades ago, in a classic Federal style, bigger than any of the other more Tudor-style stone homes in the neighborhood, to prove to anyone who drove down the main road that "Just because I'm Catholic, and from Irish stock, doesn't mean I don't know what it means to be American."

Oh, Daddy. You never did stop, did you? Even now you're trying to prove your mettle.

The closest Grace came to her hoped-for moment with her father was the day before he died, and it was actually with her mother. The two of them were in the kitchen making sandwiches and iced tea, and Margaret had set down her knife on the cutting board and rushed over to her daughter, given her a tight hug, and cried, "I'm going to miss him so much. And you, too, Grace. Please stay."

This outburst of emotion was so unlike her mother, Grace saw right away what death had the power to bring out in a person. The two of them stood in the

504

kitchen a long time while Grace and her mother clung tightly to each other as Margaret Majer Kelly cried, and Grace was glad she'd fallen apart with Fordie earlier so that she could be strong for her mother now. Margaret cried so much that afternoon that when the day of the funeral arrived, she smiled wryly at Grace and said, "I don't have any tears left. Those sandwiches tasted so salty."

She didn't ask her daughter again to stay in Pennsylvania, but when Grace's suitcase was packed and it was time for Fordie to drive her to the airport, Margaret sat down on Grace's squishy bed with the faded pink matelassé coverlet, and patted the space next to her. Grace sat and felt her heart speed up as she tried to fill her lungs with air.

"Thank you for coming. And for staying," her mother said. "It's been . . . Having you here has made it easier to —" And here her voice cracked, and Grace could see her mother's eyes get watery.

Taking her mother's hands in hers, Grace squeezed and said, "It's all right. I understand. It's why I can't wait to get home to Caroline and Albie." She'd spoken to them on the phone that morning, and her heart had cracked open with love and grief.

Her mother squeezed Grace's hand in reply, and her grip felt strong. She felt connected to her mother, with more than just their hands, and hoped this could be the start of something new and enduring between them.

Margaret looked around Grace's room and cleared her throat.

"What next?" she wondered aloud.

"Plan a visit to Monaco," suggested Grace.

Her mother sighed, and Grace could hear the East Falls society lady coming back to herself. "Eventually," she said with resignation. "I wish I had the luxury of running away from my real life, but there are things I must attend to."

Ignoring the ignorant dig on her own life — she'd never "run away" from a damn thing in her entire life — Grace kissed her mother on the cheek. She couldn't expect everything to change in a moment, could she? But she left feeling hopeful, and that was enough.

CHAPTER 32

1962

Grace selected the blue gown for the party at the Onassis villa. Rainier used to like seeing her in blue, and he'd been so testy recently, she didn't think she could take it if he criticized her dress on top of everything else.

Stop speaking English to the children. You need to practice your French as much as they do.

That perfume is cloying. Please shower it off.

Albie has better things to do than take music lessons in town. Leave it to me to schedule his afternoons.

Why don't you smile more, Grace? I only want you to be happy.

Rainier was under considerable strain, Grace reminded herself. De Gaulle had threatened to cut off all electricity to Monaco if Rainier didn't impose certain taxes

507

on businesses in the principality, and Aristotle Onassis, whose two cents often put Rainier in a foul humor, was constantly calling and offering unsolicited advice. She squelched the voice inside her that said, *He wasn't being very nice before the crisis, either.*

Still, ruling a principality that was so stuck in its ways was a challenge, and Rainier was passionate about modernizing the country. Grace felt it was her duty to cut him every break possible, to make her own needs invisible to him, and to try to help him in any way she could. The problem was, every time she made a decision without consulting him, he found fault with it.

We might live in a palace, Grace, but this is far too much to spend on flowers for an event at a hospital.

In these moments, she felt replies rise like viper attacks to her tongue, but she swallowed them back. She certainly wasn't about to tell him that she thought some of the decisions he was making, especially to allow so much construction in their little principality, were unwise and short-sighted. In her view, what made Monaco so alluring to the wealthy people who'd long visited and poured money into its economy was its natural beauty and relative seclusion. She felt he should capitalize more on Monaco's coastal glamour and offer tourists more cultural opportunities, instead of allowing every free space to be cemented over with ever more hotels, apartments, and banks.

Her despair and confusion about her marriage spilled over into her time with her children. She couldn't help it, and hated herself for it. On edge all the time, she found herself yanking things like snuck cookies or off-limits toys out of Caroline's and Albie's hands, scolding them harshly for going against her wishes. Once, her nerves were so frayed, she actually bit Caroline's arm to teach her not to bite Albie. She'd done it gently, but she'd still done it, and she'd said, "See what it's like? You don't want your brother to feel that way, do you?"

My God, I sound just like him, she admitted to herself over glasses of wine she sipped tearfully at the end of another interminable day. In the morning, she would try to snuggle with the children in the nursery longer, read them more books, to make up for her behavior the day before. But somehow, by the end of the new day, she'd have become hopelessly impatient with them again.

It was hard to pinpoint when things had gotten to this point between her and Rainier. There had been no one defining moment, but rather a series of incidents. No one incident on its own seemed so bad; each one had its own story and explanation. But now that she had begun to feel their cumulative effect, Grace felt exhausted from the effort of constantly trying to figure out which choice was less likely to anger Rainier. She'd married him because he made her feel loved and protected. But she felt that way so rarely now, she found she had a hard time trusting it when she did.

She realized now that her biggest mistake had been to close her eyes on the issue of her career, and not insist on a clause in their contract that would allow her to return to acting — because now, after six years of marriage, she couldn't even fathom bringing up such a topic. As months rolled relentlessly forward, it seemed there would never be a time other than now. Now was always the moment in which she was living — worrying, smoothing, cajoling, fussing. Now was completely overwhelming.

Rainier didn't comment on her choice of dress for the Onassis party, and Grace was relieved he hadn't criticized it until she realized that neither had he told her she looked good in it. When was the last time he'd told her she was beautiful? She couldn't remember. She looked down at the luminous aquamarine cocktail ring on her right hand, which he'd given her for their sixth anniversary just a few months ago, and thought, *He loves me. He might not tell me as much as I'd like, but that's just my womanly need; he does his best to show me in the ways he can.*

At Ari's dazzling villa, where all the men wore dinner jackets and all the women wore gowns and heavy jewels and everyone looked their sparkling best, Grace received many compliments on her appearance, but none from her husband. Instead, as she performed her usual duty of checking in with him throughout the night to see if he needed bailing out of any conversation, a glass of water, or an excuse to leave early, she noticed his mood slipping. First, she heard him grousing about "the vise grip of the gambling racket" in Monte Carlo; an hour later it was "I'm all for the pope and his Vatican council, but I hope his reforms don't license our children to think anything goes."

Toward midnight, Grace was sitting on a couch with Tina Onassis and her friend Rosalind Shand, whom she knew from England, and the three of them were discussing Jackie Kennedy's televised tour of the White House; though the special had aired months ago, it seemed important enough that people still wanted to dissect it.

"I think it was marvelous," said Tina. "She managed to be the little woman showing off her house, making everyone feel welcome, even though the house was the bloody White House and she lives in it with John Heart-throb Kennedy. And the press is still raving."

"The Kennedys always were maestros with the press," said Rosalind, who was several years older than Tina and Grace and had been a debutante before the war. "When Jack's father was ambassador, he managed to get everyone to love him. For a while at least. Until his policies gave him away as a snake."

"Oh, Roz, England was hardly the Garden of Eden," laughed Tina with good-natured reproach.

Grace did not want this conversation to become about wartime politics, which she'd found Europeans enjoyed rehashing. Also, she knew Jackie a bit; they'd met years ago in New York when she was a senator's wife, and Grace an up-and-coming star. Grace had always felt a little bad for her; Jackie had always seemed nervous. Back then, Grace hadn't understood the beautiful brunette's need to sound rehearsed all the time. Now she understood perfectly. "I thought she did the best she could," Grace said to Tina and Rosalind, "though she did seem a bit coltish."

Rosalind snorted. "I'm sure she wasn't given a choice. Father Kennedy put her up to it. I'd put money on it."

"Don't we all have to do distasteful things to uphold the good names of our husbands' families?" Tina mused, darting a glance in Ari's direction.

"And our own fathers," added Rosalind, with a meaningful nod at Tina, whose father was a shipping magnate just like Ari. Their marriage had been a powerful alliance for the two men.

"Yes, well," said Grace, suddenly feeling uncomfortable with the can of worms she'd accidentally opened. She'd meant for her own comment to be a more theatrical one, about Jackie's state of mind, not what she had or hadn't been put up to. "She managed to do beautifully, in spite of her nerves. Maybe I only noticed it because of my own training."

"I think other housewives weren't paying as much attention to *her* as they were to her dress and decorating skills," said Tina.

"Who is dressing her these days?" wondered Rosalind.

Grace knew exactly what designer had made the first lady his muse, but she wasn't about to open her own mouth to say it. She let Tina say the name *Oleg Cassini* as her heavily kohled eyes rested suggestively on Grace's face, which she hoped was like a sphinx.

At that very moment, Rainier perched beside Grace on the arm of the couch where she was reclining. She jumped in fright, putting a hand to her chest, feeling her heart lurch into flight.

"I didn't mean to startle you, darling," said Rainier. "Or was it the mention of your old flame that jolted you?"

"Goodness," she said, catching her breath. She dared not comment on Oleg or Rainier's tease — in which she'd heard quite clearly the derision.

"We were just talking about Jackie Kennedy's tour of the White House," said Rosalind, jovially including Rainier in the conversation.

"Ah, yes, John Fitzgerald Kennedy's wife and savior," Rainier said, arms outspread, tone sarcastic. "Everyone knows it's a marriage of convenience, poor man. He's always carried a torch for Marilyn Monroe, hasn't he, darling? What was that story you told me once?"

Poor man? Grace was overcome with a desire to throw her drink in Rainier's face. If only getting angry at an ungallant comment was as easy in real life as it was in the movies. She'd often wished she could have the satisfaction of the on-screen slaps she'd given to Clark Gable and William Holden.

But as usual, Grace had only herself to blame for this comment of Rainier's, which invited her to tell a story she'd been forced to recount on so many occasions. Once Rainier mentioned it, she could never figure out how to reclaim the story, to turn it around somehow. That night, she'd had enough. Icily, she said, "Why don't you tell it, darling?"

Apparently oblivious to her tone, and pleased that the other women's husbands had joined in and expanded his audience, Rainier smiled and said, "Well, John the senator was in the hospital after one of his back surgeries and Grace, being Grace, wrote to Jackie to say how sorry she was to hear of her husband's condition and was there anything she could do." He paused, clearly to absorb the looks of rapt concentration on Tina and Rosalind's faces. "And so Jackie invites Grace to visit John, somewhat as a joke on him, because he'd been complaining about the homeliness of the nurses

515

in the hospital. But Jackie astutely wondered what he would say if *Grace Kelly* came to call wearing a nurse's uniform."

Rainier chuckled and went on. "So Grace donned a costume from a friend, and went to call on John at the hospital, and Jackie greets her warmly. But what does Grace see when she gets to his private hospital room but a life-size poster of Ms. Monroe stuck to the ceiling above him." Rainier burst into his familiar appreciative laughter, and Grace could hear how so much tension from the evening was sloughed off in that laugh.

Ari and Rosalind's husband, Bruce, joined Rainier, while Rosalind sipped her drink, poker faced, and Tina looked at Grace, eyes wide and scornful. *But what else should we expect, chérie?* Grace tried to meet her friend's gaze. *I know.*

"And so," Ari asked Grace, "what did he say when he saw *you*?"

"Nothing," said Grace, making her voice as light as possible. "He was so sedated, he never even opened his eyes."

But Rainier and Ari and Bruce hardly heard her reply, they were laughing so hard.

In the car on the way back to the palace, Grace looked out the window silently, responding little as Rainier recounted various conversations he'd had throughout the evening, at last coming to his triumphant rendition of the John and Marilyn story. When Grace only replied with a brief smile and a "Well done," Rainier was silent for a minute.

Grace could feel the air in the car go cold and dank. *Let it go. Please, just let it go.*

"I suppose you think you could have told it better?" he snapped.

"Of course not," she replied, too quickly, too irritably. It was late; her defenses were low. She just wanted to shut the conversation down, but she was too tired — and yes, too angry — to reach for her usual smile and soothing tones.

"It was like you set me up," he said, "asking *me* to tell the story, then not even laughing at the punch line."

"Because I don't think of the story as one with a punch line. It's not a joke, Rainier," she said, the words tumbling out before she could stop them. "I thought you understood that when I first told you what had happened." She was sure he had. Hadn't he said, *Poor Jackie?*

He shook his head. "I've always seen the humor in it," he said. "Pity you can't."

Right, because I'm a humorless ice queen.

"I don't want to talk about it." Her whole body felt cold, and yet she was sweating.

The skin of her arm felt clammy beneath her hand.

"Of course you don't. You never want to talk about anything anymore."

Was that true? It might have seemed that way to him, because it was true she didn't want to talk about many of the things he did — his zoo, the casinos, construction in Monaco, his goddamn car collection. But it was equally true that he didn't want to talk about anything important to her — the hospital, the gardens, starting a cultural center in Monaco that would focus on the performing arts.

"That's because anytime I offer an opinion on anything," said Grace, "you tell me it's wrong."

"That's not true, and it's not fair," said Rainier. "You just don't like it when I disagree with you."

You just did it again, Grace thought. But instead of feeling angry, she felt short of breath, as if she was being drowned from within, like a current was rising inside her, threatening to engulf her completely. Her mind cast about wildly: what was the fastest way out of this conversation?

"I'm sure you're right," she said, trying hard to see his point. It was true enough that she didn't like disagreements. She'd avoided them her whole life. Perhaps she should be more . . . what? Open? It was just so hard when she felt like she was being pushed underwater. She'd try to work on that, too. Anything to get out of this conversation.

He didn't reply, waiting for her to say more.

She put a chilly, damp hand on his warm, dry fist on the black leather seat between them. "I'll try," she said.

He didn't reply, but the conversation was mercifully over.

Silence, she told herself. *Remember the old lesson.*

Silence is much better than this.

Chapter 33

Grace knew what it was the moment she laid eyes on it. A script. It arrived unceremoniously in a pile of mail that sat on her desk like any other solicitation or felicitation, but its manila plainness practically glowed neon to her eyes. "Her Serene Highness" was scrawled in fountain pen, in Hitch's familiar hand.

How could he have taken her seriously? When they had spoken on the phone the week before — just one of their periodic catch-ups, nothing premeditated about it — she'd said, "I miss the thrill of getting scripts from you, Hitch. What I wouldn't give for one more." She'd meant it, but hadn't intended it as an invitation. It had been more of a lament.

Slicing open the top of the heavy envelope, she breathed in the paper scent, the possibilities contained within, then reached in and pulled out the stack of pages.

"MARNIE" had been typed across the cover page. Six letters. The world.

Grace pushed her glasses up the bridge of her nose and began to read.

It was pure Hitch: theft, love spurned and gone wrong, blackmail, characters driven to the point of violent madness by their obsessions. The title character was nothing like Lisa Fremont or Margot Wendice, nor was it a stretch in the direction of Georgie Elgin. Marnie was sexy and disturbed, like no one she'd ever played before, and quite possibly altogether wrong for her.

She'd never wanted a role so badly in her life.

The idea of doing *Marnie* — of saying those lines in front of a camera, working with Edith and Hitch, staying at the Chateau Marmont, feeling free — took hold of her like nothing else in years. In fact, she couldn't remember ever wanting to do anything so much, except perhaps to leave East Falls and attend the Academy in New York.

But the idea of even mentioning the possibility to Rainier turned her insides to liquid. All the questions he was likely to ask flooded in: *Who will be your leading man? Who will take care of the children? Who will perform your duties as Princess? How do we*

521

explain it to our subjects? Is this a onetime thing, or do you want more? How dare you be so selfish?

Grace forced herself to take a deep, steadying breath. No one knew about this yet. She had some time. And questions needed only carefully planned answers.

She took a large pad of paper from a drawer, along with her favorite fountain pen from Uncle George, and began writing down all the questions and protests Rainier might ask. Then she began composing answers.

When she was finished, the day was nearly over; it was time to collect Caroline from school. For the first time in years, she felt whole and full of purpose. When she rose from her desk and shrugged on her jacket and put her hair over the collar, she felt inches taller, her legs stronger.

She could do this. She *had* to do this.

It was almost like he knew what she was going to ask. She'd set the scene as perfectly as she could, complete with the children in bed and his favorite home-cooked meal, including pie and cold American beer, in the hopes of putting him in mind of the running gag from their early correspondence — anything that could remind him of the woman he'd fallen in love with seven years ago. *It had been love, hadn't it?* Whatever it was, she wanted to remind him of it.

He seemed amused by the beer, and grateful for the steak and scalloped potatoes, as she rarely served red meat and creamy sides these days after having had two children. As he was nearing the end of his first helping, she made her prepared speech, adopting as strong and even a tone as she could.

"I had a bit of a surprise the other day when Hitch sent me a script for his next film," she began, and to her surprise he didn't stop eating or look at her in any kind of suspicious manner. Somehow, this made her more nervous, but she went on.

"I was absorbed in the script from the start. I couldn't put it down, and I thought it would be a new sort of challenge for me. A different kind of role." As he kept eating, she sped up her talking, wondering if he was listening at all. "And now that Caroline and Albie are older, and in school, I thought perhaps it's time for me to do this work again. Think of the tourists that flocked to Monaco after our wedding. I wonder if a return to film — good films, of course, like the ones Hitch makes — could actually *help* Monaco, attract the right kind of attention. And" — she paused, hoping it was all sinking in — "I would not take any time off from my duties here to make the movie. I have always taken a vacation in the spring with the children. I — or we, if you can join us — could take the vacation in California this year. I'd put up my mother and maybe also Peggy or Lizanne, and the children can play with their grandmother and cousins. I'll only be gone a few hours a day for filming."

It took a few seconds after she stopped talking for him to set down his knife and fork, pat his lips with his napkin, and look at her. She searched his face for emotions — anger, fear, worry, *anything* — but he looked so . . . blank. Her heart was thundering in her chest, her ears, her brain.

From the list of questions she thought he might ask, he only voiced one.

"Who would be the other star? A man, presumably?"

"A Scottish actor. Sean Connery. He's not well-known in American movies yet, though I've heard he's going to be in a new series of movies based on the James Bond novels."

"I'm not sure I agree with you about the effect this will have on Monaco," he said, though without malice. "However, I've been expecting you to ask for this for a long time. I was surprised you didn't sooner."

Ah, she thought, realization dawning. *So this was why he didn't seem surprised, and just let me talk. He's been rehearsing this conversation longer than I have.*

"If you had asked me this three years ago, or even one, I would have said no," he went on, and her heart galloped at the hope implied by his words. "But you have been so miserable lately, so difficult to reason with, so unlike the woman I married, I began wondering if perhaps you needed to do another movie."

Her heart pounded faster, though less with hope than with resentment: *Miserable? Difficult?*

But did it matter, if he let her do it? She remained silent, let him go on.

"If you can figure out a way to make Monaco accept their Princess in a movie, I will support it."

"Isn't that a bit chicken and egg?" she replied, as this was a problem she'd anticipated. "Monaco will be more likely to support it if you do."

"Have a press release drafted and let me see it."

"It will have to say that you are excited to see me return to the screen," she said, suddenly feeling as she had when hammering out the terms of her contract with Jay and

Dore a decade ago. Her *unfulfilled* contract — another complication she'd have to contend with, as *Marnie* was not an MGM movie. But that seemed like nothing compared to the quiet battle she was having right now, at dinner with her husband.

"Am I excited to see you return to the screen, or am I excited to see you do one last movie?"

This was the one question she had been hoping he would not ask. But she had prepared an answer. "There's no reason to get ahead of ourselves," she said sweetly. "You're happy to see me do one more movie."

"I'm not," he said. "But you can say it, if it means you will be yourself again."

"I really do think this is what's been missing from my life," she gushed, relieved if not exactly grateful for the direction the conversation had taken. "Thank you, Rainier."

"You're welcome, Grace."

The day she called Hitch to say yes, Grace felt euphoric. In the afternoon, she sat on the floor and built a city of wooden-block towers with Albie and Caroline, and she found joy in every clink of rectangle to rectangle, every silly design suggestion her children made, and when Albie got out a plastic truck and knocked it all down, she laughed till tears spilled from her eyes. A week ago, she'd have scolded him for wrecking all their hard work.

Maybe she had been behaving miserably. Maybe Rainier was right. Some small voice inside her told her his assessment had been unfair, incomplete somehow, but she shushed it and tried to figure out how to thank him. They hadn't been on a romantic getaway in ages, she realized. Perhaps that was what they needed.

She worked with her assistant to perfect a press release, and asked Hitch to wait until she gave the go-ahead before his office made any announcements. Amazingly, everything was going according to plan. Rita, Maree, Carolyn, and Judybird were all thrilled for her when she called with the news. Peggy said she'd start packing her bag then and there. "I need a vacation," she said. "And you and your career have always made the perfect excuse. Remember the fun we had in Jamaica?"

Only her mother pointed to a dark cloud above. "Are you sure, Grace? You've worked so hard to get where you are. Why would you want to go backward?"

"Backward?" Grace repeated with genuine

surprise. She'd thought, after her father died, that she and her mother had reached a new and deeper understanding. She even relished her widowed mother's recent visits to Monaco; it was like, without her father around, Margaret Kelly was free to please only herself, her daughter, and her grandchildren.

"I never intended to stop acting," added Grace.

"Well, Rainier made it quite clear he expected you to. I'm surprised he said yes to this, unless . . ." Her voice trailed off.

"Unless what, Mom?"

"Nothing, nothing."

"Come on, Mom, that was not nothing."

"I just hope he's not . . . setting you up."

You set me up. Those had been Rainier's words in the car after Ari's party. He'd accused her of doing it to him. She hadn't, of course. Why on earth would he do it to her?

"You're being ridiculous, Mother."

Her mother didn't reply right away, then said, "As long as you're sure." Grace thought she sounded serious, but the long-distance line was a little crackly that day, and it was hard to tell.

"Anyway, you can come to California in the summer? Haven't you been saying you want to take the children to Disneyland?"

"I'm sure I can," her mother said, and Grace could hear the hedge despite the static. *I can do it alone if necessary,* she told herself. *It won't be the first time.*

CHAPTER 34

The release leaked before Rainier's final approval, before they'd had a chance to discuss the inevitable questions and how they would answer them.

"How did this happen?" Grace demanded, thumping down on her assistant's desk three different newspapers announcing in bold print, "Grace Kelly Returns to Film"; "Grace and Hitchcock Together Again"; "The Princess Descends Her Tower."

Her assistant, Marta, already looked close to tears when Grace stormed into the room. Phones all over the office were ringing.

"I don't know what happened," she whispered. "I'm so sorry, Grace."

"He hates it when the papers use my maiden name," Grace seethed, her heart beating wildly, her face hot. She could see it all play out between them: Rainier's fury, the yelling, the blame — she hadn't been careful enough; she'd been Princess long

530

enough to know better; she'd obviously been appallingly careless.

And he'd be right. She'd failed. Miserably. And she'd pay with her one shot at getting back her career — her freedom.

Grace felt so sick, she actually heaved over the toilet for a few minutes, but there was nothing in her stomach. She hadn't had her usual oatmeal or coffee yet, and she hadn't eaten much the past few days anyway, so heightened was her sense of anticipation about the announcement and the very prospect of doing the film.

Who would do this to her? Rainier's sister, Antoinette, came to mind. She'd never liked Grace. But how would she even have known about this movie? Grace had been careful to keep the secret among a select few. On the other hand, she knew how treacherous families could be, and she wouldn't put it past Antoinette to have planted a spy in her orbit.

But who? Not Marta, who appeared as distraught as Grace at the news. Grace went back to her office, where Marta was adding to the growing stack of messages from journalists calling for comment.

"One of them," she told Grace, "said that even Hitchcock was surprised by the news. Pleased but surprised."

Grace groaned. Rainier would be home from Paris later that day. She'd have to make some progress on this mystery by then. The more she thought about it, the more convinced she became that it must have been Antoinette. "Has anyone spoken to Rainier?" Grace asked.

Marta shook her head. "He's been meeting with de Gaulle all morning."

A reprieve. "Good," she said. "Have you spoken to Rainier's secretary?"

"He's also making no comments until we get an official word from you and the Prince."

Grace nodded. "Does *he* know how it happened?"

Marta shook her head solemnly.

"Has anyone spoken to Antoinette's staff?" Grace whispered.

Marta's eyes widened. "No," she said, catching Grace's drift right away.

"Maybe you and Pierre could find a way to . . . get some information? Together?" she asked.

Clearly thankful to have a task other than answering the phone, Marta nodded. "Right away," she said, rising from her desk, looking down at the phone that had started ringing again.

"Let it go," instructed Grace.

A few hours later, Marta reported that she and Pierre had made inquiries with Antoinette's staff, and no one over there knew anything about the leak, either.

"Do you believe them?" asked Grace.

Marta shrugged. "It's impossible to discern."

Grace wondered desperately if proof was even necessary. Antoinette had made other bids to depose and destabilize her brother over the years. She planned to suggest her as the culprit to Rainier; Grace was convinced it was her, proof or not.

After a long day of nervous pacing, thinking out loud with Marta, and finally taking a long walk on the grounds to escape the infernal phone ringing, then choking down nothing but a small portion of plain spaghetti with her children at dinner, Grace tried to watch a television show while she waited for Rainier to come home.

When at last he did, it was dark, and their wing of the palace was quiet. He didn't appear angry. In fact, all he looked was surprised. "I didn't expect you to be up," he said, crossing the room to pour himself a glass of whiskey from the crystal decanter.

"I . . ." Her mouth was dry. "I wanted to see you before I went to sleep. Could I have one of those?" she asked, nodding at his glass.

He poured her one with a slight smile, and said, "Tough day?" And he handed her the glass. The smoky liquid burned her tongue, throat, belly.

"I'm sure you know why," she said. *Why isn't he angry?*

"I read the papers," he said; then he shrugged. "What did you expect? You must have known this would happen."

She was so confused; he was acting like this was all perfectly normal. "I hadn't authorized the release yet," she said. "You hadn't approved it."

"Grace, we both know it didn't matter what I would have said. You were determined to do this. I left it in your hands."

"You asked to approve the release, and I intended for you to do so," she said, experiencing again that feeling of confusion she sometimes felt in conversations with Rainier.

"It doesn't matter," he said.

It doesn't?

Once upon a time, she would have been grateful for his apparent acceptance, his flexibility and forgiveness. But now she knew better; he'd expect something later. She thought back to the expert ways he'd wooed her, the way he'd made her feel accepted and loved, only to say in front of all those reporters that the Princess of Monaco would have more important duties than moviemaking. Then unilaterally banning all her movies from the principality they were supposed to rule over together.

"How do you want to reply?" she asked, wanting to do as he said from this point on in the hopes of limiting his inevitable future anger.

"The only thing I asked in all this is that you would be yourself again," he said. "So far, that hasn't happened. So far, this whole thing has turned you into a nervous wreck. You decide. Can you do the movie and find yourself again? Or will it put so much stress on you that you cannot perform any duty well? I would hate for your performance to suffer, for the reviews to be bad, as much as I would hate for Monaco to miss their Princess."

"I would, too," she said quietly, wondering why his speech had pushed her under the water again. He was looking out for her. He wanted her to succeed and to protect her from failure. Why, then, did she feel that success was impossible?

Despite Marta's sleuthing, Grace was never

able to come up with any proof as to who had leaked the release, and as the press whirled itself into a tempest around *Marnie,* not a single thing she or Hitch or Rainier said satisfied anyone. Some papers went so far as to print outright lies, such as that Monaco was broke and Grace had to do the movie to make money for the principality; to this accusation, she replied that this was so untrue, she would donate her entire salary to charity to prove it. MGM quickly leapt into the fray, pointing out that while the studio was thrilled by the idea that Grace might return to the screen, they had not been asked for, nor had they given, permission for her to do a film with Hitchcock at Paramount.

Shaky and jumpy, Grace felt queasy most of the day, and rehearsed answers and excuses rather than sleeping at night; she hadn't lost this much weight or felt this strung out since her wedding.

After nearly a month of it, Jay called.

"How're you holding up, Graciebird?"

"Not well," she admitted. "I can't seem to win on this one."

"What does Rainier say?"

What a good question. Nothing. Incredibly, nothing. When he wasn't busy talking to French officials about the future of

Monaco, he simply told her, "It's your decision."

"He says it's up to me," she replied, thinking of the quote he'd approved recently saying how absurd it was in this day and age that any husband might stand in the way of his wife having a career. *But you have,* part of her wanted to scream, *if not now, then when we got married!*

"Good man," said Jay.

At this compliment of her husband by her agent, something clicked into place. She didn't have to wonder anymore what Rainier was getting out of this, because she saw exactly what he was getting: he appeared to be the supportive husband, when in fact he was letting her drown in the storm. Because how could she explain what was really happening between them? How he said she could do as she pleased, then gave her no assistance, no love or support. He was doing nothing.

Or had he done worse than nothing? Had he, as her mother suggested, set her up to fail?

"Yes," Grace agreed, seeing the need to keep up appearances if she was going to get what she wanted out of this. Now that she knew what the game was, maybe she could win it. "Poor Rainier," she cooed, "he has enough to deal with, without my silly movie needling him."

"I've been thinking," said Jay, and Grace could hear the caution in his voice. "This isn't the only opportunity that will come along, you know. And this one had needless complications. For instance, I could get you a terrific MGM script, which would eliminate the problem on their end."

"Jaybird, I'm not going to start reading packets of scripts again. Hitch is special. This movie is special." *It's my only chance. If I blow it, that's it for me and movies.* She knew the truth of this in her bones, and also knew it was impossible to explain to anyone else. Especially now that the stakes were so high and so public. If she didn't do *Marnie,* she'd never do another movie.

"I disagree," said Jay. "Think about it, Grace. This might not be the right time."

"I'll think about it," she promised. But that wasn't what she was going to think about at all. What she planned to think about was how to turn the tide. She'd done it once before, with Howell and his Jamaica photos, when she'd stood her ground with Dore and gotten what she wanted out of MGM. She could do it again.

But last time, she wasn't a mother. Wasn't a wife, didn't have *subjects,* for Christ's sake. Already, the people of Monaco were being interviewed and polled, and the overwhelming feeling in the principality was that Grace was not one of them, never had been one of them, and doing a movie all the way in California would only prove the hunch they'd always had that she would desert them one day. She was still *la princesse américaine,* not *notre Princesse bien-aimée.* Every time an idea occurred to her — and all her ideas boiled down to instructing her office to ignore the press, then doing the movie without further comment — she kept thinking of how that decision would affect her life.

Every single time, what she came back to was the children. Leaving Rainier to do the movie — and more movies — was out of the question, for she knew exactly what was in her marriage contract about that: she would never see Caroline and Albie again. Much as she welcomed the idea of never seeing Monaco again, and even found the Shakespearian notion of being banished romantically appealing, she could not imagine never seeing her children again.

If she did not leave him, but upset him by doing the movie against his wishes, what was to stop him from *effectively* taking Caroline and Albie away from her? He'd already done it with their son, she thought bitterly. She rarely saw Albie, except on vacations and weekends, because his schedule was so full of activities befitting a young heir to the crown. Rainier could do the same thing with Caroline.

Grace thought back to their courtship letters, to all they had said about how they wanted to raise their children. Of all the tests to which she'd been subjected before they wed, that had been the most important, she realized now. She'd written that what she wanted more than anything was to give her children a life with the freedom he himself had described. He had been the first man to help her picture that life, to invest her in the power of the childhood neither of them had had. And now that she had two perfect children, little people who didn't yet know the selfishness and mistreatments of the world, she believed in that vision all the more, felt inside herself the most profound desire to protect them as long as she could. To let them be children.

Did Rainier really believe in that portrait of childhood he'd painted for her? She thought he did. *That* had not been a lie. Surely.

His desire for her, his admiration for her, hadn't all that been true, too? It must have been, for he hadn't been trained to act as she had.

Though he had been trained as a prince, and perhaps there was no difference.

She'd never been one to drink away her troubles, but she'd never felt so trapped inside her own body or mind. A stiff drink was the only way she could think to escape. She mixed herself a gin and tonic and drank it quickly, feeling its effects immediately on her empty stomach.

Whatever his real feelings for her or about fatherhood or any of it, she realized now, what had mattered most to him was that *she* believed those things. She'd been willing to *pay money* for those things, to leave her career and country for them. He'd seen that willingness in her, a kind of desperation for the life he purported to offer, and *that* had been important to him.

She drank another gin and tonic, and felt drunk.

Much as she wished to talk to someone, to pour out her heart and receive some comfort in return, whom could she possibly call? She couldn't *admit* any of this. To anyone.

She called Marta and thought she kept the drink out of her voice just enough to say she was feeling sick, and could she cancel her calls and let the nanny take care of the children that evening? One more gin and tonic and she was asleep on the couch in her office.

When she woke, it was dark, though it was only nine in the evening. Mercifully, the children were asleep, and Rainier was away. After drinking a large glass of water and eating a chunk of baguette slathered with butter, she poured herself a glass of wine and took it outside. Without heading anywhere in particular, without even thinking about where her feet were taking her, she found herself in the gardens. But even the scent of the honeysuckle, the light breeze rustling through the leaves of the trees and bushes and climbing roses, did not soothe her. Instead, she tuned in to the distant sound of the Mediterranean rushing against the sand. Crash and retreat, crash and retreat.

She stopped walking at the same spot where she and Rainier had chatted seven years before, when for a moment she'd forgotten the *Paris Match* cameramen following them around, forgotten the ugly dress she'd had to wear, forgotten that she was anything other than a girl meeting an attractive, intriguing man on a spring day.

Leaning on the stone wall and dangling

her wineglass over the edge, the wide, delicate bowl of it between her thumb and middle finger, Grace tried to remember what it had been like to be that girl. She'd just won an Academy Award; she was decorating a beautiful apartment in Manhattan; she was looking forward to meeting a clandestine lover later in the evening. But none of that mattered as much as what she didn't have. What she had now. That girl hadn't felt any freer than the woman she'd become.

Instinctively, she gripped the glass tight and reeled back her arm, spilling the liquid on her jeans and sweater. Then she hurled the glass as far as she could. She watched it disappear, engulfed by the shadows of the night.

A clink rang out when the glass hit a rock, followed by a tinkling shatter as it went to pieces somewhere below.

It wasn't enough.

Doubling over, hands balled into fists, she howled into the night curses that were swallowed by the vortex of the water, until she was out of breath and discovered that she was on her knees, and they had been scraped and dented by the rough stones that formed the road.

Staggering back to the palace, she shut herself again in her room.

■ ■ ■ ■

Grace didn't emerge for days, except to play with Caroline for an hour or two every afternoon. She always made sure to bring a box of Kleenex as testament to the cold she claimed to be nursing. Her nose was certainly red and stuffy enough to convince anyone she was sick.

After about a week, during which Rainier left her almost totally to her own devices, except to ask, perfunctorily each evening either by phone or from the other side of their bed, "Is there anything I can do?"

Divorce me. Let me be free in a way that I can still see my children.

"No," she replied.

One fresh and sunny morning, she woke and remembered something Fordie had said after her father died.

They love you, and you treat them like the prince and princess they are. Keep that up. That's what'll heal the hurt you're feeling inside you now.

I hope you're right, Fordie. I sincerely hope you're right.

After a scalding shower, in which she scrubbed herself raw with a sponge and fragrant rose-scented soap, Grace dressed as she had not in weeks: a casual but pressed cotton dress, a sweater tied around her shoulders, jewelry, makeup, perfume. In the nursery, Caroline ran to her mother and flung her arms around her, and Grace felt gummy emotion clog her throat. She cleared it, knelt on the floor, and hugged her daughter in return.

"Mommy, you look so pretty! And no more Kleenex!"

Grace laughed and touched her daughter playfully on the nose. "You are a perceptive girl, Caroline. Yes, Mommy's feeling much better." This was a lie, but she knew the only way to feel the role, to be convincing, was to perform it. "Let's pick Albie up from school," she suggested.

Her five-year-old daughter's eyes went wide. "Really?"

"Yes," she said. "And then let's get ice cream!"

Caroline whooped with delight and ran to get her favorite doll ready to bring with them. Grace told the head of Albie's security entourage about her plan, and as the guard reached out to pick up the phone, presumably to okay this with Rainier, Grace stopped him by saying curtly, "I'm his *mother*. I can pick him up from school." He nodded, and even though Grace was sure he'd call Rainier as soon as she left, it had felt so good to say it, so good to defy expectations.

The three of them had a perfect afternoon, complete with extra-large gelato cones and rolling up their pants and getting them wet anyway as they ran across the beach. Grace even enjoyed taking them to Rainier's zoo to check on Albie's favorite animals. The children challenged each other to races through the gardens, and Grace thought to herself how much her own father would have liked to see them doing that, just like the challenges he used to stoke between his own children. They were exhausted at bedtime, and she read them her own favorite bedtime books on Caroline's bed — the two of them sat on either side of her, their heads heavy against her chest. She could smell their hair, the light fragrance of the baby shampoo, as well as the sun and salt that still clung to the strands. Their bodies were warm, soft, and relaxed.

Just as both of them were dropping off to sleep, Rainier popped his head in and Albie jumped up. "Papa!" And he ran to Rainier with a hug. Caroline followed.

Grace was left on the bed, bereft and resentful that their perfect little moment had been shattered.

"Don't let me interrupt," said Rainier, though he beamed at the affection of his children.

Grace stood, her legs sore and her joints stiff from their raucous afternoon. Watching Caroline and Albie cling to their father, after everything she'd come to realize that day, made Grace's heart feel heavy and bruised when all day it had felt light and full. "Time for bed," she said, sounding more strict than she meant to, even a little annoyed. She didn't want to act frustrated with her children. That was the whole point. But she was too tired to tend to that problem right now.

Eventually, she got them to sleep. Rainier was waiting for her in their bedroom.

"I heard you picked Albie up from school," he said, his voice as neutral as it had been for weeks.

"Yes," she said simply. "And I plan to do it more often."

Rainier was silent.

She sat at her vanity and started taking off her earrings and rubbing cold cream onto her face.

Then he said, "How will you do that if you're making movies?"

"I won't be making movies," she said flatly. "I'm going to back out of *Marnie.* I'll send out a statement tomorrow."

Rainier didn't respond right away. She could see him in the mirror, behind her. His face was inscrutable. Finally, he said, "I'm sorry it worked out that way."

"I know you are, darling," she said, wiping the cream off her face with a tissue, along with the makeup and grime of the day.

Then she turned in her seat to face him. "But before I send the statement, I want to have a meeting with you about the children. And about Monaco. If I'm not going to use my talents in film, I need to use them elsewhere. And you need to listen to me."

Her blood coursed through her like waves in the ocean — she could hear it in her ears. But she didn't feel like she was drowning this time.

Her husband pressed his lips together, then said, "It'll have to be early tomorrow. I have a busy day."

"I'll be up," she replied.

The cold cream hadn't been enough to make her feel clean, so she took a shower and felt better. In her nightgown, she padded barefoot down the hall and looked in on Caroline, then Albie. Both of them were fast asleep, breathing deeply, blissfully unaware of what had transpired between their parents.

CHAPTER 35

1964

Grace was amazed to discover that Rainier actually listened to her and even took her advice about a few things. She was most surprised to discover the respect he had for her opinions about Monaco and its future, and on her suggestion, he curbed the construction in order to preserve the principality's natural beauty. And he was allowing her more freedom to pursue her own interests, without requiring his approval. She had already founded a charity called AMADE, or the Association Mondiale des Amis de l'Enfance, which touched the lives of children in need all over the world by providing medical care and education, and she was well on her way toward forming a local foundation for the arts that would focus on dance, and also the crafts of Monégasque artisans.

"I don't need another father," she'd told

him before she officially turned *Marnie* down. "I don't need supervision. If you have suggestions, please do me the favor of treating me at least as well as a colleague. Or assume I won't take your advice."

Curiously, this warning had made him leave her alone almost entirely. He didn't get involved with AMADE or the foundation. Once in a while, he would tell her that he'd heard this or that compliment on her work, and she told herself to be content with that — and for a while, she was. As long as her work reflected positively on him, she learned, she was free to continue. And it was work she was learning to relish. It got her up every morning. It wasn't the same as acting. But it filled her life with purpose, and for that, she was thankful.

The sticking point was still the children. He'd promised to let her have more time and influence with Albie, but now she could see that he'd told her this only to placate her. First, Rainier arranged special language lessons for their little boy in the afternoons, without consulting Grace, and the lessons limited the extra time with Albie she'd recently been enjoying with him and Caroline after school.

"I thought we agreed to discuss these matters first," Grace said, unable to keep the ice out of her tone.

"He needs the lessons, Grace. And I'll pick him up in the evenings," he'd said dismissively, "since it's close to my offices in Monte Carlo. We'll be home for dinner."

"No," she said. "I don't agree."

Rainier sighed imperiously. "I don't know what you remember, Grace, but I never agreed to let you call the shots about Albie."

"You're twisting my words," she said. "I never asked for that. I asked that we *discuss* Albie."

"You say *discuss*, but what you mean is that you want me to agree with you."

She knew this wasn't true. But she also knew that there was nothing — nothing — she could say to convince him.

"You cannot have everything you want," he went on. "Anyone would say you have more than enough already, and that you're lucky to have a husband who's interested in helping to raise the children."

"The children?" she couldn't help but shriek. "You leave Caroline entirely to me, except to tell me all the things I'm doing wrong, and then spoil her rotten with sweets and dolls." She'd pointed this out two years before, after *Marnie,* and for a short time, the situation had improved. He'd said, and

she remembered this so clearly, "I know you're right, Grace, and I'm sorry. I'll try to be more present for Caroline, and for you with her."

But now he said, so calmly, not even responding to Grace's anger, "She's my sweetest darling. Can you blame me for spoiling her? I can't help myself, really."

Grace opened her mouth to speak, but couldn't find the words. She wanted to throw heavy objects around the room, wanted to scream. But what good would it do? She laughed in that moment, thinking of the absurdity of awakening any man with tears, screams, slaps, or even by shining like a star. What man had ever shown an ability to change in that way? Certainly not her father. Not Oleg. And not her husband.

It was all a fiction.

Children really were the crux of it all, weren't they? There was nothing like the love they gave, and the love she could give to them. She felt connected to Albie even as Rainier tried to keep him from her, and she felt their mother-son love so strongly whenever they were together. Despite Rainier's hypocrisy about Caroline, Grace secretly enjoyed having their daughter to herself.

She hoped their next — and last — child would be a daughter for that very reason.

She was pregnant again. For the third time in two years. The other two — well, she couldn't think about the other two. In recent years, she'd become extremely good at locking unpleasant thoughts away; she couldn't survive any other way.

Excited as she was about the prospect of another child, she felt deeply superstitious and had vowed not to say anything to anyone until the first trimester was complete. When it was, she felt healthy and energetic, and told Rainier one morning over coffee and rolls while the children watched a television program, "I have some wonderful news, Rainier. I'm pregnant again, and I feel certain this time it's going to stick."

He smiled indulgently, and she wondered if he would bestow one of his rare compliments, for that had been one of the things she'd asked for two years ago as well: "You dwell entirely on the negative. I need for you to be positive, about me and the children. I need you to say we're doing well, to express your love and pride in us. You used to be able to do that so well." And again, for a while, she'd been showered with compliments. But those, too, had dwindled. The last time he'd given her a piece of jewelry, she gave it back to him and said,

"I'd rather have words." He'd looked at her with sad eyes and said, "My beautiful darling, please don't make me into someone I am not."

Now, her big news hanging between them, she looked at him expectantly, eyebrows raised, hope burbling like a spring in her chest.

"I did wonder when you would tell me," he said.

"You knew?" she asked, surprised.

"Of course, *chérie*. You always glow, but you're even brighter when you are with child."

His eyes lingered a little longer on her, and she felt their warmth sink into her skin.

Then he turned his eyes back to his paper, and Grace sat wishing for more until she told herself not to be selfish. Then she rose to find out what Albie and Caroline were up to. The television had been switched off, and the two of them were arguing over what game to play next.

"Mommy can decide!" Caroline said as soon as she glimpsed Grace in the doorway, clearly thinking this would give her an advantage. Remembering the way her own parents had played favorites with her and her siblings, Grace suggested a coin toss instead. Albie's choice, Chutes and Ladders, won the day. Grace promised to play Caroline's game next, and the three of them sat on the floor and played companionably for the next hour. It wasn't the set of Hitchcock's next film, but it was her best shot at reshaping her own life. She swore to devote herself to her children as she had to the stage and then the screen. Mother, wife, princess . . . they were all roles, even if she hadn't fully digested the script when she accepted the part.

Putting a hand on her belly, she thought, *Hang on in there. I promise to do everything I can to make you feel loved and seen. And protected. You'll have the life I never could. I love you already.*

Even though it was too early for such signs, Grace could have sworn she felt the little one swim around inside her in reply. She laughed to herself. Already, this one had perfect timing.

CHAPTER 36

1976

"Poetry? At the Edinburgh Festival?" Grace hadn't even realized there *was* such a thing.

"I just spoke to John Carroll, who organizes all the literary events, and he would be *thrilled* if you agreed," said Gwen. The words came down the telephone line like a prayer, but in Latin, like in the old days. Grace could hardly understand. Her? Read poetry on a stage in front of thousands of people?

"Peggy Ashcroft's done it," urged Gwen. "And Ralph Richardson."

Poetry, Grace found herself thinking, virtually around the clock. Poetry was not film. It was *literature.* What was more respectable than poetry? And Peggy Ashcroft! Grace had adored her in so many things, most recently a television drama series from England doing marvelous work with Shakespeare, *The War of the Roses,* in which she'd played Queen Margaret.

Grace carried the secret of the poetry reading around like a loose diamond in a pocket, feeling the hard, sparkling promise of it in the soft folds of her mind. She opened her mouth to discuss it with Rainier many times, but always wound up changing the subject in her throat, before any words like *poetry, theater,* or *festival* could come out. *No,* she kept thinking to herself. *Silence. Don't ask.*

She hadn't asked for permission to go to the Academy thirty years ago. She'd applied, gotten in, then presented her acceptance to her parents as a fait accompli. Oh, they'd given permission at some point — and revoked it, memorably. But she was almost forty-seven years old now, for heaven's sake! And this was *poetry.* Nothing risqué or untoward about it. Something Rainier would sleep through in any case — no doubt about that. And hadn't she promised herself that she would give some thought to who she was now? She wasn't Grace Kelly anymore, but she had the sense that that girl, that persona, was her calling card — much more so than Her Serene Highness, Grace de Monaco. It was Grace Kelly whom John Carroll wanted to read at Edinburgh.

Before she could think it through further, she was calling John Carroll and babbling *yes* and *thank you* and *won't it be marvelous,* she loved poetry, just loved it, and she couldn't wait to begin.

Then she really did have to tell Rainier, and the mere thought of doing so made her oatmeal go gluey in her stomach. *You can always back out,* she told herself. *Lord knows you've gotten good at that.* Making excuses. But Grace Kelly didn't make excuses. Grace Kelly had negotiated her contract with MGM, had made sure she got the part of Georgie Elgin in *The Country Girl.* Yes, she'd had to do *Green Fire* in exchange. There was always an exchange.

She continued not to tell him. Yet. Instead she ordered boxes of books from George Whitman, whose Paris shop, Shakespeare and Company, was modeled on Sylvia Beach's long-shuttered store by the same name and was *the* resource for books in the English language in France. Wordsworth, Tennyson, Byron, Bishop, Dickinson, Cummings, O'Hara (one of Uncle George's favorites), Sexton (because she was feeling bold). On Whitman's suggestion, she added in a few books by a poet named Maya Angelou.

When the books arrived, she secreted

them away in her office. First, she set them on her desk with a satisfying *thud,* using her stainless steel scissors to slice the wide tape that held the seams of cardboard together. Parting the flaps of the box released a scent of ink and freshly cut paper, and she breathed it in deeply. *I Know Why the Caged Bird Sings* was on top, and she picked it up and let the tight pages fan out beneath her thumb, sending a light breeze onto her face. She found the title poem, which she'd read years ago and forgotten. Grace nearly choked when she got to the line "a caged bird stands on the grave of dreams." She put her hand over her mouth as she read the rest, her eyes running swiftly over the short stanzas, looking for hope, an answer. There wasn't one, not exactly, for a lesson from school came back to her as she read: poetry doesn't offer ease and comfort, but depth and recognition, which she found in Angelou's free bird that "dares to claim the sky."

She'd done that once.

Dare.

That was it, wasn't it?

Daring.

The morning she was to leave for Edinburgh, she sat down with Rainier to a fine breakfast — yogurt, berries, muesli, toast, cured meats, and cheese.

"What's the occasion?" he asked, hungrily tucking into a bowl of peaches and yogurt drizzled with honey. Grace sipped at her coffee, her own plate of fruit and cheese and bread untouched. She might have to take a box of breakfast with her in the car that would be driving her to the airport.

"Well, I thought I'd leave you with plenty of your favorite things, while I'm gone for a few days," Grace replied.

"Remind me where you're going?" he asked as if she'd already mentioned this trip, and it had slipped his mind.

"The Edinburgh Festival," Grace said, as if it was nothing. The market.

"Going to take in some culture? Meet some friends?"

"I am meeting friends," she affirmed with a nod. "Gwen, and Cary, you know. But I'll also be appearing in the festival myself." Grace's blood was pounding in her ears.

Rainier stopped chewing and looked at her. He swallowed. "Oh?" he asked.

"I'll be reciting poetry," she said expansively. *What a lark. A whim. Nothing to bother about.*

"Reciting poetry?" He blinked uncomprehendingly. She couldn't very well blame him for not grasping it right away. The idea had seemed incredible to her as well. "Like Caroline and Albie did in school?" he further clarified.

"Not precisely like that, no," said Grace. "I'll be performing with Richard Kiley and Richard Pasco of the Royal Shakespeare Company. It's all very upper-crust," she said in an English accent. "I can't wait," she added in the same accent.

"Performing," he repeated her word, as if groping around for some of his own.

Grace looked at her watch and said, "Oh my, look at the time. Must dash to catch the plane." No time for the to-go box. There were worse problems.

Sliding off her kitchen chair, she went over and pecked her startled husband on the cheek. "I've left a ticket for you on your bureau, in case you want to join me. My hotel suite will be more than big enough to accommodate both of us. It might make a nice getaway." She tried to layer promises she didn't really feel into her voice. But the risk was low, since she knew he would never come. And if he surprised her, well then . . . maybe the surprise of his arrival would ignite her desire.

It had been years since she'd seen the castle in Edinburgh, that magnificent medieval

562

fortress atop a rocky hill. In that way, it reminded her of the palace in Monaco: both were the geographical crowns of their respective kingdoms. *Well, in Monaco's case, a principality, not a kingdom, but why quibble with details like that?* she thought as she stood in her richly upholstered and tapestried hotel room, looking out the picture window at the castle, a pot of tea steeping on the table behind her.

Though Monaco was by far more colorful, Grace felt right at home in the predominantly gray stone and green grass of the Scottish capital. It was mid-August and blazing hot in the home she'd left behind, but Edinburgh was bright, blue skied, and barely warm enough for short sleeves, reminding her of late September in Pennsylvania. She could wear a jacket outside if she wanted to.

After that one private moment in her quiet hotel room, Grace's agenda was filled with engagements, as was typical of festivals. But for the first time in ages, she didn't resent the events. Alone in her room, she bathed and dressed herself — though she did hire a local woman, a real magician, whom Gwen had suggested, to do her hair and makeup before her performances. Then she floated from her rooms, down the antique elevator, and into the much-perfumed lobby, where she waved at familiar faces or exchanged a few words with the concierge before hailing a cab to her destination. Because the city was jammed with famous performers that week — actors, rock stars, and socialites galore — no one paid her much attention. She felt like she was twenty-three years old again in New York City.

The first time she stood on the intimate stage at St. Cecilia's Hall for a rehearsal with Richard Kiley and Richard Pasco, both of whom greeted her warmly, as if she were one of them, Grace nearly cried. But she swallowed it back as she shook the actors' hands and said, "Goodness, I haven't been on this side of a theater in so long."

"Too long," said Richard Pasco. *"Rear Window* is one of my all-time favorites."

"You're too kind," said Grace, flushing with embarrassment at the compliment. "Hitch did make movies feel more like theater. The rigor, and also the fun. The camaraderie." Even though Grace was overcome with the memory of how special she'd known *Rear Window* was, it was Georgie Elgin's words from *The Country Girl* Grace heard in her mind now: *There's nothing quite so mysterious and silent as a dark theater, a night without a star.*

Rehearsing with the Richards was not a facsimile of those early plays and movies; it was its own theatrical experience; but it pulled out of her all the lessons about drama and acting and *re*acting to her fellow players that had lain dormant inside her for so long. She left their first reading breathless with excitement, ravenous for more. There simply could not be enough, especially since their program was short compared to a play or a film.

Of all the poems she read during those exhilarating days, her favorite was Elinor Wylie's "Wild Peaches," which was so profoundly American in its celebration of Chesapeake Bay and "brimming cornucopias" and "the Puritan marrow" of the poet's bones, Grace feared she might get choked up when she performed it with the ironically British Richards. To help distance herself from the material and protect her heart and voice just enough from the way the poem touched her, she gave herself a character with a slight Southern accent and was amazed at the way her old skills came back to her. Oh, she still did impersonations and little monologues from time to time as a party trick with old friends who asked for it, but to *create* a character from Wylie's poem was an exercise she hadn't attempted in more than two decades. It felt like un-earthing a favorite old sweater found in the corner of a closet, and discovering that it was still soft and miraculously intact, nary a moth hole in sight.

Still, the accent was risky. The night of their performance, her stomach was churning so riotously she thought she might actually be sick. Unlike in the old days, she didn't have an image or goal in mind for the night — it wasn't like her father was going to rise from the dead and sit in the front row, and she didn't even fantasize about the unlikely event of Rainier appearing with an armful of long-stemmed roses. No, what she was really worried about was embarrassing herself in front of hundreds of people. Tripping on the words, flubbing the accent — or, worse, doing what she thought was a great job and then reading in the paper the next day, "Grace Kelly should have stayed in Monaco."

When she stepped onto the stage and felt the hot white light from above, the rapt silence of the audience was palpable. They were waiting . . . for her. For her to reclaim herself or to make a complete fool of herself. What had she been thinking, trying something like this? Though as Princess she regularly appeared in front of crowds larger than the one she was in front of that night, she never expected to feel as inexperienced and *naked* in front of an audience as she had in her Academy days. When she swallowed, her saliva trickled down a parched throat. It was now or never. With a smile, she looked out at the audience, a blessed blur as always without her glasses. And then she began to speak. Using the accent from rehearsals, she recited the poetry with Richard Pasco and Richard Kiley, and just as had been true in her old theater days, she eventually stopped feeling the intensity of all the eyes on her. She became immersed in her work, overtaken by it and the interaction with her fellow players.

When they finished speaking, there was that telltale beat of *Really? It's over?!* silence before the audience erupted into applause and whistles, a standing ovation of gratitude for a job well done.

Grace smiled widely again, her nerves gone, her body so light on the stage, she might have floated away, had she not been holding hands with the Richards for a bow. The audience kept clapping. Kept whistling. Slowly, Grace began to feel her body again, beginning with her cheeks, which burned from the width of her smile. Gallons of hot, celebratory blood rushed through her veins.

She couldn't believe it. She was home.

If there was a price to be paid for this pure joy, it would be worth it.

CHAPTER 37

If there was a price, it was Rainier's silence. Not only did he not come to Edinburgh, but he asked nothing about her reading, nor did he comment on the rave reviews. He said nothing about the next reading or the next — for the invitations came pouring in. His muteness had a different texture from the silent treatment her father had used to punish her when she was young. It didn't feel mean-spirited, but rather utterly clueless, as if Rainier had decided a few poetry readings just weren't worth arguing about. Grace guessed that someone close to him had told him exactly what Grace herself had thought about the readings: it's poetry. Great Works. No violence, nothing sexual. The engagements required little of her in the way of rehearsals, and each performance was a one-shot; no long runs in theaters away from home. For each, she could be there and back in just a few days.

Though, usually, she stayed longer. "I think I now understand what you always saw in London," Grace said to Caroline on the phone. "Harvey Nichols and Selfridges are wonders, and how did I live before Fortnum and Mason's tea?"

"Are you really saying your beloved Fauchon isn't as good?"

"Weeeelllll," Grace said lightheartedly, "they are equal. Let's leave it at that. Before, I couldn't have agreed to that. But now I see the error of my thinking."

Caroline laughed. "It's nice to hear you so happy, Mom. Is it really Wordsworth and Shelley that have done it?"

"Yes, them, and the other actors I've discovered who love them as much as I do."

"Do you think it'll lead to anything else?"

"I haven't even thought about that," Grace said, surprised to discover it was really true. "I'm just enjoying it for what it is."

At another time in her life, Rainier's indifference to her new passion would have wounded her or made her feel lonely. But the poetry was its own reward; she kept quiet, contented company for many hours with poets whose collections were always stashed in her handbags and sitting around the living quarters of the palace. The volumes became her most sought-after company, for they never failed to help her feel less alone. She was always underlining phrases and stanzas that spoke to her deeply, like Robert Duncan's lines from "Childhood's Retreat": "my secret / hiding sense and place, where from afar / all voices and scenes come back."

When Grace and Rainier were together, they didn't need to discuss poetry in any case — there was plenty to discuss when it came to the problem of Caroline and Philippe Junot. Their daughter's relationship was only becoming more intense, and Grace and Rainier could talk for long stretches about what to do about it. "No one seems to know what it is he does," grumbled Rainier one early-fall evening at Roc Agel. Grace was filthy from a day spent in the garden, pruning and weeding and selecting the best of the late-season blooms for her dried flowers. She'd taken to combining these two loves of hers by reciting poems as she performed the ritual of preparing blooms for drying. Elizabeth Barrett Browning, "Beloved, thou hast brought me many flowers," and of course Shakespeare, "Summer's lease hath all too short a date."

"What are we going to do about him?" Rainier asked as he poured her a cup of Bandol.

"I wish I knew," sighed Grace, plopping into a chair next to Rainier and peeling off her gardening gloves. This little table was their favorite spot on an overgrown hillside near the house. "I've been trying to distract myself away from it, as you've always advised. I'm attempting not to hover."

"There's a time for hovering," he said moodily.

"What makes you think this is it?" she asked, draining her tumbler of water before picking up the wine. A breeze riffled the long grasses and wildflowers around them, and bees buzzed toward a hive nearby.

"I've never seen her so smitten with anyone," he said.

"But she's only nineteen. Well, close to twenty now," said Grace, surprised at this reversal in their parenting roles. The wine was delicious, and the day had been warm and productive. Her lungs were full of fresh air.

"I know a cad when I meet one," snarled Rainier. "This Junot, he wants something from her."

"But what? He seems to have plenty of money."

"*Seems.*"

"Ah," said Grace, her husband's concern becoming clear. She took another sip of wine. Goodness, it was delicious — and strong. She'd need to go easy. And eat something soon. She couldn't remember when she'd last eaten. "And none of your contacts have heard of him? That *is* strange." Because the world they inhabited was rather small.

"Supposedly he is some sort of *investor.* But what does he invest in? And where does he find the time? He's out every night if the papers report correctly."

"Maybe he's a vampire," said Grace, surprising herself at her own playfulness.

"Be serious." He glared at her.

"I am!" said Grace. "And you know better than to believe those rags that call themselves newspapers. Frankly, I'm relieved she's decided to continue her studies instead of drop out. She'll see sense with Junot, just like she did with school."

Rainier pursed his lips. Secretly, Grace was glad he was finally getting a dose of the anxiety she'd been experiencing for years about their daughters, even if it was only a thimbleful by comparison. It appeared that after all the years of worry, she'd developed a gift for patience and waiting things out that Rainier did not possess.

Well, she thought to herself, there had to be a silver lining in all that strife somewhere.

■ ■ ■ ■

Nineteen seventy-six was turning into quite a year, Grace reflected as she buckled her seat belt in first class and asked for a glass of champagne. *Why not?* She had things to celebrate. Her poetry readings, her new détente with Rainier, a period of relative calm with her daughters, and now a trip to New York to sit on the board of Twentieth Century Fox that would include a long weekend in Massachusetts with old friends and then Albie, who was living in a dorm at Amherst.

When Jay Kanter, who was now at Fox himself, had called to offer her the position, Grace's jaw had nearly dropped open. "You'll be the first woman on the board," he'd said. "We need someone with experience not just in the industry, but in running a big show. And what show's bigger than Monaco?"

She very nearly said that her husband was really the one running that show, but then stopped herself because in fact she *was* responsible for a great number of important things in their principality. Her charity work, which had started in once poor and now world-class hospitals and eventually branched into the ballet, the theater, and now the Princess Grace Foundation, kept her very busy and was — she saw suddenly, talking to Jay — experience that could be applied to the board of a motion picture company.

Unlike the sporadic poetry readings, a board seat was a big enough commitment that she felt she ought to run it by Rainier first. She described it as "a natural extension of my behind-the-scenes work in the arts. And what a tremendous excuse to see Albie more often! He won't feel like Mummy's just coming to check up on him."

To her surprise, Rainier agreed without a fight. "I hope it sets an example to Caroline and Stéphanie," he said. "That they can aspire to greater things than *boys.*"

Grace bit her tongue, but Rainier's unexpected fatherly feminism irritated her. He'd never been able to see her acting career this way. Why was it different for his daughters? The answer came to her in a flash: because boys would take his daughters away from him in a way that work would not. Romantic love was just about the only thing that could supplant filial devotion.

Don't get sidetracked, Grace. Poetry readings, board meetings, nearly adult children with interests and passions of their own.

Those are what's important now. It was *good* that Rainier wanted the girls to cultivate their interests.

The plane began to taxi and Grace took a sip of champagne, and wondered to herself if maybe — just maybe — she might find herself on the cover of a magazine again, not for being Princess Grace, but for one of her new pursuits. Maybe that *Ms.* magazine she sometimes found in Caroline's room. "Grace Kelly, Film Mogul" or "Not Just a Pretty Face: Grace Makes Waves in the Boardroom." But no, she sighed, a publication like *Ms.* would never feature someone as old-fashioned as her, board of Fox or not. She'd settle for *Vogue* and an article that didn't include a box about tourist attractions in Monaco.

She quickly discovered she'd have much to tell any journalist who wanted to ask about her new position. At her first board meeting, in a room that felt like it was floating in the center of Manhattan, with a view all the way to the Statue of Liberty on the clear day they met, Grace listened hard and took many notes. Her new colleagues were discussing the upcoming slate of movies, including a big gamble they were taking on an upstart young director named George Lucas, who was making what Jay described passionately as "a whole new kind of science fiction picture."

Dennis Stanfill snorted and said, "The script reads more like a Western with robots."

"George Lucas?" asked Grace. "Didn't he do *American Graffiti*?"

"One and the same," said Jay. "It's good to know he has some name recognition."

Grace nodded, thinking back to the drama about the teenagers in a California town somewhere in the northern part of the state. "That movie's a far cry from outer space," she observed.

"Lucas is a genius," said Alan Ladd Jr. matter-of-factly. "You should see his work with models and camerawork, Grace. What he's doing is truly *new,* a bit like Hitchcock in his time. Plus he's one of the most talented writers I've seen in years."

"Well, I was certainly impressed by his other movie," she said, moved by Alan's enthusiasm, and inclined to believe him. "He took a subject and a place and a cast of characters that I knew nothing about, and made me care about them. Maybe he can do the same thing with robots."

"Let's hope so," said Dennis, "because we need a win, badly."

"I like the way she thinks," said Alan,

ignoring Dennis and smiling at Grace. Shooting Jay with his index finger and thumb, he said, "Good call, man." Then, turning back to Grace, he added, "And Alec Guinness has signed up to play an important role. Kind of a monkish warrior type. Weren't you in a movie with him back in the day?"

"Yes! *The Swan,* which was in fact his very first American movie," Grace cried with satisfaction.

And just like that, Grace was rooting for George Lucas and his Western with robots, hoping her instincts would be proven right.

When she told Albie about it over burgers and fries at a diner in Amherst two nights later, his eyes widened and he exclaimed, "Mom! Do you think you can get us tickets to the premiere? That would be amazing."

Grace laughed. "You've actually heard of this movie?"

"Mo-om, of course. Anyone who reads sci-fi, or watches *Star Trek,* or anything like that is just waiting for this movie to come out."

"Alan Ladd Jr. will be very glad to hear that," she said. "Do you watch *Star Trek*? I had no idea."

"Everyone's seen *Star Trek,*" he said chidingly. But her son's ribbing had such a different quality from that of Rainier or the girls. It was gentle, without malice or competition or fear.

"Everyone except your uncool mom who only watches BBC dramas," she replied, all lighthearted self-deprecation. "Tell me why I should watch it," she said, then listened as her son tripped over his words extolling the virtues of Captain Kirk and Spock, a conversation that wound its way to a book called *Stranger in a Strange Land* by a writer named Robert Heinlein, and then — to Grace's relief, to Huxley and Orwell and Bradbury. "Now, *Fahrenheit 451* I know something about," she said. "Everyone in New York read it when it came out in the early fifties. I would get into a subway car, and half the faces would be hidden behind it."

Albie appeared shocked by this revelation, his rosy lips hanging open. His handsome, fair face was soft and unlined beneath his wavy blond hair — the only one of her children to inherit her coloring, and the one she knew the least. But maybe that was about to change. "How old were you when it came out?" he demanded.

"Oh, I don't know. What year was it published?"

"Fifty-three, I think," he said.

"Then I was twenty-four," she said, amused by her freshman son's youthful cluelessness. "Albie," she suddenly thought to ask, "do you know when I was born?"

Chastened and wide-eyed, he closed his mouth and shook his head.

"Nineteen twenty-nine," she said.

"The year of the stock market crash," he said, as if giving an answer on a TV quiz show.

"Yes," said Grace, "though that's not how I like to remember it, especially since your grandfather was a very smart man and didn't have anything in stocks when it crashed. So we were fine. Financially, anyway."

"Wow," said Albie reverently. "I didn't know that."

"It's too bad you couldn't know your grandfather Kelly," said Grace, feeling a pang of sorrow about her father for the first time in many years. "I think you two would have gotten along famously." Secretly, she was also relieved her father couldn't sink his poisonously vengeful teeth into her children. He'd ruined poor Kell. And Peggy, his other favorite, was on her second unhappy marriage, her elder daughter, who was a mother herself, a stranger to her. Grace might not have been her father's favorite child, but here she was enjoying burgers and ice cream with her own son, and that meant the world to her. It meant she'd gotten somewhere in her life.

"Yeah," agreed Albie. "He was in the Olympics, too, right? He won a gold medal. I can't even imagine doing something like that."

Grace reached across the table to tuck a thick lock of hair behind her son's ear. "You'll do your own amazing things, Albie. I know it." Grace remembered how much it had meant to her to have the support and belief of Uncle George, and wanted so much to give that to her own children.

He blushed and said, "I hope so. It's not easy, you know, being half Grimaldi and half Kelly. There's a lot of history on both sides. A lot of people who've never met me sometimes expect things of me, just because of who I come from."

"I can only imagine," she said, finding it curious that she was having this conversation with Albie and not with the girls, whom she was often trying to coax into confessing their fears and anxieties. "You're young, though. It'll happen in its own time. It might take you longer *because* of whom you come from. And I want you to know that's all right with me."

"Thanks, Mom," he said, looking down and smiling at the sundaes Grace hadn't even realized had arrived.

Emboldened by her moment of closeness with Albie, Grace decided to broach the subject of Philippe Junot the next time she met Caroline in Paris. After some careful orchestration, including a jaunt to buy some new fall clothes and a late lunch at a bistro of Caroline's choice, Grace said, "Darling girl, you look wonderful. How is school?"

"I keep telling you, Mom, it's not *school*. It's university."

"I do keep forgetting," Grace laughed off her oft-made mistake, and told herself not to scold Caroline for her tone — which, Grace had noticed recently, bore striking resemblance to the one Rainier took when *he* was reprimanding her. "In America, it's all school. And I never even went to university."

"I know," said Caroline, and again Grace had to squelch the words that rose to her mouth: *What's that supposed to mean?*

"But of course the Academy was terribly rigorous," Grace said, a touch defensively. The waiter arrived with their meals: sole meunière for Grace and steak au poivre for Caroline. They shared a plate of sautéed spinach and another of crisp, salty potatoes. Steam rose off the plates, the scents of each mingling into one buttery, winey mixture — rich and sharp at the same time as only French cuisine could be.

Caroline rolled her eyes as she picked up her own fork and knife and made herself a bite of steak and spinach.

Ignore that. "Tell me about Philippe," Grace said brightly. "What sorts of things do you do together? I assume it's not all parties, as the papers would have us think." *Those naughty papers, whom we all hate. Remember, darling girl, we're on the same side!*

Caroline swallowed and took another bite before answering. "He likes to eat," she finally said. "So we go to a lot of restaurants. And to shop." Shimmying her shoulders, she added, "In fact, he bought me this blouse."

Grace hadn't liked the blouse as soon as she'd seen it, but had resisted saying anything in the interest of the more important conversation she needed to have with her daughter. Though it was long sleeved, the blouse was made of so fine a material that everyone in the restaurant could see her daughter's bra through it. She wished Caroline had worn a camisole over the lacy white lingerie, but Grace smiled and said, "It's very pretty."

"You don't like it," Caroline countered knowingly.

"I do! And what do I know about fashion these days anyway? You've long since replaced me on all the best-dressed lists," Grace said, which was after all true. She often consoled herself that those lists were a cosmic reminder that had she remained in Hollywood, she'd be out of work now for sure.

Placated by her mother's compliment, Caroline said, "Philippe has great taste. Everyone's always asking for his advice on what to wear, what to buy next."

"That *is* a handy quality," Grace said, reaching for the nicest thing to say that popped into her mind. Was Philippe perhaps like Oleg? In this flash of connection, she realized with nauseous clarity that Caroline and Philippe were lovers.

"Do you ever go to movies?" Grace asked, hoping to find something innocent and youthful in her daughter's relationship. "Walks through the Tuileries? Exhibits at the Louvre?"

Caroline shrugged. "I do that stuff with my friends. Philippe's too busy. He just wants to cut loose when he has time off."

Grace had eaten half her sole without tasting a bite. Setting down her knife and fork, she said, "As long as you're happy, darling."

"I am," Caroline said earnestly. She took a long drink of red wine.

Grace believed her. Caroline was happy. And what was the harm? Grace had survived her share of lovers and heartache. Caroline would, too. Suddenly, the heavier warning she'd planned about Junot felt unwarranted. Perhaps even counterproductive.

Grace fixed her eyes on Caroline and said, "You know I'm always here if you need me, right?"

"Mom! I'm fine," Caroline said, shivering a bit with discomfort. But Grace was sure she'd heard her, and that was the best she could do. For now.

CHAPTER 38

Do not behave like Mother.

It had become something of a mantra since Caroline had become engaged to Junot. And even though her own motivations for behaving badly with regard to her daughter's wedding were far different from those of Margaret Majer Kelly, Grace could now understand the maternal impulse to lash out at anyone or anything that got in her way. Her own mother had been happy with Grace's choice of husband, but unhappy about being marginalized and having to give up her dream of a royal wedding in Philadelphia, which she could rub in the faces of all the Main Line women who'd snubbed the wife of upstart businessman John B. Kelly. By contrast, Grace feared for her daughter's future happiness. No one except Caroline herself thought that Philippe Junot was the right man for her. The marriage was doomed, at best.

But Grace remembered how alone she'd felt during her engagement, how she couldn't come to her mother with anything but the required questions about outfit and flower colors, and she didn't want Caroline to feel that way.

When Caroline had told Grace and Rainier about the engagement, her face had been so full of youthful excitement and affection. She'd sat the two of them down in the living room, where they used to play Monopoly and Clue, and said, "I know Philippe isn't your first choice for me, but I love him. I really do. He makes me laugh, and makes me think of the world in challenging ways. That's what I want for myself — love, and fun, and to always be thinking in new ways."

Grace felt as though her heart was oozing a sticky, thick love for her daughter, and she recognized that she'd felt this same way when each of the children had been born, as if her body was manufacturing something that would cost her and protect them at the same time. She felt hot and craved skin-to-skin contact with her daughter, but Caroline was not a baby she could cradle in her arms anymore. She was a long-limbed adult who sat almost primly across from her parents, hoping for a positive reaction.

For once, Grace was the one to offer enthusiasm first — and she reflected that Rainier must really have been perturbed by their daughter's announcement, even though they'd both known it had been coming, if it trumped his compulsion to always beat Grace to the praise. Rising from the couch, she went to hug Caroline, who also stood and met her in a tight embrace. "My darling girl, congratulations," she said in her daughter's ear, as she felt Caroline's soft, slick hair against her cheek, inhaled the scent of lavender from her soap. When they each pulled away, Caroline's eyes were damp with tears. She said, "Thank you, Mom." This feeling of being loved by and in communion with her daughter would be worth the explosion from Rainier she knew was coming from the way he was sitting, frozen, on the couch.

Almost mechanically, Rainier stood, too, and hugged his daughter. "If it's what you want," he said.

Later, in their bedroom he raged, "How can you act like this is okay?"

"How can I not?" The vehemence of Grace's own words and tone startled her. She found she simply didn't care what Rainier thought about the way she would love their daughter through this ordeal. It was terrifying and freeing: *I don't care what you think.* Had it always been coming to this?

She went on. "She's our *daughter,* and she's made up her mind. The best we can do is let her know we love her no matter what. Even if she makes a huge mistake."

"You agree, then? This is a huge mistake?"

"Of course I do. How many times have we talked about it?"

He frowned and looked away. Grace could hear his mind whirring. He was so used to Grace being the heavy, the one willing to say no. *Not this time,* she thought.

Grace kept her smile on for all the shopping, showering, thank-you-note writing, gift wrapping, and seat arranging. Curiously, the more she smiled, the more honestly happy she felt for her daughter. It helped that Caroline responded so positively to the attention. Rainier kept his distance. "It's all women's work anyway," he grumbled. "And you've been in Monaco long enough to know how everything should be done. Just keep it small, for God's sake. We still don't even know who this Junot is, and because of Albie, Caroline will never be the Princess in any case. Best not to go overboard."

Despite not wanting to go overboard, Rainier finally said he'd come to one of her poetry readings, at St. James's Palace in London, because he wanted at least one member of the English royal family to attend his daughter's wedding. It had always bothered him — still it bothered him! — that not one member of the most famous and beloved royal family in the world had attended their wedding in nineteen fifty-six. "It's disrespectful," he'd said on their honeymoon. "Shows they give us no credit." But now that Monaco had survived a few crises with France and its sovereignty was secure, Grace knew her husband hoped for more recognition from the other European monarchies, especially the House of Windsor.

She felt more nervous than ever before her performance that night at the palace, but also happier than she had in years. Perhaps this was the new leaf. Regardless of his reason for attending, this was a chance for him to experience firsthand her joy in being onstage. Surely he would be touched by the poetry and his wife reciting it. He would feel, and participate in, the applause thundering around him; he'd be proud of her, and perhaps experience for himself a little of what it was like to be appreciated by a theater full of people. A wall that had long been stalwart between them would crumble. *It seems I do still care what you think,* she thought warmly before she took the stage, ready to see her husband beaming proudly at her.

When she stepped out under the warm white lights that night, she felt like her decades-younger self stepping onto a Broadway stage for the first time, knowing her parents were in the audience and wondering what they would think. Her stomach was a riot of nerves, and her throat felt tight. How would she get the words out?

She raised her eyes to the box where Rainier was sitting — for she was wearing her glasses and could see — and saw her husband's head lolling on his shoulder, lips soft and parted, eyes closed.

Asleep. Even as loud, enthusiastic applause greeted her.

The nerves buzzing throughout her body stopped. For a moment, she couldn't even hear the applause. She nearly opened her mouth to scream at him, "I'm only the third reader! You're my husband!"

Instead, Grace moved her eyes to the faces of people in the orchestra seats — all wide-awake and smiling expectantly. *Well,* she told herself as she straightened her shoulders, *what does it matter if he's not watching?* His slumber put her in an elite category that included the finest opera singers and ballet dancers in Europe. A familiar hardness formed inside of her, a fist of anger that had been closing protectively around her heart since she was a girl.

Grace drew in a long, fortifying breath as she lifted her eyes to where the Queen Mother, in whose honor she was reading, looked down at her beatifically, expectantly. Grace found the words to the Keats poem that started her program: "Bright star, would I were as stedfast as thou art — / Not in lone splendour hung aloft the night . . ."

Despite Grace's secret wish that it would not, Caroline's wedding day arrived — without a Windsor in attendance. Her eldest child, her first daughter, looked almost saintly in her modest embroidered dress, which fairly glowed white against her tan skin and dark hair, which had been swept back and fastened to a veil with a curve of small white flowers at the sides of her head. Grace tried to look at Philippe as little as possible, because to see the two of them together only drove home how mismatched they were, even physically — Caroline so young and delicate, all small points and angles, and Philippe, who was so much older, which showed in the lines of his face, his politician's smile and heftier features. *How ironic*, Grace observed, *that I should spend so many years in thrall to much older men on-screen and off-, but it should be my daughter who actually marries someone entirely too old for her.* Whatever criticisms she had of Rainier, none had ever been that he was too old.

"Caroline told me how much it means to her that you're both here today," Albie said to Grace and Rainier as they waited in one of the chambers of the chapel before the ceremony began. Stéphie was also there, sitting on a desk and swinging her legs and chewing gum like the schoolgirl she was.

"Our little diplomat," Grace said, smiling and patting her son's cheek. She felt a flush of tears at his words, but was determined to hold them in even though she'd instructed her most trusted makeup artist to use only waterproof products for this momentous day. "Thank you for telling me that."

The ceremony, mass, and photographs, the endless receiving line under the waning but still hot Monégasque sunshine, seemed to stretch the day out interminably. Caroline, who usually detested this sort of pomp and formality, appeared to be relishing every minute of it now that the attention and compliments were directed at her. She smiled with genuine gratitude and kissed or grasped hands with everyone, no matter who they were, and Grace recognized something in her daughter that reached down into her gut like a hand scraping out the innards of a Halloween pumpkin. *She feels seen.* In spite of all her instructions to herself not to be like her own mother, had she made Margaret Majer Kelly's mistake anyway? Did Caroline also feel unseen? Was this the stage her daughter felt she needed to step upon to get her mother's attention?

The hand scouring her insides went to work again when Grace watched as Rainier took Caroline to the dance floor when the band struck up "Sweet Caroline," which had been their daughter's household theme song since its release nearly a decade ago. Rainier and Caroline smiled at each other in that way that excluded everyone else at the reception, that way that simultaneously said *je t'aime, papa* and *je t'aime, ma fille.* "And when I hurt," sang the front man of the band, "hurting runs off my shoulders. How can I hurt when holding you?"

A fierce maternal jealousy filled Grace, and she wondered what Philippe thought when he saw his bride with her father. Grace scanned the crowd for Caroline's new husband; it took longer than expected because he was toward the back near the tiers of intricately decorated cake, not even looking at his new wife but laughing riotously with some other unctuous, false-smiled businessman type.

I'll be right here when you need me, Grace thought at her daughter, hoping that she'd finally be up to that task, hoping she could give her daughter what she needed, when she needed it.

The palace was eerily silent after the wedding. Grace took off for Roc Agel alone, needing the healing touch of the long grasses and wildflowers. She had told the rest of her family, whom she left behind at the palace, that anyone was welcome to join her if they felt so moved. No one had volunteered, and so she'd left, taking with her a new volume fresh from Shakespeare and Company by the Irish poet Seamus Heaney. She'd recently become interested in Irish writers, following a binge on the poetry of Yeats.

It was a warm late-summer afternoon, and Grace stood in her studio surrounded by fresh cuts of flowers she planned to dry and press into designs and patterns that pleased and soothed her, when she was startled to hear Stéphanie's voice from the doorway behind her say, "Mom?"

"Oh, my goodness," Grace said, whirling around, her hand on her galloping heart. "Stéphie! I'm so glad to see you, but so surprised!"

Her younger daughter laughed. She looked enough like Caroline to give Grace a fresh pang of the sadness that had dogged her since the wedding. "Sorry," Stéphie said, "but I wanted . . . I just thought maybe we could keep each other company."

Grace almost wept at this surprise. Her beautiful, popular daughter had surely turned down many invitations for more glamorous locales and company than Roc Agel and her washed-up actress of a mother.

Crossing the room, she hugged Stéphanie. "I couldn't be happier to see you."

"Do you want help with your flowers?" Stéphie asked. This offer was also unprecedented. *Goodness, what other pleasures will this evening bring?* Grace wondered.

Though the idea of talking flowers with her daughter, and also of getting some of that work accomplished, was appealing, she didn't want to risk boring Stéphanie so that she'd never be tempted to repeat this daughterly offer of company and companionship.

"Actually," said Grace, "I'm starving. How

about you?"

They spent an hour in the rustic kitchen, chopping fresh herbs and tiny tomatoes they gathered together from the garden, boiling water for pasta, and nibbling on a chunk of a local goat cheese and crostini with *l'eau pétillante.* They traded funny stories about the wedding, and Stéphie opened up about some of the girls at her school and how it bothered her when they excluded her from certain parties and outings. "I don't always want to actually go," her daughter said, "but I want to be invited."

"Yes," Grace agreed, "it's always nice to feel included." She remembered so well how it had felt *not* to receive invitations to the usual Hollywood parties as soon as she moved to Monaco. Of course, she couldn't have gone, but it would have been so nice to feel that her friends missed her so much that they invited her anyway. Not being invited made her feel forgotten. The long list of invitations she had to decline had so swamped her in recent years, she'd forgotten how hard that other feeling had been for her, and she tried to offer Stéphie as much understanding as she could.

When at last they each had bowls of steaming, fragrant spaghetti smothered in herbs sautéed with anchovies in oil, it was dark. "Want to see if there's a good movie on television?" Grace suggested, and when Stéphie nodded with an eager smile, they went to the living room and sat cross-legged as Grace used the new remote control to find a channel that might have a decent movie. In minutes, she located a choice so perfect it was almost divine intervention: *Roman Holiday* with Audrey Hepburn. It was only about fifteen minutes in.

"Have you ever seen this?" Grace asked her daughter, who stared at the screen in rapt attention as she slurped a mouthful of pasta and shook her head.

"Shame on me, then! This movie is a must."

She only wished Caroline was there. At the first advertising break, Grace filled Stéphanie in on the start of the movie she'd missed. "So," her daughter asked in disbelief, "this is really about a princess of a small country in Europe who wants to run away from her life?"

"It is," Grace affirmed, hardly able to believe the parallels herself. The first time she'd seen the movie had been when it released in 1953, and she'd been twenty-four years old — exactly the same age as Audrey. How clearly she remembered sitting in the dark theater, watching Princess

Ann enjoy her ice-cream cone and new sandals and impish haircut, little freedoms Grace could have walked out of the theater and enjoyed herself at the snap of her fingers. Little had she known that in three years, the young actress who'd sat in envy of her contemporary's luck in landing this prime role would trade those very freedoms for the life Audrey was playing in the movie.

Now, twenty-five years later, Grace was watching the movie again with her own little princess, laughing with recognition as sheltered Princess Ann got into all manner of trouble throughout Rome alongside Gregory Peck's Joe Bradley, who was utterly won over by the girl's naïve charm. When the movie ended and Ann chose to resume her stifling life as sovereign, with all the luncheons and interviews she abhorred, Grace and Stéphanie were blowing their noses and dabbing their eyes with tissues. When the credits rolled and they finally looked at each other, they burst into laughter and went into the kitchen to eat ice cream, standing in their bare feet.

"Too bad Caroline didn't meet a Joe Bradley," mused Stéphanie.

I was just thinking the same thing. "I'm sure Philippe is showing her a terrific time on their honeymoon," Grace said. "And maybe *you* will meet a Joe Bradley someday."

Stéphanie grinned, and she looked as excited and carefree as Grace had ever seen her. "That would be fun," she said.

As she lay in bed in the velvety darkness, with her windows open to the symphony of crickets and cicadas, a fan delicately whirring in the corner of her room, gratitude welled up in Grace. After everything she'd given up, life was finally giving her something back — the Fox board, the poetry readings, and now an intimacy with her daughters she'd always craved. Caroline's marriage might not last, but it had afforded Grace the opportunity to support her daughter and to be close to her other two children.

Before she knew it, Stéphanie would also be a grown woman. And maybe another director, someone of Hitch's caliber, would show her a script. And it wouldn't matter what Rainier said, or what some decades-old piece of paper dictated. Her adult children, whom she loved, couldn't be kept from her. They could choose to get on a plane to California. And they would. Surely they would.

CHAPTER 39

Twenty-five years. Their so-called wedding of the century had been a quarter of a century ago. And later this spring, England's Prince Charles would marry Lady Diana Spencer in a wedding heralded as the biggest thing in nuptials since her own. It was very strange to be the bride against whom others were measured, especially when she hardly even remembered wearing that dress, taking all those pictures, walking down the aisle, and bowing her head so regally beneath her veil. Even she was impressed at herself, looking at the pictures that were still sprinkled into newspapers and magazines. The pictures proved she had indeed been a fairy-tale bride, but what they couldn't show was that every molecule in her body had been yearning to be on Rainier's boat, sailing away from it all.

Grace was to meet Lady Diana later that

day, at a poetry reading at Goldsmiths' Hall in honor of her groom, Prince Charles. She had half a mind to take the young man aside and tell him to be nice to that young thing he was marrying, for she looked like a frightened rabbit in every single photo that was taken of her. And like everyone else in their circles — everyone except Diana herself, Grace assumed — Grace had heard the rumors that he was still involved with his college sweetheart.

Rolling out of her feathery-soft London hotel bed, Grace padded to the bathroom and stared at her face in the mirror. Every morning she hoped to see something different, especially if she'd woken many times to use the toilet, as she had last night. She kept hoping the bloat in her face and torso would be gone, the excess water flushed down long pipes and into sewers, far away from her own body.

But every morning she was disappointed. She hardly recognized herself. The hormone specialist she saw regularly in Paris had put her on what he promised was the absolute latest in treatment for menopausal women. When she complained that the regimen of pills was making her face and body fill like water balloons, the doctor kept saying this effect would subside; she just needed to be patient. Patient, patient. She was so tired of waiting all the time.

For God's sake, *when* could she expect to look like herself again? Through all the trials of her life, one thing she'd always been able to depend on was looking in the mirror and seeing herself every morning. It was disconcerting to see this fun-house version of herself look back at her, when her face was the one thing she'd never had to struggle with in her life. The choices she'd always made to stay out of the sun, not to smoke, not to drink too many cocktails or eat too many desserts had sometimes been a hardship, but as a result her face had been stable her whole life.

It was beyond vanity, the way these changes unsettled her. What she felt was more like being shipwrecked, marooned on an island where nothing was familiar, all her usual defenses and helpmeets destroyed. She had to figure out everything anew.

The change was making her cranky, which she was not proud of, but hadn't been able to help. She had been extra critical of her girls lately, after a few months of unexpected calm following Caroline's divorce from Philippe Junot last year. Grace and her elder daughter had been like storybook princesses locked in their palace, shutting themselves in from everything else outside. Grace stroked Caroline's hair as she cried; they burrowed under duvets and watched movies and ate chocolate ice cream; they took long walks in the hills near the palace that reminded her of her treks with Rita in the hills near Sweetzer when she was her daughter's age; then they would take cooling swims in the pool. Eventually, they made plans for the relaunching of Caroline's life: graduate school, Paris, and a foundation for children that she could pour her energies into. "I want to be so busy, I don't even think about men," she said to her mother. Full of hope, Grace cupped her daughter's beautiful face in her hands and said, "I'm so very proud of you."

But hardly six months had gone by, and Caroline again became a regular feature in the tabloids: worse, the photographers were now also attacking Stéphanie with a vengeance now that she was a regular on the party circuit.

Unlike the last time they'd had this conversation, Rainier was in favor of Grace taking up residence in Paris with their girls. "They must behave," he said irritably. It was the most he said on the subject, as he was pouring all his parenting energy into Albie, who would soon be graduating from

Amherst and was becoming more and more interested in the sports he'd always casually pursued. He'd even taken up a little-known Olympic event called the bobsleigh. "Can you imagine?" Rainier had chuckled. "The prince of the sunniest country in Europe competing in the winter Olympics?"

"It is ironic," Grace agreed. "But his grandfather would be very proud." She wondered if this was really true, however, for Jack Kelly's grandson was more of a dabbler than a focused athlete. Albie was good at many sports, which pleased and reassured Grace. Having seen what happened to Kell, whose fanatical dedication to rowing had kept him from enjoying his own life, Grace had never asked Albie to choose between tennis and swimming and track. Not for the first time, Grace felt grateful that her father had died before he could pass any sort of judgment on her own children. She had enough of his voice in her ears even from the grave. Then she felt terribly guilty for feeling that way.

In the shower, Grace massaged a large, fragrant cake of soap over her skin, lathering her puffy body in foamy white bubbles. Then she let scalding-hot water rinse the bubbles into the drain. She sighed. A makeup artist would be arriving soon to do what she could with her face. She longed for the days on movie sets when she had to plead for less makeup. Now she had to make sure there was enough.

Gwen Robyns kissed Grace on both cheeks under the soft yellow lights shining down on Goldsmiths' Hall's marble Staircase Hall when the poetry reading was done. They had been corresponding and speaking on the phone lately about doing a book on flowers together, but she hadn't actually seen her friend in months. "It's so wonderful to see you," said Grace, holding her friend's hands tightly in her own. Both sets of hands betrayed her age and her friend's — chilly to the touch, with loose, thin skin and more pronounced knuckles. The Cartier diamond Rainier had given her nearly a quarter century ago was constantly falling into the crook between her finger and palm.

"I can't wait to catch up properly tomorrow," said Grace. She never liked to schedule too many meetings before a performance, preferring to use the time to rehearse or immerse herself in other poems by the same author. So she had added time in London on this trip to see more of Gwen, as well as a few other friends who happened to be in the English capital.

"What do you think?" Gwen whispered to Grace, nodding over at Diana, who stood beside Charles in a stiff blue dress meant to show off her milky skin and delicate collarbone — but the girl stooped, curving her shoulders inward, her nose preparing for a downward dive into her glass of sparkling water.

"I wish I could send her to Edith and Sandy for crash courses in how to wear clothes, and how to act like a princess when you don't feel like one," Grace said, her heart breaking for this young swan. How different she was from Caroline and Stéphanie, who had never been wallflowers, who had always stood tall and thrust out their chins for the cameras. Grace wondered if this was because her own daughters had been raised in the spotlight, whereas Diana was being shoved into it. She could see why, of course; the girl was lovely. Grace wished only that she could show her how to hide her insecurities.

Grace and Gwen couldn't speak long before they were accosted by a number of appreciative earls and dukes and Royal Shakespeare players, each one full of praise and questions and invitations to upcoming productions. At last Grace had to excuse herself to use the ladies' room, and she found Diana standing in front of a mirror sniffling back tears as she tried to adjust the bodice of her gown with her long, soft arms.

She looked so distressed, Grace approached her and asked, "Is there anything I can do to help?"

"Not unless you can let it out," Diana said softly, her voice damp and blunted by her stuffy nose. "They made me wear it a size too small."

"Well, that's wretched," Grace said, putting what she hoped were comforting hands around the girl's rib cage, and trying to gently move the fabric so that it would rest more comfortably. It was stuck tight to her clammy skin, though.

"It's not going to budge," said Diana.

"If it makes you feel any better, you look absolutely gorgeous in it. I'd never know it was too small," said Grace. The two women were looking at each other in the mirror, rather than directly into each other's faces, and still Diana avoided eye contact, even in this indirect medium. Grace was surprised to realize that despite the age and extra weight that were so obvious in her own appearance, she wouldn't have traded places with this beautiful young creature for anything in the world.

"They never listen to me," Diana said, her

voice clearing a bit, strengthening as she made this statement.

How Grace wanted to help her! "I have always found it best not to let anyone know they've gotten the better of me," Grace said, groping around for the best of a lifetime's worth of advice and coming up short.

Diana sighed as if Grace's entreaty was entirely beyond her. "Does it ever get better?" she asked, finally lifting her eyes and staring straight into Grace's. Searching, afraid, sad. This was a girl who wanted — and needed — the truth.

Grace put her arm around Diana and laughed with as much warmth as she could muster. "Oh, my dear girl," she said, "I'm afraid it only gets worse."

Diana's chin trembled.

"But you can get through it," Grace said firmly. "You will be Queen Diana someday. And in the meantime, when it does get worse, I want you to call me."

Diana nodded, swallowed valiantly, then reached for a tissue from the box on the table in front of them. After blowing her nose and blotting under her eyes, she said to Grace, "You can count on it."

"My door is always open to you, if you need a place to get away."

Diana nodded, Grace patted her on the

back, and the two of them reentered the fray, the younger woman standing just a fraction straighter than before.

"You really won't go?" Grace asked Rainier incredulously, holding the unassuming card on which was engraved their invitation to the wedding of Charles and Diana. "I thought it might be fun, this time, to *attend* the so-called wedding of the century and laugh together at the absurdity of it all."

Rainier shrugged, then took a handful of almonds from the dish near his elbow. He ate a few, then sipped his Scotch and soda. They were sitting on the patio of Roc Agel, a luscious sunset falling pink and orange all around them, a vase of wildflowers on the table where they would later eat dinner.

"They didn't come to our wedding, nor to Caroline's," he replied. "I see no reason to put myself out to go to this. Think of how terrible our own wedding was, Grace. This promises to be just as bad, and this time I'm not required to attend."

So many emotions competed for Grace's attention — frustration at his shortsightedness, hurt that he couldn't see the irony and potential fun in attending this wedding of all weddings with her, resentment of his usual self-centered pettiness — and combined, they felt like a hot, gassy flame in her chest. She hated feeling this way, and so she threw anger at herself on the pyre inside her. *You're being selfish. Maybe he has a point.*

And: *How can he look so calm?!*

"If it means so much to you," said Rainier, his tone so casual, so easygoing, as if they were discussing a golf tournament, "go by yourself. Or take Albie. It will be good for him to be seen at such an event."

"And if they ask where you are?"

"Tell them I wasn't feeling well." Rainier snapped his fingers, and Grace practically saw the lightbulb go on above his head. "In fact, that's perfect. We'll RSVP yes for both of us, but I'll come down with something" — he coughed for effect — "at the last minute, and you'll have to take Albie instead."

"I'd much rather go with you. Dance with you," she said, her voice cracking. She hadn't felt like she wanted, let alone needed, Rainier at an event in years. Why now? Why this one?

Rainier clicked his tongue. "Come now, Grace. We're beyond this, aren't we? You know you'll have more fun without me anyway."

"That's not true," she protested, her

throat singed by the emotion burning inside her. But wasn't it true? She didn't want it to be true.

"We'll have fun at Frank's place next month," he said, his voice less patronizing, a little more solicitous. Grace wondered if he could see that she really was distressed and wanted her to feel better, or if he just wanted the scene to end. Heaven knew, she wanted it to end, too. But differently.

Rainier was glad to go to Frank and Barbara Sinatra's because it was easy, familiar. He wouldn't have to stick his neck out. And the event would be about him. Well, *them*. The twenty-fifth-anniversary celebration of their wedding.

Grace sighed. "I'll make sure Albie's schedule stays clear for the end of July." *And I'll see if I can book another reading in England.* This thought doused the flame inside her ever so slightly.

CHAPTER 40

Before she went on to Frank's place in Santa Barbara to meet Rainier and her children for the big party in April, she met with the Fox board in Hollywood. She still relished these meetings — every one of them, even the contentious ones in which they discussed hiring and firing and pulling the plug on movies that weren't going as planned. After the latest, she had lunch with Jay at Musso & Frank, which looked just as it had in 1955 when they'd opened this room adjacent to the original, which had been called Francois since 1919 — in fact, Paul, the maître d' in his red vest with the black lapels, still called it "the new room," when he seated them. "Miss Kelly, what a pleasure to see you again. Would you like to sit in the new room?" It was all dark wood paneling with a wide strip of toile wallpaper toward the ceiling, and not a single window, giving it a nighttime feel all day long. The red leather of the booths was still slick and crackled when her weight hit it.

Her old agent — well, Grace supposed he was still her agent, since it wasn't as though she'd ever gotten a new one — looked fit and tan despite what appeared to be his habit of ordering martinis with lunch. Well, she corrected herself, martini lunches weren't exactly her habit, either, but she had ordered one today because it sounded so Los Angeles "power lunch." Wasn't that what they called them these days? Cautiously, she took only a few sips, while Jay waited for his second. She had a moment's fleeting sadness that Judybird wasn't with them, as in the old days. But she was with her third husband, Don Quine, and seemed happy. Grace had seen her just a few months ago at Bemelmans Bar, after a reading in New York.

"I probably shouldn't tell you this," said Jay, "but I still get calls about you. More so now that you're doing these poetry readings."

"Oh, do tell," she said, giddy with the very idea of these calls, the promise and possibility contained in that little one-syllable word. How many other calls had changed her life?

"Most of them aren't specific," he said. "They're from directors and other actors wanting to know if you'd be ready to make a comeback for the right script."

"And what do you tell them?"

"I say nothing is impossible. Lately, I've also said I'll ask you directly the next time I see you." Jay reached out and twirled the stem of his fresh martini glass, watching the two olives wobble in the clear, icy liquid as he waited for her reply.

"Are they directors and actors I'd want to work with?" She was playing with a little ball of fire, and she knew it, but it was so tempting.

Jay nodded. "I think so."

Grace inhaled deeply, feeling the air inflate her chest. She'd have to do something about this face of hers, but without knives. Hollywood's default to surgery was so dishonest. She'd prefer to play a crone to a Norma Desmond.

She began the calculation she'd found herself repeating lately, as if it might somehow change. Caroline and Albie were practically finished with school, and adults, in any case, who could fly wherever they wanted to go, and to whomever they wanted to see. They didn't need their father's permission to see their mother. And Stéphanie was fifteen; in three more years, she would be eighteen and beginning university. With two older siblings to help her, she would be able to make her own choices about where to be and with whom.

It was a terrible position to put her children in. But was it better for them to have a mother who lived a life of "quiet desperation," to borrow a phrase she'd recently read in Thoreau's *Walden,* in which she'd recognized herself so strongly? If their mother was truly happy, would her children not be free to be happy as well?

Three years. She could be free of the contract she'd signed in 1956 in three years. She'd be only fifty-four years old. Katharine Hepburn was fifty-five when she did *Long Day's Journey into Night,* and older when she won her second and third Oscars for *Guess Who's Coming to Dinner* and *The Lion in Winter.* Audrey, who was also born in 1929, still made the occasional movie, and Lauren Bacall, who'd been at the Academy just a few years before Grace, was still going strong. Ingrid Bergman, her old idol, to whom Grace had so often been compared, had done quite a lot of work through her fifties and sixties.

Give me one more year, Jay, Grace very nearly said, though instead she sighed and the words "I suppose you never know" escaped her lips. She had time. The process of making movies had slowed considerably since Hitchcock's heyday of shooting two, sometimes three, pictures a year. She wasn't ready to say it out loud, but perhaps she could start quietly reading scripts in a year; it would take her a while to find the right one, then more time to agree and actually start shooting. Meanwhile, she would continue to enjoy the stage with her poetry readings, as she spoke to lawyers and prepared herself for the next phase of her life. That was one great irony of all this — she no longer had the stamina it required for a multiweek theater run. She really could only do the poetry readings or movies. One-offs.

Jay cocked an eyebrow and echoed her words with his glass raised. "I suppose not."

Grace lifted her own glass and clinked it to his, feeling its musical ring reverberate through her whole body.

April 18, 1981, found Grace in the company of many of the friends she'd shared the same day with twenty-five years before. But even in the singer's beloved Palm Springs, at Frank and Barbara Sinatra's secluded compound on a slope of the San Jacinto Mountains, far from everything, the day couldn't have felt more different from the original in Monaco, where they'd been surrounded by water, lush sprays of cut flowers, and crowds of strangers. Here were only people they'd known for years. The surroundings were dry and the vegetation scrubby, but Frank and Barbara had made sure their home was an oasis of local cacti and trees, a glittering blue swimming pool, stone patios, and enormous windows with spectacular views of the mountains and desert below.

"Now, this is a man who knows how to get away," Rainier said admiringly, standing on the lower deck and surveying the vast panorama, a coupe of champagne in his hand.

"I've always been amazed at how huge the sky feels in California," added Grace. "And here, I feel it even more." Endless possibilities. As far as her eyes could see. She thought of her conversation with Jay a few days before. And with Diana not long before that. With all eyes on a new young princess and her future, who would even care if Grace and Rainier were to call it quits? Whatever that would even mean. Perhaps they would only live apart, and not divorce. How different would that be from what they were doing now? They led such separate lives as it was. Perhaps they would even celebrate fifty years in another twenty-five.

It would all be up to Rainier. Her mind was made up. It was strange to be thinking of the end of her marriage on this day when she was supposedly celebrating its longevity, but the anniversary gave her an ironic sense of peace. She'd hung in there a long time. No one would be able to fault her for throwing in the towel too soon. She took real pride in that.

Rita and Cary and Ava and Jim and Katy and Judybird all came to the party, among a hundred others. There were toasts and laughter, congratulations and exclamations of wonder — but less for the fairy tale than for the number of years that had passed. *Can it really have been twenty-five years? How young we all were. . . .*

Before they were seated, someone — she never knew whom — called on her to her to recite a poem. It became a chant, "Po-em, po-em."

"In Clark Gable's voice!" demanded Frank, and she had a flash of imitating Coop for Frank and Clark and Ava all those years ago.

"Well, since you are our host," she said, with a courtly bow and a hand on her heart. Then she raised her glass, and took a sip to thundering applause. When someone produced a step stool, she alighted, and there was complete silence. She began, hands in fists on her hips, arms akimbo, chest thrust out. Someone hooted in appreciation.

"All the world's" — she paused for effect — "a stage," she began, hitting Clark's nasal, masculine twang pretty well, she thought. Egged on by the appreciative whistles and claps of her audience, she went on with Jacques's speech to Duke Senior from *As You Like It,* improvising a bit when she couldn't remember a phrase or two:

"And all the men and women merely players; / They have their exits and their entrances; / And one man in his time plays many parts, / His acts being seven ages. At first the infant . . . / And then the lover, / Sighing like a furnace, with a woeful ballad, / Made to his mistress's eyebrow. . . . / And the last scene of all, / That ends this strange eventful history, / Is second childishness and mere oblivion, / Sans teeth, sans eyes, sans taste, sans everything." She paused again, then ad-libbed, "Except that line for which the player was bestly known, 'Frankly Scarlett'" — she paused, cupped one hand to her ear, and used her other to conduct her audience in reciting along with her — " 'I don't give a damn.' "

The room exploded with applause, stomps, whistles, and shouts of "Encore!"

No one clapped louder than Rainier. His expression was one of singular admiration and love, and — was it really? — regret. As if he knew. He knew what he had made her give up.

And he'd done nothing.

Hamming it up with her bow, Grace put out her hand and said, "Have to know when to exeunt," as she stepped down from the stool, her legs shaking a bit.

Albie was the one to steady her, letting her lean on him as he gave her a kiss on the cheek and a "That was amazing, Mom."

She kissed him in reply and whispered, "Thank you, darling."

Soon enough, the room calmed down and it was time for supper. Once everyone had dined on roasted vegetables and quail, Rainier stood up, tapping his water glass for attention. In seconds, all eyes were on him.

After thanking everyone for coming, and thanking Frank and Barbara for their friendship and gracious hosting, he looked around and said, "On this day in nineteen fifty-six . . ." Then he stopped, shook his head, and cleared his throat. When he went on, it was clear he was struggling to keep his emotions in check. Grace put a hand automatically on his arm and smiled up at him encouragingly. She felt fizzy and happy, and was as curious as anyone else about what Rainier was about to say; it surprised her that he was so choked up, but she attributed it less to a quarter century of love than the just dawning realization of what those years had cost.

"On this day in nineteen fifty-six," he said again, his voice a bit bolder, "I married Grace Kelly. All the headlines read that this talented American actress had found her prince, but no one seemed to realize that the truth was that *I* had found my princess. *She* is the one who kissed me awake." He looked down at her with an admiring smile and put a hand on his heart as a few guests quietly blew their noses. Grace smiled up at him, surprised that his words could disarm her after all these years. But then he'd had time to plan and write this speech, as he had his letters twenty-six years ago.

"I was not fully alive, not fully myself, until I married Grace," he went on, looking back out at the guests in the sparkling candlelight. "For she has brought out the very best in me, and in Monaco. Our country has flourished under her radiant smile, but more importantly, our three beautiful children have her intelligence, her golden heart, her poise, and — yes, dear, I must say it — your *grace*. . . ." Here he paused for effect, letting their guests *pshaw* and chuckle appreciatively, though he didn't look at her as he said it. He cleared his throat again and said, "Since poetry has meant so much to you in recent years, I wanted to close with a few lines from Elizabeth Barrett Browning." Now he looked at her and recited, "How do I love thee? Let me count the ways. / I love thee to the depth and breadth and height / My soul can reach, when feeling out of sight / For the ends of being and ideal grace."

She was amazed at how these words moved her, even the emphasis he placed on the word *grace.* Emotion welled up in her like the old familiar flood, filling her chest and making breath difficult to catch. When he finished, "I love thee with the breath, / Smiles, tears, of all my life; and, if God choose, / I shall but love thee better after death," the flood had risen all the way to the crown of her head, and a tear leaked out. All around them were honks and sniffles into tissues, just as there had been on this day plus one twenty-five years ago.

With a hand on her heart, Grace stood and kissed Rainier, and their own tears mingled where their lips met, sealing or melting promises. She could no longer honestly say she knew the difference.

EPILOGUE

September 13, 1982

She hadn't felt this good in ages. True, the busy weekend with visiting friends at Roc Agel had had its tensions, what with Stéphanie declaring she wanted to give up fashion-design school for race-car driving with her boyfriend, Paul Belmondo, but Tuesday dawned quiet and bright at their cottage on the hill. Everyone else having left, at last it was just Grace and Rainier, Stéphie, and Albie. She and Rainier stood in the kitchen and drank coffee together, and she said to him as he stewed about Stéphanie again, "We've been here before, darling." Putting a hand on his arm, she assured him, "We'll get through it again." And she believed it. He was the same man he'd always been, but she felt different. This time, this crisis, would be different.

Life seemed miraculously full of possibilities that morning. Once Rainier left for the palace and a full day of meetings, the house was silent except for the chirps and trills of a few birds outside. With her second cup of coffee warming her hands, Grace padded barefoot onto the patio and breathed in the scent of rosemary and lavender, felt the gritty stones beneath her toes, and let her eyes rest on the wildflowers dappled by the morning light. *I caught this morning's minion, king- / dom of daylight's dauphin, dapple-dawn-drawn Falcon . . .* Grace often found herself reciting this opening to Gerard Manley Hopkins's poem when she caught the serene, spectacular beauty of morning here, her favorite spot on earth. For it truly was her favorite, and it gave her pause about her plans. Roc Agel, its flowers and its peace, had been her escape for more than two decades.

But there could — would — be other gardens, other places where the sun filtered through the trees just so. She recalled the immensity of the California sky, and her breath caught.

She showered, then dressed. She was starting to reconcile herself to her fuller face, and she was looking forward to giving another poetry reading at Windsor Castle later in the week, and seeing Gwen and Diana again; she thought she also might join

Caroline at the spa where she was relaxing in the English countryside.

Jaybird had even called her with news of a promising script; she'd read a few he'd sent in the past year, but none of them had felt worth the fallout. But she had a feeling about this next one — there was just something about the way Jay talked about it. She could wait, though. If she'd learned that much in twenty-six years of marriage, it was how to wait. She had plenty of time, after all. She was only, nearly, fifty-three.

Grace loaded the backseat of their Rover with dresses and boxes of hats, most of them new and needing adjusting in Paris. By the time she was finished and Stéphie was groggily ready, there was room for only the two of them in the driver's and passenger's seats. Albie was still asleep, bless him.

"I'll drive to the palace," she told the chauffeur.

"I cannot let you do that, Madam," he replied.

"You can and you will," she said as kindly and firmly as she could, knowing that had this been Fordie, she'd have figured out a way to make room. She wanted to be with only family that day, and the full backseat was a convenient excuse to drive with just Stéphanie, to whom she wanted to speak privately so she could better understand why her daughter wanted to give up something for which she had such gifts — fashion — for something so reckless. She knew a thing or two about shortsighted decisions.

"Are you sure you want to drive, Mom?" Stéphanie asked, blowing on her mug of fresh coffee as she settled into the seat next to Grace.

"Of course," said Grace, counseling herself *not* to tell Stéphie to be careful with the mug of hot liquid. *She's not a child anymore,* Grace reflected, admiring her daughter's fine features and tanned skin. "I don't get a chance to spend time with you alone often enough."

Her daughter, understandably reticent after a weekend of being regaled by one parent with all the reasons why race-car driving was inappropriate for a girl and a princess, only sighed.

Grace turned the key in the ignition and slowly drove onto the road. The views on the way back to Monaco were spectacular, with glimpses of the Trophée des Alpes in La Turbie and the Mediterranean coastline with its dramatic slopes and medieval towns, but Grace kept her eyes fastened to the asphalt. Even after twenty-six years, Rainier's prediction that she'd be comfortable driving this road had never quite come true. The hairpin turns were just a little too steep for her to ever completely relax. Still, she'd driven the route countless times, and she felt confident enough.

"It hardly seems like back-to-school time, does it?" said Grace, hoping to lighten the mood.

"You always say that, Mom," her younger daughter teased, and Grace stole a sideways glance to see she was smiling. Then, imitating her mother with perfect pitch, Stéphie went on. "Oh, in Philadelphia, the leaves will just be starting to change color, and the scent of sharp pencils would be in the air." She laughed, then said in her own voice, "I should think you'd be used to the heat here by now!"

"You would think that, wouldn't you?" Grace said, relieved that the two of them were settling into the drive so quickly. This had been the right decision. "But the sunlight here has always been a bit much for me, to be honest," Grace told her daughter.

Stéphanie shook her head and giggled, and Grace remained silent. Maybe she wouldn't bring up Paul or racing after all. She asked about her plans for her school week in Paris instead.

As her daughter talked, Grace began to

feel strange. She'd been having headaches lately, but this was different. Her pulse quickened, almost as though she was nervous about something, but she wasn't *that* concerned about the drive. And everything with Stéphie was fine at the moment — they weren't anywhere near a fight.

Then she began to feel hot. *Damn menopause,* she cursed to herself. Soon, she could hardly focus on what Stéphanie was saying; it was as though she'd entered a kind of echo chamber, and her daughter was in another one far away.

When her vision began to blur despite the fact that she was wearing her glasses, Grace began to panic. "Mom! Slow down!" she heard Stéphanie shout.

"I . . . I can't," she replied, hearing her voice full of fear and confusion, again from far away. Her foot was on the brake. Wasn't it? But they seemed only to be going faster.

"Mom!"

Her daughter's scream was the last thing she heard, her daughter's fingers brushing hers on the steering wheel was the last human contact she felt, as the car lurched off the road. The clear blue sky — *it's been just as vast here, too, all along* — seemed to engulf them.

Like a bird, Grace's body flew free, losing

all contact with the seat just before everything slammed down with a force and a sound she'd thought only movies could make.

And then, all was dark.

AUTHOR'S NOTE

I was lucky enough to get to travel to Monaco while I was researching and writing this novel, and one of the most important and entirely unexpected moments came at the very end, in the cab ride from my hotel in the Larvotto to the airport in Nice. I got to chatting with the driver, a native Monégasque, and when he asked what had brought me to Monaco, I told him about this book.

"Oh," he sighed, clearly under the weight of some heavy memories, "the day she died was terrible for Monaco."

I asked him to explain, and he went on to tell the story of how he had been a young chauffeur in his late teens the day it happened, and how sad her death had made him. "We loved her," he said, speaking for his principality.

I ventured to ask if that had always been true, for I knew of her struggle to fit the role she had married into.

With a pooh-pooh frown and a casual wave of the hand that only Europeans seem to be able to carry off, he said, "But of course in the beginning, we did not know what to think of her. But once we knew her, we could not help but love her."

We could not help but love her. His breathless, heartfelt statement stuck with me through the next drafts of this book, as I explored the many ways in which Grace loved and was loved in return.

I like to think there is a continuum in the genre of historical fiction, and on one end are the works of pure fiction (with made-up characters and the made-up events of their lives) set against the backdrop of real-life settings and locations, often with magical elements (think *Outlander*). On the other end are novels that stay so close to the real events of real people's lives, the books are often mistaken for biographies even though plenty of imagination went into the emotions, actions, and reactions of the characters, who happen to have names everyone recognizes (think *The Paris Wife* or even my last book, *The Kennedy Debutante*).

Though *The Girl in White Gloves* stars such a real-life person, and delves into the well-known events of her much-documented life,

I can assure you that this novel falls much closer to the middle of the continuum than the near-biography end — despite the first of the two suggestive epigraphs that open the book, which I accepted as a kind of dare.

I took many liberties in the writing of this novel, for a variety of reasons. For one thing, since I was writing scenes from thirty-three years of Grace's life, I needed to implement some dramatic compression strategies, which meant making manageable the truly staggering cast of characters who were her friends, colleagues, and employees. To this end, I created composite characters with fictional names like her assistant Marta, and even her childhood friend Maree Frisby, who was one of her bridesmaids and a real person, but who in this book is a combination of other bridesmaids and childhood friends I discovered in my research.

I also — *ahem* — adjusted the time line in a few instances to suit my dramatic needs. For instance, Albie started Amherst in 1977, not 1976, but I couldn't resist the (entirely made-up) conversation he had with his mother about *Star Wars* that could only have taken place in seventy-six; in that same fateful year, I had Caroline meet Philippe Junot a bit earlier than she actually did. And

Grace likely started on the board of Fox before she took the stage in the Edinburgh Festival, but it made more sense for me to reverse them. Similarly, I took liberties with her extremely busy comings and goings — for instance, sometimes she didn't go back to New York City between movies in 1954, but to keep the pace of the novel going, I needed her to be with Oleg and other characters at certain intervals. In my defense, I'll say that exact dates were hard to come by in any case since she didn't leave behind a diary I could check.

Nor was I able to lay my hands on many letters to or from her — and yes, that means that the letters between her and Rainier are all fictionalized. They *did* court each other in letters for the second half of 1955, but those letters appear to be lost, so I wasn't able to read any. Despite writing to numerous historical societies, museums, biographers, and relations, I wasn't able to find many letters at all in her own hand. The best of the bunch were in the Margaret Herrick Library of the Academy of Motion Picture Arts and Sciences in Beverly Hills, California. However, thanks to the work of biographers who interviewed her directly, knew her personally, and/or gained access to correspondence no longer in the public domain, I was able to piece together a coherent picture of Grace and cut through the tremendous amount of speculation about her life. To that end, the most essential biographies I read — and would recommend to anyone looking for more information about Grace — were J. Randy Taraborrelli's *Once Upon a Time: Behind the Fairy Tale of Princess Grace and Prince Rainier,* Donald Spoto's *High Society: The Life of Grace Kelly,* and Judith Balaban Quine's *The Bridesmaids.*

Since I suspect many readers are wondering about the romantic relationships from before her marriage, I want to say that like everything else in this book, I very much had to *choose* which relationships to portray and how to portray them. There weren't any flies on the walls during her dates, and the etiquette of her time kept her from divulging too much to even her closest friends (a difference between her life and those of modern city girls like Carrie Bradshaw that I have to thank Judith Quine for illuminating in her book). So I admit to a certain amount of speculation, and picking and choosing which partners to explore in the interest of a coherent and suspenseful narrative arc.

I suspect some modern readers raised an

eyebrow at Grace's relationship with Fordie, the Kelly family chauffeur — a real person whom Grace loved and respected. I thought a great deal about whether, then how, to portray their friendship, which was imbalanced in all the ways that make twenty-first-century readers uncomfortable (including me!). I was determined not to be anachronistic, however, and I wanted to include Fordie because he was an essential person in her life, and I wanted to do it in a way that felt true to the times and to Grace's character. History isn't always a comfortable place to be, and I hope this relationship, and any other behaviors and attitudes of these mid-twentieth-century characters that might cause us discomfort, will spark productive discussion.

Perhaps the most illustrative *fictional* moment is the final one, in which Grace has a medical event that experts describe as something like a stroke and drives off the road. No one can truly know what she thought, or noticed, in those horrible final seconds of consciousness. But sometimes a writer gets to give her character a gift, and mine to Grace is a final sensation of freedom and theatricality, a dramatization of Georgie Elgin's words that became for me a guiding light in this novel, that "There's nothing quite so mysterious and silent as a dark theater, a night without a star."

ACKNOWLEDGMENTS

Mom and Dad, it was such fun touring Monaco and sharing the first drafts of this novel with you — I feel lucky that you get as excited about my subjects as I do, and want to be in on the adventure. Here's to many more! And, Elena, thank you for your energy and endless inspiration, and for the huge compliment of wanting to write a book with your mom.

Thanks to my many incredible friends on whom I leaned for moral support during the writing of this book, which also happened to be a tumultuous time in my life. To those friends who also read drafts, often more than one, and sometimes on a tight deadline, I'm deeply grateful for the insights and long conversations that arose from the time you took to read Grace's story: Danielle Fodor, Lori Hess, Elise Hooper, Diana Renn, Laura White, and Kip Wilson. I'd like to give a special shout-out to Alyson Muzilla as well as Ellen, Tony, and Derek Spaldo, who are not only amazing readers but actors who reality checked my theater scenes. And Mike Harvkey — I owe much of my knowledge of classic Hollywood to you and your suggestions for where to take myself for drinks. And thanks once again to Margaret O'Connor (and your cat Grace Kelly!), for helping to make this dream come true.

For their assistance in helping me locate — or sometimes confirm the absence of — Grace Kelly's letters and other written materials, thank you to Mark Vieira; Louise Hilton of the Margaret Herrick Library; Thomas Fouillerion of the Archives of the Palace of Monaco; Cady Miriam at the Philadelphia Museum of Art, Library and Archives; Alex Bartlett at the Chestnut Hill Conservancy; the East Falls Historical Society; and the Ocean City Historical Museum.

Kate Seaver, my wonderful editor, thank you for your thoughtful suggestions, which vastly improved the book; I so enjoy our conversations about Grace, summer vacations, and conference fun. I look forward to our next books together! Dasia Payne: this book owes a debt of gratitude to your keen eyes and incisive feedback at a critical juncture. And Kevan Lyon, wow do I feel lucky to find myself on your agency's crew, and thank you for reading this book and providing feedback and guidance.

To my amazing team at Berkley — Diana Franco, Danielle Kier, Sarah Blumenstock, Fareeda Bullert, and Mary Geren — thank you so much for helping me build a readership, and for patiently answering my many, many questions about the publication process. Craig Burke, Jeanne-Marie Hudson, Jin Yu, Ivan Held, Claire Zion, and Christine Ball — I still have to pinch myself to remind myself that this is really happening, that I really am on your team. Vikki Chu, your cover design is beyond my wildest dreams, and seeing it for the first time was the most fun thing that happened to me at Disneyland. Heartfelt thanks to Frank Walgren, Lynsey Griswold, and Kayley Hoffman for setting my mind at ease with thorough edits.

And to all of you who are holding this book in your hands, THANK YOU. If you're also blogging, tweeting, bookstagramming, reviewing, and/or telling your friends about *The Girl in White Gloves* (and/or if you did it for *The Kennedy Debutante*), I'm more grateful than I can possibly express in words. You're the reason I get to do this amazing work, the reason any writer can see their name in print. So, seriously, thank you for reading and for spreading the book love far and wide.

ABOUT THE AUTHOR

Kerri Maher is the author of *The Kennedy Debutante,* which People magazine described as "a riveting reimagining of a true tale of forbidden love," and *This Is Not a Writing Manual: Notes for the Young Writer in the Real World* under the name Kerri Majors. She holds an MFA from Columbia University and founded YARN, an award-winning literary journal of short-form YA writing. A writing professor for many years, she now writes full time and lives with her daughter and dog in a leafy suburb west of Boston, Massachusetts.

The employees of Thorndike Press hope you have enjoyed this Large Print book. All our Thorndike, Wheeler, and Kennebec Large Print titles are designed for easy reading, and all our books are made to last. Other Thorndike Press Large Print books are available at your library, through selected bookstores, or directly from us.

For information about titles, please call:
(800) 223-1244

or visit our website at:
gale.com/thorndike

To share your comments, please write:

Publisher
Thorndike Press
10 Water St., Suite 310
Waterville, ME 04901